The Caspian Gates

By the same author

WARRIOR OF ROME:

Fire in the East

King of Kings

Lion of the Sun

ANCIENT WARFARE:

A VERY SHORT INTRODUCTION

The Caspian Gates
A Warrior of Rome Novel

DR HARRY SIDEBOTTOM

MICHAEL JOSEPH
an imprint of
PENGUIN BOOKS

MICHAEL JOSEPH

Published by the Penguin Group

Penguin Books Ltd, 80 Strand, London WC2R ORL, England

Penguin Group (USA) Inc., 375 Hudson Street, New York, New York 10014, USA

Penguin Group (Canada), 90 Eglinton Avenue East, Suite 700, Toronto, Ontario, Canada M4P 2Y3
(a division of Pearson Penguin Canada Inc.)

Penguin Ireland, 25 St Stephen's Green, Dublin 2, Ireland (a division of Penguin Books Ltd)

Penguin Group (Australia), 250 Camberwell Road,
Camberwell, Victoria 3124, Australia (a division of Pearson Australia Group Pty Ltd)

Penguin Books India Pvt Ltd, 11 Community Centre,
Panchsheel Park, New Delhi – 110 017, India

Penguin Group (NZ), 67 Apollo Drive, Rosedale, Auckland 0632, New Zealand
(a division of Pearson New Zealand Ltd)

Penguin Books (South Africa) (Pty) Ltd, 24 Sturdee Avenue,
Rosebank Johannesburg 2196, South Africa

Penguin Books Ltd, Registered Offices: 80 Strand, London WC2R ORL, England

www.penguin.com

First published 2011

1

Set in 12/14.75pt Dante
Typeset by Palimpsest Book Production Limited, Falkirk, Stirlingshire
Printed in Great Britain by Clays Ltd, St Ives plc

A CIP catalogue record for this book is available from the British Library

ISBN: 978-0-718-15591-9

www.greenpenguin.co.uk

To my aunt Terry and the memory of my uncle Tony

Contents

N

W E

S

North
Sea

ANGLES

RUGII

BRITANNIA
INFERIOR

FRISII

Franks

Elbe

BRITANNIA
SUPERIOR

Atlantic
Ocean

GERMANIA
INFERIOR

Colonia
Agrippinensis

BELGICA

Rhine

Alamanni

Juthungi

LUGDUNENSIS

Agri
Decumates

Danube

RAETIA

NORICUM

PANNONIA
SUPERIOR

AQUITANIA

GERMANIA
SUPERIOR

1

Cularo

Mediolanum

Siscia

2

Ravenna

DALMATIA

NARBONENSIS

3

HISPANIA
TARRACONENSIS

ITALY

LUSITANIA

Tarracona

Rome

BAETICA

M e d i t e r r a

Tauromenium

MAURETANIA
TINGITANA

MAURETANIA
CAESARIENSIS

NUMIDIA

Carthage

AFRICA
PROCON-
SULARIS

0   100   200   300   400 miles

0   200   400   600 kms

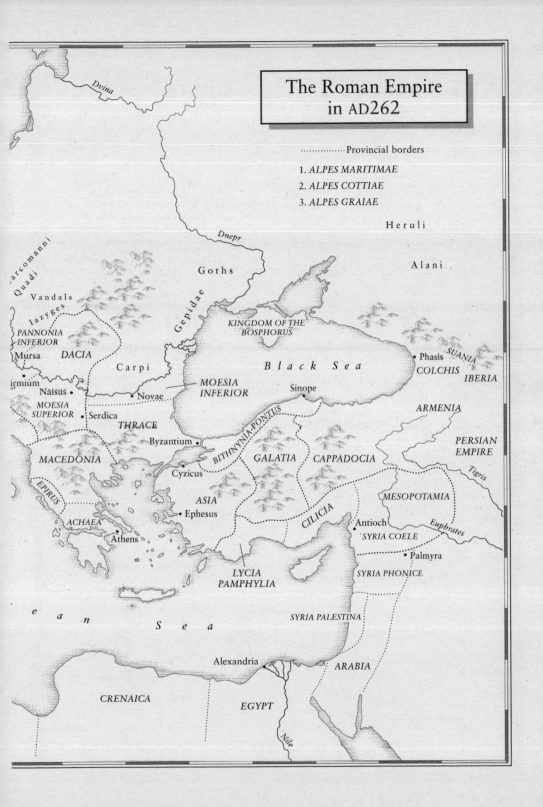

The Roman Empire
in AD262

.... Provincial borders
1. *ALPES MARITIMAE*
2. *ALPES COTTIAE*
3. *ALPES GRAIAE*

Dvina

Heruli

Dnepr

Goths

Alani

arcomanni

Quadi

Vandals

Iazyges

PANNONIA
INFERIOR

Mursa

DACIA

Carpi

KINGDOM OF THE
BOSPHORUS

Gepidae

Black   Sea

Phasis

SUANIA

COLCHIS

IBERIA

irmium

Naisus

MOESIA
SUPERIOR

Serdica

Novae

MOESIA
INFERIOR

Sinope

ARMENIA

THRACE

Byzantium

BITHYNIA-PONTUS

GALATIA

CAPPADOCIA

PERSIAN
EMPIRE

MACEDONIA

Cyzicus

Tigris

EPIRUS

ASIA

MESOPOTAMIA

ACHAEA

Ephesus

CILICIA

Antioch

Euphrates

Athens

SYRIA COELE

Palmyra

LYCIA
PAMPHYLIA

SYRIA PHONICE

e   a   n

S   e   a

SYRIA PALESTINA

Alexandria

ARABIA

CRENAICA

EGYPT

Nile

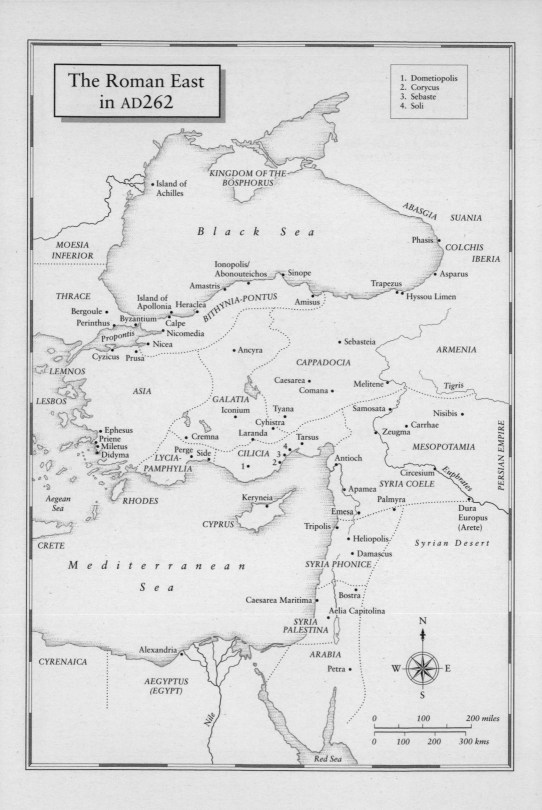

The Roman East in AD262

1. Dometiopolis
2. Corycus
3. Sebaste
4. Soli

KINGDOM OF THE BOSPHORUS

Island of Achilles

Black Sea

ABASGIA   SUANIA

Phasis •   COLCHIS

MOESIA INFERIOR

IBERIA

• Asparus

Ionopolis/ Abonouteichos   • Sinope

Trapezus •

Amastris •

Hyssou Limen •

THRACE

Island of Apollonia   Heraclea

BITHYNIA-PONTUS

Amisus •

ARMENIA

Bergoule •   Byzantium •   Calpe

Perinthus •   Nicomedia •

Propontis   • Nicea

• Ancyra

• Sebasteia

Cyzicus •   Prusa •

CAPPADOCIA

Tigris

LEMNOS

ASIA

Caesarea •

Melitene •

LESBOS

GALATIA

Comana •

Nisibis •

Iconium •

Tyana •

Samosata •

Carrhae •

Cyhistra •

Ephesus •   Priene •
Miletus •   Cremna •

Laranda •

Tarsus •

Zeugma •

MESOPOTAMIA

Didyma •

Perge •   4

Side •   CILICIA   3

Antioch •

Euphrates

LYCIA-PAMPHYLIA

1 •   2

Circesium •

SYRIA COELE

Apamea •

Palmyra •

PERSIAN EMPIRE

Aegean Sea

RHODES

Keryneia •

Emesa •

Dura Europus (Arete) •

CYPRUS

Tripolis •

Syrian Desert

CRETE

• Heliopolis

Mediterranean

• Damascus

Sea

SYRIA PHONICE

Caesarea Maritima •

• Bostra

Aelia Capitolina •

SYRIA PALESTINA

N

CYRENAICA

Alexandria •

ARABIA

Petra •

W   E

AEGYPTUS (EGYPT)

S

Nile

0   100   200 *miles*

0   100   200   300 *kms*

Red Sea

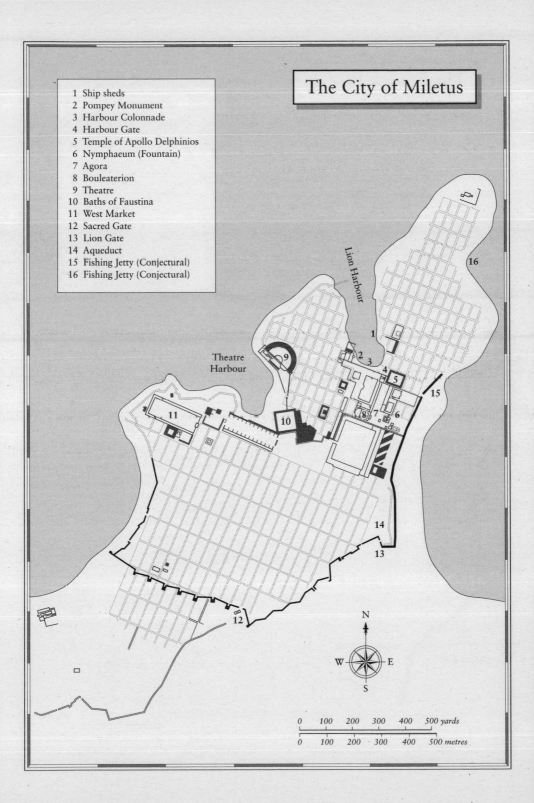

The City of Miletus

1 Ship sheds
2 Pompey Monument
3 Harbour Colonnade
4 Harbour Gate
5 Temple of Apollo Delphinios
6 Nymphaeum (Fountain)
7 Agora
8 Bouleaterion
9 Theatre
10 Baths of Faustina
11 West Market
12 Sacred Gate
13 Lion Gate
14 Aqueduct
15 Fishing Jetty (Conjectural)
16 Fishing Jetty (Conjectural)

Lion Harbour

Theatre
Harbour

N
W E
S

0   100   200   300   400   500 yards
0   100   200   300   400   500 metres

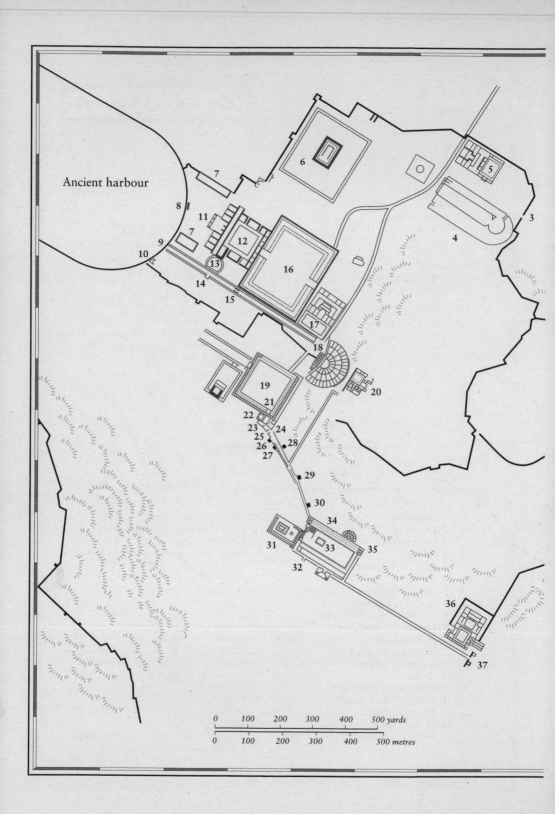

Ancient harbour

6

5

3

4

7

8

11

7

9

12

10

13

16

14

15

17

18

19

20

21

22

23

24

25

26

28

27

29

30

34

31

33

35

32

36

37

| 0 | 100 | 200 | 300 | 400 | 500 yards |

| 0 | 100 | 200 | 300 | 400 | 500 metres |

The City of Ephesus

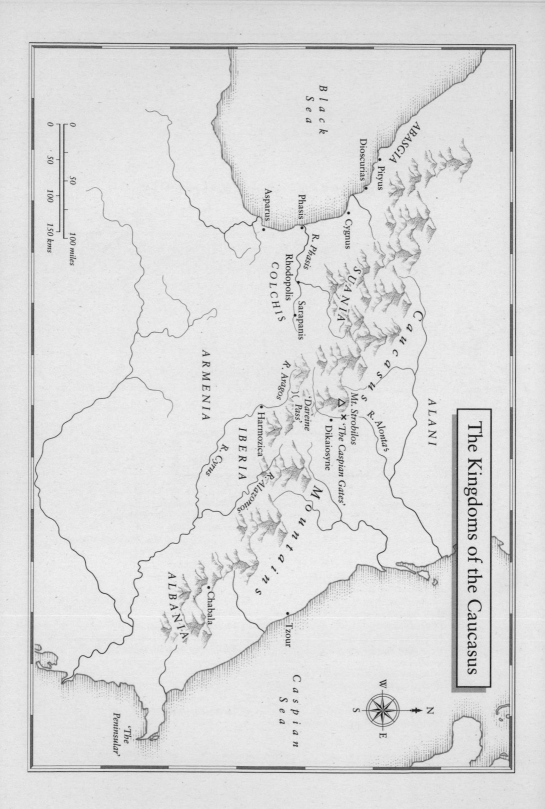

The Kingdoms of the Caucasus

Black Sea

ABASGIA
Dioscurias
Pityus
Asparus
Phasis
Cygnus
R. Phasis
Rhodopolis
Sarapanis
COLCHIS
SUANIA
Caucasus
R. Alontas
ALANI
R. Argos
Mt. Strobilos
'The Caspian Gates'
Dikaiosyne
'Dar
eine
Pass'
Harmozica
ARMENIA
IBERIA
R. Cyrus
R. Alazonios
Mountains
ALBANIA
Chabala
Tzour
Caspian Sea
'The Peninsular'

N
W   E
S

0
50
100
150 kms

0
50
100 miles

Exile, it seems, is a gift. I thought it was a punishment.

–Seneca, *Medea* 492

Prologue

The Caucasus, Autumn AD259

A family formed by crime must be broken by more crime.

–Seneca, *Medea* 55

He was wounded and unhorsed, but he was alive. At the top of the slope was a stand of mountain pines. In cover, back against a tree, the man tried to listen for the pursuit. He could hear nothing over his own agonized breathing.

The shaft of the arrow had snapped when he crashed from his mount. The arrowhead was embedded in his left bicep. The blood still ran hot down his arm. The pain came in sickening surges.

He was a fool to have agreed to hunt bear. Lonely wooded glens, many armed men; it was all too easy to become isolated, then all too easy for an *accident* to happen. He was a fool to have trusted his brother. There had always been something not right about the youngest of them. The presence of their sister and her retinue had lulled him. If only he had remained close to her. His brother and his followers would have attempted nothing then. The man knew he had been a fool, and now he would die. He despaired.

This was not right, not for a descendant of Prometheus. The man tried to control his sobbing. On the peaks above, Prometheus had been persecuted. Spiteful Zeus had hung him in chains. Every day, with the sun, the eagle had come, its cruel, sharp beak lunging into the soft flesh, tearing, slicing, gobbling down chunks of Prometheus's delicate, dark liver. With the night, the eagle left. As the cold winds blew and the snow flurried, miraculously, the liver was healed. And then, with the dawn, the eagle returned. Thirty years of torment until Heracles had shot the eagle and freed the man's ancestor.

Prometheus was a lesson in endurance, in suffering overcome, of ultimate redemption. Who should learn it better than his distant offspring? The man drew a slower, deeper breath; still ragged, but more in control. He forced the pain away and kept very still. He listened. All was quiet; so quiet you could follow a mosquito by its hum.

The hunters were out of earshot, at least temporarily off the trail. After the ambush, he had ridden some distance before the moment of pain-induced inattention and the low branch that had swept him off his horse. The horse had bolted. He was alone.

The man looked around. The copse was shot through with shafts of weak sunlight. It was quite considerable, and not of pine alone. Here and there blazed the autumnal reds and golds of beech, maple and birch. There was no undergrowth, but the trunks and low branches, the odd fallen tree, all gave some cover.

The man turned his attention to the arrow. Thinking of it brought back the pain. He forced it down again. His left arm was almost useless. Using his teeth and the dagger in his right hand, he cut the sleeves of his sheepskin coat and linen tunic away from the wound. He had to bite his lip hard when the material pulled clear. The blood started to flow fast again.

The man unstoppered his wine flask. Not pausing to dwell on it, not giving cowardice an opportunity to undermine his resolve, he poured the alcohol over the wound. The pain was searing. He drummed his heels, clenched the discarded sheepskin in his teeth. Not crying out, he cleaned the wound.

The pain, the stench of greasy sheepskin, its revolting lanolin taste – the man spat and then retched. The convulsive movement made the pain worse. He fought for control. He used the mental tools at his disposal. Imagine the pain as a red-hot ember, his arm as a fennel stalk. Force the ember down inside the stalk. Let it glow there in the dark, smoulder, do its worst; you can carry it for miles, the surface of the fennel barely warm to the touch.

The pain somewhat mastered, the man sniffed the wound. Nothing, just blood and wine; the homely waft of sacrifice. Relief ran through him. They had not used the most potent of local poisons, not the one whose mere scent could injure or blind. If they had employed another, it probably mattered little. Every morning, like all his family, he had climbed the ladder to the top room of the tower. There his father had unlocked the big, bound chest, had measured out the potions. Every morning the seven of them – father, mother, the four boys and their sister – had drunk down a little draft of every poison, all except one that was known in the region. It took a time: there were many poisons known in Suania. Endless innocent mornings vitiated by nausea and pain, but all worth it on a dreadful afternoon such as this one.

There was an inch or so of splintered shaft protruding. It was inscribed with strange markings. The arrowhead was barbed. It could not be pulled out. He could cut it out. But he would scream, and bring the hunters down on him. He sat and thought.

He unbuckled his bow case and quiver. They were useless to a one-armed man. He took two straps from them. One he tied tight above the wound. The flow of blood slowed almost instantly. The other he fashioned into a sling. He regarded the bow case for a time. He considered his weapons. On his belt a sword and dagger; another two daggers, one hidden in a boot, the other in the lining of his coat. He pulled a bowstring from the case and, gripping one end in his teeth, made it into a lariat.

Somewhere in the distance, a hound gave voice and a man called. The main body of the hunt, or the assassins? There was no way to tell. It was time to move, time to decide what to do.

Leaving the bow case and quiver, the torn scraps of clothing, the bloodied ground, the man moved off through the trees, away from the direction in which he had come. He tracked up the slope until he came to a small glade. Through the break in the foliage he could see the sky: a hard, distant blue. Darkness would fall within two hours. He looked north to the mountains. The Croucasis lived up to their Scythian name; in the cold sunshine their flanks were still 'gleaming white with snow'. But the mountains were smoking. Wisps of vapour curled up towards the peaks, coalesced into a dark cloud at the very summit. The first snows would fall here in the upland valleys in an hour or so. Darkness would come early. Not long to stay alive.

The man felt sick again; sick and weak. He thought for a moment, then, taking a slightly different angle, stepped back into the trees the way he had come. He cast about for a place to lie up. A great fallen beech, its dying branches fanned upwards, abutted a standing evergreen. He settled himself into the space between the screen of dying deciduous leaves and the grey, lichened trunk of the pine.

The man was shaking slightly. He did not know if it was from the cold, or from fear and the shock of betrayal. Fumbling, he fed himself some cold pheasant and a little flat bread from the pouch on his belt. He had never trusted his youngest brother, not since childhood. Somehow, he had always known things would not go well for him if he fell into his hands. From the wine flask he poured libations to Prometheus, Heracles and Hecate, and prayed; especially to the dark goddess of revenge.

It was still dead calm in the wood. The storm would not get here very soon. He had to decide what to do. Hiding here did not seem good. He would get colder and weaker. He would be discovered and killed. He needed to be on the move. But where to?

Listening hard, he shut his eyes and thought once more. He could try to get back to the main body of the hunt. Among his own retainers and his sister's men he would be safe. He would have to avoid the assassins. His brother would have them spread out, searching – maybe they were already following his trail. He did not know how many there were; he had seen only two. Had there been several more, unwounded, the man would have put money on ghosting past them. He had always been good on the hill and in the forest. But he was wounded; slowed down and in pain.

There were sledge tracks in the grass off to the left. The first snows next to never closed the nearest pass. Despite the lateness of the season, there would be Scythian nomads, Alani or, more likely, men from their subject tribes, still driving their herds back north over what they called the Croucasis.

If the man could fall in with a group of Scythians, he would be safe. Obviously, they were aware of his father. Last spring, they would have handed over to his father's men fleeces, hides and slaves to be allowed to make the passage south. It might be that his own name was not unknown among the Scythians. The nomads would protect him. Of course, he would have to cross the mountains with them, spend the winter out on the plains. And come next spring, they would not need fleeces or slaves. His safe return would open their way. But the man cared nothing for that. He would be alive to be ransomed; alive to take revenge on his youngest brother.

A strange languor was creeping over him. The Scythians would be in a good mood, the bellies of their animals full of the

5

sweet meadow grasses of Suania, their own saddlebags stuffed with apples and pears. They would be going home. A winter with the Scythians would not be so bad, a winter spent drifting after the flocks across the wide plains of the nomad sea. Their tents would be snug; braziers lit, a pleasant fug of conversation, food and drink. The women of the Alani were said to be tall, beautiful and wanton. Their men were complacent. All you had to do was hang your quiver outside her tent, and the husband would go off and leave you in peace until you had finished enjoying his wife.

The sharp ring of metal on metal snapped the man's eyes open. He held his breath, listening. Nothing. Slowly, he turned his head from side to side, eyes wide. Nothing. He knew he had not imagined it. Up above, the top branches were stirring with sluggish menace. The storm would get here soon.

His arm hurt like a Christian on the pyre. He tried to push the red-hot ember back into the fennel stalk. Careful not to make a sound, he wriggled his toes, with his good hand massaged his thighs, tried to get feeling back into his legs.

Another sound. Off to his right, a careless footfall. In the gloom, the man grinned. He had always been good on the hill. Yet another sound. There was his brother's creature, not above twenty paces away. Alternately, the hunter bent to peer at the ground, following the trail, and stood scanning ahead. He had a bow in his hands, arrow notched, half drawn. His jerky movements betrayed his nerves.

You are right to be nervous, thought the man. If I had two good arms and a bow, you would already be dead, shot as easily as a sitting pheasant. Even with one arm, I have marked you out for Hecate.

The hunter stopped at the edge of the glade, just as the man had hoped a pursuer would. The open ground was an obvious

6

place for an ambush. Anyone would fear that, as you stepped into the clearing, an arrow might whistle out from the tree line ahead. Only the deepest thinking would suspect anything from behind.

The man eased himself to his feet. Oddly, his left arm, though still incapacitated, had ceased to hurt. He studied the way first he then the hunter had come. The wind hissed through the branches. Nothing else: no human movement or sound.

The man glided forward, feet placed carefully, the lariat in his right hand. The gathering storm covered his approach.

The hunter still hesitated. The man closed behind him. An innate intimation of danger; the hunter began to turn. Too late. With fluid movements, the man slipped the noose of bowstring over the hunter's head, yanked the slip knot tight around his neck, pulled as hard as he could.

Instinctively, the hunter's fingers scrabbled at the cord biting deep into his throat. There was no purchase to be had. Blood ran down his neck.

The man, left shoulder braced between the hunter's shoulder-blades, exerted all his strength. Boots slipped and stamped on the forest floor. The man's breath came in harsh, animal pants. The hunter's was a death rattle. Convulsions, then a heavy stillness. A foul smell of voided bladder and bowels. The man continued to choke the lifeless corpse.

'Impressive, brother, you have killed him five times over.'

The man's youngest brother emerged from the shadows of the wood. Above him, branches whipped this way and that. The tails of his long native coat were thrown back, the sleeves hung empty. In his unencumbered hands was a drawn bow.

The man turned, dragging the body round to act as a shield. 'This will not look like an accident.' He spoke to buy time, to distract. Slipping his injured arm from the sling, despite the pain, he took the weight of the dead man with it. Out of sight, his right hand drew the dagger from his belt.

'Indeed not, brother. It is no accident. You were waylaid by a band of Alani. A tragedy.'

Fifteen or so paces on either side of the speaker, two more hunters materialized up the hill out of the darkening wood, hoods up, menacing, like creatures from Hades. The three bowmen were well spaced. Grudgingly, the man recognized good tactics.

'Who can say what happened?' his brother continued. 'Everyone knows those nomadic barbarians are irrational, bloodthirsty – eaters of flesh. Robbery, ransom – who knows what they were after? Perhaps you resisted: you always were the brave warrior, our father's favourite. Whatever happened, they killed you. Shot you down like a deer.' He smiled, gloating. 'Have you noticed that the arrow in your arm was made by the Alani?'

The man did not answer the rhetorical question. While his body was perfectly still, his eyes flicked this way and that, measuring, estimating. He did not intend to die here, not at the hands of his brother.

'We have more than enough Alanic arrows. Do you not admire my foresight? You were always the brave one. I was always the one with foresight. Do you remember how our old tutor always admired my disquisitions on the quality of *pronoia*? Odd how the old Greek's philosophical idea seems so much more real here than it ever did in the classroom.'

The first snowflakes were falling, twisting and turning in the gusting wind.

The man grimaced through the pain in his arm. 'And did the philosopher's lessons in ethics not do you any good? Who should you love if not your brother?'

'Oh, but I do, brother, I do. Both love and admire.' The voice was unctuous. 'Because I admire you, I think it certain you will follow the heroes to the Islands of the Blessed. And because I love you, I will send you there forthwith.'

'My death will do you no good.' The man's thoughts were racing. The dialogue had to continue, had to win him time. 'Our father will not name you his heir. If I am dead, he will turn to one of our brothers. Failing that, old Hamazasp of Iberia or whoever our sister marries. The council of three hundred would be happier with any of them than with you. The members of the *synedrion* will never willingly accept you.'

The darkness was gathering. Straight ahead, thought the man. Throw the dagger; kill or wound my brother. Run straight ahead. The bowmen on either side should be reluctant to shoot and risk hitting my brother or each other. Prometheus, Hecate, hold your hands over me.

'Enough talk.' A new voice: female. Out of the gathering storm walked their sister. Her face was very pale, her lips a deep red in the half-light. She too held a drawn bow.

The man knew then that it was all over.

'Enough philosophizing.' She addressed herself to the younger brother. 'You are not now the least of four boys sat at a teacher's feet. Stop your ears to clever words and remorse. Show yourself a man.'

It was all over with him, but the man was not going to go quietly, not like a sacrificial animal. In one move, he let go of the corpse, threw the dagger and launched forward. The dagger spun through the falling snow. The younger brother twisted his head. The dagger caught him in the face; opened up his cheek. He dropped his weapon, reeled away, howling.

The man had made three steps when the first arrow hit in the thigh. He managed another two steps before his leg gave way. The late-autumn grass rising up, bruising his face. The thump and searing pain as another arrow found its mark in his back.

9

Fingers clawing in the turf, pulling him forward. Prometheus, Hecate . . . The pain of another arrow, and another, and another. The fingers stopped working. The darkness surged up.

The snow was falling heavily in the glade. It was settling in the sightless eyes of the corpse. The living siblings of the dead man stood close together, right hands clasped. One of the two hunters had tied their thumbs together. The brother had a knife in his left hand. Deftly he cut the tips of their thumbs.

'Neither with steel nor poison,' he said. Leaning forward, he licked the blood from his thumb then that of his sister. 'Sealed and countersealed in blood.'

The girl repeated the words. She dipped her head, her red lips parted and her tongue curled around his thumb.

PART ONE
The Humane Land

(Ionia and the West, Spring AD262)

*Ionia has other features to record besides
its temperate climate and its sanctuaries.*

–Pausanias 7.5.4

I

'A snake,' said Maximus. 'A fucking big snake.'

Everyone looked to where the alarmed Hibernian pointed, out into the atrium.

It was a fucking big snake all right: long, scaly, brown. And – if you knew snakes at all – completely harmless. But it was agitated, obviously disturbed, twisting and writhing here and there in the lamplight that illuminated the big open space at the centre of the big house in Ephesus.

Ballista asked Hippothous to get rid of it. Seeing the reluctance on his secretary's face, Ballista remembered that many Greeks and Romans kept the creatures as pets. Possibly, he suggested, the *accensus* might just put it out of the house. Certainly get it away from Maximus. Hippothous went off to find a slave or two to actually catch the thing.

Ballista sat down, and called for his new body-servant Constans to shave him.

It was odd, the attitude to snakes of these Mediterranean types. On their account, the creatures had a bad parentage, born from the blood of the Titans, enemies of the gods. And they kept bad company: the hair of the petrifying Gorgons was alive with them. And then there was unhappy Philoctetes, bitten by a snake on the island of Lemnos, the smell of the suppurating wound so bad the other heroes abandoned him there when they sailed on for Troy. Yet despite all that, often Greeks and Romans would feed the scaly things by hand, offer them cakes, twine them fondly around their necks and set them up as guardians of houses, tombs, springs and altars. The fools.

The perspective of a man such as Ballista, born beyond the northern frontiers of the *imperium* in the misty forests and fens of Germania, was much more straightforward. There was not a snake in Middle Earth that did not share the old, cold malevolence of Jormungand, the world serpent who lay coiled in the icy darkness of the ocean waiting for Ragnarok, for the day when it was fated the serpent could return to dry land and the gods would die.

A snake without venom regretted it. Certainly, Maximus overdid things, but he was not a complete fool. Not about snakes anyway.

Constans came in carrying the shaving apparatus. He placed a heavy silver bowl of warm water on the table. Condensation ran down the side. Ballista repeatedly scooped the water up and splashed it on his face. He took his time; dousing his cheeks, admiring the bowl's embossed images of the Persian king hunting a lion.

Constans busied himself with the whetstone, putting a fine edge on the razor.

At length, face glowing, Ballista leant back. Constans draped the napkin around his master's neck. And, with just a little reluctance showing, Ballista offered his throat to the blade. Through the steam he could see his two freedmen, Maximus, with his short beard, and old Calgacus with his ugly face with its patchy stubble. Both were looking at him, and both were smiling. The bastards.

Constans leant over and got to work, skilled, diligent and slow. *Schick, schick*, the razor traversed the pulled-tight skin. Constans was a godsend. His dexterity meant that Ballista was spared visiting the public barbershops. It was not the expense, exorbitant though it could be, and it was not the idlers sat around on their benches, the endless gossip, or the enforced proximities that Ballista minded. His dislike of such establishments was more visceral. A shout, an accident in the street, a moment's distraction, even a stone thrown by a mischievous youth or boy – it had happened – and you left minus an ear, or at best looking like a man with a bad-tempered wife with sharp nails.

Constans had repaid his purchase price in another way. A couple of years earlier, Ballista had freed Calgacus, along with Maximus and his then secretary the Greek boy Demetrius. After that, it somehow seemed wrong to have old Calgacus shave him. And, truth be told, the old Caledonian had never been much good with a razor. All too often recourse had to be made to spiders' webs soaked in oil and vinegar to plaster the nicks, if not staunch the flow.

Out of Ballista's line of sight, a caged bird was singing furiously. It was irritating. Hopefully it would not distract Constans.

Ballista knew it was ridiculous. A man such as himself. The first sixteen years of his life he had been brought up to be a warrior among the Angles, the tribe in which his father was war-leader. He had stood in the shieldwall when just fifteen. Killed his first man the same year. Most of the following twenty-four years, although technically a hostage, he had served in the Roman army. He had broken his ankle and jaw once, ribs twice, and his nose and the knuckles of his right hand more times than he could remember. There were scars scattered over the front of his body, and the back of his right hand was seamed with them, as you would expect of a swordsman. In Africa, he had won the mural crown for being first over the enemy wall. Again and again, he had stood with the front-fighters in hot battle. And yet he was nervous – no, be honest – he was scared of the barber.

Hippothous and two slaves appeared outside. The lamps were paling. Soon it would be dawn. The three men stood in a huddle, heads to one side, debating how to go about cornering the snake. The creature had plenty of room for manoeuvre. The atrium was big. The whole rented house was big. It was a house fitting the *dignitas* of a senior member of the equestrian order, the sort of house a sometime Praetorian Prefect would rent for his *familia* while waiting for the sixth day before the *ides* of March and the opening of the sailing season, waiting to start his voyage home to retirement in a comfortable villa in Sicily. Naturally, the *Vir Ementissimus* was paying a high rent. But that was of little concern to a man who two years earlier had defeated the Persian King of Kings at the battle of Soli and captured his treasures and harem. Of course, all such booty, legally, went straight to the emperor. But it was often striking how much never reached him.

Out in the atrium, the two slaves went to catch the snake.

'You not going to help them?' Calgacus asked Maximus. 'A big strong bodyguard like you, ex-gladiator and all, quick on your feet; aye, very helpful you would be.'

'I am not fucking scared of fucking snakes. It was just he was a bit fucking big.'

'Aye, I know, and there were none of them where you grew up.' Calgacus was enjoying himself. 'You lying Hibernian cunt,' he added amiably.

The slaves were not having an easy task of it. The snake did not want to be caught. It was probably long steeped in cunning. Certainly it was quick, slithering out of the questing hands. The slaves shouted at each other. Hippothous shouted at both of them.

Ballista hoped again that it was not going to distract Constans.

The slaves were running around like actors in a bad mime. The unholy row would have woken anyone – except the entire household was already awake: Ballista and the men in the *andron*; his wife, Julia, and her maids in the women's quarters; the domestic slaves throughout the house wielding an arsenal of cloths, sponges, feather dusters, brooms, buckets, poles and ladders. A blur of sawdust tipped out, then swept up again, a cloud of chased dust; the usual frenzy of domestic economy.

Ballista had instructed the bell rung early this morning, with a good two hours of the night left. It was not a day to be late. It was the anniversary of the accession, one hundred and one years earlier, of the divine emperors Marcus Aurelius and Lucius Verus. It promised to be a grand day: sacrifices, a procession, singing and dancing, all sorts of entertainment, more sacrifices, speeches and a feast. It was a day on which the imperial cult would be celebrated, on which the expression of loyalty and religious sentiment would meld together.

It was not a day for Ballista to be late. Everyone knew what he had done the previous year – turned his hands on a man who, no matter how briefly and how very wrongly, had worn the purple. He had thrown Quietus – may his name be damned – from a tower, a cliff, the pediment of a temple; had stabbed him, strangled him, beaten him to death with a chair leg. In one lurid version, he had torn his heart out on an altar. The details of the execution might vary, but everyone agreed what had happened next. The soldiers had acclaimed Ballista emperor. Certainly, the barbarian had laid down the diadem after just a few days. And certainly, Odenathus, the king of Palmyra, who now oversaw the eastern provinces of the Roman empire in the name of the true

17

emperor Gallienus, had pardoned him. But a man who has killed an emperor, or even an ephemeral pretender, will always be the object of curiosity and some suspicion. Not a man who can afford to be late for a festival of the imperial cult.

It was all rather worse than the idlers in the bars and baths had it. As soon as the deed was done, Ballista had written to the emperor Gallienus: a letter of explanation, a request for *clementia*, a plea to be allowed to retire into private life, to live quietly in Sicily. The *cursus publicus* would have taken the letter west at about fifty miles a day. It had been sent months ago. There had been no reply.

As youths, Gallienus and Ballista had both been held at the imperial court as sureties for the good behaviour of their fathers. The young men had got on well. They could even have been counted friends. Ballista had hoped it would help. He had hoped he would be allowed to live quietly as a private citizen, that he would not be convicted of treason. If declared guilty of *maiestas*, Ballista hoped his property would not be confiscated, that his sons might inherit. If the verdict was bad, he hoped for some form of exile rather than the executioner's sword. For months, Ballista had hoped all these things, but there had been no reply.

That was not all. Many years ago, Ballista had killed another emperor. Not many people knew of the young Ballista's role in the death of the terrible Maximinus Thrax. Most, if not all, the other twelve conspirators were dead. Ballista had only told five people. One of them was also dead. Three of the others were still with him: his wife Julia, his freedmen Maximus and Calgacus. But, worryingly enough, the fifth one, his ex-secretary Demetrius, was now in the west; precisely, in the court of Gallienus. It would not be good if a report arrived there that Ballista had been anything other than punctual for a festival of the imperial cult.

With a final, slightly disconcerting flourish, Constans finished the shave. Ballista thanked him, avoiding the eyes of Maximus and Calgacus. On cue, their breakfast arrived. The Jewish slave woman Rebecca put out bread, cheese, soft-boiled eggs, as well as honey, yoghurt and fruit. A substantial *ientaculum* for a Roman or Greek, nothing too taxing for the three northerners.

'Tell me, darling girl,' said Maximus, 'are you frightened of big snakes?' He spoke to Rebecca but was looking at Calgacus. She blushed and shook her head. Calgacus ignored him. 'Sure, you must be getting used to them,' the Hibernian continued, all wide, blue-eyed innocence. 'Living here, I mean. I heard tell there was one hereabouts built on such a heroic scale it won applause when its owner took it to the baths. Ugly-looking thing, though, it was.' Rebecca left as quickly as possible.

'Bastard,' said Calgacus.

'Poor girl,' said Maximus, 'ending up with you on top of her.'

Hippothous came in to join them. The snake was gone. They all started eating. The magpie was hopping about in its cage, squawking annoyingly.

'I hate caged birds,' said Ballista.

'You have always been a sensitive soul.' Maximus nodded. 'There is a terrible sadness in their singing.'

'No, it is the smell – bird-droppings, moulting feathers: puts you off your food. I would wring that fucking thing's neck, if it were not for my wife.'

Breakfast finished, Constans and three other slaves helped the men into their togas. The draping, winding and folding took a long time. The Roman toga was not something you could put on without help and, once arranged, the heavy thing curtailed any sudden, unconsidered movement. No other people wore such a garment. Ballista knew those were three of the reasons the Romans set such store in it.

Eventually, the four citizens were appropriately accoutred:

gleaming white wool, deep-green laurel garlands, the flash of gold from Ballista's mural crown. There was no sign of the women and the children. The magpie had not let up.

'Tell the *domina* we will wait for her outside, down on the Sacred Way.'

Outside, a cold pre-dawn, no wind; the stars paling, but the Grapegatherers still shining faintly. There was a hard frost over everything as they walked down the steep steps. Dogs barked in the distance.

The Elephant was no more expensive than the other bars along the *Embolos*. Nothing was going to be cheap along the Sacred Way. The heavy wooden shutters were open. Hippothous and Calgacus went inside.

The sky was high, pale blue, silvered in the east, streaked by a lone long stretch of cloud, like a straight line carefully drawn. The swallows were high, wheeling and cutting intricate patterns.

'One day, do you think the sky will fall?' Maximus asked.

'I do not know. Maybe.' Ballista carried on watching the swallows. 'Not in the way you Celts think it will. Maybe at Raknarok, when everything falls. Not on its own.'

'Your cousins the Borani and the other Goths, they think it will fall.'

'Not my cousins. Nothing but ignorant refugees.'

'And they speak highly of you,' smiled Maximus.

The others came out with the drinks: four cups of *conditum*. The ceramic cups were hot to hold. The steam smelt of wine, honey and spices.

'Calgacus, do you think the sky will fall?' Maximus asked.

'Aye, of course. Any day now.'

As a Hellene, Hippothous, unsurprisingly, looked superior.

Ballista regarded his friends. Calgacus, with his great domed skull and thin, peevish mouth. Maximus, the scar where the end

20

of his nose should have been pale against the dark tan of his face. And then there was Hippothous. Things were not the same with him as they had been with Demetrius. Of course, Hippothous was older – most likely about Ballista's own age. Yet possibly it was more a question of origins. While Demetrius had come to Ballista as a slave, Hippothous had been born a free man – according to his own account, a rich young man that misfortune had turned to banditry or something close to it. It could be the latter was just too new an addition to the *familia* yet to be a friend. But there was something about Hippothous, something about his eyes. Ballista was far from sure about his new secretary.

The chariot of the sun hauled over the shoulder of the mountain. Up above, the swallows flashed gold and black. Along the *Embolos*, many of the early risers turned to the east and blew a kiss. A few went further, prostrating themselves in the street in full *proskynesis*. None in Ballista's party moved. Each to his own gods, some to none.

'*Dominus.*'

Ballista turned, and there was his wife. Julia looked good. Tall, straight, what the Greeks called deep-bosomed. Her hair and eyes were very black against the white of her matron's *stola*.

'*Domina.*' He greeted her formally. Her black eyes betrayed nothing. Things had not been comfortable between them for a year or so. He had not asked why. And he was not going to. It might be to do with a girl in Cilicia called Roxanne. The unease had appeared after that, after he had come back from Galilee, where he had been sent to kill Jews, when Julia had returned from the imperial palace in Antioch. Someone there might have told her about Ballista in Cilicia, about Roxanne. Things were not comfortable. But the daughter of a senator never made a scene in public, and she did look good. Then there were their sons.

'*Dominus.*' Isangrim stepped forward respectfully. He was a tall boy, just turned ten. And he was quick. He knew his mother expected a certain formality between father and son, expected him to behave with the *dignitas* appropriate to the descendant of a long line of senators on her side. But he knew it irritated his father. Having held the dignified pose for a moment, Isangrim grinned. Father and son clasped forearms, as Isangrim had seen Ballista do with Maximus, Calgacus and the other men he had served with. They hugged.

It was all too much for Dernhelm. The three-year-old escaped the hand of Anthia, one of the two maids with Julia. The boy launched himself at his father and brother. Ballista scooped both boys up. He heard a tut of annoyance from his wife. Ignoring it, he swung the boys high, burying his face in the neck of first one then the other, hair flying, all three laughing; deliberately defying her.

As Ballista set his sons down, another small child barrelled into them. Wherever Dernhelm was, Simon, the Jewish boy Ballista had brought back from Galilee, was also likely to be found. They were much of an age; both full of living. Rebecca started forward to retrieve her charge. Ballista smiled and waved her away. He hugged Simon as well. He had been told often enough by his wife that it was a bad idea to treat a slave child as if it were free, to make a pet of it. He knew it was true. He would have to do something soon. Modify his behaviour or manumit the child. Then there was Rebecca herself. She had been purchased down in Galilee to look after Simon. With her, it depended on what Calgacus wanted. Soon Ballista would have to ask him.

The Caledonian himself came forward. 'Aye, that is it, why not mess up your toga.' Calgacus often seemed to be under the misapprehension that, if he adopted a muttering inflection, his voice, although pitched at a perfectly audible volume, would not be heard. 'After all, it is not you that has to sort it out.' Quite good-naturedly, he shooed the children away.

'And it is not you either these days.' Ballista gestured to Constans. The voluminous woollen drapes of the barbarian's toga rearranged just so, Constans collected Rebecca and Simon and went back up the steps that ran between the blocks of housing that clung to the terraced hillside. Ballista, his wife and two of her maids, his sons, his two freedmen and his *accensus* set off up the Sacred Way.

The *Embolos* ran away uphill in front of them, the smooth, white base of a vertiginous ravine of buildings climbing the slopes on either side. Now there was activity along its length. Precariously up ladders, men fixed swags of flowers from pillar to pillar, garlanded the many, many statues. Others were bringing out small, portable altars, readying the incense and wine, kindling the fires. The air already shimmered above some of them.

All the Ephesians were taking pains over this festival, none more so than the members of the *Boule*. The four hundred and fifty or so rich men who served on the city council had paid for the flowers that festooned all the streets and porticos. They had paid for the frankincense and wine the ordinary citizens would offer as the procession passed, and the much greater quantities of wine they would drink when it was gone. It had cost a great deal – Ephesus was a large and populous city. Yet it might prove worth every *obol*. The city had been on the wrong side in the latest civil war. The year before, it had supported Macrianus and Quietus against Gallienus. Of course, it had had no real choice. But that had not always helped in similar circumstances when the winner was feeling vengeful, or simply short of funds. If imperial displeasure fell on the city, it would fall on the members of the *Boule*. Rich and prominent, serving for life, there was no way they could escape notice.

No one had more reason to be generous than the current *asiarch* in charge of the day's festival. As high priest of the imperial cult in Ephesus, the metropolis of the province of Asia, Gaius Valerius Festus could not be more prominent. He was one of the very richest men in the city. Recently, he had pledged a fortune to dredge the harbour. He had been one of those whose homes had been deemed palatial enough to entertain the pretender Macrianus and his father when they travelled through on their way to the west to meet their fate. To add to his sensitivity, his brother was a Christian. The deviant brother had disappeared from jail and had been in hiding abroad for more than two years. He had reappeared shortly after the fall of Quietus. The emperor Gallienus was known to be extraordinarily relaxed about such things, but the family reunion had caused no great pleasure in the soul of the *asiarch*. It was no wonder Gaius Valerius Festus had invested a huge sum in the festival: choirs, musicians, several leading sophists – and the gods knew *they* did not come cheap – and a whole herd of oxen to be sacrificed and provide a roast meal for everyone in the city.

They had made no distance at all, had not even got past the temple of Hadrian at the front of the Varius Baths on their left, when they were brought to a halt. Up ahead, a muleteer was having problems with his charge. Long ears back, the beast was circling. It had shed its load of flowers. Now its narrow hooves were stamping and slicing the fallen blooms into a muddy mush.

Ballista checked that his sons were out of range. A mule finds it easier than a horse to strike out in any direction. Seeing the boys safe, Ballista put it out of his mind. He looked back the way they had come, down to the library of Celsus, and beyond to the harbour. Just a few days, and they would take ship for the west. There was no point in waiting in Ephesus for Gallienus's decision. It would find them wherever they were. That was part of the god-like power of an emperor. *Allfather, Death-blinder,*

Hooded One, let the decision be good: no worse than exile, with the estate to my sons.

Ballista was half aware that Maximus was giving the party a lengthy account of breeding mules in Hibernia. It all seemed to hinge on cutting the mare's mane and tail before taking her to the donkey – it humbled her pride; would probably work on women too. There was a small stream of water running down the *Embolos*. Idly, Ballista's eyes tracked it back up the hill, past them and under the careering mule. The rivulet ran on beyond where the driver's stick was being employed in anger. The water was coming from the left-hand side of the Sacred Way, from the Fountain of Trajan.

Twice the size of a man, Trajan soared up, his head and shoulders reaching level with the second storey of the building. He was near naked, as befitted a god. Other, smaller deities peered out at him from their columned niches. In the big pool at his feet, barbarians cowered. It was from this pool that the water was coming.

Odd, thought Ballista. The Romans were so good at hydraulic engineering. The water was starting to pour over the rim of the big basin at a prodigious rate. It was thick, brown, muddy. The mule, stamping and splashing, whinnied; a high call ending in a frightened hee-haw.

Realization came to Ballista in a rush: the fountain and the mule; before that, the snake and the caged bird; it was spring, a dead calm, no rain for days. Allfather, all the signs were there. They had to get out of here, get to a place of greater safety. The mule, sharp hooves flying, blocked the way ahead. On either side, the buildings crowded up on top of each other: a death trap. It had to be downhill. To where? The open orchestra of the theatre? No, definitely not; not with the tall, delicate stage buildings and the monuments looming above the seats. The gate into the commercial *agora*, the Gate of Mazaeus and Mithridates? It was a good structure, solidly built. No, of course not there – beyond it, the *agora* itself.

'We are going to the *agora*.' Ballista's words cut across the prattle of Maximus. The *familia* stared. 'We are going to run. Calgacus, you go in front; get people out of the way. Maximus, you carry Dernhelm. Isangrim, with me: hold my hand. Julia, you and your women, keep close. Hippothous, bring up the rear.'

Julia made as if to question all this, but stopped as the two freedmen and the secretary obeyed the instructions. In position, the men hauled up their unwieldy togas. A moment's hesitation, and the three women more demurely rearranged their costume. High on Maximus's shoulder, young Dernhelm was roaring with laughter.

'Time to go.'

Bystanders gawped, reluctantly moved out of the way as the *familia* set off, slow at first, down the street. 'Faster! Move faster!' Ballista shouted. Aided by the slope, they picked up speed.

Out in front, Calgacus was yelling: *Vir Ementissimus . . . diplomata . . . shift it, you soft southerners*. The fine details may have been lost on most pedestrians, but the general intention was clear. The crowd stepped to the sides, pointing, laughing, treating it like a prelude to the festivities. As he ran, Isangrim's hand sweaty in his, Ballista thought how embarrassing this would be if he were wrong.

They pounded on; past the tomb of Arsinoe, past the *Heroon* of Androclos. The noise came as they reached the Gate of Hadrian: a great clattering rattle, like an empty wagon or chariot driven fast over cobbles. The bystanders looked this way and that, searching for the source of the noise. There was nothing in sight, just the big man and his *familia*, garments ridiculously hitched up, tearing past as if Hecate herself were after them.

As they hurtled into the square in front of the library of Celsus, the noise changed to a strange, hollow rumble, like distant thunder. The paving stones shifted. Ballista and Isangrim stumbled. Holding each other's hand, their momentum helped keep them upright. Maximus was holding Dernhelm just ahead; Calgacus still out in front; the others behind, still on their feet. They all ran.

The noise surged, changed again – now a bull roaring in a cave. The ground punched up into their feet. Ballista lost his grip on Isangrim. Down, scrabbling on the gritty stones. People falling, screaming all around them; Ballista reaching for his son. Between the paving slabs, earth was thrown up like chaff from a winnowing sieve. The slender columns of the library of Celsus swayed. The air seemed to tremble.

Ballista and Isangrim clasped hands, clawed to their feet. They could see Maximus's back vanishing into the gateway. High on the pediment above the Hibernian's head, the statues of Augustus and the first imperial dynasty shifted and moved – a sinister, stiff ecstasy of primitive priests about a macabre blood ritual.

'Come on!' Ballista shouted.

Together, father and son ran into the shadow of the vaulting – a terrible crashing behind – on under the colonnade. And then . . . And then they were clear; out in the open spaces of the commercial forum. Nothing here to threaten them. Keep away from the equestrian statue of the emperor Claudius in the middle, and there was nothing but wooden stalls little higher than a man. Nothing to fear.

Calgacus and Maximus had pulled up in a clear space. They were doubled over, panting like animals, hugging Dernhelm. The little boy was wide eyed, silent. Ballista and Isangrim joined them.

Ballista kissed both his sons, and looked around. Hippothous and one of the maids had joined them. Julia? He looked around again. Where was Julia? He directed his gaze further afield. People everywhere: standing, milling, some running. No sign of her.

'Isangrim, stay with Calgacus.'

'No,' shouted Maximus. 'I will go back.'

'No, look after the boys.'

Ballista headed back, against the gathering flow of humanity. Still no sign.

The din was deafening: shouts, screams – humans and animals – the horrible grinding as the works of man fell in ruin. But now the ground was still. For how long?

Back under the colonnade. Ballista shouldered his way under the gateway. Allfather, where was she?

A man ran blindly into Ballista. He was shrugged aside. Ballista fought through to the other side, desperately scanning the square.

There! Off to the right. Julia was kneeling by a fallen statue, and under the statue lay the maid Anthia. Dark blood pooled out.

Touching Julia's shoulder, Ballista said something. She took no notice.

Ballista let his bunched-up toga drop. The white folds fell in the blood. He reached down to see if the girl was alive. What if she was? He could not lift the solid marble statue. He felt for a pulse. Guiltily, he was relieved she was dead.

Ballista started to straighten up. He stopped. Had his fear overcome his senses? He looked up. Another statue was poised on the very edge of the gate. He remembered another gate, another city. The great temple at Emesa, the statues turning in the air, rigid as they fell; the heavy, brittle impacts; the carnage among his men; the slicing pain in his leg. Now, the ground in Ephesus was still. For how long?

Again he bent down, felt for a sign of life.

'She is dead. Come.'

Julia did not move. Inexplicably, she began to recite Latin verse:

'Why, victor, celebrate?'

Ballista put his hands under her armpits.

'This victory will destroy you.'

Ballista got his wife to her feet.

Quid, victor, gaudes? Haec te victoria perdet.

Half-carrying her, Ballista pulled Julia away.
Back in the *agora*, they reached the others.
Nearby, above the cacophony, came the sound of a hymn:

Poseidon, Earth-holder, steadfast stabilizer;
Avert your anger,
Hold your hands over us.

Fools, thought Ballista: wrong reason, wrong deity. The gods had chained Loki deep in the earth, suspended the serpent above his head. Loki's good-wife caught the venom in a bowl. But the bowl must fill, must be emptied. And then, in the dark, the poison gathered on the fangs, balled out and dropped on the Evil One's unprotected face. Loki screamed, and hopelessly fought the chains and the rocks that secured them.

No point in praying. Nothing to be done.

II

It was dark in the *agora*. Well past dawn, and darkness had returned. Thick clouds of dust and smoke had rolled under the gate, billowed down past the theatre from the mountain. The sun could not break through. The choking yellow-brown fog had turned the Tetragonos *agora*, the commercial heart of Ephesus, the metropolis of Asia, into something from beyond the Styx.

The ground had stopped moving, but in the crowd some still staggered like sailors trying to recover their land legs. Near to Ballista, a man clutched a market stall and vomited. The trades-man made no objection; like many, he just stared blankly, overwhelmed by the enormity of what had happened. Here and there, individuals screamed incoherently or ran pointlessly, their wits unhinged. From the gloom came snatches of hymns: *Posei-don, Earth-Holder* . . .

'*Dominus*.' It was Calgacus. '*Dominus*, the house, the rest of the *familia*. We must get back.'

Ballista tried to get his thoughts in order: the house, Constans, Rebecca and Simon, the others . . . the horror. Of course Calgacus was fearful – Rebecca.

Hippothous drew near. His sandy hair was dusty, his blue eyes shot with red. '*Dominus*, with an earthquake this severe, there is never just the one shock. All the subterranean wind cannot force its way out at once. Air is bound to be left in the narrow places of the earth. The ground will shake again as it escapes.'

Ballista stroked the heads of Isangrim and Dernhelm. He tried to think.

'The boys' – Hippothous gestured – 'the women, they will be safer here in the open. If you go with the men, I will look after them.'

Ballista looked around through the thick, jaundiced air. There were no buildings, and it was flat here, all the way down to the harbour. 'After a shock, there can be a tidal wave.'

Hippothous nodded, an oddly calm and judicious nod, as if he were discussing a proposition in a philosophical school. 'Not always, and we are hundreds of yards from the sea. There is only a tidal wave if there is an onshore wind opposing the escaping air. The sky is calm today.'

Ballista did not reply at once. He looked at the crowds standing vacant, occasional eddies of imbecilic motion in the murk – all irrational, possibly dangerous. He could not leave his sons here. He would not be parted from them now.

'We will all go,' Ballista said.

The Gate of Mazaeus and Mithridates loomed out of the gloom. On its top, some statues still stood. Ballista eyed them suspiciously. The square beyond the gate was a deserted shambles. To the right, tendrils of smoke issued from the façade of the library of Celsus. Ahead, the big Parthian war monument had collapsed; the barbarians and their conquerors, both indiscriminately hurled to the ground. Ballista quickly led the group away to the left. He hoped the boys had not noticed the fallen statue and the crushed body of Anthia.

31

Emerging into the Sacred Way, they saw the scale of the destruction and its inhuman randomness. Some buildings stood pristine; next to them, a whole block had imploded. The temple of Hadrian and the Varius Baths appeared untouched. The block opposite, the *insula* of their rented house, had given way.

'Gods below . . .'

The street itself was partly blocked. Clambering over the debris, they reached the foot of the slope where the rented house had stood.

Ballista took stock. There were people here, many rooted in shock, but others moving more purposefully. Scurrying like ants over the ruins – rescuers or looters, you could not tell. The *familia* closed up around Ballista. They were waiting, except Julia, who continued blank-eyed with shock. Why could someone else not take the decisions? Ballista pushed aside the childish thought.

'Isangrim, stay with your mother.' Ballista turned to the remaining maid. 'Rhode, take good care of Dernhelm; stay close to your *domina*. Hippothous, guard the women and children. Keep out of the lee of the buildings, try to stay in the middle of the street.'

Ballista grinned resignedly at Maximus and Calgacus. 'We had better do what we can.' He gestured at their bedraggled togas. 'These will not help. We should leave them here.'

As the three men began to strip down to their tunics, Ballista realized that, somehow, the mural crown was still on his head. He passed it to Hippothous. 'Look after it. I lost one once in Antioch; cost a fortune to replace.' The bloodshot eyes of the *accensus* gleamed. Ballista wondered if he was one of those men with a passion for gold. Certainly, he had been little better than a bandit back in Cilicia.

'We should take the togas,' said Calgacus. 'They can be tied into ropes.'

'Allfather, you are right.' Ballista shook his head. 'We have nothing, not even a weapon between us.'

His freedmen both smiled. From somewhere or other, Maximus produced a serious knife. Calgacus had two. The old Caledonian handed one to Ballista, who gave it over to Hippothous.

'You really are nasty, dangerous bastards.' Ballista laughed.

'Sure, and you have always been too trusting,' replied Maximus.

The three men gave their attention to the slope. The path between the two blocks of houses was gone. Walls had toppled sideways to bury it. But most of the buildings had collapsed forwards, sliding down the hillside. They would have to climb over the fallen roofs, the exposed beams and masonry.

The material of his toga knotted over his shoulder, Ballista set off. They climbed spread out, careful not to get in front of each other. The ruins were hideously unstable. If one of them caused a slip, anyone behind him was liable to be crushed as well. It was painfully slow going. Every hand and foothold threatened injury; jagged tiles and exposed nails were everywhere.

Allfather, this is near-suicide, thought Ballista. The whole lot could go at any moment, even without the terrible likelihood of an aftershock. Out of nowhere came the realization that he was clambering over the dead and dying – even worse, over the uninjured and trapped. He inched upward.

The house, when they eventually reached it, was just recognizable: a weirdly truncated version of what it had been. It had shifted forward, and the floors had collapsed down on top of each other. The headroom of each chamber had been reduced to no more than a couple of feet. The beams of the ceilings stuck out in rows just above each other. It did not look as if it had ever been a real house. It reminded Ballista of one of those fancy Italian cakes built in layers.

They got on top of it, tore away tiles, called down into the rubble. They listened. Nothing came back from the house; just distant shouts and screams, and far too close squeals and sharp cracks as timber and masonry settled or fell. There was a half-scented smell of woodsmoke.

There was a dip where the atrium had been. Digging down from the top of the house was hopeless. With few words, they crept towards the hollow. Maybe they could tunnel in from the side.

A deep menacing roar rose from below. They stopped, gazed down. A breeze had got up, was blowing away some of the Stygian gloom. A lone figure was haring up the Sacred Way. He ran heedless, scrambling over obstructions, pausing for nothing. At no great distance behind him came the pursuit, a throng spilling out from the *agora*, past the smouldering library of Celsus. The mob was baying for blood – the worst sound in the world.

The man was heading straight for Julia and the boys. Paralysed with impotence, Ballista watched. *Allfather, Deep Hood, Death-blinder, let them be safe.*

Hippothous had seen the man coming. He was herding the *familia* back behind the columns of the façade of the small temple of Hadrian. The man tried to dive in after them. Hippothous stepped out from the central arch. His arm moved; sunlight glinted on the blade. The man sheered off, ran on. He looked tired, not moving well.

The mob was gaining. They surged past the temple of Hadrian. They were yelling, giving voice to their hatred. Snatches floated up to Ballista: *Kill the arsonist, the atheist . . . Christians to the lion.*

The man broke stride by the turning into the path up to the governor's palace. Deciding against it, he ran on up the *Embolos*.

He only got as far as the Fountain of Trajan before they were on him. A hurled stone brought him down. He tried to get to his feet. Someone kicked him down again. He disappeared: the centre of surging, kicking frenzy.

'Gods below!' said Maximus. 'See the women.'

Ballista saw it was worse than the Hibernian had said; there were even children in the lynch mob. He looked away down the street. Hippothous was doing well. He was keeping the *familia* back in the temple of Hadrian, sparing the boys the sickening sight.

The crowd parted momentarily. The man was on his feet again. They were clawing at him, beating him, pulling him this way and that. He was not young. Now he was bloodied, beyond pleading.

'Poor bastard,' said Maximus.

The man went down once more. The mob closed in, like hounds breaking up a beast.

'Poor bastard,' said Maximus again.

> *Poseidon, Earth-holder, steadfast stabilizer;*
> *Avert your anger,*
> *Hold your hands over us.*
> *Phoebus Apollo . . .*

The celebrants of this impulsive blood rite held their stained hands to the sky. Their hymn drifted up; to the three men watching on the slope, above to the Olympian gods. Presumably, the deities on high would be pleased – if they existed.

Down on the *Embolos*, the knot of humanity began to unravel. Men, women and children drifted away. At a distance, they started to look more deflated than exalted.

In the misty spring sunshine the body lay abandoned in the middle of the Sacred Way.

Up on the slope, the three men did not speak of it. There was

35

nothing to say. With no words at all, they resumed their delicate traverse to the hollow of the atrium.

Before he shifted over the edge, Ballista looked down on the *Embolos*. He was pleased Hippothous had got the *familia* out of the temple of Hadrian. Ballista did not trust its slender columns to withstand another shock. The corpse lay in the street not far from them, but that could not be helped. It was the manner of the slaying he had wished his sons not to see, not its happening or its aftermath. After all, what child had not witnessed violent death, in the arena or elsewhere, had not seen the bodies on the crosses outside virtually every town in the *imperium*?

The sides of the depression were seamed with jagged rents like badly cut niches in a tomb. Some of the openings were no bigger than a baby; others could admit a man. They clambered perilously, peering into the dark, dust-choked holes, calling, listening for signs of life.

'Here.' Maximus summoned the other two. Muffled sounds; crying – an infant?; a woman's voice – *Help, somebody help*.

'I will go,' said Maximus. 'All the good living has left you two as fat as gladiators.'

Ballista felt a surge of gratitude. Maximus was one of the very few who knew his fear of confined spaces.

They cut and rolled one of the togas into a rope, tied it around Maximus's waist, spliced another to it.

'Three sharp tugs, and we want you out of there,' said Ballista. 'You do the same, and we will start pulling you out.'

Maximus nodded. With no discernible hesitation, he levered himself into the hole.

Maximus's progress was slow. He worked small chunks of brick and timber along his body with his fingers and toes, pushed them out behind him. Eventually, his feet disappeared.

Ballista waited, playing out the makeshift, woollen rope.

Calgacus was silent beside him. There was a faint but definite smell of burning. Up above, in a clear blue sky, the swallows wheeled and darted.

For a long time the rope did not move. Ballista could hear Maximus grunting, scrabbling, coughing. Every so often the nearby sharp crack or groan of moving rubble made both the watchers jump.

At long, long last they heard Maximus returning. Calgacus leant into the fissure, dragging out the rubble as Maximus booted it. Maximus's feet reappeared. As he wriggled out, the sound of crying squalled after him.

Maximus slumped down. All across his body, bright-red gashes showed through the dense paste of sweat and dust.

Calgacus reached in and, like some nightmarish midwife, brought the child into the light. He passed Simon to Ballista, and leant in again. As tenderly as he was able, Calgacus pulled Rebecca out. The ugly old man cradled her in his arms.

'Constans is in there,' Rebecca croaked. She could hardly speak. They had not thought to bring any water. She disengaged herself from Calgacus, and took up Simon.

Ballista looked down at Maximus. The Hibernian nodded, an expression of much doubt on his face.

'Calgacus, take them down to the others.'

Ballista helped them up to the lip of the hollow. Below, Julia and Rhode, Dernhelm on her shoulder, were in the open. For some reason, Hippothous was leading Isangrim apart, back behind the façade of the little temple.

'Calgacus, get Isangrim and that Cilician fool back out of that death trap. And you take care on the way down.'

Calgacus waved a hand in response.

At the base of the depression, Maximus sat, eyes shut, panting like a dog. It was stupid not to have brought water.

Ballista's hands went to untie the improvised belt at Maximus's waist. He resisted the half-hearted attempt to stop him. 'You are all done.'

'Sure, it will not work.'

'Maybe, but what can you do?'

With the rope around him, Ballista lifted his torso into the opening. Straightaway, his own body shut out most of the light. Awkwardly, he dragged himself further in. When his feet were in, he stopped. He lay still for a time, telling himself he was allowing his eyes to adjust. He tried not to think of the crushing weight of the unstable rubble above and all around him, tried not to let the terrifying constriction of his movements enter his mind at all. The tunnel was little wider than his shoulders, all its surfaces rough and catching. He wondered if he could carry on.

Like an animal with its back legs broken, he dragged himself forward with his arms, feet flippering ineffectually behind. A jagged piece of rubble sliced through his tunic. He felt the warm blood smearing his stomach. He let the pain rise; concentrated on that, used it to blot out the fear.

The deeper he went, the faster and shallower his breathing became. The air might be getting bad, or it could just be him. Keep going. *Do not think, just act.*

The ghastly tunnel opened out just a little. His hands, as much as his eyes, told him there was a lintel or the like overhead. It must have saved Rebecca and Simon. Beyond, the space felt no bigger than a rabbit hole.

'Help.' The voice was soft, but shockingly close.

'Constans?'

'Help! Zeus, it hurts.'

Ballista could make out something pale in the near-total darkness in front. He reached out. It was a hand and forearm; warm, gritty to the touch. They extended out of the rubble.

'Constans, can you move?'

'Zeus, Athena, all the gods, get me out of here.'

Ballista was finding it hard to breathe. He forced himself to talk soothingly, as he would to a horse. What he said he did not know. Slowly, not to startle him, he let go of Constans's hand. Ballista ran his fingers over the rubble, trying to form an impression of what was there.

The opening was indeed little bigger than a rabbit hole. Ballista slid his arm in alongside that of Constans; there was next to no room for anything else. He patted the trapped man on the shoulder. Above the hole seemed to be one large block of masonry. With no equipment and no room to work, it would be impossible to break it up or move it. Below the fallen material was more fragmentary. Possibly it could be dug out, but then the unsupported block above would come down.

Ballista lay still again. His breath came in short gasps, making staccato the platitudes he continued to address to Constans. Ballista was not nearly deep enough for the air to be foul. As he talked, he thought about this specific tunnel. He thought about tunnels in general. His mind went back six or seven years, to Arete. Discussing with his friend Mamurra how best to ventilate tunnels. Mamurra, the friend he had left to die in a tunnel. There had been no choice. The Persians would have broken in, killed everyone. No choice at all. But, at times, the moment he had ordered the pit props knocked down, had the entrance caved in, came back with a horrible clarity. Not then, but later, the Persians had broken in anyway. They had killed everyone they caught.

A sharp tug on Ballista's waist, then another. The northerner lay waiting – maybe he had missed the first pull on the rope. He said something to Constans; something reassuring, nothing valedictory about it at all. Ballista started to move backwards.

At first, he moved slowly, not wishing to unsettle Constans.

39

Then he realized this was madness. Hands, elbows, knees, feet working furiously, he propelled himself away. He felt the sharp things; the abrasions, nicks and cuts blossomed all over his body.

Maximus caught him as he shot out feet first. The Hibernian set him down. Ballista was retching, wiping his eyes. They should have brought water.

Maximus pointed to the side of the depression. Smoke issued from at least a dozen vents. One streamed out in a jet, as if from a crack in a charcoal burner's stack. Another gave out distinct puffs, like an angry chthonic god signalling catastrophe.

'We cannot leave him,' Ballista said.

Maximus nodded, hoisted himself into the opening.

Ballista knew what Maximus was going to do. Should he stop him? Ballista drew back from the abyss of the huge moral dilemma. He looked over the ruins; perilous and transitory. Ballista shut his eyes.

There came the sound of scrabbling. Maximus was back. He got out, re-sheathed the knife.

'Time to go.'

III

'*Dominus*, have you decided what to do with Ballista?' At the words, a silence spread through the dining room of the requisitioned house in Byzantium.

The Roman emperor, the pious, invincible Publius Licinius Egnatius Gallienus, did not respond to his *a Studiis*. The responsibilities of Voconius Zeno were to aid the emperor in his cultural studies, duties which did not stretch anything like so far as this.

'The man has killed a pretender, had the temerity to assume the purple, even for only a few days,' Zeno continued.

Gallienus selected a pear from the low table by his couch. Who has bribed you? he thought. How much did this question cost?

'Ballista is in Ephesus, waiting for the start of the sailing season to take a boat and return to Sicily. In five days he will be gone. He is not coming here to the court,' said Zeno.

Gallienus turned the fruit in his hand. It had a lustre in the spring sunshine. Biting into it, he took in the other men in the room. There were fourteen apart from himself: five civilians; heads of imperial chanceries, including Zeno; and nine military men. It was a small, intimate lunch after the formal *consilium*.

The serious business of the morning was done. They had discussed at length the imperial decision, as implacable and irrevocable as that of a god, concerning the city of Byzantium.

'Of course, *Dominus*, I am not suggesting a course of action.' Zeno was losing confidence in the face of continued imperial silence. 'It may well be he should be rewarded, rather than punished.'

Gallienus noted that, while all were quiet, only one of the others seemed especially interested. It was not Rufinus, the *Princeps Peregrinorum*. As head of the secret service, Rufinus should have been all ears. The man who was paying close attention, although hiding it well, was Censorinus, the deputy Praetorian Prefect.

It could be time for a change, thought Gallienus. Censorinus may be a low-bred individual, his misquotations of Homer the talk of the court, but he had served as *Princeps Peregrinorum* to both Gallienus's father, Valerian, and the short-lived pretenders Macrianus and Quietus. He was a political survivor: untrustworthy, but ruthless and efficient. Gallienus knew he needed men with the latter qualities, and he had never been one to hold a man's birth against him.

'Try a pear,' the emperor said to Zeno. 'You know how I enjoy things out of season.'

A servant passed the silver fruit platter, and Zeno helped himself. Gallienus suppressed a smile. It may well be that Zeno detested pears, but an imperial suggestion always had the force of a command. And – the urge to smile was hard to resist – Zeno would be turning over all the possible meanings of what he had said, and must recognize the dangerous implications of 'things out of season'.

'My mind is not yet made up,' Gallienus said. 'But now I want my *comites* to advise me on my *decennalia*.'

Unsurprisingly, given the nature of the subject, it was a civilian, one of the heads of chanceries, who began. '*Dominus*,' said Caecilius Hermianus, the *ab Admissionibus*, 'your ten glorious years on the throne demand a fitting, magnificent spectacle.'

'Indeed,' replied Gallienus. 'Although I was hoping for more specific suggestions.' The pleasure of crushing men with words was insidious. He must keep it in check. He did not want to become like Tiberius or Caligula: kingship and tyranny were two sides of a coin.

'It will have to wait for the autumn, when the campaigning season is over.' The senior Praetorian Prefect, unlike his deputy, Censorinus, did not affect the accent and manners of the upper class. Volusianus was a military man through and through. He had started out as a cavalry trooper, and he was proud of it. He was one of the few men Gallienus trusted unreservedly. How the senate had loathed it when he had made Volusianus consul the year before.

'Which gives us time to plan a truly wonderful occasion.' The urbane voice of Palfurius Sura, the *ab Epistulis*, was full of enthusiasm. 'Obviously, it must open with a grand procession: the senate and equestrian order, in togas, selected matrons of good character; torch-lit, at night, ascending the Capitol.'

'White oxen with gilded horns, white lambs: two hundred of each – a holocaust to thank the gods of Rome for their providence in watching over the best of emperors in these difficult times.' Achilleus, the *a Memoria*, nodded at his own sagacity and plain speaking in even alluding to the chaos that disfigured the empire.

One of the military officers spoke. 'The standards of the legions and auxiliaries, the prisoners-of-war: Persians, Goths, Sarmatians.' Aureolus, the Prefect of Cavalry, once a shepherd boy among the Getan tribesmen up by the Danube, was another tough military man whom Gallienus trusted.

'Elephants,' said Achilleus. 'They would add grandeur to the procession; and golden cloaks for the matrons.'

'There must be at least three days of spectacles.' The *ab Admissionibus* Hermianus clearly wished to win back ground after his earlier rebuff. 'Circus races – a full programme of course; gladiators – fewer than 1,200 would not be right; and theatrical performances of all kinds: mimes and buffoons, as well as pantomimes and serious actors.'

'Buffoons putting on a Cyclops-performance, and boxing. Your people love both.' Zeno was on good ground; all knew the emperor's liking for such things – nothing out of season here.

'Excellent,' pronounced Gallienus. 'Excellent. The gladiators will march in the procession, and the boxers and pantomimes can be exhibited on wagons.'

There was a tiny pause, as the *comites* assured themselves that the emperor was serious, before a great deal of decorous agreement.

'And buildings – an emperor must provide work to feed his people – there must be buildings.' Some of the glacial self-control customary with an emperor slipped. Architecture was one of Gallienus's keenest passions, along with philosophy, poetry, oratory, women, his patron god Hercules, and several other things; he was a man of many and varied passions. 'The architects have been commissioned to draw up plans for the new colossus on the Esquiline Hill. The foundations at least must be ready to be dedicated by the *decennalia*. But more is needed. I wish to construct a portico along the Via Flaminia. It will extend as far as the Mulvian Bridge. It should be four columns deep, the foremost bearing statues of the great men of Rome.'

The *comites* murmured their appreciation of his kingly vision.

'But, Quirinius, can our *fiscus* afford such grandiose plans?' Gallienus laughed, self-deprecatingly – if he had not been an emperor.

The *a Rationibus*, in charge of the finances of the *imperium*, did not hestitate. 'Celebrating your *maiestas* is without price and, as you know, *Dominus*, plans are in hand to debase the precious metal in the coinage again. It will be a few months before the merchants catch up.'

'Things must be done open-handedly, even if the *fiscus* is short.' Gallienus was quite serious now. 'We cannot ever appear short of money, or our enemies would take heart.'

Rufinus cleared his throat. 'The confiscated estates of the recent round of deluded traitors, and those of their families, can be sold. Celsus in Africa, Ingenuus and Regalianus on the Danube, Valens and Piso in Greece, the Macriani in the east – they were all rich men, with rich friends.'

'The wages of treachery,' nodded Gallienus. Perhaps Rufinus still had some usefulness yet as the spymaster in charge of the *frumentarii*.

A slave glided up to the *ab Admissionibus* and whispered in his ear. Hermianus rose to his feet and announced that, if the most noble emperor had finished his lunch, the leading men of the *polis* of Byzantium were awaiting him in the hippodrome; almost all the members of the *Boule* had been rounded up.

The councillors of Byzantium, a hundred and fifty or so of them, were standing in a ragged line on the chariot-racing track. They were surrounded by soldiers. All the members of the *Boule* looked terrified. They were right to be. The previous year, Byzantium had joined the wrong side in a civil war. When the advance guard of the armies of the Macriani arrived, the city had opened its gates. That need not have been fatal. Many cities had done the same. Those cities were now paying reparations to the *fiscus* of Gallienus set at two to four times the contributions previously extracted by the pretenders. A punishment as mild as potential financial ruin was not a likely option for Byzantium.

When news had come from the west that both the young usurper Macrianus and his father, the sinister Macrianus the Lame, the real power behind the revolt, had been killed outside Serdica, the city of Byzantium had held fast in the faction of the remaining usurper, the young Quietus, who was far away in Syria. This misguided adherence had not been removed either by the arrival before the Byzantine walls of an imperial force commanded by the African general Memor, or by the setting up in front of the main Thracian Gates of the severed heads of the Macriani, father and son. By the time word came that Quietus had been killed in Emesa, it was too late. The siege had begun. By the usage of war, when the first ram touched the walls, the only surrender could be unconditional; all the men could be killed; the women and children sold into slavery. Some held they could be killed too.

The siege had continued into the winter. Gallienus had sent two more of his *protectores*, the famed siege engineers Bonitus and Celer. It had not appreciably hastened things. Byzantium was rich, well supplied. It occupied a very strong position. It was surrounded by the sea on three sides; the Bosphorus, fast-flowing, to the east. There was high ground for its acropolis. To the west, its land walls were substantial, watched over by tall towers, well equipped with torsion artillery.

The wealth of Byzantium and the strength of its position had long fed the contumacy of the city. Two generations earlier, the *polis* had defied the emperor Septimius Severus and the might of the whole empire for three years. It looked fit to do the same again. The siege had dragged into the spring. The birds had long since picked the skulls of the Macriani clean.

Gallienus himself had broken the deadlock. He had arrived suddenly from the west, accompanied only by the cavalry of the guard. After a herald had arranged a truce, he had ridden alone up to the Thracian Gates. He had not offered terms, but had sworn he would prove more merciful than had Septimius Severus.

The latter emperor had ordered many killed, sections of the walls and most public buildings razed, and had reduced Byzantium to the legal status of a village ruled by its neighbour and rival *polis* of Perinthus. After a brief debate, to try to avoid such things happening again, the *Boule* had recommended that the people throw themselves on the *clementia* of Gallienus. Now, getting to their feet after performing adoration, sweating as the early-afternoon sun beat down in the hippodrome, the councillors were more than anxious about whether they had made a good decision.

'Those two in the middle,' Achilleus, the *a Memoria*, whispered to his emperor, 'the ones standing a pace in front of the others.'

Gallienus regarded the men. Both were tall, with full but neat beards and heads of hair. They were clad in Hellenic *himation* and tunic, right arms decorously wrapped in the cloaks. They clung to their self-control for dear life: only their eyes – ever moving, circling – betrayed them.

In the morning, the *consilium* had expressed the view that Byzantium was too venerable and too important, both as a crossing point between Europe and Asia and as a bulwark against the barbarians from the Black Sea, to be destroyed. A swingeing fine and the execution of the ringleaders should suffice. These two men, Cleodamus and Athenaeus, had led the defence. They should die. The deaths of these two rich, honourable and potent men would cow the others. Their estates would enrich the imperial *fiscus*.

Gallienus looked at them steadily. One word, and they were dead. He felt the intoxicating rush of power. One word, and all the members of the *Boule* were dead; one word, and life was ended for any he chose of his own *comites*. Such god-like power

47

was dangerous. Of course, every slave owner had the power of life and death. But that was over instruments with voices, of little more significance than drowning a cat. These were free men. His was the power of an Olympian. It was not to be used without consideration. Even Hercules, Gallienus's particular divine companion, had often been too hasty. The sack of sacred Delphi, the killing of his guest Iphitus: in both, Hercules had been too hasty. Gallienus would learn from the errors of his immortal friend: nothing hasty, nothing ill judged.

Shifting his attention beyond Cleodamus and Athenaeus, Gallienus considered the other councillors. All were rich and honourable, but lacking the drive and initiative to head the defence of their own city; followers not leaders. When the bad times came, as they would when the tribes from the north attacked again, who would be more use?

'From that bald head, to that one over there.' Gallienus's pointing finger swept along about twenty of the main line of councillors. 'Kill them all. They are guilty of *maiestas*, their entire estates are confiscated. Proceed with the executions.'

Soldiers herded the condemned men out from the spared. Some begged, some cried, a few went with dignity. One by one, they were forced to their knees. Steel shone bright in the sun. The sickening sounds of the blows; the blood spraying very red in the air then, dulled, draining into the soiled sand.

There had been no reaction from the *comites* behind the emperor. They knew as well as Gallienus that while an emperor was expected to listen to the views of his *consilium*, he was in no way bound to follow them. The will of the emperor was law; arbitrary and untrammelled. It always had been thus, and so it would be for ever.

IV

The soft, blue sweetness of a Mediterranean spring night hid a multitude of things. Ballista stood on the terrace of the governor's palace, high on the slope of the central mount of Ephesus. Darkness had not long fallen. The offshore breeze hissed through the ornamental shrubs and the scrub of the hillside; the gubernatorial and the unclaimed – the wind made no differentiation.

He looked out. To the left, lights shone from the residential district that climbed the opposite slope. Above them, the mountain loomed dark blue, the sky eggshell blue above that. In front of him and below, past the pale semicircle of the theatre, the famous fifty lanterns illuminating the street that ran arrow-straight to the port. There were lights down by the water, too, not enough to mask the silver-black harbour. Beyond, in the Aegean, the lamps of the fishing boats drifted out on the offshore breeze. Off to the right, more lights: in the open spaces of the exercise ground, the Harbour Baths and the Olympeion; more outside the city itself, out on the plain of the Caystros river.

In the gloaming, if you did not know what had happened, it all looked good. But Ballista did know, and it was all far from good.

There were too few lights in the residential district and the port; too few lights out to sea. The lights off to the right, in the grounds of the Harbour Baths and the other places, were the campfires of the homeless. The flaring street lanterns were little more than civic bravado.

It was eight days since the earthquake. There had been no tidal wave. But there had been four big aftershocks. Among the many rescuers and looters scrabbling among the ruins, many more had died. As ever, it was not the earthquake that had killed but the buildings. More fires had broken out as homeowners raked through the debris, desperately searching for their loved ones or possessions.

Yet everything that could be done had been done. The governor of Asia, Maximillianus, had put the two hundred and fifty auxiliary soldiers in the town at the disposal of the civic authorities. Corvus, the *eirenarch* of Ephesus, had deployed them with his fifty men of the watch. Fires had been doused, the most dangerous ruins that could be got at had been pulled down. Looting and lynching had been discouraged by means of some exemplary executions in prominent places.

The meeting Ballista had just left had addressed the longer-term concerns. The governor had gathered a small *consilium* of men of rank: the scribe to the *demos* Publius Vedius Antoninus, the *asiarch* Gaius Valerius Festus, the wealthy notable Flavius Damianus, the *eirenarch* Corvus, and Ballista himself. Ballista knew all these men except one from his previous time in Ephesus. Three years before, he had been there, serving as deputy to the governor. Ironically, the governor was the one man he had not met previously. One thing he knew of the others was that they disliked each other strongly. *Inamicitia* was rife among them; in some cases, it had run in their families for generations.

Yet today, personal and familial animosities mainly set aside, in something almost approaching collegiality, the men had spent hours in discussion. How to prevent rioting and rapine, and how to avoid pestilence and famine – the problems were grave, but the consensus among the *hegemones* present was that they were not insuperable.

Maintaining public order was always an issue in a city such as Ephesus, whose population was often estimated to approach a quarter of a million. One aspect of the discussion had surprised Ballista. Flavius Damianus, the Christian-hater, whom Ballista detested of old as a man who took perverse pleasure in the physical suffering of others, had proposed that proclamations be posted announcing that attacks on those who might be thought to have brought down the anger of the gods be banned from the city on pain of death. It might be, thought Ballista, that Flavius Damianus hated the idea of the poor taking matters into their own hands even more than he loathed the atheist followers of the crucified Jew.

The imperial priest Gaius Valerius Festus had raised serious concerns about the great temple of Artemis outside the city. On the one hand, it was filled with incalculable treasures, both sacred and profane; not for nothing was it known as the bank of Asia. On the other, it had an imperially recognized right of asylum and, because of that, as was ever the case with such places, in its grounds abided a horde of murderers, kidnappers, rapists, and other lesser criminals down on their luck. Either way, it was a potential source of serious trouble. After due deliberation, and acknowledging that it would stretch the tiny force of armed men thinner still, Maximillianus ordered fifty of the auxiliary soldiers to reinforce the civilian temple guards. No one had suggested that the goddess might look after her own.

Ballista had recommended that the troops be brought in from their individual billets, which were spread across the city, and gathered in two or three requisitioned barracks so that the largest possible numbers could be sent out quickly in the event of serious disorder. The *consilium* was divided. Publius Vedius Antoninus and Flavius Damianus supported the notion: only a fool trusted the fickle hoi polloi. But in the end, the governor had been swayed by the views of Corvus. Given that there were no sizable bandit groups in the nearby mountains at the moment, and that there had been a robust investigation of all lower-class clubs in the city, with any suspicious *collegia* being suppressed, just the previous year, a more visible presence of armed men throughout the city would have a calming effect. Ballista had to acknowledge that there was something in the local *eirenarch's* view.

Everyone knew that pestilence followed an earthquake like vulgar abuse followed a philosopher. Already the governor's palace was hung with swags of laurel, that sure preventative of plague. Ephesus possessed public slaves whose sole duty was to carry the dead out of the city. But the number of corpses visible, let alone those still buried in the ruins, was far beyond anything with which the *libitinarii* could deal. The scribe to the *demos* was assigned just twenty soldiers to assist the *libitinarii*, but he was to have the authority to compulsorily recruit as many privately owned able-bodied slaves as he felt necessary. Areas of public land out on the Caystros plain were designated for anonymous mass graves.

The aqueducts and water supply had been less damaged than might have been expected, but not all was as it should be. Clean drinking water might stave off disease. Flavius Damianus promised to put things to rights, using his own slaves and tenants, at no cost to the city or the imperial *fiscus*. The governor's *accensus* wrote out a commission, which Maximillianus had signed there and then.

No apocalyptic vision was complete without famine. Hunger was the terror that constantly gnawed at all the cities of the *imper-*

ium. To assuage their fear – on occasion to ameliorate the harsh reality – frequently they stripped the countryside bare, reducing peasants and poor tenant farmers to eating strange, sometimes noxious roots and leaves. The three rich men in the *consilium* stepped up. They would feed their city. They would scour their estates, empty their granaries, have their dependants transport the produce to Ephesus.

Given the potentially ruinous magnanimity of their gesture, it was only right that the governor had allowed Flavius Damianus to discourse at some length on how such generosity and love of the *polis* ran deep in his family – had not his eponymous ancestor, the famous sophist, planted his lands with fruit trees and given the *demos* free access to them? After that, naturally, both Gaius Valerius Festus and Publius Vedius Antoninus were granted similar indulgence.

Ballista's thoughts had wandered. Could it be that a disaster such as this transformed the love of honour with which the Greek elite so often credited themselves into a practical reality? Yet looked at in a more sardonic way, this engrained virtue of *philo-timia* was nothing if not competitive. By this signal act of generosity, these three *eupatrids* were elevating themselves far above the rest of the rich men in the *Boule* of Ephesus. The *demos* could not but praise them: their action would reach the ears of the emperor.

Was there an *imperium*-wide pattern to be found here? Was there a small group of incredibly rich men rising up from the ranks of the larger oligarchy in each city? Ballista remembered how, in Arete, his friend Iarhai had told him that there used to be a dozen or so leading men in that city. When Ballista had arrived at that town, there had been just three. Maybe, but Arete had been a special case. Situated perilously but profitably between the great empires of Rome and Persia, its notables owed their status

53

to their abilities in deploying armed force. And now, had this earthquake not made Ephesus also something of a special case? Of the four hundred and fifty members of the Ephesian *Boule*, forty-seven were dead or unaccounted for. Unsurprisingly, finding this out had been one of the first acts of the authorities.

When Publius Vedius Antoninus launched into an ample review of the buildings with which past members of his family had adorned the city, some might have considered he had strayed rather from the point. Maximillianus urbanely interjected to thank most, most sincerely each of the *eupatrids*. He was sure many decrees of the *Boule* and *Demos* of the Ephesians would be passed extolling their virtues. It may well be that when the *Heroon* of Androclos was repaired, the heroic founder would have to share his quarters with statues of men still living. Their munificence was unparalleled: Hellas and poverty might be foster sisters, but one should not forget that Croesus had reigned here in Asia.

After the admiring laughter which acknowledged the governor's playful allusion to the aphorism of Herodotus, Maximillianus had brought proceedings to a close with a brief speech intended to keep up everyone's spirits. A unit of auxiliary cavalry, double strength, one thousand-strong, was en route from the interior. Letters had been dispatched to the emperor; soon the bounty of Gallienus would ease their troubles. All would be well.

Maximus walked out on to the terrace and up to Ballista. 'Sorry I was not here when you came out. I waited, but one of the governor's men said you would all be at it for hours. So, I . . . I went for a wander.'

'Went for a wander?'

'Yes, a wander.'

'And was it good?'

'Sure, it was magnificent.' Maximus smiled. 'You cannot be

praising too highly the dedication and enthusiasm of the girls of this town. Straight back to work, putting their backs into it. Now, if your public servants learnt a trick or two from them, the place would be back to rights in no time.'

'You really are a sadly deluded man.'

'Well,' considered Maximus, 'you might say that, but not if you had any knowledge of philosophy. Does not each one of us recreate the world in our own minds based on what our eyes and ears tell us? Now, I know that some of your Stoics hold that only the wise man gets it right. But they themselves will admit that a wise man is harder to find than a virgin in a whorehouse. So, given that most of us are going to get it wrong, and given it is up to us, what sort of fool would you be if you did not make the world you perceived into the sort of place that suited you?' He waved a dismissive hand. 'I am surprised at an educated man like you – do you not have any understanding of sense perception theory at all?'

'Have you been talking to Hippothous again?'

'Well, not just now, luckily. But, it has to be said, he does like to philosophize. Just like little Demetrius he is: cannot get enough philosophic dialogue. Mind you, he is also very keen on that phys– physiog–'

'Physiognomy – reading people's characters from their faces.'

'That is the one. A noble science, infallible in the hands of a skilled practitioner, so he says. Loves it, he does. Tells stories that would make your hair stand on end.'

'And that probably tells him a lot too.'

'Where is Corvus?' Maximus asked.

'The governor held him back for a private conversation.' Ballista leant on the parapet. Maximus joined him. Together they looked out at the sea, all quiet under the waxing moon.

Ballista's thoughts ran back to the casualties among the *Boule*:

nearly one in nine dead. Now, if the death rate across all the citizen body were about the same magnitude, and there really had been about 250,000 in the city, that would mean around 28,000 corpses, by far the majority still to be unearthed. But it is the collapsing houses that kill, and a rich man's house is likely to be better built. Yet what about the poor who lived in huts? They were easier to get out of; there was not much to collapse. There were no simple answers.

Out to sea, the light of one of the fishing boats winked and went out. Ballista's thoughts continued on their way: to his own household. Seven of the eight people who had been with Ballista had survived. A few others had lived. The cook and a kitchen porter had been shopping in the *agora*. They were shaken, but unhurt. The day after the earthquake, a stable-boy had reappeared. No one could tell what had happened to him. His wits were gone. They had dug Rebecca and Simon out of the ruins, but with Constans and the others they had failed. Twelve of them – men, women and children, almost half the *familia* – all gone. Constans, the boys' pedagogue, Julia's *custos*, three of her maids . . . the rest – all gone.

After the fire had burnt itself out, Ballista, Maximus and Calgacus had returned again and again to the wreck of the house. Hippothous had joined them. With insane dedication, running ridiculous risks, they had climbed over and dug into the teetering ruins. Repetition had not dulled the fear. Each time, Ballista had found it harder to force himself up the slope, to cram himself into the black, tomb-like niches in the rubble. They had scraped and burrowed, always calling out for survivors. They had retrieved many of their possessions: the strongbox, their weapons, much of Julia's jewellery. But no voices answered their calls. They came across just four corpses, mangled and charred. They had left the sad things where they were, a coin pressed between their teeth.

It was Corvus who had released them from their Sisyphus-like labours. The house of the *eirenarch*, on the other side of the Sacred Way, was in a block miraculously unscathed. Corvus straightaway had taken the remnants of Ballista's *familia* into his own household. On the fifth evening of their fruitless digging, he had invoked his powers as head of the watch to order them not to return to the site of their former home. Ballista had seldom felt such simple gratitude to another man. Words could not touch it.

A burst of lamplight shone out across the terrace. Just as suddenly, it was shut off as the door closed again. After a moment or two, the bulky figure of Corvus, stepping carefully, joined Ballista and Maximus. He leant by them on the parapet. In the silence, their eyes adjusted to the night. Out on the silver-black sea the lights of only two fishing boats were to be seen. They seemed to be returning to port. Above the pale moon and amid a myriad of other stars, the nine gems of Ariadne, the newly risen constellation of the Cnossian Crown, one of the harbingers of spring.

Corvus spoke. 'They say Electra ceased to shine in grief for Troy. Now there are only six Pleiades.'

Maximus looked up. 'But they do not rise until–' Ballista, not unkindly, silenced his friend with a hand on his arm.

Corvus seemed not to have noticed. 'But others say the missing Pleiad is Merope, the wife of an oath-breaker, hiding herself in shame.'

Corvus paused. The others did not speak.

'Grief and shame,' Corvus continued, 'they go well together. The day before the earthquake, as *eirenarch* of the Metropolis of Ephesus, all I had to worry about was a couple of thefts and a missing girl. Her father was a potter. They lived out by the Magnesian Gate. By all accounts, she was a pretty thing, good natured, trusting. The neighbours suspected an old fraud of a fortune teller who had a hovel out there. I had my men tear his place apart. There was plenty of evidence of illegality – magic symbols, an alphabet board, some black chickens, a trench dug in one room, chicken shit all around it. But no sign of a missing girl. We gave him a beating. Nothing. He did not do it. The locals suspected him because of his trade, because he was not an Ephesian. He was Etruscan; the way those charlatans often are, or pretend to be, if they are not claiming to be Chaldaean. Gods below, I so wanted to find her. It was consuming me. She was five years old.'

Again Corvus relapsed into silence. Ballista could see only one of the fishing boats coming into the harbour.

'Just one small girl' – Corvus's thoughts continued on their path – 'easy to lose in a city of a quarter of a million people. It seems a small thing now in a city where tens of thousands are dead or missing. But in a way I despise myself for thinking that. Can grief be quantified, measured by numbers?'

Ballista had been watching the remaining fishing boat. Its light had disappeared. Now, a new, brighter light flared down on the quayside, off to the right. Half hidden by the Harbour Baths, it had to come from the market at the northern end of the harbour.

'Would her parents have cared if the whole city had fallen, if all the stars had faded from the sky? Would their grief have been worse?' Corvus was lost to his emotions.

Another light down by the water. This time more central: an ominous glow.

'What has happened – that girl, the earthquake, the lynchings?' Corvus shook his head sadly. 'If I were not already an Epicurean, I would become one, or turn to atheism. It would make anyone realize the gods are far away or do not exist.'

'Fuck,' said Maximus. 'The Harbour Baths are on fire.'

The flames could be seen clearly now, already clear of the high roofs, sawing in the wind.

'Fuck.' said Corvus. 'The gods are far away.'

The three men studied the scene in silence.

'At least the breeze is offshore,' Corvus eventually said. 'It should not spread. I will get my men down there.'

'No,' Ballista said quietly. 'It is too late for that.'

Ballista was staring down, past the fire, past the central harbour gate, out by the jetties. The dark shapes, matt black against the glittering reflection of the flames in the water. His mind had gone back to the very first time he had sailed into Ephesus. Behind him, Maximus had been teasing young Demetrius; something about the gods. Always that, or sex. Ballista himself had not really been listening. He had been looking at the open harbour, the wealth on board the moored ships and stored along the quays. He had been looking at it through the eyes of his barbarian youth. Cut out one or two merchantmen, and go, but, if your fleet were big enough . . .

The Harbour Baths were burning furiously now. Men were running past them, up the arrow-straight road that led to the heart of the town. Beyond, there was more than enough light to see the dark shapes out on the water, a vast number of them, a prow at both ends. Northern longships.

'The Goths are here.'

V

Ballista had admired Corvus from the first. The *eirenarch* did not go down in his estimation now. He bore this latest disaster like a man. With no hint of panic, he surveyed the dark panorama, took his time, obviously thinking hard.

'How many ships do you think?' Corvus's voice was steady.

'At least fifty,' Ballista replied.

'I think more than fifty,' Maximus said.

'He is probably right. His eyes are good.'

'How many men?' Corvus asked.

'A longboat carries at least thirty, the biggest up to a hundred.' Ballista shrugged. 'Say fifty to a ship.'

'Two thousand five hundred.' Corvus actually laughed. 'Our soldiers are scattered, and outnumbered by at least ten to one. Well, that is the end of it.'

'Not necessarily.' Ballista failed to keep the special pleading out of his voice. 'Get the citizens in the residential areas up on the roofs. A tile thrown by an old woman can kill as well as a soldier. All warriors hate fighting in such places.'

Corvus laughed again. 'Ballista, my friend, all these years, and you still do not understand us Hellenes. We are not like you northerners. It is not that we are cowards, as the Romans often say. But it has been centuries since war came to this city. The Ephesians would fight, but they would need some days to get used to the idea. No, it is over.'

The *eirenarch* looked around in the gloom. Other than Maximus, there was no one in earshot. Corvus turned and held his arms out to embrace Ballista. The northerner did not move.

'Ballista, go to the house. Collect my *familia* and yours. Leave the town by the Magnesian Gate. Collect animals from my villa on the road south. Go to Priene. It is on the side of a mountain, still has good walls; the safest town in Ionia. Ask for Marcus Aurelius Tatianus, son of Tatianus. He is my guest-friend. He will take care of you all.'

Corvus stood, his arms still extended. Still Ballista did not move. 'You can come with us.'

Corvus shook his head. 'You are not Ephesian. I am the *eirenarch* of this *polis*.'

'Think of your wife, your daughters.'

Corvus laughed yet again, seemingly with genuine amusement. 'You mistake me, my friend. I do not intend to die here, unless the fates decide. I will fetch the governor. He has a few troops with him. We will see if we can defend a high place behind the palace. The Goths will be more interested in loot and rape than fighting trained men. If not, I will get Maximillianus to safety. Sooner or later, death comes to the coward as to the brave man.'

Ballista stepped forward and was enfolded by Corvus's arms. They kissed, on each cheek, the lips. 'I will keep your family safe.'

'I do not doubt it.' Corvus stood back, and shook Maximus's hand.

In the dark, Ballista grinned. The barbarians might be inside the gates, but the social hierarchy of the *imperium* held. Maximus was a freedman.

The path down from the palace was steep; to the right, a precipitous drop. Ballista and Maximus kept close to the wall on the left. The steps were wide, awkward to run down, ankle–jarring. Ballista called ahead to Maximus to slow down. No point in risking a fall. 'I do not want to carry you.'

'I am not sure I *could* carry you, you fat fucker.'

'Fuck you too. I am just not quite in fighting trim. Anyway, you should show your *patronus* more respect.'

'Certainly: *Patronus*, you fat fucker.'

When they reached the Sacred Way, it was eerily deserted. Momentarily, Ballista wondered if he and Maximus had run into a different reality – one in which the Goths had made a different choice, had sailed to another town. Every choice made opened up a different path. Could they all in some way exist in different places?

Some figures ran round the corner from Marble Street. No steel in their hands. They were fleeing. Ballista and Maximus turned to their left and, holding their scabbards out so as not to tangle their legs, they ran. Past the Fountain of Trajan, its waters still and black. The Sacred Way climbed up. It drained the energy from their legs.

Not far, and they swerved left into the alley. Narrow, steep; they pounded up its steps.

The house, like all Mediterranean houses, showed a blank wall to the outside world. Ballista doubled up, panting hard. Maximus hammered on the big oak door with the pommel of his sword.

The grating of the bolts and the bar, and Corvus's porter swung back the door.

Ballista straightened up. 'Wake the household. Your *dominus* has ordered us to leave. Tell everyone to bring only what they can carry.' The porter left. 'Maximus, get our kit. Bring it to the atrium. I will get Julia and the boys.'

It was dark in the bedroom. Julia turned in her sleep and muttered. Ballista gently put a hand on her shoulder. She twisted, alarmed in her sleep. He moved to the boys. Isangrim was sitting up, rubbing his eyes. Ballista put his arm around him, spoke softly in Greek. 'Isangrim, we must be men.'

The ten-year-old looked back solemnly. 'Let us be men.' He was doing well learning Homer.

Ballista looked at his younger son. Dernhelm was fast asleep, one hand straight above his head. In the big bed, Julia was stirring.

Bringing his lips close to Isangrim's ear, Ballista whispered in his native tongue: 'We will be warriors.' The boy beamed. Julia had not approved of her sons being taught a barbarian language, but Ballista knew the child saw it as a code, one shared with him by just his father, brother, Maximus and old Calgacus. Noisily jumping out of bed, Isangrim started hunting for his miniature sword. That woke Dernhelm. Ballista scooped him into his arms before he could cry, kissed the top of his head, smelt the warm small-child smell of him.

Julia was sitting up. Ballista answered her unspoken question. 'We are leaving. The Goths are in the city.'

She took the news calmly. 'Are there Borani among them?'

'I do not know.'

Julia nodded, and got to her feet.

Ballista passed Dernhelm to her. 'As quickly as possible. Only bring essentials. Meet me in the atrium.'

She nodded again, more peremptorily, as if his words were unnecessary. At times like this, Ballista thought, she was her old self: practical and assured. She had instantly remembered the bloodfeud between her husband and the Gothic tribe of the Borani.

There was pandemonium in the atrium. Members of both *familiae* were rushing here and there, carrying some things, dragging others. They were getting in each other's way, cursing loudly. In the middle of it all, seemingly perfectly at ease, Maximus stood with a mound of armour and weapons.

As Ballista and Maximus helped each other to arm – shifting the weight of the mail, tying laces – Calgacus appeared. The Caledonian was fussing over Rebecca and Simon. Ballista told him to get armed. The words came out more brusquely than intended. It was natural that Calgacus was worried – everyone was worried. And if there were Borani among the Goths, it would make everything worse. Ballista had not sought the bloodfeud. But on that boat, all those years ago, the Borani would not surrender. Ballista had not sought it, but it was real. Bloodfeuds had always been a reality in a northern warrior's life. If the Borani discovered Ballista was here, they would try to kill him. Of course, that would not end it. If they lived, Isangrim and Dernhelm would inherit the feud when they grew to manhood.

'Stop snivelling.' The voice of Corvus's wife, Nikeso, cut across the din. Nikeso was a tall woman. She was making her way, stately through the confusion. The daughter spoken to dabbed her eyes. The other two huddled behind, cowed.

'*Kyria*,' said Ballista.

'*Kyrios*.' Nikeso was collected. 'My husband says we are to go with you.' It was only notionally a question.

'Yes, the Goths are in the city. I am to escort you to Priene.'

'So be it.'

'We must go on foot until we reach your suburban villa. There will not be enough animals and carts there. We will try to find more on the road.'

Nikeso turned to one of her slaves. 'Put all that stuff down. Make sure you have your *kyrios's* strongbox and my jewellery.

And bring out all the weapons in the house, the hunting ones and the heirlooms. The *Vir Ementissimus* Marcus Clodius Ballista will distribute them. Leave everything else.'

Waiting, Ballista half-drew his weapons – first the dagger, next the sword – then snapped them back in their sheaths. He touched the healing stone tied to the scabbard of his sword. He was completely unaware of what his hands did. He was wondering if he should have told Corvus about his bloodfeud with the Borani.

Julia and the boys came out.

'Is everyone here?' Ballista asked.

'Yes,' said Julia.

'One of Corvus's boys is absent.' Nikeso spoke with no obvious emotion, but a woman sobbed among the *familia* behind her.

'Where is he?' Ballista addressed the crying slave woman.

'I do not know, *Kyrios*.' She fell to her knees, arms outstretched: the classic pose of a suppliant. '*Kyrios*, he is my son. He is just a boy.'

Ballista was silent, thinking.

'We cannot wait.' Nikeso's voice was flat.

Ballista nodded. He raised up the slave woman. 'He will be fine. It is a big city. The Goths will not be everywhere.'

There were thirteen in the *familia* of Ballista, just four of them fighting men: Maximus, Calgacus, Hippothous, and Ballista himself, already armed. The *familia* of Corvus was larger – twenty-two in all. Two members of the watch lived with his household. These *diogmitai* had their big, wooden clubs. Ballista told them to take any other weapons they wanted from the pile. Five of the male slaves, including the porter, looked capable of bearing arms. Ballista told them also to select the weapons that suited them. If they did well tonight, their *kyrios* would hear of it, and he might give them their freedom.

Ballista got them all into some sort of order. Hippothous

would lead. The five armed slaves would keep the women and children together. Ballista, Maximus and Calgacus, with the two *diogmitai*, would bring up the rear. If anyone got separated, they were to go out of the Magnesian Gate and make their way to the villa of Corvus just south of town, then over the mountains to Priene. Ballista told them this twice, slowly, trying to make it stick despite the darkness and the fear.

Through the door, they shuffled down the alley and turned left up the Sacred Way. There were people there now; running, jostling. A man ran into Maximus, who casually punched him to the ground.

Keeping moving, Ballista glanced back over his shoulder, down towards the library of Celsus. Most of those in sight were Ephesians – darting here and there in their terror, like animals before a bush fire. But beyond them, not far from the temple of Hadrian, were men with steel in their hands. Some of the Goths were turning aside to loot, but the majority were pressing purposefully up the hill. They must have heard about the wealth to be found in the temples and public buildings situated around the civic *agora* which lay between Ballista's party and the Magnesian Gate. Someone must have told them. There had been stories of locals going over to the Goths. A persistent rumour spoke of a Greek called Chrysogonus, a leading man from one of the cities up towards the Black Sea, throwing his lot in with the pirates, guiding them on their raids. It was said he had led the Goths to the sack of Nicomedia a few years earlier.

Ballista stumbled; the pavement was uneven. He could see the backs of the crowd ahead. He felt a surge of fear until he saw the heads of his sons. The rag-tag column was moving too slowly. The Goths would overhaul them before the civic *agora*. There was no point in urging more speed; it would just cause panic, further delay. There was nothing else for it: the Goths would somehow have to be delayed. They would have to be faced.

Not far, and the path bent to the right. It was narrow there, further straitened by the fallen statues and drums of columns which had been dragged to the sides. The part-ruined monument of Memmius jutted into the road on one side. There was a fine fig tree on the other. The distance between them could be held by four determined men side by side. Ballista shouted for Maximus to push his way through to Hippothous. Have the column halted just beyond the monument. Make sure Hippothous kept them together. Get back down here.

Ballista positioned himself, Calgacus and the two *diogmitai* across the path. He was fighting to control his breathing. Maximus was right: he had been living too easy. Having checked that the *familiae* were shepherded together where he wanted them, Ballista drew his sword and hefted his shield. He was the right-hand man, hard up against the big ashlar blocks of the base of the monument. Calgacus was to his left, the two *diogmitai* beyond that. Maximus reappeared. The Hibernian took his accustomed place at Ballista's left shoulder. Calgacus shuffled over. The end one of the *diogmitai* dropped out of the line. Ballista shouted at him to hold himself ready to replace anyone who fell. The man of the watch waved his agreement, his demeanour less than enthusiastic.

The Goths were still a distance away. Ballista used the time to make sure of his bearings. To the right was the monument of Memmius. The earthquake had done it no good. Of the upper storeys, only a few isolated columns and fragments of masonry remained. The lower two storeys were heavily damaged; much of the sculpture had crashed from the walls, and truncated caryatids were left hanging, legless and deformed. The thing was a ruin, but it guarded his right. To the left of his men was the fig tree, up against a wall. No way round there. Hold the line, and they would be safe. Far off to the left, across a square and above a big imperial temple, Ballista could see the dark bulk of the mountain, its safety very far away. If the line broke, they would all die.

Seeing the men standing across the way, the Goths pulled up about twenty paces short. In the gloom, it was impossible to judge their numbers. They were a dark phalanx, backlit by torches and more distant fires. Swords glittered in their hands; the curved outlines of shields glinted. Some of the Goths wore helmets. The raking torchlight made deep, crazed shadows in the empty pavement. Ballista noted it. The earthquake had lifted and moved the broad slabs of the road.

'Watch your footing,' Ballista said softly. Maximus repeated it. So did Calgacus. Ballista smiled. They had spoken in his native language. It would mean nothing to the *diotigmai*.

'Come on, girls,' called Maximus. 'Do you want to dance, you arse-fucking cunts?'

A babble of voices. Their attention caught by the use of a dialect of their own language, the Goths all called out: a jumble of threats, boasts, questions, less certain things. An individual stepped forward. The orange-red light swam over his mailed shoulders, the steel of his helmet, the blade in his hand. His face was shadowed. His helmet was adorned with the skull of a small, fanged animal. He held up his hand, and the noise dropped.

'I am Tharuaro, son of Gunteric. I lead the Tervingi longboats in this Gothic expedition. Who are you?'

Maximus filled his lungs but, before he could answer, Ballista restrained him.

'I am Dernhelm, son of Isangrim of the Angles. The Romans know me as Ballista.'

A deep muttering – *hoom, hoom* – came from the Goths: recognition, maybe grudging respect, but no warmth.

'The man who was king of the Romans for a day,' Tharuaro shouted. 'We know you. It is lucky for you we are here. There are two crews of Borani with the fleet. They would want to eat your heart raw. But we Tervingi have no particular desire to kill you. Now, stand aside. My men have been at sea for three days, they want what they have come for.'

Ballista did not speak at once. A bat flitted between them. 'Will you give safe passage to those with me? All of them – men, women and children?' The bat banked back, hunting. 'And the things we carry?'

Tharuaro snorted. 'You are trading from a bad position, Angle.'

'Will you take an oath to your high gods Teiws and Fairguneis?'

'We will let those with you go unmolested. But we will take your weapons and your goods.'

'No.'

'Like all your people, you are a fool. Lay down your swords.'

'No.'

'I see five of you. There are thirty or more of us.'

'But here only four can fight.'

Tharuaro spoke no more words to Ballista. The Gothic *reiks* turned his back, conferring with his men.

'They would kill us anyway,' Maximus said quietly. 'Easier if we are disarmed. Fuck them.'

The Goths milled, sorting themselves out. Ballista wondered how they would go about it. If they advanced in a wedge – the boar's snout of the north – even uphill their momentum would certainly smash through a line only one deep. But the road surface was deeply pitted, treacherous. If one man tripped, the close-packed ranks of the boar's snout would pile up in chaos.

They might find themselves sprawling at the feet of Ballista's men. Then it would be like killing netted fish. Like killing tuna – fish that bled a lot.

Maximus's *gladius* flashed as he tossed the short sword from hand to hand. Under his breath, he was singing in Latin, a Roman marching song:

'Thousand, thousand, thousand we've beheaded now.
One man, a thousand we've beheaded now.
A thousand drinks, a thousand killed.
So much wine no one has as the blood that he has spilt.'

Four Goths emerged from the ranks. Tharuaro was no fool. He had seen the danger posed by the road. It would be man to man.

Tharuaro had taken his place opposite Ballista. The next Goth was festooned with bracelets and necklaces, obscure amulets braided into his hair: he must be one of their priests. This *gudja* would face Maximus. The other two were proven warriors. Mail-coated, their arms shone with the golden rings Tharuaro or some other *reiks* had given them.

The Goths advanced at a walk, evenly spaced, room to use their weapons. They rolled their shoulders, flexed their necks, made passes with their blades. They moved workmanlike, a ploughman going to his team. They had done this many times before.

Ballista got into a fighting crouch: left leg forward, shield held well out, sword back and raised, the leather thong from the hilt over his wrist. He checked the paving around his feet. The stones were mainly smooth, their surfaces very shiny. A couple of paces in front, one was cracked and tilted; another just behind his right foot stuck up, uneven. He found he was muttering a prayer: *All-father, Death-blinder, Spear-thruster . . .*

Three paces out, the Goths roared and lunged forward. Ballista's world shrank to the few feet that enclosed him and his enemy. Tharuaro swung down a blow to the neck. Ballista hunkered down behind his shield. A sudden step, Tharuaro slid to his right knee, his blade now singing below Ballista's guard, towards his left leg. Hurriedly, Ballista got the shield down. The impact jarred up his arm. Splinters of wood flew. Ballista brought his right wrist over, thrust at his opponent's face. Tharuaro took the edge of the blade on the rim of his shield, forced it up.

Surging to his feet, the Goth slammed his shield-boss into Ballista's body. Ballista's heel caught on the uneven pavement and he staggered back, winded. Arms wide, he floundered to regain his balance. Tharuaro thrust savagely into his chest. Ballista twisted convulsively, the point of the blade punched home. A hammer blow – white, burning pain – it broke some of the close-forged metal rings, driving them into the flesh. The point snagged, then slid off across the surface of the mail coat. Tharuaro was within Ballista's shield. Fighting for breath, the Angle let go of his shield-grip and used his left arm to draw the man in; with his right he smashed the pommel of his sword into the bearded face. A metallic snap as the nasal on the Goth's helmet broke. A softer, more sickening sound as his nose shattered. A grunt of pain. The scent of blood.

They were wedged together, Tharuaro's sword arm trapped between their bodies, Ballista's uselessly high in the air, their breathing hot in each other's face. The Goth reacted first. A kick to the right shin and Tharuaro dropped his shield and crunched the heel of his left hand into Ballista's chin.

As Ballista staggered back again, the other warrior used the time to scoop up his shield. The northerner, shieldless, got into a low crouch, sword two-handed out in front.

Gasping, they eyed each other, motionless in the guttering

light, time not moving. Next to them, the clang of steel on steel, the stamp of booted feet, the rasping breaths of frightened men fighting for their lives.

Tharuaro spat. The blood was black in the gloom. His eyes flicked away across the road. Ballista's eyes never left the Goth's blade. Tharuaro laughed.

Ballista feinted forward, winning time to glance to his left. Maximus and Calgacus were still there. But one of the *diogmitai* was down; head half severed, dark blood coursing over the road, the slabs slick with it. The other was being driven back. A blur of blows from the Goth. The despairing defence of the man of the watch would only end one way, and at any moment.

Ballista gave all his attention back to the *reiks* facing him.

'The dance is nearly over, Angle.' Tharuaro's front teeth were gone. Ropes of bloody spittle hung in his beard. Ballista knew in his heart the Goth was right. When, any moment now, the second of the *diogmitai* was downed, Calgacus, who was still trading blows with his man, would find himself outflanked, fighting two to one.

Maximus and the *gudja* had drawn apart. The Gothic priest's shield was gone, the mail on his left arm broken, a great gash showing through. A warrior behind him called for him to let a fresh man take his place. The *gudja* did not deign to reply.

'Thousand, thousand, thousand . . .'

The demented Hibernian was still singing; breathless, the lyrics staccato, but still singing.

Maybe, thought Ballista, one last, united effort from the three of them. Better that than nothing. Call to Hippothous to get the combined *familia* moving towards the gate. Should have told them to keep moving from the start. But in the chaos of a sacked city, one fighting man and a few slaves cannot hope to guard about thirty women and children. Too late for regrets. Allfather, look to my boys. Let them join me in Valhalla – not now, not soon. Now, we will try to buy them just a little time. Get the only other fighting man down here.

'Hippothous!' Ballista shouted.

Ballista was drowned out by a choking scream from his left. He pretended to cut at Tharuaro's head; flicked a look across the road. The last of the *diogmitai* was still on his feet. His hands were holding the long, grey ropes of his own intestines. Hopelessly, he was attempting to force them back into the slit in his stomach.

'Hippothous!'

With precision, the Gothic warrior chopped a leg from under the wounded man. Once the watch man was on all fours, two heavy blows to the back of the head sufficed.

The other six combatants, out of the corner of their eyes, watched as if the gruesome tragedy of a saga were being acted out.

The Goth flicked the blood from his sword, turned inwards. Without words, Calgacus, Maximus and Ballista stepped back, rearranging themselves in a half-circle, back against the high base of the monument.

The Goth jerked around, swinging his sword up the hill. Too late. It was smashed out of his grip; went ringing against the far wall. Another blow and he reeled back, clutching his right shoulder. Hippothous lunged. The Goth leapt back. His feet slipped on the blood-slick stones. He went down, hard. On his arse, boots finding little purchase, he scrabbled towards his comrades.

Hippothous came forward. Calgacus, Maximus and Ballista fanned out to join him. The line was re-established; the road blocked again.

'You were right, Tharuaro. The dance should end.' Ballista

spoke quietly. 'You said you have no particular desire to kill me or my men. You and your Tervingi came for treasures, for women. There are many of both in the street behind you. Take them. There are many more in the civic *agora* behind us. In a little while, we will be gone, the way open to you.'

'The Borani will be glad we have not killed you, Angle.' Tharuaro looked at the *gudja*, as if seeking his approval for words not yet spoken. 'There is no bloodfeud between the Tervingi and you. It is not a matter of honour. Go now – quickly.'

Ballista told Calgacus to lead the *familia*. When they were moving, Ballista, Maximus and Hippothous turned and began to trudge up the hill.

The Goths watched them go, hard eyed, their thoughts unknowable.

VI

Gallienus walked out into the walled garden. Even here, in the wilds of Thrace, well to the north-west of Byzantium, the plants seemed to apprehend that spring was approaching. Gallienus yawned, stretched and took in the view. The sun was warm on his back. It was a rare luxury for an emperor to be alone. It had been a tiring time.

The imperial *comitatus* had remained in Byzantium for three days after the city had surrendered. It had been three hectic days of smoothing the return of the city to imperial allegiance, of reassuring the surviving councillors that there would be no further reprisals, of convincing the leading men, Cleodamus and Athenaeus, that their industry in the defence of the town and their loyalty to the Macriani, terribly misguided though it had been, would bring them not punishment but advancement.

The confiscation of the estates of the twenty executed councillors had also demanded close attention. The influx of wealth had proved timely. Two days before the *comitatus* left, news had come of the earthquake that had hit Ephesus. An emperor was nothing if he was not open-handed. The property of the condemned was sold, the proceeds to be sent to the devastated city. As ever, the emperor took with one hand and gave with the other.

There had been a disquieting rumour of an unusual concentration of Gothic pirates in the Aegean, but it could not be helped. Far more pressing issues called for the presence of the emperor in the west.

The *comitatus*, consisting of just high officials and the cavalry of the guard, had made good time. They had spent the second night in the city of Perinthus. From there, they had struck inland, riding fast through the rich farmland of the *campus serenus*. On the fourth evening, they had reached the small town of Bergoule and Gallienus had called for a day's halt to rest the horses.

This morning, the one before the *ides* of March, had brought Gallienus no respite. First, at dawn, there had been a solemn sacrifice to celebrate this day forty years before, when the divine Aurelius Alexander Severus had been named Augustus and accepted the titles of *Pater Patriae* and *Pontifex Maximus*: to the divine Alexander an ox. Gallienus half remembered Alexander Severus. Although Gallienus had still been a child, had not yet been given the *toga virilis*, by the end of that reign he had already been at the imperial court, a hostage for the good behaviour of his father. In his memories, Alexander was a weak-looking young man, too reliant on both the senate and his mother. It was said that when the mutineers, led by Maximinus Thrax, had burst into the imperial pavilion, Alexander had died sobbing, blaming his mother, clinging to her skirts. Not a good role model for an emperor such as Gallienus sought to be but, officially, Alexander was a god, and as such had to be honoured.

After the duties of religion, the mundanities of the imperial office. Wherever an emperor went, embassies appeared. Two had been from local communities, each requesting protection from unlawful exactions for the *cursus publicus*. Abuse by officials and soldiers of the *diplomata* which authorized them to requisition men, animals and carts for the imperial posting service had always been endemic. Palfurius Sura, the *ab Epistulis*, had drafted the looked-for imperial pronouncements, weighty and full of warnings. Gallienus had signed them in purple ink. Doubtless, the communities would inscribe these responses in stone, set them up where all could see. Once the emperor was no longer in the vicinity, Gallienus wondered how much good that would do.

Three further embassies had been seen. Two, one from Achaea, the other from North Africa, had both been granted their petitions for tax relief: five years each. Neither community was particularly large or prosperous, so imperial munificence could be advertised loudly, while the *fiscus* lost little.

The final deputation had been more diverting. The people of an isolated village high in the Rhodope mountains had found a satyr sleeping in their fields. They had stoned the creature to death. As was always the way with the wondrous, they had brought the remains to the emperor. It was a pity the skin had not been better preserved. But the emperor and his *comites* had studied it closely. Although it resembled a man, the tail and hooves were still to be distinguished. Gallienus thanked the peasants graciously: it would form a fitting addition to the miraculous menagerie – the dead tritons and centaurs, the skeletons of heroes, the feathers of the phoenix, and the living dwarfs and giants, human and animal – exhibited at Rome in the palace and stored in its cellars. The rustics left rewarded with more coins than they had ever seen in their lives. Roman government had to be personal, and it had to be bountiful.

Now it was late morning and, the *negotium* of political audiences over, the stately schedule of the imperial day moved to *otium* and the pursuit of culture. Rather than reading, Gallienus had felt moved to philosophic discourse. As *a Studiis*, Zeno had been dispatched to find a philosopher. Even in a town such as Bergoule, in the middle of nowhere, it should not prove too difficult. As someone had said, these days it was easier to fall over in a boat without landing on a plank than look around without seeing a philosopher. The question was: would Zeno find one of any worth?

Philosophers did not travel, at least not at the behest of authority. Longinus could not be persuaded to leave Athens, nor Plotinus Rome. In fact, when Gallienus was in Rome with his wife Salonina, it was the imperial couple who had traversed the eternal city, not the lover of wisdom. Freedom of speech and self-sufficiency were keystones of the soul of a philosopher of any sect. *Parresia* and *autarkeia*, as well as a suitable contempt for the moral irrelevancies of wealth and fame, were well demonstrated by a philosopher declining an imperial summons. In a sense, if a philosopher did come running when an emperor called, it might be thought to demonstrate that he was not a philosopher at all. It remained to be seen what sort of creature Zeno would unearth.

The garden was pleasant. Gallienus inspected the budding fruit trees. Zeno had not brought up again the matter of Ballista. Gallienus had made inquiries with Rufinus. The head of the *frumentarii* did not think Zeno and Ballista had ever met. The former had been governor of Cilicia at the time of the revolt of the Macriani. But he had left the province before Ballista arrived. If the men had never met, it was unlikely there was personal animosity between them. In which case Zeno most likely had taken a bribe to raise the issue of Ballista.

Despite that, Zeno was right: something must be decided. A man who had worn the purple attracted conspirators like rotten fruit did wasps. If a man had once been thought capable of ruling the empire, he might well be considered so again: once *capax imperii*, always *capax imperii*, as Tacitus might have said.

Gallienus was unsure. Ballista was an old friend. Gallienus freely admitted, in the silence of his heart, that he owed much to the big northerner. Yet Ballista, at the very least, had to be watched. The emperor's thoughts were running towards exile. He would have liked to impose the lesser form: *relegatio* from Italy and native province, with property untouched. But that did not answer. Ballista did not have a native province in the *imperium*, he already had a house in Sicily and, free to roam, he would be hard to monitor. No, it would have to be the more draconian form: deportation to a designated place – a small island where *frumentarii* could keep a close eye on him and his connections. Usually, deportation involved the confiscation of property. But Ballista was an old friend. Let him hold on to his worldly goods; let his family live with him. Ballista, like Gallienus, was known to love his family. Ballista had often said he hankered for a quiet, retiring life. Gallienus would choose a comfortable, out-of-the-way island for him to live out the time the fates granted him.

Hermianus, the *ab Admissionibus*, ushered into the garden Zeno and another man. The latter looked the part: staff and wallet, cloak and no tunic. Judging by his beard and hair, roughly chopped short, he was of the Stoic persuasion.

'*Dominus*, this is Nicomachus the Stoic.'

The philosopher bowed and blew a kiss from his fingertips, the more restrained form of adoration.

Gallienus turned the full light of the imperial gaze on the philosopher. Nicomachus neither flinched nor looked ostentatiously disrespectful; maybe he would do.

'Would you like a drink?' Gallienus asked in Greek.

'Thank you, *Kyrios*, watered wine.'

Not one to parade asceticism, thought Gallienus. That was good, and the man appeared clean. Gallienus signed that Zeno and Hermianus could retire. The drink would arrive presently.

The emperor sat on a stone bench next to a portrait bust of Diogenes. He asked if the philosopher would like to sit.

'No, thank you, *Kyrios*.' Nicomachus leant on his staff, one leg crossed, like a figure from an antique vase. As they waited without talking, Gallienus wondered if the philosopher had been searched.

A slave of the imperial household emerged, served the drinks, and departed.

'Tell me your views on exile,' said the emperor.

Nicomachus remained silent for a time while he collected his thoughts. He was very still, and frowned a deep frown of philosophic concentration. A creditable performance so far, judged Gallienus. If the words matched the gestures, this could be enlightening.

'The majority of mankind thinks of exile with nothing but horror and fear. You are torn from your home, family and friends. Everything you love, everything you know is taken away. You are thrust out to wander, dusty-footed in abject poverty, among uncaring or hostile strangers: misery and loneliness leading to an unmarked grave.

'If it was only the ignorant hoi polloi who saw exile as an unmitigated evil, it need not detain us. Only demagogues and fools care what the masses think. But other men, the most revered of men, have expressed similar views. Did not the divine Homer portray the pain of Odysseus: clinging to the shattered raft; sitting alone, weeping by the shore? Ten years of unhappiness, of dashed hopes and unfulfilled dreams.

'Think of the lines Euripides wrote on exile. Electra asks her brother, "Where does the wretched exile spend his wretched exile?" He replies, "In no one settled region does he waste away." He might have bread, "but strengthless, exile's fare."

'Yet others have seen it differently. Many philosophers, and those ones the most distinguished, have considered exile as neither bad nor good. It is nothing but an irrelevance. The good man is good no matter where he is, in no matter what circumstances he finds himself. Like wealth or poverty, like sickness or health, it cannot touch the inner man or his moral purpose.

'Then again, some philosophers – highly thought of, if misguided – argue that exile is the inescapable lot of all men; cast out, as they say, from our own dear country, by which they mean from the divine. I will not trouble you, *Basileus*, with such recondite theories. These philosophers hold that a king must always be a philosopher. They are wrong. The philosopher is one thing, the king is another. It is enough that the ruler listens to philosophers. The *basileus* ever has weighty practical matters on hand; no time for arcane speculation.'

Gallienus allowed himself to smile. His fondness for the Platonist Plotinus was well known. Nicomachus had made a neat swipe at the followers of Plato, combined with an elegant, understated appeal for his own imperial favour. Zeno had done well to discover him; the Stoic Nicomachus would go far.

The philosopher's face lightened. 'Finally, we should examine how exile may actually work to a man's advantage, may be a positive good, if not an absolute blessing. Musonius, himself exiled by Nero, rightly saw that, all too often, men of position are addicted to high living. An exile is in straitened circumstances. He must live more simply. Musonius pointed to Spartiacus the Lacedaemonian. He suffered from a weak chest. In exile, he had to renounce luxury, and he ceased to be ill. Exile cleanses, toughens the body.

'And exile can be morally good, an education in virtue. Condemned by Domitian, Dio Chrysostom wondered if exile was good or bad. He sought the advice of the Delphic Oracle. Apollo told him to carry on doing what he was doing. At first, Dio did not understand that his *relegatio* had forced him to think about the most important question of all: how should a man live? Clad in humble attire, Dio wandered and, as he tells us, some men mistook him for a philosopher. They came up to him and asked him to tell them about good and evil. To answer, Dio had to think deeply about these profoundest of things, and in doing so he actually became a philosopher.

'Let us end by returning to Odysseus. We have seen his wandering, but what were its effects? He had fought at Troy – he was no weakling – but there he was more known for his cunning than his skill at arms. Ten years of suffering refined and toughened him in body and soul. When the gods granted him to return to Ithaka, he was a different man. Virtually alone, Odysseus had both the physical and moral strength to slaughter the many enemies who had invaded his home.'

Nicomachus finished. He leant on his staff, imperturbable.

Gallienus asked the philosopher no questions. There was little point in an emperor attempting Socratic dialogue. On one side, the autocrat whose will was law; on the other, one of his subjects, whose life hung by a thread. Neither free speech nor the truth was likely to be attained. The words of the eunuch philosopher Favorinus still rang true: 'You give me bad advice, my friends, when you do not allow me to think the man who commands thirty legions to be right about anything he chooses.' Gallienus would mull it all over by himself.

The emperor graciously thanked the philosopher. Was there any benefit he could grant?

'Just that you think on my words and, if possible, the further pleasure of your company.' It was well said; for a philosopher to ask for material benefits undermined his very claim to philosophic status.

From wherever, out of sight, he had been listening, Hermianus emerged. The philosopher accepted the honour of kissing the imperial seal on the proffered ring. Relinquishing Gallienus's hand, he blew the kiss of *proskynesis*. Hermianus escorted him out.

Alone in the garden, Gallienus sat and thought. Exile might not break a man; it *could* change him. Odysseus had returned and killed without mercy those who had done him wrong. More recent history furnished examples of men returning in arms to take revenge on those who had exiled them: Dio of Syracuse driving out the tyrant Dionysius; Marius bathing the streets of Rome in blood. Ballista had never shown either the ruthless ambition of the latter, or the driving principles of the former. But he was an excellent general, a fine leader of men. Three times he had defeated the Persians; once, the King of Kings in person. Ballista had killed the tyrant Quietus. He had been hailed emperor: Marcus Clodius Ballista Augustus. Embittered by exile, he would appeal to the disaffected, would make an excellent figurehead for a revolution: once *capax imperii*, always *capax imperii*. Rome had always welcomed men of violence who fought her cause and espoused her values. Already Gallienus could hear the insidious sophistries of the courtiers of the new regime: Ballista, the new Aeneas, come from abroad, sword in hand, to sweep away the soft and the decadent from the seven hills, come to return Rome to her antique, martial virtue.

Exile alone would not contain Ballista. The Romanized barbarian would remain a threat to Gallienus himself. Mutilation might be the solution. No man who was deformed could sit on the throne of the Caesars. Cut off his ears and nose. But Ballista had been a friend. Just the nose then.

Gallienus shook his head, took a drink. What was he thinking? He remembered the story of an eastern prince in Tacitus. The young man had been raised as a hostage in Rome. Politics had

83

dictated that the time had come for him to be sent back to his native land, to rule as a client king in Parthia. His subjects had not cared for his foreign, western ways. But they had not killed him; instead they had cut off his ears and nose. Such, Tacitus had written, was Parthian *clementia*. Gallienus knew himself an autocrat, but he still appreciated irony.

Mutilation was not the answer. Such behaviour was the 'clemency' of a cruel oriental despot, not the emperor of the Romans, a *basileus* of the Greeks. Death – that was the answer.

VII

The escape from Ephesus was easy. Ballista and the others had walked up to the civic *agora*, crossed it, and taken the street which led past the East Gymnasium. The crowds at the Magnesian Gate had caused delay but no danger. Outside, the *familia* had headed south. Even with the women and children, in under half an hour they had reached the villa of Corvus.

That was how it had gone: completely uneventful. But it was not how Hippothous remembered it. He remembered the slow trudge up the claustrophobic street from the Memmius monument; the uneven, deceitful pavement; the echoing tumult of nearby chaos; the reek of burning. He recalled trying not to look too often over his shoulder; the milling crush at the town gate; beyond the walls, willing the *familia* to move faster; the ever-present fear; the terrible anxiety that every sound at his back was the coming of the Goths.

Hippothous knew he was no coward. But a long career in banditry had taught him that running away should be done with all speed. He had no number to the times he had been chased. But never had he moved as slowly. In all those times in Cilicia,

Cappadocia, Syria, Egypt, even Aethiopia, if the women and children had slowed him up, he had left them by the path or killed them. Hostages for ransom, his own followers: it made no difference. A life among the *latrones* did not encourage sentimentality.

Alongside Hippothous at the rear of the small knot of refugees, Ballista had walked steadily. Hippothous could not help but admire the big barbarian's self-control. At the villa, Ballista had been all cool capability. The domestic staff were gathered, the animals led out. As the latter were harnessed, Ballista made much of the grey gelding he had stabled at the villa. The old, infirm and very young were helped into the saddle. Ballista insisted Julia ride his horse; he would walk. Two burly male slaves were left to prevent casual looting – they were to take to their heels if the Goths came. The rest of the staff, about a dozen, were added to the column, and they set out again.

From then, Hippothous's mind had been more restful. There was no real likelihood of the Goths venturing so far inland, not when there was so much still to pillage in Ephesus. He knew nothing of Goths but a great deal of men plundering.

Ballista had led them south on the main road. When it turned to the east, inland towards Magnesia ad Maeandrum, they had taken to the hills; the path climbing and leading south-west. They had spent the night in the sacred site of Ortygia, their sleep disturbed by the fervent prayers of the priests and the panicked locals. *Zeus, Apollo, Athena, all you Olympians, protect us from the fury of the Scythians.* The next day, they had skirted the foothills of Mount Thorax, come to the flat lands and billeted themselves in a decayed village called Maiandros. A final morning's march, less than ten miles, easy going on a flat road, and they had reached Priene. It was the *ides* of March.

Hippothous was hot and irritable, his patience wearing thin. They had not outrun the news of the Goths. They had been told that the north-east gate of Priene would remain closed until the chief magistrate, the *stephanephoros* Marcus Aurelius Tatianus, came and made a decision. That had been nearly an hour earlier – more than long enough for Hippothous to take the measure of the place.

The passageway of the gate was narrow. Even if open, a couple of determined men could hold it. It was flanked by towers. The walls were old, the stones pockmarked with age, weeds growing in the cracks and joins. They had seen no work for generations. But it was a tribute to the original builders that the great, close-fitted ashlar slabs still stood. While a nimble individual could probably climb them – say, scale them at night when no one was looking – if defended, they would still pose a formidable obstacle. To Hippothous's left, the wall dog-legged out, providing further enfilading against any attacker ascending the ramp to the gate. Beyond the dog-leg, the wall curved away, following the foothills above the plain. To the right, they zigzagged wildly up the steep slope. They stopped when they came to the mountain cliff. No need for walls there. An outcrop of Mount Mycale reared up three hundred feet or more: pale-grey rock, too sheer for vegetation. At the top was the acropolis. Corvus had been right: Priene was a hard place to take.

Although Hippothous had not been in Ionia before, he knew the outline of the story of Priene. Once one of the leading towns of the Ionian Greeks, Priene had been betrayed by the Maeander. The silt brought down by the many-channelled river had created a wide plain, driving back the sea. Left landlocked, Priene and its port of Naulochos over the years had sunk into provincial obscurity. Hippothous hoped that very obscurity, and the distance from the Aegean, would keep it safe now.

There was a stir at the gate. A voice boomed out from the battlements. 'I am Marcus Aurelius Tatianus, son of Tatianus, *stephanephoros* of the *polis* of Priene. Who are you?'

'Marcus Clodius Ballista and his *familia*, with the *familia* of Marcus Aurelius Corvus. My friend Corvus told me to come to you, his guest-friend, to find shelter from the fury of the Scythians.'

The gates were opened, and Tatianus walked out. Greetings and introductions were given and taken. Hippothous regarded Tatianus – regarded him very carefully. The *stephanephoros* was a tall man, dressed in a Greek *himation* and tunic. His walk and movements were those of a *eupatrid*: slow, considered, exhibiting the self-possession of the elite. When not in motion, he stood still, hands clasped in front of his body, for all the world an image of a statue of Demosthenes.

But Hippothous saw through it all. This attempt to personify ancient civic virtue was a sham. Tatianus's eyes were never still. They shifted rapidly, circling about. This was the sure sign of a man who has done some foul act, such as killing a relative or committing a forbidden thing, something proscribed by the gods, such things as had been done by the son of Pelops or by Oedipus, son of Laius. Tatianus would have to be watched. What was physiognomy for if not to guard against the vices of the bad before having to experience them?

Tatianus bade them leave their animals. His servants would see to them. On foot, he led the way under the vaulted gate. Blank walls and occasional shadowed doorways faced the narrow street, which climbed sharply. At least they were shaded from the early-afternoon sun. In the intervals between buildings, to their right, the acropolis cliff loomed over everything.

As they walked, Hippothous continued his physiognomic musing. The eyes of Tatianus reminded him of those of the people of Thrace from the regions around Byzantium and Perinthus, the two *poleis* in which Hippothous had come to manhood. Their eyes also were ever circling about and moving, and their character was notorious – only their innate cowardice usually restrained them from the evil acts they desired.

When they reached the theatre, the street levelled out but grew narrower still. Tatianus asked if Ballista would care to see the theatre: there was a wonderful view to the south, out over the plain and the sea towards Miletus and the island of Lade. Ballista said he would be delighted, but possibly at a later time; his people were tired and hungry. Of course, of course; Tatianus had already sent men ahead to prepare the house and set out a meal.

Hippothous thought of Perinthus and Byzantium, two *poleis* filled with evil men, two *poleis* he could never visit again. He thought of Aristomachus, the man he had killed in the latter. Remorse was not in his mind. He thought of the news of Gallienus's massacre of city councillors at Byzantium. It had filled Hippothous's heart with fierce pleasure.

Beyond the theatre, the street began to dip down. They came to a deep flight of steps. Hippothous saw why they had had to leave the horses. A few paces further and in the right-hand wall, massive stone slabs framed a doorway.

'Welcome to my house.' Tatianus addressed Ballista, full of urbanity. Together, they stepped over the doorstep and into the cool of the corridor. Hippothous and the others followed. The porter emerged from his cubby-hole, bowed, blew a kiss from his fingertips and, having performed his *proskynesis*, disappeared again.

At the end of the corridor, set off to the left, was the bright light of an atrium. As they processed towards it, they passed steps up to a passageway which ran off to the right towards another atrium. Clearly, Tatianus or one of his ancestors had incorporated at least two houses in order to make a home fitting the family dignity.

In the shade of the peristyle, couches and tables were set out.

Slaves appeared with bowls and ewers. As they washed the hands of the more respectable, Tatianus efficiently allocated quarters to the newcomers, his eyes shifting all the time. Ballista politely requested just one room for himself, his wife and their sons. He did not wish to impose any added burden on his host. His two freedmen and his *accensus* could share a room.

As the northerner spoke, Hippothous caught a look from Julia. Ballista's wife seemed about to say something, but she did not. Hippothous knew things were not good between them. Her eyes gave it away. They were black, and that was seldom good. They had a lack of depth, almost an insubstantiality, about them which often pointed to a deep, tightly controlled anger. And they were dry, the sure sign of immorality. The eyes were the gateway to the heart.

Yet it was far from certain that all lay with her. Ballista's eyes were heavy lidded, sloping at the outer corners. When he spoke, especially when talking to his wife, he often sighed. The great physiognomist Polemon had identified such a combination as characterizing a man contemplating evil. But Hippothous was not sure yet about Ballista. As Polemon had also said, one single sign will not suffice; your judgement should not be confirmed until you have considered the testimony of all the signs.

The *humiliores* among the new arrivals dismissed to the further reaches of the house, the honoured guests took their places on the couches. Tatianus poured a libation, spoke a short prayer, and reclined on the most honourable couch with his eldest son and Ballista. Neither Corvus's wife Nikeso nor any other woman was present. The freedmen had a couch near the back. Old-fashioned ways held in the provincial town of Priene.

The wine was *Aromeus*, one of the best of the Ephesian region. The bread was warm. In addition to the inevitable hard-boiled eggs, the first dishes were local clams, grilled scallops with vin-

90

egar and Median silphium, and samphire conserved in brine. Hippothous decided that the rusticity of the latter was designed to emphasize the exquisite good taste of serving the shellfish at the optimum season and the hideous expense of the imported spice. Many men got rich importing silphium from the distant recesses of Asia. The Maeander plain may have reduced the town of Priene, but it had created rich farming land. If you owned enough of it, as Tatianus obviously did, poverty was far from the door.

Tatianus was treating Ballista to an exposition of the sights to be found in Priene: the temple of Athena and Augustus, that of Demeter and Kore, the Alexandreum – the latter, down by the West Gate, the very house in which the Macedonian had stayed when he was besieging Miletus.

Having not eaten since before dawn, when they set out, Hippothous addressed himself with a will to the food and drink. He was hoping there would be more good things to follow, and that the *Aromeus* would not give him too much of a headache later.

There was a commotion out by the door, movement in the dark corridor, and a messenger ran out into the atrium. Blinded by the sudden glare, the man stood blinking, peering at the indistinct figures in the shade of the peristyle.

'*Kyrios.*' Unable to identify Tatianus, he addressed those on the couches in general. '*Kyrios*, Flavius Damianus has arrived from Ephesus. He is to speak to the *Boule*. The Goths are sailing south.'

In the *Bouleuterion*, Flavius Damianus was on his feet, speaking. The descendant of the famous sophist of the same name, Flavius Damianus clearly considered that he knew how to make a good speech. Sonorous and weighty, the Attic words poured out like a river in flood. Arcane ancient history was paraded. Courage had always been the virtue of the men of Priene. This *andreia*, instilled by nature and training, had thrown back the barbaric fury of the Galatians. It had confounded the combined forces of Ariarathes of Cappadocia and Attalus of Pergamum when those monarchs, most impiously, had attempted to seize the city.

Seated by Ballista in the front row, on the speaker's right hand, Hippothous knew that Flavius Damianus would continue for some time. He surreptitiously picked food out of his teeth, and looked around. The council chamber was high and dark. It smelt of antiquity. Some one hundred men sat on the banked seats that filled three sides of the room. There was room for many more. Five hundred? Six? The town may have decayed, but Hippothous wondered if it could ever have boasted a *Boule* of anything like that number.

Flavius Damianus had settled into an extended excursus on the unchangeable nature of northern barbarians. Galatians, Goths, Scythians, they were all the same: fierce, yes, but irrational as they were, they lacked the true moral dimension of courage, as possessed by a Hellene. Just as they had no moral fortitude, their big, pale bodies could not endure the heat or hard labour.

Out of the corner of his eye, Hippothous checked how Ballista was taking all this. The northerner was staring impassively at the low fire smoking on the altar in the centre of the room. Probably he had heard the like many times before. Hippothous worried at a fragment of lamb stuck in his teeth. He had a slight headache.

At last, Flavius Damianus finished, with a rousing panegyric of the men of Priene, the descendants of the heroes of the battle of Lade. What did such men have to fear from a drunken rabble of Scythians?

There was a murmur of applause, rather muted. Carried away by his rhetoric, Flavius Damianus possibly had forgotten that the Ionians had lost the battle of Lade. Not the man with an oration your ancestor was, thought Hippothous. That is the problem with us Hellenes: forever dwelling on the distant past. Maybe the Romans are right: we Hellenes talk too much and do too little.

Tatianus thanked Flavius Damianus, and called the *Vir Ementissimus* Marcus Clodius Ballista to take the floor.

Hippothous sat forward. He knew what Ballista was going to say. Although he did not understand the reason for it, he was interested to see what reaction it would provoke.

As Ballista stood, collecting his thoughts, a shaft of light came from the door at the top of the northern steps. Ballista waited as the latecomer found his seat.

'Councillors of Priene.' Ballista spoke Attic Greek well, with no barbarisms and almost without a northern accent. He had, after all, been educated at the imperial court in Rome. 'Your city lies some miles inland. The Goths will not go far from their boats. If they lose them, they are cut off in a hostile land. Further down the coast, the city of Miletus and the sanctuary of Didyma have much to fear; the city of Priene little. Should the Goths come here, you have stout walls. The Goths have come to plunder, not to besiege. I believe, if sensible precautions are taken, that the city of Priene is safe. So safe that I intend to leave my *familia* – my beloved wife and small sons – here while I travel to Miletus. As an experienced military officer, I will offer my services in their defence.'

Ballista stopped. There were cries of protest. What malignant daemon had put this in his mind? Ballista should stay here and help them.

The northerner shook his head. 'My mind is made up. I will take just my *accensus* Marcus Aurelius Hippothous and my freed-man Marcus Clodius Maximus. The rest of my *familia* I entrust to your protection. They will stay at the house of my friend Marcus Aurelius Tatianus. May the gods hold their hands over all of us.'

Outside, walking through the Sacred *stoa*, Hippothous recalled the parting at Tatianus's house. Ballista's sons had behaved well.

The younger, Dernhelm, might be too young to realize the full import, but the elder, Isangrim, had been brave. There had been few words spoken between Ballista and Julia: brief platitudes, a simple kiss. The atmosphere had been tense with things unsaid, thoughts never to be formed as they had not been uttered. At the last, Ballista had embraced old Calgacus, they whispered close – fierce, strong things – and it had been done.

Leaving those you loved – Hippothous had done it many times. But two stood out. Tauromenium, all those years ago: the last, brief meeting with Cleisthenes, upstairs above a bar, in a room rented by the hour, time running out, the retainers and hired toughs already out looking for him. The youth crying, pleading to leave with the man he loved – he would not care when his family disinherited him, if the whole world called him a *cinaedus*. Hippothous was moved, but he knew Cleisthenes did not mean it or, if he did, he would soon change his mind. He had loved the boy one more time, and set off for the docks.

Cleisthenes, dear boy though he had been, was nothing compared with Hyperanthes. They had grown up together. Hippothous and Hyperanthes, *ephebes* of the city of Perinthus; their families rich, well connected. Possibly, if they had not been the same age, the *polis* would have looked more indulgently on them – as the older *erastes* and his younger *eromenos*, a throwback to the great days of free Hellas, the time of Harmodius and Aristogeiton, Alcibiades and Socrates. Maybe then Hyperanthes' father would not have sent him away to Byzantium into the so-called care of Aristomachus. Even then, after Hippothous had killed Aristomachus, even then it would have been well but for the shipwreck. Not a night passed that the memory did not haunt Hippothous. The dark waters off Lesbos, the life slipping from Hyperanthes in the cold, the boy slipping away in the dark.

They reached the crossroads to the north-east of the *agora* where the horses were waiting, and Hippothous came back to the present. The two slaves Ballista had hurriedly purchased held the bridles of the five horses and two pack mules. The animals looked up from the fountain, mouths dripping.

Ballista had asked Tatianus to provide a messenger to go to the governor Maximillianus. The man was there. Ballista led him away from the fountain, away from the others, then called for Maximus to join him. He did not ask Hippothous. The horses went back to drinking.

Ballista talked earnestly to the messenger. Hippothous watched. He felt jealous of the northerner's intimacy with Maximus, angry that Ballista should trust that ignorant Hibernian and not his *accensus*.

The messenger left. Ballista and Maximus came back, and they all mounted. Ballista played with the ears of his pale horse. 'Time to go.'

They rode west, the ordered columns of the Sacred *stoa* on their right, the *agora* to the left. The half-witted Hibernian was singing a song about a woman with five accommodating daughters. They passed the steps up to the great blue and red temple to Athena and Augustus. The street fell away before them.

The full decline of Priene was evident. Shops on one side, houses the other; most ruined, roofs fallen. It was not recent. Tall pines thrust up through some of the broken buildings. There were very few people about.

Hippothous had no idea why Ballista had taken this dangerous course. There was little in his physiognomy that suggested the hero. His eyes were very dark blue, almost bluish-black. Often, they caught the light, shone like the rays of the sun. It was a combination that suggested caution about everything, if not cowardice and fear, as well as an unseemly companionship with the poor. Still, one single sign will not suffice.

Yet, no matter how illconsidered their expedition was, the sun was shining, swallows cut through the air, the pines gave shade. Life could be worse.

A black man suddenly walked out from one of the sheer, stepped alleys to the right. In the lead, Ballista's horse shied. It backed, rear hooves stamping dangerously close to the broken slabs covering the drain on the left of the street. Hippothous could not suppress a shudder. A bad omen. Black was the colour of the underworld; of ghosts and daemons, of triple-faced Hecate and the terrible Eumenides. Before the battle of Pharsalus, Brutus's men had come across an Aethiopian. They had run him through with their swords. They had lost the battle.

Ballista got his grey under control, spoke soothingly to it. The Ethiopian bowed, blew a kiss to the mounted men. Ballista nodded and moved on. The others followed. The Ethiopian watched them go.

They rode on slowly, in silence. Even Maximus was quiet. Hippothous thought that some of the warmth had gone out of the afternoon.

They were nearing the West Gate when Ballista reined in and spoke to an old man squatting by the side of the street. Was the Alexandreum nearby? The ancient unfolded himself and shuffled to an alley off to the left. He gestured: come, come.

Ballista and Hippothous swung down. Maximus said he would stay with the animals.

The entrance to the alley was narrow, largely overgrown. The old man was waiting some paces down on the left. He pointed to an open door.

Ballista's hand went to the wallet on his belt. With an air of the greatest dignity, the old man demurred and returned the way they had come.

Hippothous followed Ballista into a courtyard. It was dusty

96

and empty, with the sad air of neglected festivals. On the door-post was an inscription: *You shall enter this sanctuary clean and dressed in white*. Hippothous noted that Ballista was wearing black.

A priest appeared from a doorway in the south wall. He walked unhurriedly. Disconcertingly, he gave the sense of having expected them. He welcomed them formally, talked briefly with Ballista and graciously accepted some money.

After the priest had left, they stood waiting. The courtyard was still, hushed. Ballista was not in the mood to talk.

In due time, the priest reappeared with a small boy carrying the offerings. They ushered the men towards a door in the north wall, into the sanctuary itself. The room was dark; three columns down the middle. In the north-east corner was a low platform. They mounted the steps. On the platform stood a marble table. On it were statues: Alexander reaching for his sword, Cybele, other divinities. The table stood over a crevice in the rock.

Ballista took the small cakes and placed them on the table. He took the unmixed wine he had requested and tipped it down into the crevice.

Alexander lives and reigns.

With no further ado, Ballista turned and left. Hippothous followed him.

Outside, a fresh wind had got up. The alley afforded a magnificent view out over the city walls, across the Maeander plain and the Aegean, to a range of hills. Misty and blue in the distance, the last of those had to be the peninsular of Miletus. Alexander, it was said, had gone from this very house to conquer Miletus. Hippothous did not know what Ballista was thinking, but he wondered if the bad omen had been averted.

VIII

Ballista looked at the moon. It was big, one night before full. Over the starboard bow was the small, three-humped island of Lade, dark and quiet. To the other side, no distance across the water, the lights of Miletus twinkled all over the slopes of the peninsula. The water ran down the sides of the boat, spun out behind, the wake bright on the dark sea.

It was late. Ballista was tired. They had ridden out of Priene, past the landlocked port of Naulochos, to a village called Skolopoeis. There they had sent one of the slaves back to Priene with the animals. Having hired the fishing boat, they had waited for the coming of the evening offshore breeze. Ballista stretched and yawned. It seemed an age since they had set out before dawn that morning to travel to Priene.

Seated in the bows, Hippothous was telling Maximus about Miletus. Like a good Hellene – like Demetrius, the previous *accensus* – Hippothous seldom missed an opportunity to parade his knowledge of distant Hellenic history. 'The land here was ruled by a local, a Carian chief called Anax or something barbarous like that. Then warriors from Crete came. They were led by

98

Miletos, the son of Apollo and Areia; although some say his mother was Deione or Acacallis.'

'Strange,' said Maximus. 'It is usually the father a fellow is not so sure about.'

Hippothous ignored the interruption. 'Of course, some say the founder was Sarpedon, but that is obvious nonsense.'

'Obvious to the most benighted fool.'

'Anyway, the Cretan newcomers settled down with the local Carians and things were fine between them. But things were very different when the Ionians came under Neileus, son of King Kodros of Athens. They killed all the men and took their women. And that is why, to this day, the wives of the Milesians will neither sit at table with their husbands nor call them by name.'

Maximus nodded admiringly. 'Sure, these Milesians are on the right track, but imagine if they could get the women not to talk to them at all.'

It was strange how often Hippothous and Maximus talked. Of course, over their months together in the *familia*, they had shared salt, but much about them suggested that they disliked or even despised one another. Yet there was something that made each seek the other out. Now Hippothous was telling Maximus how the Milesian philosopher Thales thanked the gods for three things: that he was human, not an animal; a man, not a woman; a Hellene, not a barbarian. The teasing did not run all one way.

Ballista hoped the slave had got Pale Horse back to Priene safely. Allfather, he hoped he was right about the safety of Priene. He knew Calgacus would die before he let any harm come to Julia and the boys. Nothing melodramatic about it, he just knew it. If the Goths went there, the acropolis looked impregnable, and Tatianus struck him as capable. But Flavius Damianus was a very different case. The man had done well after the earthquake, but Ballista still mistrusted him from the previous time in

Ephesus. Still, Julia and the boys staying there and him going to Miletus was the right thing.

The old fisherman was in the stern with the steering oar. The remaining slave was asleep in the bottom of the boat. Ballista unhitched himself from the mast and asked Hippothous what he knew of the defences of Miletus.

'"Once, long ago, they were brave, the men of Miletus."' Hippothous recited the iambic verse. 'The words of Phoebus Apollo have become a proverb. For twelve years, the army of the kings of Lydia invaded the land of Miletus. It did them no good; the city held. Since then things have not gone so well. The Ionians lost the naval battle off Lade and the Persians took the city. Alexander's fleet anchored at Lade and the city fell. A later Macedonian king, the Antigonid Philip V, took Lade, and Miletus went over to him.'

'So,' Ballista said, 'if the attacker has control of the sea, the city falls.'

'The Goths have a few boats.' Maximus laughed. 'Well, that is grand. As Calgacus would say, we are all going to die.'

'The men of Miletus are not what they were,' said Hippothous. 'By the time of the Romans, the Milesians had sunk so low that their island of Pharmakousa was overrun with pirates. Notoriously, they held the young Julius Caesar for ransom.'

'Although,' countered Ballista, 'in the story, once released, Caesar raised boats from Miletus, returned and crucified his captors.'

'That would be more down to him than the men of Miletus.'

Ballista shrugged. 'All stories change in the telling.'

The boat drove easily through the slight swell. They were getting close. Moving to the stern, Ballista stood by the fisherman. He studied the city of Miletus. Here, in the north-west, the peninsula sloped steeply down to the sea. In the moonlight he could make out the walls. They appeared sound. So far, so good.

The fisherman tacked to bring the boat around into the narrow mouth of the Lion Harbour. On either side, crouching in the gloom, the large statues which gave the haven its name. By them were winches and chains. Once, they would have closed the entrance; now they lay in sad disrepair. The city walls continued into the harbour but ran out before the quays at the far end. To the left were ship sheds to house war galleys. They were derelict.

Ballista thought back to another arrival at another town, years earlier. He had been sent to defend Arete on the Euphrates. He had told the *Boule* what had to be done, told them of the necessary destruction and impositions as sympathetically as he could. They had not liked it. Cries of outrage – some of them shouting that it would be no worse being captured. Maybe in some ways they were right. Had he thought that then, or was it something fitting he now added? Memory was a slippery thing.

As the boat glided in, there was a stir on the quayside. A *telones* – something about them always betrayed them as customs officials – led a group of auxiliary soldiers to the edge of the water. There were no more than half a dozen soldiers; useful for arresting smugglers, less good for a *hansa* of Goths.

The old man docked the boat. The *telones* shouted – something peremptory befitting the nature of his calling. Ballista ignored him, let Hippothous browbeat the official with the sonorous titles of Ballista's exalted Roman status. The soldiers saluted smartly enough. The *telones* managed to appear both fawning and vaguely aggrieved.

Ballista stepped ashore. As the others tied up the boat, he asked the *telones* to summon the *Boule* of Miletus.

The official bridled. '*Kyrios*, it is late. The councillors will be asleep.'

'Then wake them.'

'They are men of influence.' The *telones* sounded outraged. 'It would be unseemly.'

Ballista turned and spoke in Latin to one of the soldiers. 'Go to the *curia*. There should be public slaves in the council house.'

'*Kyrios*, the councillors must not be disturbed,' the *telones* interrupted, still in Greek. 'They will be angry.'

Ballista continued addressing the soldier. 'Send the public slaves to rouse the councillors.'

'No, *Kyrios*, you must leave this until tomorrow. You have no authority over these troops.'

Ballista looked at Maximus, nodded his head at the *telones*, and continued giving orders. 'If there are no slaves in the *curia*, find out where a prominent councillor lives.'

Maximus approached the *telones*, put a fraternal arm around his shoulders and, pulling him close, drove his knee into the man's crotch. The official crumpled, clutching his balls. Maximus took a step back and effortlessly kicked him to the ground.

'Hammer on the councillor's door until someone answers.'

Maximus had lined up to bring the heel of his boot down on the *telones'* ear, when Hippothous restrained him. The *accensus* handed over his walking stick. Maximus thanked him.

'When you have woken the councillor's *familia*, send his slaves to summon the rest of the *curia*.'

There was a swish as Maximus swung the walking stick through the air, a solid crunch as it landed. The *telones* yelped.

'Is that clear, *Miles*?'

'Perfectly, *Dominus*.'

Swish – crunch, swish – crunch; Maximus was going about his work with skill and commitment.

'Take two of your boys with you.'

'We will do what is ordered, and at every command we will be ready.'

The soldiers had done well: barely a smile. There were few things soldiers enjoyed as much as watching a civilian getting a good beating.

'Enough,' Ballista said. Maximus handed the stick back to Hippothous.

'Thank you,' said Hippothous. 'Done most philosophically. One day, when we have time, I will tell you how the great doctor Galen recommends one beats people.'

The three remaining soldiers began to help unload the baggage from the boat. The *telones* got to his feet and limped off. Maximus sang as he caught and stacked things. Hippothous, such manual labour being beneath a free-born *accensus*, polished his walking stick.

Ballista set his back to the sea and surveyed the harbour. Off to the right was a large monument on a stepped circular base. It boasted several ships' rams in marble. There was a colonnade behind it that turned and ran across in front of him. Its shops and warehouses were all shuttered bar one – probably a drinking den. Where the colonnade stopped to the left was a tall gate, the sort of elaborate, impractical thing commissioned in civic pride in the days when peace seemed immutable. Beyond that, running back towards the water, was the plain wall of a sacred enclosure. It was pierced by just one ornamental gateway. Behind it rose the round roof of the actual temple. It had to be the home of Apollo Delphinios, the patron god of sailors.

Ballista strolled over to the monument on the round base. An inscription recorded its erection to honour Pompey the Great for ridding the sea of pirates.

'All done,' Hippothous said.

Maximus, the slave and one of the soldiers shouldered the various bags and shields. The mail coats and everything else were both bulky and heavy.

Through the Harbour Gate was a broad paved road, now empty. The men's footsteps echoed back from the colonnades on both sides. There was always something unnatural about a city at night.

A walk of a few moments and the roadway opened out into an *agora*. The soldier pointed to an imposing building to the right. Miletus was, and had always been, a more important *polis* than Priene. Its *Bouleuterion* was correspondingly grander. The outer gate through the *propylon* was open.

Inside was a wide courtyard, porticos with Doric columns on three sides, a tomb or shrine in the middle. On the fourth side the several doors of the actual council house were hermetically shut, although lights could be seen through the high windows. The soldiers who had gone ahead sauntered out of the shadows under the columns. Public slaves had been sent to find the councillors. There was nothing to do but wait.

Overhead, the moon rode across the sky, putting the stars to shame. In the mundane sphere, ox skulls sculpted on the tomb threw back its light. Ballista slipped into an elegiac mood. He thought about defending Miletus, his reasons for coming to this *polis*, about the Goths. It would not be the first time he had faced them. That had been many years before. He had been a Roman officer when the general Gallus had thrown the Goths back from the walls of Novae up near the Danube. Gaius Vibius Trebonianus Gallus – what a general he had been; what an emperor he would have made, if the fates had not struck him down so soon after he reached the purple.

The night was not having such a melancholy effect on the others. 'You may well like this town,' Hippothous said to Maximus. 'It is a sink of depravity.'

'I can but hope.'

'And your hopes may be rewarded. The divine philosopher

Apollonius of Tyana tried to bring the Milesians to virtue. He sent them a letter: "Your children lack fathers, your youths old men, your wives husbands, your . . ."'

'Well, if their wives are lacking husbands, I am their man.'

"'. . . husbands rulers, your rulers laws, your . . ."'

'And I am sure you will be looking after the youths.'

Hippothous sighed an exaggerated sigh. 'I am far from sure Thales was right. It might be better to be born an animal rather than a barbarian.'

'Maybe some of the husbands too.'

'Of course, you will not know that this town has given its name to a whole type of erotic story. Would you like to hear a Milesian tale?'

'That depends,' Maximus said suspiciously.

'"There was once a boy of Miletus, the first blush of down on his cheeks—"'

'No, I really do not think I would enjoy that.'

'Then how about this? "Once there was a woman of Miletus—"'

'Better already, much more my end of the *agora*.'

Hippothous spun the tale, a depraved Penelope weaving an obscene account: a virtuous widow starving herself to death in her husband's tomb; outside, a soldier guarding a crucified corpse; his blandishments; her acquiescence; the unspoken horror of their lovemaking by her husband's decaying remains.

Maximus was listening intently, although with lines of suspicion on his face.

The disappearance of the corpse from the cross, the widow volunteering her husband's cadaver to take its place, the discovery of the substitution, the laughter of the townsfolk, the unresolved ambiguities of the tale's ending . . . What happened to them? Was he punished? Was she? Was the laughter enough to save them?

'You Greeks are all fucking liars,' Maximus exclaimed.

'I think you will find that is just Cretans,' Hippothous replied suavely.

'You stole that story from Petronius's *Satyricon*, and it happened in Ephesus.'

'No, it is likely he took it from Aristides' *Milesian Tales*.'

'The Romans are right about you – thieves and liars, every fucking one of you.'

The acrimonious literary debate was cut short.

'Health and great joy.' The man appeared like an apparition conjured out of nothing. He was in middle age, respectable, right arm wrapped in his *himation*. 'I am Marcus Aurelius Macarius, *stephanephor* of Miletus, and *asiarch* of the imperial cult in this *polis*.'

'Health and great joy,' Ballista replied formally.

Macarius smiled. He was good-looking, with a cleanshaven face reminiscent of a polished artefact of considerable value. 'It is an honour to welcome Marcus Clodius Ballista, *Vir Ementissimus*, victor of Circesium, Soli and Sebaste, to Miletus.'

'It is an honour to be here.'

'If it is convenient, the *Boule* wishes to have your advice.'

Inside, the *Bouleuterion* was the shape and scale of a theatre. Curved tiers of seats banded up to the shadows of the tall beamed ceiling, upon them some two hundred men. There was room for six or seven times that number. Ballista noted the two doors high up in the back wall. That was how the councillors had got in unseen.

Macarius offered a little wine and a pinch of incense to the gods, and then made the proposal.

The men of Miletus had done well. Seven years ago, when the Goths had sacked Nicomedia and the other cities in Bithynia, the *Boule* and *Demos* of the Milesians had begun the repair of the walls. The number of men chosen for the watch had been doubled. Proper military training had been reintroduced to the instruction of the *ephebes*. Three days ago, when the news had come from Ephesus, they began stockpiling food. The men of Miletus had done well, but one thing had been lacking, a thing now made good by the providence of the gods. The city had lacked a man of proven military skill and experience to command the defence. Now, in answer to their prayers, the gods had sent such a man. Macarius called on the *Boule* of Miletus to appoint Marcus Clodius Ballista, the hero of Circesium, of Soli, of Sebaste, to be *strategos*, to save the city from the fury of Scythian Ares.

The councillors shook back their cloaks and applauded. The proposal was passed without debate, unanimously. Macarius called on the *Vir Ementissimus* Ballista to take the floor.

Ballista had been thinking about what he would say, but he had not prepared a speech. No stranger to what was expected, he would let the words come.

'Once, long ago, they were brave, the men of Miletus.'

Unease ran through the *Bouleuterion*. No one knew the proverb better than the honourable men assembled. Who was this barbarian to insult them?

'Once, long ago, they were brave, the men of Miletus, and they are brave still.'

Recognizing the rhetorical ploy, the councillors were mollified. They settled to listen.

'What makes a people brave? We should believe Herodotus: it is geography, the nature of their land. The Maeander Plain may have grown, but the mountains and the sea do not change. The back-breaking limestone mountains, and the deep, widow-making sea remain. While they endure, the Milesians do not change.'

A murmur of approval came from the councillors. This general from the north spoke their language.

'For twelve years, the Milesians defied the Lydian kings. It took the might of Persia and the genius of Alexander to take the walls of Miletus. There is no shame in going down fighting against overwhelming odds. Men do not speak ill of Leonidas and the three hundred Spartans at Thermopylae. Athens fell to the Persians, Rome to the Gauls. There is no shame in it. Where would Rome have been if the Milesians had not avenged Julius Caesar and crucified the pirates? The Goths who will come are not a host led by a Darius or Alexander. They are no more than the pirates your forefathers routed on Pharmakousa.'

Again the cloaks were shaken back and applause rang to the gloomy rafters.

'I cannot tell yet what measures may be necessary but, be warned, they will be a bitter medicine. But we have time. The Goths will not be here for several days.'

As soon as Ballista finished, before the sounds of approbation had died, Macarius was on his feet. 'How do you know the Goths will not arrive for days?'

Ballista smiled. 'I know too much about Goths.'

IX

Ballista looked at the lights on Lade. They were clustered down on the shoreline, some few straggling up the three low mounds of the island. They were the camp fires of the Goths.

From the roof of a tall house on the hill up above the theatre of Miletus, Ballista had a good vantage point. Lade was in full view, not much more than a mile away. To his left was the Theatre Harbour and to his right the Lion Harbour. Their waters were as still and dark as those of a well. It was a calm night, even on this high place on the peninsula. There was just the merest hint of an offshore breeze. It was different up above. Lines of clouds from the west marched across the face of the moon, like the tattered ranks of a disordered legion. The moon was still big. Counting inclusively, as almost everyone did, it was four nights since it had been full.

Ballista knew the ways of the Goths. When he had spoken to the *Boule* of Miletus, he had known the city had a few days' grace. It had been the night before the full moon. The Goths marked the full moon with their festival of *Dulths*: animals were sacrificed, great and terrible oaths taken, a feast consumed and vast amounts of drink downed. The next day, they were always hung over. Sure enough, their sails had appeared before Miletus late on the day following that. The rest of that day and today they had remained quiet by their boats on Lade.

All in all, Ballista had had four days as *strategos* to organize the defence. First, he had learnt all he could about Miletus. Surprisingly, the *Boule* had produced a well-drawn, detailed map. Miletus was a planned city made up of neat, Hippodamian squares. Possibly that accounted for the existence of the map. Ballista had not contented himself with that. He had taken a small boat, and had himself rowed all around. On foot, he had surveyed the walls and tramped up and down the streets and open spaces.

Miletus, the ornament of Ionia, occupied a broad but tapering peninsula running towards the north-east. The Aegean lay to the west, the gulf of Latmos to the east. Gratifyingly, in the north and north-west, the land dipped sharply down to the sea. There were just six places where it would be practical to land a sizable force, such as a *hansa* of Goths. On the west was the long inlet of the Lion Harbour, the broader and deeper Theatre Harbour and, outside the land walls, a wide beach at the foot of a hill topped with suburban villas and temples. On the east there were two small bays with a few jetties used by local fishermen, and another open beach beyond the walls. It could have been a great deal worse.

What had already been accomplished by the *Boule* pleased Ballista. The walls were in good condition, and the stocks of food ample for several weeks. Best of all, they had persuaded the prefect of an auxiliary unit of Dacian spearmen in transit to the east to remain with his men in the city. The unit was less under strength than some, having three hundred soldiers with its standards.

Ballista had been busy – more than busy: he had worked himself to exhaustion. He had ordered the hasty construction of a wall along the quayside to close the inner end of the Lion Harbour. Stakes had been driven into the bed of that harbour and the one below the theatre. Large stones had been dragged up on to all the wall walks, ready to be dropped on approaching Goths. Acquiring the stones, as well as the need to provide construction material for the new wall, had involved the knocking down and smashing of quite a few monuments and many statues. As soldiers would, the Dacian auxiliaries had gone to it with a will. Any number of large metal pots and cauldrons capable of being placed on a fire had been requisitioned. Together with the combustibles and the sand to be heated, they also now waited on the battlements. Arrows with tar-soaked rags tied around their heads were stacked nearby. The aqueduct which entered the city through the south-eastern wall was blocked. At this, the members of the *Boule* had protested: the waters would not run in the famous *nymphaeum*; the Baths must be shut. Hippothous had intervened: they could still drink; were not the Milesians justly proud of the sweet water from the deep Well of Achilles?

Physical resources were one thing, manpower was another. Ballista had set about augmenting the three hundred auxiliaries. A sweep of the town, mainly the bars and brothels, turned up regular soldiers detached from their units. These *stationarii* – on special assignments, on leave or overstaying it – added another ninety trained men. There were one hundred men chosen for the watch of Miletus, and another hundred young men being trained as *ephebes*. To these Ballista added three thousand citizens, volunteers for the most part, some of whom had in their day received a little military instruction when *ephebes*. Lastly, there were fifteen hundred slaves, who were provisionally offered their freedom, depending on their performance.

The raggle-taggle defence force had to be armed. The stocks

of the few weapons dealers were confiscated. Spears, swords, shields and armour long dedicated in the temples were brought forth, although many of these turned out to be useless with age. Arms kept in private homes, as heirlooms or for hunting, were collected in the *agora*. All over the city, carpenters and leather-workers were put to making shields. Night and day, the streets were loud with the clangour of blacksmiths beating out javelin and spear heads.

With the limited means at his disposal, Ballista had shaped his plans. The armed citizens and slaves were distributed evenly around the walls. They could throw and drop things; some of them had bows and knew how to use them. But there was little point in keeping any back as a reserve; they would be no use hand to hand against Gothic warriors. The men chosen for the watch and the *ephebes* had been mixed in with the Dacian auxiliaries and the *stationarii*. The idea was to pad out the number of the latter and stiffen the former.

Ballista had thought long and hard about how best to deploy his inadequate number of trained men. The first decision he had taken, and he still considered it his best, was to station a hundred and fifty of them in the temple of Apollo Delphinios. There they could cover both the Lion Harbour and the small fishing jetty to its east. Less obviously, they could also prevent any Goths coming down into the main city from the more northerly of the eastern fishing harbours. That this implicitly meant abandoning the northern residential districts to the enemy was something he carefully failed to mention.

Another group of one hundred and fifty he quartered in the Baths of Faustina. These protected the Theatre Harbour and, similarly, they could try to stand in the way of any Goths who had scaled the land walls at the base of the peninsula. Again, in the latter case, the fate of the southern area of houses was not discussed.

From the remainder, he had created six small units of forty men. These were ordered to various important places around the walls: one at each of the two fishing jetties on the east, one where the aqueduct crossed into the city, one each at the Lion Gate and the Sacred Gate in the southern wall, and one in the Western Market.

This left just fifty trained men. Forty of them were to remain with Ballista as his bodyguard and the only reserve. The final ten, aided by a large number of labourers, were to operate the two siege engines he had constructed.

At the siege of Arete, Ballista had seen pieces of artillery which had been hit by enemy projectiles. One had been smashed and had fallen on its side. One of its torsion springs lay horizontally on the ground. The image had stuck in his mind.

An artillery piece was a complicated bit of equipment, hard both to build and to maintain. Two vertical torsion springs each had an arm which powered a slide which threw the stone or dart. Here, Ballista had overseen the creation of two new and radically simplified weapons. A huge torsion spring, made from the long tresses of Milesian women, was set horizontally in a stout wooden frame. Its one arm was winched back almost flat to the ground. A stone was placed in a sort of bowl at the end. Released, the arm sprang vertically. When it hit an upright retaining bar, the stone was hurled.

These improvised artillery he had placed at the foot of the theatre, covering that harbour. There had only been time for a couple of test shots before the Gothic sails had been sighted. The weapons had worked, if with alarming inaccuracy. Ballista hoped the latter would prove less important than the factor of surprise.

Standing on the hilltop in the cool night air, Ballista stretched and yawned. He knew he had done all he could. He had just over five thousand defenders. They outnumbered the Goths in the region of two to one. But only one in ten of his men had any real training. In fighting men, the Goths outnumbered the Milesians about five to one. But the walls would make a difference, and so should the artillery.

High above, the moon fled through the sky. At the end of time, when the snows of Fimbulvetr, the winter of winters, lay across the world, the wolf Hati would run the moon down and devour it. Ballista shrugged the image from his mind. That lay in the future, as did the fight for Miletus. Ballista knew the ways of the Goths. They did not attack at night. He called Maximus and Hippothous to him. They were all bone tired. They might as well get some sleep.

Ballista woke with a feeling of profound dread. Although next to no breeze came through the open window, somewhere in the house a door clicked. Outside, the leaves of the ornamental shrubs rustled. The very air seemed to heave like a swelling sea.

Unwillingly, he forced his eyes open. Nothing. He sat up, looked all around the bedroom. By the faint light of a low lamp, he could see the room was empty. Unsatisfied, he got up, checked the room again. Still nothing. He stepped to the window, felt the cool night air on his face. Nothing disturbed the tranquillity of the moonlit atrium. The humped shapes of the men of his bodyguard slept peacefully.

Ballista lay back on the bed. Strangely, he felt almost disappointed. For most of his adult life he had been haunted by the daemon of the emperor Maximinus Thrax. Intermittently, but always in the dead of night, Ballista would wake to find the huge, hooded figure regarding him.

Julia, true to her Epicurean upbringing, had tried to argue it away: it always happened when Ballista was tired and under extreme pressure; it was no apparition but a figment of his mind. Ballista did not believe her. Twenty-four years earlier, he had broken his oath and killed the emperor he had sworn to protect. The body of Maximinus Thrax had been mutilated, denied burial. Barred from Hades, it was only too likely the dead emperor's daemon would walk the earth, seek out the one responsible.

Ballista had not seen the daemon since he had killed Quietus. As he fell asleep again, Ballista wondered about the shade of that ephemeral emperor. Another *sacramentum* broken, another mutilated corpse, another daemon whispering revenge.

'Wake up!'

Ballista was sunk deep in sleep; it was hard to surface.

'Wake up, you lazy bastard.'

Ballista forced his eyes open. Maximus's concerned look and the gentle hand on Ballista's shoulder belied the Hibernian's harsh words.

'At fucking last.'

Ballista threw back the sheet, swung his feet to the floor. 'The Goths are in the city?'

'No,' said Maximus, 'but they are moving.'

'You could have let me sleep until they got here.'

Maximus laughed. 'Sure, are you not the brave one.'

'What can you do?' Ballista, having laid down fully dressed, pulled his boots on, reached for his sword belt. 'Time to go.'

'No, not until we are armed.' Maximus hauled the softly shimmering pile of mail towards the bed. '*You* might want to go down in history as one of the stupid fuckers who runs out bare-arsed at the first alarm and gets a stray arrow in his balls, but I do not. We have got some time.'

They helped each other into the heavy mail coats, then each started to buckle and tie their own various straps and laces.

Ballista's fingers fumbled with his left shoulder guard. Maximus fussed his hands away and fastened it for him.

'I have said it before,' muttered the Hibernian, 'but if I were as frightened as you before a fight, I would not do it.'

Ballista grinned ruefully. 'I was not aware I ever had a choice.'

Maximus said nothing, because it was the truth.

Up on the roof, Hippothous was waiting. From somewhere, he had acquired a fancy, antique Greek helmet. Its inlaid face mask hid his features. Wordlessly, he pointed to the north. The moon was still up, and the clouds had blown away. In the clear, still, azure night, the longships were easily seen, but harder to number. At least a dozen, maybe more. Evidently, they intended to round the tip of the peninsula and attack at some point on its eastern flank.

Hippothous turned dramatically and gestured south. Out beyond the land wall, the Goths had already come to shore. The boats were beached out of sight, but the first fires glinted apricot in the dark. Above, straight as a spear shaft, the first columns of smoke rose from burning buildings.

There was no need for Hippothous to point out the other two divisions of Goths. One, about fifteen ships roughly in line, although still some way out was wheeling to run in towards the Lion Harbour. The final group of raiders was closer. More than twenty of them, their oars whitening the wine-dark sea, they were pulling hard to the Theatre Harbour.

'There are more of them than at Ephesus.' Hippothous's voice came muffled from behind the narrow 'T' opening of his helmet.

Ballista grunted. He was thinking.

'Success breeds success,' Maximus said. 'Every northern pirate in the Aegean will have joined them, maybe some locals too.'

Ballista took a final look all around. For once, the priorities seemed straightforward. With luck, the southernmost Goths would be diverted by looting. They might be intended as no more than a diversion anyway. Those rounding the peninsula would have to be ignored for now. The longships heading for the Lion Harbour would take a little time to arrive.

'Rouse out the bodyguard.' Ballista's voice was decisive. 'We will go to the Theatre Harbour.'

Hippothous turned to go.

'And send a runner ahead. Get the men from the Baths of Faustina on the walls, and tell the artillery not to shoot until we are there.'

At the head of the stairs, Hippothous acknowledged the order.

'One more thing – tell them to light the fires, if they have not done so already.'

Hippothous vanished below. Soon the clattering of equipment and the thud of boots floated up. Ballista and Maximus stood in silence. Beyond and to the right of Lade, across the water and the plain, the mountains were a dark, serrated mass. Ballista thought he could just make out the pale line that was the acropolis of Priene. The Goths were here, not there, and that was good.

'Ready,' Hippothous called from below.

They plunged down the steps of the theatre, along corridors three times the height of a man. The noise of their passing reverberated back from the vaulting, torches throwing misshapen shadows across the great stone slabs.

Emerging from the theatre, they ran to their left. Along the wall, the levied men shifted nervously. The regulars from the Baths of Faustina cheered. The militia joined in, but tentatively, uncertainly. A night they had prayed never to see had come.

The two new siege engines stood ready, monstrous, sharp-angled things in the light of the fires. Their throwing arms were winched back, loaded. They smelt of fresh-cut wood and tar.

Panting, Ballista asked the *optio* in charge if all was ready.

'We will do what is ordered, and at every command we will be ready.'

'Wait for my command, then reload and shoot as fast as you can.'

Ballista and his bodyguard climbed the steps to the wall walk. They fanned out to either side. The levied men shuffled aside gratefully.

The Gothic longships were closer than Ballista had expected. Low and sleek, they were at the harbour mouth, not much more than a couple of hundred paces out. Lines of white splashes showed where their oars broke the water. They were rowing hard.

'Wait, wait!' Ballista found himself shouting. Unconsciously, he dragged his dagger an inch or so from its sheath and snapped it back, repeated the procedure with the sword on his left hip, then touched his fingertips lightly on the healing stone tied to his scabbard.

The longboats cut through the water. Ballista had ranged the artillery for a hundred and fifty paces, the limit of effective arrow-shot. He cursed himself for not thinking to place some marker out in the harbour. Gallus had done so at Novae. He had done the same at Arete. Allfather, he was a fool. It was harder to judge distances over water, and at night.

'Light the missiles.'

Along the wall, bowmen touched their fire arrows into the torches. A smell of burning. From behind came louder sounds of bigger things catching fire.

'Release!'

The flaring tips of dozens of arrows shot away, bright in the night. Most fell short; some flew wildly askew. A derisive cheer started across the water.

A heartbeat or so later, a great double twang and thump from behind the wall. With a terrible whooshing, the incendiary missiles of the artillery raced overhead. They rose, then dipped and fell like meteors trailing sparks.

One dropped short. The other had the range. It did not hit a ship but splashed, hissing, into the middle of the fleet.

Cries of surprise and alarm came from the Goths. The splash of the oars faltered. The ships lost way. The Gothic *reiks* were bellowing at their warriors. In no time, the oars restored their rhythm. The longboats surged forward again.

Arrows whickered out. One or two were finding targets. Here and there, red fire blossomed momentarily on the boats, before being doused by the crews.

Ballista could hear the squeal of the winches dragging back the arms of the artillery. How long could it take? He did not look round. All his attention was on the still, dark water in front of the leading longships.

Suddenly, with a terrible splintering and tearing unmissable above the din, one of the leading longboats shuddered to a complete halt. Those behind it swerved. Two of them collided. Yells of consternation from the Goths. Another boat embedded itself on a sunken stake. The longboat behind it rammed into its stern.

The water creamed, as the crews dug their blades into the water, desperately bringing the longboats to a halt. Arrows continued to hiss among them. Confusion reigned in the harbour. Some *reiks* and warriors roared forward, others screamed retreat. Some boats turned, uncertainly. Most lay dead in the water.

The double twang and thump came again. The great burning missiles arced through the night. One fell almost dangerously short, spinning down to fizz and sink just beyond the dock. But the other, as if guided by the hand of a god, plummeted inexorably down towards a stationary longboat. The world seemed to hush for a moment. Then it exploded in a fury of sound: the crash of timbers, the roar of flame, the pitiful screams of burning men.

There were brave men among these Goths, but it was over. The unseen dangers below the surface, the all too visible threat from the heavens, the growing accuracy of the bowmen: all made it irrevocable. Some longboats stayed in place, trying to rescue those they could from the crews of the three irreparably damaged vessels. The rest backed water, turned and hauled back towards Lade. With those from the stricken ships who had not drowned dragged on board, the last few boats fled. Arrows and intermittent artillery shot pursued them all until they were well out of range.

Ball-is-ta, Ball-is-ta. The chant echoed down the defences; full throated with the exhilaration of relief. *Ball-is-ta, Ball-is-ta.*

'I am of a mind that one swallow does not make a summer,' said Maximus.

'For once, I am inclined to agree with you.' Hippothous had pushed the bronze helmet to the back of his head. His eyes glittered.

That is a man who enjoys killing, Ballista thought. 'Hippothous, gather the bodyguard and round up about fifty of the regulars here. We need to get to the Lion Harbour.'

As the men were collected, Ballista briefly inspected the artillery. As he had suspected, one of them had broken on its second shot. He praised the men there, and told them not to relax; the Goths might come again.

They pounded down a dark street. At least the grid plan of the town made directions easy. After about three hundred paces they came to the south wall of the *Bouleuterion*. Ballista called a stop. He told them they needed to get closed up – who knew what they would find around the next corner? But, equally pressing, he had to get his wind back. Running in full armour was always exhausting, but he was far from campaign fit, and he was not so young any more. Forty winters were taking their toll.

Turning left, the tall, many-columned edifices of the *agora* opened up around them. All was empty and quiet where they were, but the north end was a very different case. Men were fighting and dying along the battlements of the hastily constructed wall which blocked the quay of the Lion Harbour. The bowel-clenching sounds of steel on steel, of agonized screaming, washed down the colonnades towards them.

There were some two hundred paces to go. It was too far to run; they would arrive fragmented, out of breath.

'Form up on me,' Ballista said. 'We walk until I give the order.'

Nearly one hundred armoured men, close packed, stepped forward. Ballista was at their head; Maximus on his left, Hippothous his right. Going to meet something very frightening, it was hard to walk slowly. Every instinct screamed: run, get it over and done. Twenty paces gone, thirty – just let it be over.

More Gothic warriors were appearing on the wall walk. A few had fought their way down some steps and were trying to cut their way to the gate. If they got that open, it was all over.

Sixty paces, seventy. Unconsciously, Ballista quickened the pace.

A knot of Roman auxiliaries was fighting with their backs to the inside of the gate. More Goths were pressing on them. Blades flashed, rising and falling in the eerie torchlight.

Ninety paces gone, a hundred.

The fight at the gate was nearly over, but a handful of Romans was still on their feet. They could not last more than moments.

'Charge!' Ballista drew his sword and launched himself forward.

The paving stones hard under the soles of his boots, scabbard banging against his left leg, Ballista forced his legs faster. The weight of his shield was dragging on his left arm. Faster, faster.

Ballista had pulled clear of the line; Maximus and Hippothous half a step behind. The charge was shaping itself into an arrowhead: the wedge or boar's snout beloved of the northern sagas.

The last Roman had been chopped down. Only twenty paces to go. Four of the Goths moved to lift the bar of the gate. The others, twenty or thirty, turned to face the onslaught.

The warrior facing Ballista set himself, long braided hair and beard, eyes glaring above a red shield. Ballista, legs pumping, shield well out, crashed straight into him. The impact stopped Ballista. The Goth staggered a step or two back. Someone thumped into Ballista's back. Knocked forward, the northerner's shield dipped as he fought for balance. The Goth raised his blade for the killing blow. Dropping the shield, still off balance, Ballista side-stepped off his left leg. The Gothic blade thrummed just past his ankle. It rang, sparking on the stone. Feet slipping, still toppling forward, Ballista shot like a ferret between his opponent and the next warrior in line.

Not glancing back, a hand to the ground, Ballista regained his balance and let his momentum carry him on.

The Goths at the gate, their backs to Ballista, strained as one. The bar lifted a fraction. Ballista aimed at the nearest warrior. At the last moment, the Goth looked over his shoulder – too late. At a flat run, Ballista drove the point of his sword two-handed into the small of the man's back. Mail rings snapped and the steel went deep. Ballista's momentum crashed them both against the wooden boards.

Ballista wrenched his blade free. Some instinct made him spin to his right, wheeling the blade backhanded. It deflected the thrust inches from his nose. The impact ran through his arms. He dropped to one knee and brought his blade back, scything at his opponent's knees. The Goth leapt backwards.

Ballista rose to his feet carefully. For what seemed an eternity, they watched each other, like fighting cocks after the first pass. Then a blow from behind took the Goth in the back of the neck. As he collapsed, Ballista heard the thump of the bar falling back into place.

Maximus grinned at Ballista. The Hibernian's front was a bloody mess, none of it his own. Ballista smiled back and took the shield proffered by Hippothous. The Greek had pushed his archaic helmet back again. He was whooping with joy. So much for your Hellenic self-control, thought Ballista. He looked around the shambles. There was not a Goth still fighting inside the wall. Those that still moved, and some that did not, were being cut to pieces.

'I am thinking it is still not safe,' said Maximus.

From the top of the wall, Ballista looked out and recreated the events from what he saw. Just one longship was skewered and broken out in the standing. The stakes had failed. He remembered the men embedding them saying that while the Lion Harbour was shallow, its bottom was thick mud. The wretched stakes must have toppled or sunk.

Sixteen double-prowed ships were moored at the dock, a skeleton crew on each. The majority of the Goths were just in front. They never liked to venture too far from their boats. The warriors on land had formed a shieldburg. The first rank was kneeling, their shields planted on the ground; the second standing, the bases of their shields resting on the bosses of those in front; the ones behind holding their shields overhead. It was a daunting sight, as firm and unyielding as a rock, virtually arrow proof.

It was hard to count the Gothic warriors. There were some eighty shields overlapping in the front rank, but the shieldburg could be as many as ten or twelve deep. That was a lot of dangerous men.

The twenty or so paces of the quayside between the Goths and the wall were littered with the dead.

Nothing moved. It was one of those disconcerting calms that often punctuated a battle, when both sides, as if by mutual consent, drew back and waited. Seeing the Gothic corpses, Ballista knew it would take a lot to get them to assault the wall again. But if their *reiks* were determined, it would take a lot to stop them a second time.

The sky was lightening with the false dawn. The torches along the wall were paling. Away in the distance to the right, from behind buildings on a rise in the ground, smoke chuffed up. The northernmost flotilla of the Goths had not been idle. The stalemate in the Lion Harbour did not favour the defenders.

As he leant thinking, Ballista noticed that the battlement under his elbows was made from a block of carved marble. It depicted a triton holding a steering oar, his fishy tail long and impressive. It was ironic, the monument boasting of Pompey the Great sweeping pirates from the water smashed and reused for a makeshift defence against a new threat from the sea. All the deeds of men were transient. Ballista wondered if anyone in the future would see that stone and draw a similar conclusion.

There was a stir in the Gothic phalanx. Some of the overlapping shields drew apart, and a helmeted head poked out. The man called, his tone taunting.

'And listen, Miletus, perpetrator of evil deeds; that is when
Many will feed off you and take you as their gleaming prize.'

At the Greek verse, the Milesians on the wall muttered uneasily: Chrysogonus, the betrayer of Nicomedia.

'Your wives will wash the feet of long-haired men,
And others will have charge of my temple at Didyma.'

Ballista stood straight and shouted back. 'The prophecy of Phoe-bus Apollo played out long ago when the Persians came. Your words are as false as your actions – the sophistry of a traitor.'

Ballista hoped he had identified the Delphic Oracle correctly. If he was wrong, doubtless Hippothous would put him right later. But it sufficed for now. The men on the wall jeered.

No sooner had the renegade Greek ducked down than another man stood forth.

'I am Tharuaro, son of Gunteric, leader of the Tervingi in this *hansa*. And I know you: Dernhelm, disgrace to his father Isangrim, the war-leader of the Angles. No one knows treach-ery better than you – oath-breaker, murderer of the defenceless. You are the *asneis* the Romans call Ballista.'

On the wall, Ballista was silent, eating the insults and thinking Loki-like thoughts.

'If you want men to think that you are more than a day-labourer hired for copper, the lowest *asneis*, if you have any honour left, you will come down and face me.' Tharuaro stepped clear of his men, empty handed and contemptuous. *Hoom, hoom*; the Goths growled their approval.

Ballista pulled Maximus close and whispered urgently. The Hibernian nodded. Ballista spoke in his ear again. Maximus nod-ded once more.

'I will come down.' Ballista and Maximus punched each other on the shoulder. The Angle moved to the steps. He stopped and turned. 'Remember – afterwards, only the boats.' He continued on down.

The gate remained open behind Ballista. He walked a few paces and stopped. In the gathering light, the dockside seemed very open and exposed. All was very quiet. Behind him, the torches on the wall walk fizzed and crackled.

Without glancing behind, Tharuaro held his arms out from his body. Two warriors came forth, placed a shield and spear in his hands, and faded back. Tharuaro remained, very still, arms outstretched – a parody of Christ crucified – armoured and, on his helmet, the snarling skull of a marten.

With no warning, Tharuaro took two short, quick steps, then a lengthy lunge to his left. As he moved, the shield swung across his body and the spear arced into the air.

Ballista did not flinch.

Tharuaro gracefully caught the heavily turning spear; two short, quick steps back, a lunge to the right; feet slapping on the marble, the shield in motion all the time.

Hoom, hoom; the Goths murmured their appreciation, boots beginning to stamp the rhythm of the dance – short, short, long.

Ballista could feel his anger rise. Who did this Gothic *reiks* think he was facing? A green boy? A soft southerner? Many times, Ballista had faced warriors dancing before the shieldwall. He had first done so when little more than a child in Germania, and repeatedly as a man in Roman arms – up by the Danube, before the triumph of Novae and the disaster of Abritus. There had even been Gothic auxiliaries dancing in front of the lines of the pretender Aemilianus before the battle of Spoletium which had brought Gallienus and his poor, damned father Valerian to the purple.

Tharuaro danced well. If the war dance had been in Ballista's soul, he would have answered the Goth. It was not, so Ballista stood and watched. Over the years, the Angle had observed warriors who did not dance respond to its challenge in very different ways. Some edged forwards, rattling their weapons, even gnawing the rim of their shield, everything about them on edge and ready. Others attempted nonchalance, chatting to those around them, maybe even turning their back.

Stock still, Ballista stood and watched. Tharuaro danced on, the pace increasing, the spear revolving higher, but he was not one of the Woden-inspired. Ballista knew their sort well. His own father, Isangrim, was a wolf-warrior – in front of the shieldwall, laying down his sword, baying, howling, unconscious of what he did, calling down the slathering power of the Allfather's beast. Blind to pain, hard to stop; they were the ones you could not but fear.

Tharuaro's movements were growing faster. Behind him, the low rumble of the northern war cry was beginning. Soon the dancer's limbs would become a blur, the *barritus* of the warriors would crescendo like a wave crashing on a cliff.

It was time to end this. Time for Ballista's Loki-plan. It would damn him in many men's eyes, would damn him in the eyes of the Tervingi, of all the Goths. And in that it would serve its purpose.

With no ado, Ballista raised his shield then threw himself sideways to the ground, curling under its wooden boards. Immediately, the air was full of violent sound, like the tearing of innumerable fabrics. Keeping very low, leaving the shield, Ballista scrambled back to the gate. There was a great, outraged roaring from the Goths. Missiles skittered off the pavement around Ballista. The gate slammed shut.

Inside, Ballista took the steps two at a time, but when he reached the wall walk things were irrevocable. Tharuaro's corpse, pincushioned with arrows, was being dragged away. The helmet with the feral skull had rolled off. The Gothic shieldburg had surged forward to the wall, intent on revenge. But already the warriors were falling back. The reason for their retreat was evident. Following Ballista's whispered instructions to Maximus, now every archer along the defences was shooting fire arrows as fast as he could into the Gothic longboats. The scant crews left aboard were scurrying about, but fresh flames were blossoming out faster than they could be extinguished.

Ballista watched the main body of the Goths tumble into the boats, hurl themselves on to their rowing benches. Unmoored, the double-prowed vessels pulled away from the dock, into the harbour, and out beyond the entrance where crouched the big carved lions which gave the haven its name.

A messenger puffed up on to the battlements. The group of Goths that had rounded the peninsula and attacked from the east had set on fire the jetties and the huts of the fishermen, but now also were falling back.

'Well,' said Maximus, 'if the lot in the south are content with looting a few homes and temples and do not want to try their luck against the land walls – and I am thinking they will not – that is that for today.'

Ballista grunted.

'Sure, two things accomplished: the attack driven off, and the Tervingi added to the many who will move heaven and earth to see you dead – the start of a new bloodfeud.' Maximus grinned. 'Everything you wanted.'

X

The emperor was in bed with his *cinaedus* when the rain came. Gallienus lay on his back listening to the first individual drops thumping into the garden outside the open window. Instantly, the air was full of the invigorating smell of clean earth.

Gallienus had been looking forward to reaching Serdica. The *comitatus* had ridden hard across Thrace from Bergoule; thirty miles a day or more. He had announced there would be a break of three days to rest the men and horses, to let the stragglers catch up. Serdica was a town on the rise; full of confidence, new buildings going up, even a *palatium*. Although the imperial palace was unfinished, it was a fine place to relax. There had been no time on the journey east, so Gallienus had decided it would be pleasant to spend a day inspecting the nearby battlefield where, the year before, his general Aurcolus had defeated the Macriani.

All Gallienus's feelings of ease had been vitiated by the news that had come as he approached the walls of Serdica. A messenger, grimed by tough travel along the *cursus publicus*, announced that Gothic pirates had sacked Ephesus eight days previously.

Gallienus had done what he could. There was no question of

turning back. The situation in the west demanded the presence
of the emperor. He had to tour the provinces of the Pannonias
and Noricum, ensure their loyalty, and reach Italy and Mediolanum as soon as possible, before the campaigning season was well
under way. Gallienus had written to Odenathus of Palmyra; as
corrector of the east, the Lion of the Sun should take whatever
measures were possible. The fleets in the east were in such poor
condition there was little to be hoped from them. Gallienus had
also sent one of his *protectores*, the Italian Celer Venerianus, post
haste ahead to Ravenna. The fleet there was in better shape.
Venerianus had a reputation as an admiral. He was to assemble a
squadron and proceed with all speed to the Aegean. Of course,
by the time Venerianus got there, the Goths would be long gone,
back to the Black Sea with their booty. But something had to be
seen to be done. The eastern provincials had to be reassured, had
to be shown imperial solicitude, or they might think of taking
things into their own hands. And, sure as night followed day, that
would mean yet another pretender clad in the purple; yet another
civil war, to further weaken the *imperium*.

As often when perturbed, Gallienus had turned not to the con-
solations of philosophy, as a man of culture should, but to sex. In
itself, that weakness in his character sometimes irritated him. He
wished his German mistress Pippa, his sweet Pippara, were with
him. A Marcomannic upbringing had filled her with nothing but
contempt for philosophy and its sanctimonious adherents. But
she had been left in Mediolanum. The journey had been too hard
for a woman. At least he had Demetrius.

The Greek youth was still asleep. It was the half-light just
before dawn. Gallienus turned and gently brushed a stray tendril
of hair from Demetrius's face. The boy was beautiful and cultured as well as skilled in the ways of pleasure.

Gallienus watched him sleep. The physiognomists were

wrong. In bed, Demetrius might enjoy playing the role of a girl, but there was nothing effeminate about him. His eyes were not weak. Walking, neither did he mince nor did his knees knock like a woman's. Gallienus had never seen him tilt his head to the right or adjust his hair with one finger. No palms-up, open-handed gestures. In the act of love, he did not 'snort'.

The physiognomists might be wrong but Gallienus wondered what made a fine youth such as Demetrius find his pleasures like a woman and run the risk of every man's contempt. Astrologers would put it down to the conjunction of the stars at birth; if Taurus was rising, rear end first among the Pleiades – that sort of thing. Magicians might claim to have caused it. Scratch a drawing of a castrated man gazing at his own genitals on a piece of obsidian, put it in a gold box with the stone of a *cinaedus*-fish, trick the victim into carrying it – or, much more efficacious, into eating it – and a soul was deformed.

Any number of men, charlatans or otherwise, might have any number of theories. How did you trick someone into eating a stone, in a gilded box or not? Gallienus suspended his judgement. He suspected that Demetrius's predilection was innate. Whether it was or not, for years, the boy had had no choice about the physical aspect. Demetrius said he had been born into slavery. Although very vague about his early life, once he had become an intimate of the imperial bedchamber he had spoken about the succession of brutal masters through whose hands he had passed. Gallienus had been moved to tears. The youth's degradation ended when he was purchased to be secretary to Ballista.

Ballista had treated Demetrius well. In the end, he had granted him his freedom and, although Demetrius did not realize that Gallienus knew, he had given the boy a share of the loot from the camp of the Persian King of Kings. Ballista had never taken the youth to his bed. In a Greek or a Roman, that would argue for strict self-control, but in a northern barbarian probably it was something else altogether.

Gallienus gazed at Demetrius. The emperor had never shunned Aphrodite. The gifts of the goddess of love should be honoured. There was nothing of the priggish and boorish virgin Hippolytus about Gallienus. Rather, he knew, there was a gadfly in his eyes. No sooner had it alighted on a beauty – boy or girl – than it wanted to fly again. His pleasure in Demetrius would not last. Beside anything else, the youth was shaving, using depilatories. Demetrius was getting too old.

Slowly, Gallienus pulled back the cover. Demetrius stirred, but did not wake. The boy was still beautiful. The well-formed back, the delicate moulding of the buttocks; neither too thin nor too fleshy. The straight thighs. The ringlets of dark, hyacinth hair.

Ballista had been a fool, misguided by his barbarian upbringing. The northerner was quite wrong: there was nothing unmanly about loving a boy. Gallienus had little time for the specious and hypocritical posturings of Platonic love. The noble duty of a philosophic spirit is to worship but not to touch: what nonsense. Nothing but a regime for frustration or guilt, or an unhealthy combination of the two.

No, there was nothing to be frowned at in physical pleasure for the *erastes* with his *eromenos*, as long as the older lover did not continue when the beloved became a man, bearded and tough. The very briefness of the time, from the first down to the full beard, added poignancy.

Hercules, Gallienus's particular divine companion, had not been less manly for loving Hylas. Hercules had also loved many, many women. Indeed, it had been a woman, Omphale, who had for a time enslaved him; love of a woman that had briefly unmanned him.

Demetrius woke, opened dark eyes. His cheeks shone like

amber or Sidonian crystal. The boy smiled. 'You remember your promise?' he murmured.

Gallienus kissed his lips. 'I remember.' For a moment he felt a pang of jealousy. Then it was overcome by affection. The boy was nothing if not loyal. Gallienus would keep the promise Demetrius had requested. Gallienus would not execute Ballista. Something must be done, but not that.

XI

Ballista knew Hippothous had not been happy at leaving Miletus – not happy at all.

Why, the Greek had complained, why had Ballista decided to do such a thing? The gods knew, said Hippothous, he was no coward but, largely by their own efforts, the northerner and his *familia* had saved Miletus. So, why – just two days after the Goths had been repulsed – why leave the relative safety of its walls and ride to Didyma: a place that meant nothing to them, which may well be indefensible, and to which the Goths could easily follow them? It was completely irrational; it was barbaric.

Maximus, who knew, had looked dubious, but said nothing.

Ballista, who had spent the hours before leaving closeted with Macarius, the *asiarch* of Miletus, had not felt like explaining.

For the journey, Ballista, Maximus and Hippothous had been accompanied by ten mounted soldiers and three able-bodied slaves: one Ballista's, the others belonging to the soldiers. Yet even so, it had not been without its tensions. Having left Miletus through the Sacred Gate in the southern wall, they had not long passed the tomb of Neileus, the founder of the city, when they had seen the Goths. There were small groups of the raiders scattered here and there, looting and defiling the suburban villas and temples. The Goths had not attacked, but ceased from their pleasures to stand and watch the cavalcade.

Far from slipping out unnoticed, Ballista had openly courted attention. He had had a white *draco* hurriedly made. His personal standard, its roughly hammered metal jaws snarling, had hissed and snapped as they rode. The trooper carrying it had flourished it proudly. Ballista had wondered if the man, an auxiliary called Patavinus, would have been quite so happy if he had known what had happened to most of his predecessors. Romulus, Antigonus: they had been good men, but it had not saved them. So many violent deaths. Ballista had not chosen his trade; he often thought he would have been happier in a quieter, more sedentary life.

They had ridden easily, keeping the horses in hand. There had been no danger of losing their path. The Sacred Way ran, broad and paved, up into the hills. Punctuated with milestones and rest places, it crossed the scrubby high country of laurel, box and stunted evergreen oak. Sheep and goats, abandoned by their shepherds, had looked up from their rough grazing. Once, in the distance, a pack of wild dogs loped away.

After some nine miles, the Sacred Way had dipped down to the sea at Panormos. There was no settlement there. But, in better times, boats would have been tied up to the jetties, disembarking pilgrims bound for the oracle at Didyma. There would have been a bustle of guides and hucksters vying for their money. Panormos had been deserted.

Ballista and the others had sat their horses, high on a bluff. The wind had tugged at their clothes, the smell of the sea in their nostrils. They had gazed out into the Aegean. Sure enough, across the shimmering surface, hazy, but at no great distance to the north, had been the distinctive double-prowed shapes. The Gothic longboats were no more than an hour behind.

They had ridden the last two and a bit miles south-east flanked by seated gods and priests in marble, by great crouching lions. The weathered faces of the statues, man-like and bestial, expressed the complete indifference of antiquity.

At Didyma, there was an arch with a gate across the Sacred Way. But there were no walls. The holy site was delineated merely by boundary stones. The god had not protected it from Persians or Gauls: Ballista doubted he would make a better fist of it with the Goths.

A strange deputation was waiting under the arch; a mix of robed priests and locals with makeshift weapons.

'Health and great joy.' The leader wore a wreath of bay leaves bound with white cloth. He carried a wand.

'Health and great joy.' Ballista dismounted, handed the reins to his slave. 'I am Marcus Clodius Ballista, and I have come with my *amici* and these soldiers to help you against the Goths.'

The priest beamed – an unusual reaction for a civilian encountering soldiers, a certain sign of the terrible fear abroad. 'Welcome, Marcus Clodius Ballista. Welcome indeed.' Perhaps he was partly reassured by Ballista's equestrian gold ring and his excellent Attic Greek, or it could be simply that a small party of Roman soldiers was indeed welcome in the face of a large horde of barbarian warriors.

'I am the *prophetes* of the Lord Apollo at Didyma. My name is Selandros, son of Hermias, of the Euangelidai.' The annual high priest was from one of the oldest and most prestigious families of Miletus. 'This is the *hydrophor* of Artemis, my daughter, Alexandra.' The virgin priestess was not veiled, but she kept her eyes demurely down. She was beautiful. Well, thought Ballista, the *prophetes* will fight – his worst fear would be a gang of hairy barbarians taking turns on top of his daughter. Pausanias's description of the Gauls sacking Delphi came into Ballista's mind. Worse even than the Persians, they had raped women, girls and boys to death. In one of those very rare flashes of total insight, Ballista knew that Selandros had read the same passage, that it had been in his thoughts also – poor bastard. Ballista felt a sudden quickening, his mind running back to his youth and the girl in the village of the Rugii when he was in his father's war band, back a couple of years to Roxanne, the Persian king's concubine at Soli. He savagely suppressed the atavistic urge. Years before, in Arelate, he had known a woman, a Corinthian whore, who had claimed that all men were rapists. He had thought her mad; now he was not so sure. Possibly the Greeks and Romans were not totally wrong endlessly to preach self-control. Ballista knew he had done bad things, had condoned many others, but a man can change. He was not tied to his nature or his fate like a dog to a cart.

'And this is the *hypochrestes*, and the *paraphylax*.' The former, Selandros's aide, smiled ingratiatingly. He was nothing but a frightened boy. The latter, the head of the temple guards, was older. He looked at Ballista as if he had been expecting someone else, someone better. Ballista instantly dismissed him as of no account.

'Unfortunately, the *tamias* could not come. He has much to do.' There was no surprise there, thought Ballista. The treasurer, who actually ran Didyma, would have his work cut out preparing the defence, if these were the other men of position at the sanctuary.

'The Goths will not be long,' said Ballista. 'We should go.'

Beyond the gate, there were buildings on both sides of the Sacred Way: minor temples, baths, porticos, shops and houses – all empty. Although only a village under the rule of Miletus, the settlement was of some extent. It stretched off to the right.

After a distance, the road doglegged to the east. The buildings on the right gave way to a grove of bay trees, which curved around the western end of the main temple.

The first sight of the temple of Apollo at Didyma was overwhelming: a towering phalanx of columns, a fitting home for one of the Olympians. Many had held it should have ranked as one of the seven wonders of the world.

The horses were led away, and Selandros conducted Ballista around the temple. Set in a hollow but standing on a high, stepped podium, the building was an enormous rectangle, surrounded by a double line of columns. There was only one entrance, from the east. Selandros explained how, at the first news of the Goths at Ephesus, the *tamias* had ordered the Sacred Boys – the temple slaves – to build an extra wall to narrow access.

It was a strong site. Just the one way in. There was open ground on all sides. Admittedly, if they got close, attackers would be sheltered by the partially finished roof over the columns, but the walls were at least sixty feet high and far too thick to breach except by prolonged siege works, and men in the eaves could drop tiles and stones, which would turn the space into a killing zone. The Goths might try to burn the defenders out of the temple, but that would probably destroy the plunder they were after, and the great stone building did not look particularly combustible. All in all, Ballista was relieved; it was much as Macarius had described it back in Miletus.

Before going into the temple, Ballista studied the emergency wall. It was made of well-cut blocks of stone, presumably dismantled from some nearby building. The construction looked solid enough. It closed eight gaps between columns at the previously open eastern end of the temple. The one opening still remaining was only three or four long paces wide. At the top of fourteen steep stone steps, it should be possible to hold it with four determined men in close order, maybe with just two in open order, if they had the skills. Ballista posted six of the soldiers there.

The first area inside was a forest of massive, fluted columns. Set in the inside wall was a strange big window or door, its base five or six feet off the ground. Selandros explained that it was from there that the *prophetes* gave the responses to those who consulted the oracle. 'Come.' The priest smiled. 'We will follow the pilgrim way.'

The temple was laid out like none Ballista had seen before. Selandros led them to a narrow passage against the right-hand wall. It was vaulted, dark and steep. At the far end, they emerged from the gloom into dazzling sunshine. There was a great square, open to the sky.

At the further end was a small temple. Through its open doors could be seen Apollo in bronze, naked, a stag in one hand, a bow in the other. The priestess and the sacred spring whose waters inspired her must be inside as well. The deity and his shelter were dwarfed by the huge walls around them.

Everywhere in the open were other statues: emperors, kings, priests, officials, men of honour. Hanging on the walls were innumerable desiccated wreaths of bay and, arranged below, other offerings: bowls, vases, censers, cups, pots, tripods, wine coolers – all manner of vessels cunningly wrought in precious metals. But what took Ballista aback, almost stultified his senses, were the people: men, women and children – hundreds of them – sitting, standing, a multitude of refugees, all silent and dejected.

Selandros gestured to the square. 'Usually only the servants of the temple set foot on the holy ground but, with the barbarians coming, the Lord Apollo in his love of mankind said to welcome the suppliants into his *adyton*. In settled times, those seeking divine guidance stand here and put their questions to the *prophetes* and he then consults the inspired priestess in the inner temple. Those wanting answers return the way we have come and wait at the front below the window. It is my honour to relay the divine words.'

The priest turned and led them up to the room from which the window opened. All the weapons that could be found had been heaped there. Ballista and the men of war began to sort through them.

'It should not be like this.' The voice of the *hypochrestes* was plaintive. The youthful aide spoke to everyone and no one. 'It is the fifth year, the year of the great festival. Athletes, musicians, singers, men from across the world – all should be coming to the *Didymeia*, coming in peace. Why has the god deserted us? Have we not offered enough wine and incense, enough hecatombs of shambly footed cattle? Why, despite our piety, has the god turned against us?'

'Enough.' The voice of the *prophetes* was firm. 'Apollo has not deserted us. Just as at Troy in the ancient days, the gods are divided. Warlike Ares has brought this plague of Scythians. The Lord Apollo will not submit. He who rejoices in song will not abandon those who pray to him and offer him hymns with pure and open hearts.'

The young aide seemed close to tears. 'How can that be? Are not Apollo and Ares but parts of the eternal, uncreated, undying Supreme God? Why would the timeless, immovable being . . .'

'Enough!' The *prophetes* was commanding. 'Enough of Plato, and the prattling of his foolish followers; this is a time for true religion, antique religion unsullied by speculation. Ares guided the barbarians here; the Lord Apollo will crush them.'

Ballista had taken up a huge old shield. It had been set apart, some cobwebbed dedication from a forgotten time. He hid his smile behind it. The gods aside, multiple or singular, he knew what had brought the Goths here. Obviously, there was the well-founded rumour of wealth. The renegade Chrysogonus would have told them all about that. But there was something else, something much more specific and much sharper. Revenge and honour: the true soul of the north, the blood that bound together that unforgiving land. Ballista had killed Tharuaro to create a bloodfeud with the Tervingi. With the corpse still fresh, where he went the Tervingi would follow, and the Borani with them. Those two groups would be enough to sway the whole *hansa* of the Goths. He, Dernhelm, son of Isangrim, the man the Romans knew as Ballista, had brought Scythian Ares after him, like a dog tied to a cart. And only Maximus and himself knew it, and only they knew why. If the Goths were at Didyma, they were not at Priene. Ballista's sons, his wife, old Calgacus – all would be safe.

Ballista noticed the silence. Both the *prophetes* and his aide were staring at him. He looked back blankly.

'The shield,' began the *prophetes*.

Ballista turned the ungainly thing. Leather and bronze; one of the straps had rotted and come away.

'You know who carried that shield?' The priest was strangely hesitant.

'No.'

'Euphorbus, the Trojan hero who first wounded Patroclus. In revenge, Menelaus killed him, and dedicated his shield here.'

'It is very old.'

The *prophetes* gave him an odd look. 'Euphorbus was reincarnated as the holy Pythagoras.'

'Yes.'

'The sage recognized his shield from his former life. Later, the soul passed to the diviner Hermotimas. He also pointed to the shield in your hands.'

Withdrawn into a corner, the aide was muttering, possibly a prayer.

Ballista laughed. 'I doubt a Trojan hero, having been one of the seven sages, would choose to be reborn as a warrior from Germania.'

'The gods choose,' said the *prophetes*. Inconspicuously, his aide warded off evil, with his thumb between his first two fingers.

A shout rang out from somewhere above: fire – the Goths are here.

Ballista pointed to the nearer of the two staircases set in the side walls. A roof terrace, Selandros told him. Ballista led the dash. The stairwell doubled and redoubled back on itself, replicating the labyrinth pattern on its ceiling.

As they emerged into the bright light, a flock of sparrows took wing from a nearby roof. A thought, bird-like, fluttered just out of Ballista's grasp. Sparrows, Didyma, a lesson in impiety . . . something like that. If they both lived, he would ask Hippothous. He was different, that Greek: a living encyclopaedia who enjoyed killing.

A knot of men in a jumble of ill-fitting archaic armour was looking to the north-west. Ballista followed their gaze. There were men moving around the gate through which he had ridden, lots of men. They surged in and out of the surrounding buildings. As Ballista watched, the first thin tendrils of smoke writhed upwards. The temple of Artemis, someone muttered. Others took up the words, some started praying. The smoke bodied out as the east wind tugged it away.

Sounds of commotion floated up from below, from the entrance of Apollo's temple. A local, a man with an air of competence despite his ludicrous assemblage of outmoded armour, crossed the terrace and peered down. 'Fuck,' he said simply.

Ballista joined him. Figures were appearing from the front of the temple. They were brandishing makeshift weapons – scythes, flails; a few had swords. They were rushing around the corner of the podium, heading towards the fire. Ballista looked questioningly at the man next to him. 'The stupid fuckers think to save the temple of Artemis,' the man said.

For a moment Ballista was dumbfounded. 'But the Goths will massacre them.'

'Yes,' said the man.

'Heracles' hairy arse,' said Maximus. 'You cannot save people from their own stupidity.'

'No,' agreed Ballista, 'but we will have to try.' Calling for Maximus, Hippothous and the four soldiers to follow, Ballista set off back down the stairs.

At the foot of the steps, Ballista turned towards the entrance. He slid to his arse, propelled himself down and through the great window, and ran through the avenue of columns.

A crowd jostled in his way. He shouted for them to move. They took no notice. He drew his sword and swung it. The flat of the heavy *spatha* hit a man on the side of the head. He fell. Ballista swung the sword again. A man struck on the shoulder reeled away. The crowd parted.

Reaching the entrance, Ballista turned. His men crushed in behind him. Ballista flashed the blade in a fast, complicated pattern. Its edge shone, evil in the light. The crowd drew back.

'No one leaves the temple. All of you, go back to the *adyton*.'

Their courage deflated, the mob melted away.

'What about the ones outside?' Maximus asked.

'They are fucked,' said Ballista.

It took nearly two hours for the Goths to plunder their way to the temple of Apollo. Enough time for Ballista to improvise some sort of defence. A shieldwall of eight in the gap between the columns: Ballista himself, Maximus and six soldiers. Eight close-lapped shields, two levels of four, protecting them from missiles. One soldier up on each side of the roof, trying to ready the locals to hurl things down on to the attackers. Hippothous also on the roof, tasked with going wherever he might be needed.

Ballista studied what was in front of him. Fourteen steep steps. Beyond, a flat area of beaten earth across the front of the temple, maybe twenty paces deep. Just in front and to the right of the foot of the steps, a big cone of solidified ash held by a low circular wall: the main altar. There were other altars, statues and inscriptions dotted here and there, but not enough to give the Goths much cover. They would have to cross the open ground and then attempt the steps.

The waiting before combat was always hard. The soldiers were silent, their kit creaking as they shifted their weight. Maximus whistled tunelessly, then launched into a lengthy monologue about a girl he had had in Miletus. His tone was one of mock outrage that a girl would initiate such depravity, and him an innocent boy from a distant island. It was a good job he was broadminded and had excellent stamina.

Smoke swirled around the monuments of Hellenic piety. There was a lurid yellow quality to the light, a reek of destruction. Not far away, people were screaming. Maximus kept talking.

The first Goths materialized through the smog of their own making. Helmeted, bearded, they slowly coagulated into groups.

'Come on, you little piggies,' called Maximus in the language of the raiders. 'Come and get skewered.'

Ballista reflected that the obscenity did not translate well from the Greek. As far as he was aware, in the Gothic dialect of the language of Germania, 'piggy' was not a synonym for 'cunt'.

A solid shieldburg of warriors had formed facing the temple. A warrior took a couple of paces forward. He kept himself well covered by his shield.

'I am Respa, son of Gunteric, of the Tervingi. The murdered Tharuaro was my brother. You in the temple, give up the oath-breaker Dernhelm, son of Isangrim, the *skalks* the Romans call Ballista, and you have my word you will be spared.'

Ballista laughed. Gunteric could call him oath-breaker, slave, anything he wanted. With the exception of Ballista himself and Maximus, it was most unlikely anyone in the temple understood any of it, apart from his Roman name.

A voice called in Greek from the midst of the northmen, slightly muffled but audible. Presumably it was Chrysogonus. When Respa's words had been translated, there was murmuring in the dark corners of the temple. It was cunning, but Ballista was not unduly worried. Even should they desire it, these Milesian civilians did not have the balls to try and give him up.

'I know you,' shouted Maximus. 'Respa, the one they call Cocksucker. You must miss your brother's sword in your mouth.'

'And I know you, the foul-mouthed Hibernian catamite of Dernhelm.' The big Goth raised his sword hilt-up to the sky. 'Fairguneis the Thunderer, all you high gods of the Goths, I pledge two fine stallions and a dozen oxen, if you grant Dernhelm Oath-breaker and the foul Hibernian fall beneath my sword.'

Ballista snorted derisively. 'You are long on words, but short on courage. Here we are – come and try your luck.'

Respa did not reply. At his gesture, a dozen or so warriors shook themselves out of the shieldburg. Big men, in helmets, shields, mail coats, swords, all sporting a surfeit of golden arm-rings. Men to be considered. Their *reiks* led them warily forward.

They halted, spread out by the circular altar. Respa spoke to them, too low for Ballista to hear. A single tile dropped from the roof. It shattered harmlessly. The Goths laughed, an unpleasant, wolfish sound.

Ballista silently cursed the Milesians on the roof. How much nerve did it take to throw things from a position of complete safety? What the fuck was the soldier up there doing? Where was that posturing Greek Hippothous? The Goths should be advancing through a hail of missiles.

Respa and another warrior took the lead. They reached the first step. The others fanned out behind.

'Open order,' Ballista shouted. Everyone apart from Ballista and Maximus fell back. The two of them shuffled into position, alert to the need for room for their swordplay.

Respa and the other champion came up the steps.

'Now!' said Ballista. As one, Ballista and Maximus took three paces back. Only a fool would make a stand at the top of a flight of stairs – your legs were exposed; it was further for your sword to stretch down. They both dropped into the 'plough guard': shield out, its leading edge pointing at the enemy, sword held underhand, low to the side.

Respa bounded over the top step. With horrible speed, he took two quick paces, unleashed a deafening war cry and a vicious diagonal cut down to the neck. Ballista raised his shield. Respa fluidly lowered his stroke. Ballista got his shield down just in time to prevent his left ankle being severed. Even as the wood splintered and the impact ran up to his left shoulder, Ballista struck overhand, a short-edge thrust to the face. Respa caught it on the rim of his shield, forcing Ballista's sword arm up and wide. Like a steel serpent seeking hot blood, the Goth's blade flickered across at Ballista's exposed right arm. A lifetime of training saved Ballista. Without conscious thought, he brought his shield up, round and forward, crunching into Respa, trapping the *reiks*'s blade between the linden boards and his own chest. For an instant their faces were together, their breath mingling. Ballista ducked, heaved; his knees bent, he shoved the Goth backwards. Panting, a little apart, both gathered themselves. The whole exchange had taken no more than two seconds.

The Goth who had gone for Maximus was down, moaning in pain. His companions grabbed his feet, dragged him clear. He left a bright smear of blood on the marble flagstone. Another took his place.

'Give my regards to your brother,' goaded Ballista.

Bellowing incoherently, Respa hurled himself forward, swinging a mighty overhand cut. Ballista did not flinch. Somehow he kept his nerve. Eyes on the sword, the heavy steel slicing down towards the top of his skull. At the last instant, Ballista stepped to his left, bringing his shield up and across. The metal shieldboss buckled with the blow. It almost forced Ballista to his knees. But he twisted, got his shoulder behind his shield, his whole body weight. Twisting and pushing, he drove his assailant's sword off to the right, exposing the Goth's unguarded side. There was nothing for Respa to do now but die.

With all his strength, Ballista thrust, low and underhand. There was momentary resistance, then the sharp cracks as metal rings snapped, and the wicked tip of the blade was sliding through soft tissue.

Respa screamed. His *spatha* rang on the stones. Ballista turned the blade, once, twice. The blood splashed hot on his arm. Locked in a ghastly, intimate embrace, Ballista glanced over the shoulder of the dying man. None of the Goths had a clear strike. Bracing with his shield, Ballista withdrew his blade, and pushed Respa away.

The big *reiks* tottered back. He dropped his shield. His hands went to the rent in his mail shirt; a futile attempt to staunch the blood. The gore pulsed down the Goth's legs, puddled by his boots.

A frozen moment, and then Respa fell backwards down the

steps. The man behind tried to catch him. He was knocked down. A third Goth was swept down in the tangle.

The warrior facing Maximus was stepping back. His shield was hacked, his face horror struck.

Now the men on the roof were doing their duty. Tiles, stones, scraps of metal were raining down on the steps. Sharp shards and splinters sang through the air. The Goths had their shields up, trying to cover their fallen leader, themselves. They began to pull back, dragging their dead and injured.

'*Testudo!*' yelled Ballista. He and Maximus stepped back, as the six soldiers locked their shields across the entrance.

'Are you all right?' Ballista asked.

'Never better,' said Maximus. 'I am – what was it you once called me?'

'Demented?'

'No – I have it – hideously exultant.'

'Not usually a good thing.'

'Certain, it is for me.' Maximus roared, 'I am hideously exultant!'

The soldiers laughed.

Ballista peered through the shields. The Goths had drawn back out of sight. The steps were covered with debris. An idea occurred to Ballista. He looked around, unconsciously flicking the blood in a spray off his blade. Selandros was close. The *prophetes* looked queasy.

'Selandros, get some people breaking up rocks – small, no bigger than a fist.'

The priest looked back, uncomprehending.

'I want them scattered on the steps. Make the footing as treacherous as possible. I should have thought of it before,' Ballista added reflectively.

Selandros nodded, but did not move.

'The Goths are not skilled at sieges,' Ballista continued. 'With food and water, we can sit it out in here indefinitely.'

The priest looked unhappy.

'What?' Ballista asked.

Still Selandros did not speak.

'You did get food in? The sacred spring will give us water.'

'There is food, and a few barrels of water.' The *prophetes* stopped, obviously uncertain what to say next.

'The spring?'

Selandros cleared his throat. 'The waters of Mykale have ceased to flow.'

Now it was Ballista who stared, uncomprehending. The mountain range of Mykale was, at a guess, a good twenty miles away. Priene and his *familia* were there.

'The divine water from Mount Mykale flows under the plain and the sea, to rise here at Apollo's holy place. Or it did. The spring has been dry for some years.'

XII

Ballista sat in the shade at the top of the high steps and looked down on the walled square of the temple of Apollo at Didyma. He moved the pebble in his mouth from one cheek to the other. The pall of dust made it hard to see across the *adyton*. The bright sunshine turned the fug a dirty yellow, rendered it opaque. The little inner sanctum at the far end was almost totally obscured. There was no wind. Trapped, great waves of dust slowly coiled back from the high outer walls of the sanctuary. Ballista knew the men with picks and shovels down on the ground would be finding it hard to breathe. It could not be helped; they were only slaves.

It was hot. Everyone was tortured with thirst. Despite careful rationing, the few barrels of water had run out two days after the Gothic attack. That had been the day before. They were still encircled by the Goths. No one could go outside. No one had drunk anything for more than twenty-four hours.

Ballista had been wrong in his assumption that the waters rose in the inner sanctum. The sacred spring had been just outside its doors. As soon as he had been given the news about its failure, he had got the temple slaves to work digging down to clear the channels, discover where the water had gone. So far, the Sacred Boys had found nothing.

Ballista shifted the pebble with his tongue. He was unsure if it did any good, but he could not tell how thirsty he would have felt without it. The tip had come from Mamurra, years earlier. Mamurra had been an old hand on the eastern frontier. Every time he came into Ballista's mind, there was the guilt. Mamurra, the good friend he had left to die, entombed alive in Arete.

Just as certainly as Mamurra had been trapped in the siege tunnel, so now they were all trapped in this temple. Ballista wondered if the messenger he had sent from Priene had got through and, if so, had Maximillianus, the governor, acted on it. If not, they were all doomed. The Goths need only wait for thirst to drive them out – and they would have to wait no time at all. For distraction, Ballista asked Hippothous about the sparrows of Didyma.

In a husky voice, Hippothous told the story. The Lydian rebel Pactyes had fled to the Greek *polis* of Cyme. The Persian king demanded he be surrendered. The Cymeans had asked the oracle here at Didyma what to do. Apollo had said to hand him over. Giving up a suppliant had seemed wrong to the men of Cyme. They had sent a second embassy to Didyma. It received the same answer. Now, on the embassy was a man of wisdom; Aristodicus was his name. He took a long stick and with it he went around the sanctuary knocking down all the sparrows' nests he could reach.

Ballista looked up at the towering walls. It must have been a very long stick.

As Aristodicus was about this, Apollo himself spoke in the *adyton*. How dare this man drive these suppliants from the temple? Aristodicus was not stuck for a reply. How could Apollo defend his suppliants but order the Cymeans to give up theirs? The god replied it was to hasten the impiety of Cyme and bring on its destruction; to teach them never to ask such a question again.

Sat overlooking the *adyton*, dependent on the god's house for his safety, Ballista thought it was not the place to voice his doubts over either the piety or the logic of Apollo's words. 'What did the Cymeans do?'

Hippothous smiled. 'They sent Pactyes to Mytilene. When they heard the men there were going to give him up, they shipped him to Chios. The Persians bribed the Chians with the territory of Atarneus on the mainland. The Chians hauled Pactyes out of their sanctuary of Athena and gave him to the Persians.'

'What happened to Pactyes?'

Hippothous paused, thinking. 'I am not sure if Herodotus recorded that. But nothing good.'

'And what happened to the Chians?'

The Greek frowned. 'For quite a long time, they would not use barley from Atarneus in offerings to the gods, or sacrificial cakes.'

Not the most taxing way of easing one's guilt, thought Ballista. It was just time for him to go down to the entrance and relieve Maximus when something happened down on the floor of the *adyton*. There was hoarse shouting in the murk. The mass of refugees huddled on the lower steps parted and the dust-caked figures of the *prophetes* and his aide stumbled upwards. They were both grinning.

Politely getting to his feet, Ballista spat the pebble into his left hand.

'They have struck water,' Selandros said. 'We are saved.'

With a restrained formality, Ballista and the *prophetes* shook hands. The Stygian gloom below was transformed by shouts of good omen, husky cheering. They were all indeed saved – at least for the moment.

'I am Apollo's water, to the inhabitants a gift
Given freely by the player of the golden lyre, in the Scythian war.'

The youthful aide beamed as he extemporized the poem. His role in the oracle was suddenly clear to Ballista. The priestess from the inner temple muttered the words of Apollo, this young *hypochrestes* transformed them into verse, and Selandros, the dignified *prophetes*, spoke them through the high window to the pious waiting below.

'When around the temple dashed Ares
Leto's son himself saved his suppliants.'

Selandros applauded the efforts of his aide.

'This has happened before.' The youth, buoyed up with relief, rattled on. 'The sacred spring ran dry, Alexander the Great came, Apollo opened a vein and the golden waters flowed.' He was looking at Ballista in a strange way. So was the *prophetes*. Even Hippothous had an odd look in his eye.

'No,' said Ballista. 'Euphorbus, Pythagoras, Alexander – I have been none of them.'

The *prophetes* shook his head. 'Unless you were a seer, you would not know.'

Once everyone had drunk their fill, the barrels were refilled; a spring that had failed twice could do so a third time. Ballista had the men at the entrance and up on the walls be particularly profligate with water; drinking copiously, splashing it over each other in the heat. Likewise, although the dwindling food stocks were strictly doled out, the men on view were often eating. It was important that the Goths thought the defenders were well refreshed, their morale high.

It was late afternoon. As the sun had moved down, somehow

the heat seemed to have intensified. In the relative cool of the forest of columns at the front of the temple, Ballista hunkered down with his back to the hastily erected wall. Close to exhaustion, he looked at the sparrows chattering in and out of their nests, and his thoughts went along similarly random-seeming trajectories. Euphorbus, Pythagoras, Alexander. If you believed in the transmigration of the soul, as the *prophetes* and his aide obviously did, any of the swooping birds might once have been a philosopher or a hero. Such a conviction must paralyse action. You could never tell who or what you were killing. What sort of a man would you be if you could not kill? It was better not to enjoy it too much, but circumstances sometimes demanded it be done. Belief in transmigrated souls seemed a road that must inexorably lead to pacifism, vegetarianism, and other insanities embraced by Christians and other obscure sects of Jews. Not that they held to that sort of reincarnation.

Maximus broke into Ballista's fatigue-muddled thoughts. 'What?'

'Come and watch the Goths leave.' Maximus extended a hand, and helped Ballista to his feet.

It was true. From up on the roof terrace, they saw the last of the northern raiders passing out of the gate, streaming away to the north-east towards Panormos. The Goths appeared to have little booty, were driving but a few captives before them. Something was impelling the warriors to hurry.

Wary of a trick, Ballista sent Hippothous down to the entrance to ensure that the soldiers there did not relax their vigilance. Ballista systematically scanned the rooftops and groves of Didyma but could see no evidence of lurking Gothic warriors.

Ballista gazed hard into the distance to the north and north-east. He began to smile. Out towards Miletus, some six or seven miles away, was a tall pillar of dust. Dense, isolated; he knew what it meant. A large body of mounted men was crossing the scrubby hills. They were coming south, following the Sacred Way that would bring them to Panormos. Ballista's smile broadened slowly. His message had got through. The governor had done the right thing. Maximillianus had diverted the unit of auxiliary cavalry from Ephesus and sent them south. One thousand cavalry, riding to Panormos, where the Gothic ships were moored. Threaten their longboats, and the Goths would leave.

Allfather, Deep Hood, Death-blinder; they were saved.

XIII

Gallienus thought he had overdone the poison that morning. He had been awake well before dawn. As he had been with Demetrius in the night, he had not sacrificed to the gods. Instead he had decided to go riding. While the horses were being tacked up, he had drunk some milk and eaten a little bread and fruit. With something in his stomach, he had gone to the one thing he had that was completely private. Unfastening the triple locks of the chest, he had poured out and taken a little of every poison that nature and human ingenuity provided.

Perhaps he had been careless. He had felt fine on horseback. There had been a low mist covering the Pannonian plain, the lights of Sirmium dim and haloed in the distance. Gallienus had galloped hard. His favourite hunter, Spoletium, easily outpaced the mount of Freki the Alamann, the commander of his recently created barbarian inner bodyguard. Gallienus had taken only Freki out with him. Sometimes it was good to be alone, or as near as could be for an emperor.

After a time, the sun had come up in splendour, lighting a wide blue sky with just a few high, dappled clouds. The Savus river shone, broad and placid, on the horizon. When Freki caught up, they had ridden back.

Now Gallienus did not feel so good. Sitting on the high imperial throne in the apse of the basilica in the *palatium*, he felt sick. He must have been careless. It had been ten years since his elevation to the purple. Every morning of those ten years, he had taken the poisons. His body was well used to it, his immunity strong. Emperors had died in many untimely ways but, since the time of Claudius, over two hundred years earlier, none had died by poison.

The low imperial altar with the sacred fire was in front of him. The incense burning there and the smell of horse and sweat coming off his riding clothes added to the nausea. There was nothing to be done. He would have to endure the *consilium*.

A formal speech was in progress. The man speaking was Nummius Faustinianus. Gallienus had immortalized Faustinianus by granting him the signal honour of being the emperor's colleague as the first pair of consuls to take office that year. Forever it would be known as the year in which Gallienus, for the fifth time, and Faustinianus were consuls.

The theme of the oration, as far as Gallienus's discomfort – and, it must be said, boredom – allowed him to listen, was the excellent state of the *imperium*. The rhetoric put it all down to the manifest virtues of the most noble emperor: Publius Licinius Egnatius Gallienus; more fortunate than Augustus, better than Trajan.

If only such was the case in an age of iron and rust, thought Gallienus. He considered the true, harsh practicalities of the empire. The situation was stable in the centre of the *imperium*. The Danube frontier and its hinterland were under control. After four revolts in two years – Ingenuus, Regalianus, Piso and Valens – no further usurpations appeared to be imminent. Clementius

Silvius, the governor of the provinces of the Panonnias, both Superior and Inferior; Aelius Aelianus, the prefect of Legio II Adiutrix: and Aelius Restutus, the governor of Noricum, had all been waiting dutifully for Gallienus in Sirmium. Claudius Natalianus had also arrived from his province of Moesia Inferior. Neither Veteranus of Dacia nor Valentinus of Moesia Superior had attended. Both pleaded the need for vigilance against the Goths from the Black Sea. In the latter instance at least, Gallienus knew this to be true. Apart from the Goths, the trans-Danubian barbarians were quiet, if only temporarily. Up the great river to the west, incursions were discouraged by the strong arm of Attalus of the Marcomanni. The ties were close between this German client king and the Roman emperor; Attalus was the father of Gallienus's mistress Pippa.

There seemed nothing particular to cause concern in Rome. The plebs were not rioting more than usual, nor the senate scheming. The elderly and noble Nummius Ceionius Albinus was prefect of the city. He ought to be loyal to the dynasty. He had been a friend of Gallienus's father, for what that was worth. A less formal but more efficacious eye was kept on the seven hills by Gallienus's brother Licinius.

In Africa, there was talk of strange apparitions in the Atlas mountains, whispers of tribal insurrection, the movements of peoples, incursions of nomads from the south. Faraxen, the native rebel – was he dead or not? There were rumours of a cave below a distant peak, where his disembodied head sang the old songs and talked of new things. Always something new out of Africa. Nothing here that should be beyond the capabilities of Cornelius Octavianus. As the *Dux* of all the African *limes*, he, aided by Decianus, the governor of Numidia, had dealt splendidly the previous year with the Roman pretender Celsus. And there was Gallienus's female cousin Galliena: the real mover behind the suppression of Celsus. As competent as any man, she was the emperor's eyes and ears in Africa. It was Galliena that had thought to turn a large raiding party of Franks against Celsus. Now, settled on the late usurper's estates, the German war band was a useful force against both indigenous unrest and over-ambitious Romans.

If the central body of the *imperium* was not in bad shape, the same could not be said for the west. There was no man Gallienus hated more than Postumus, no man he was more determined to kill. Two years earlier, on the Rhine, while governor of Lower Germany, Postumus had made a sordid attempt to embezzle money. Detected, Postumus had broken his sacred oath to his emperor. He had had his portraits fixed to the standards of Legio XXX Ulpia Victrix, had declared himself Augustus. The provinces of Germany and Gaul had joined him. Offered pardon, Postumus had replied with sanctimonious justifications, impertinent accusations.

At that time, Saloninus, the son of Gallienus, had been living on the Rhine in the town of Colonia Agrippinensis. Although no more than a boy, policy had dictated that Saloninus be declared Caesar, heir to the throne, and sent to show the imperial presence in the north. Postumus had besieged Colonia Agrippinensis. The inhabitants had bought their safety by handing over Gallienus's son. Saloninus's youth had not moved Postumus to pity. Gallienus's golden, beautiful boy had been beheaded. It was said his body had been denied burial. Barred from Hades, his soul would wander; alone, cold and despairing.

Gallienus had prayed to Hercules for revenge. Hercules had answered: Postumus would be struck down, his rebellion come to nothing. But the ways of the gods can be slow. Gallienus knew he should try not to be impatient – what can time mean to the immortal? Gallienus could trust the word of Hercules. The god would deliver what he had promised; he was Gallienus's special friend. But it was hard. Over the last few months, far from withering, Postumus's Gallic empire – an evil empire founded on deceit, sacrilege and child murder – had grown.

Postumus and his cronies had the presumption to appoint consuls, as if Postumus were a real emperor and they actually held Rome. The two appointed for this year told a tale. Aemilianus and Titus Destricius Juba: both senators, ex-consuls, once supposed friends of Gallienus's father. Both now rewarded for their treachery. Aemilianus, governor of Hispania Tarraconensis, had organized the defection of Spain to the rebels. Juba had done the same with Britain.

Despite Gallienus's relentless diplomacy and the outlay of precious reserves of coin, the senatorial governors of the provinces of Spain and Britain had deserted. The moral was clear: the senate was not to be trusted, the senators hated their lawful emperor, the man to whom they had sworn the *sacramentum*.

Diplomacy, even had it been successful, was far from the emperor's favoured option; it could only ever have been a stopgap. From the first, Gallienus had wanted direct military action; invasion leading to the – preferably slow and agonizing – death of the Batavian bastard Postumus. Again and again, however, something had got in the way.

The previous year, Gallienus had assembled at Mediolanum the largest field army straitened circumstances had allowed. But then the majority of it had to be marched east to fight the Macriani. Once Macrianus, father and son, were dead, Gallienus had crossed the Alps. It had been late in the season, but the campaign had begun well enough. Then the defection of the governor of Raetia, Simplicinus Genialis, had forced Gallienus to retrace his steps to guard Italy.

It was much the same this year. First there was Byzantium. The city was strategically important. It was both the best crossing between Europe and Asia, and it dominated the sea route linking the Aegean and the Black Sea. More important still, its continued defiance acted as an encouragement to any considering revolt. Gallienus's hand had been forced. He had had no choice but to go there himself.

Now there was Egypt. Mussius Aemilianus, the governor, first had gone over to the Macriani. Then, after their defeat at Serdica, even though Quietus had still been alive in Syria, Mussius had declared himself emperor. Egypt provided most of the grain which gave the plebs of Rome the first element of bread and circuses. Without it, the *plebs urbana* would riot; the eternal city would burn, and the weakness of the regime would be evident. Egypt had to be regained.

Gallienus had written to Odenathus, his *corrector* in the east, ordering him to crush the pretender. The Lion of the Sun had replied he could not. Shapur the Sassanid, although he faced rebellion from some of his own subjects somewhere near the Caspian Sea, posed too potent a threat to allow Odenathus to spare the troops to conquer Egypt. Besides, Odenathus had nowhere near enough ships, and a fleet was essential to bring Egypt back into the fold.

At Gallienus's word, warships had been gathered from the fleets at Misenum and Ravenna, and transports from the whole of Italy and Sicily. Again the majority of the field army had to be sent away. The expedition was entrusted to Theodotus and Domitianus, two of the best of the *protectores*. The former, as an Egyptian, knew the country well. They were ordered to rendezvous on Cyprus with the squadron of Venerianus once the latter had chased the Goths into the Black Sea. From there the force would proceed to Caesarea Maritima on the coast of Syria Palestina, collect what men Odenathus could give them, and then to Egypt.

Gallienus knew that, even if all went as well as it could, the Egyptian expedition could not return to Italy in time to cross the Alps before the autumn snows blocked the passes. Another year, and still Postumus would remain unpunished.

Indeed, there was another grave concern. With most of the imperial forces committed to the east, Postumus, despite his worthless, weasel words about remaining content with what he held, might think to invade Italy. At Mediolanum, the *protectores* Tacitus, Claudius and Camsisoleus had a pitifully inadequate number of soldiers. It was vital that Gallienus and the cavalry with him reached the north Italian plain as soon as possible.

Nummius Faustinianus was evidently nearing the end of his oration. Some weighty-sounding words on the theme of imperial virtues – *virtus*, *clementia*, *iustitia* and *pietas*: the ones inscribed on the golden shield which hung in front of the *palatium* – and it was done.

The *comites* shook back their cloaks. Urbane applause, nothing to concern the *silentarii* of the court, echoed around the high chamber.

Gallienus thanked his fellow consul: measured words, suitable to imperial *dignitas*. Now it was time for Gallienus to issue the orders he had formulated earlier while riding through the countryside of Pannonia.

'Our *Princeps Peregrinorum* Rufinus has brought us news of troubling developments to the east of the Black Sea in Colchis and the Caucasus mountains.'

The emperor's words, as was only right, were received with the hushed silence of anticipation, even awe.

'The *frumentarii* stationed in those parts have sent reports that the agents of Shapur have been active. With bribes and false promises, the so-called King of Kings is attempting to subvert the loyalty to Rome of the rulers of Abasgia and the kings of Suania, Iberia and Albania. The peaks where once Prometheus suffered for humanity might seem far away, but the gaze of an emperor, like that of the sun, takes in the whole world.'

The *comites* quietly murmured their assent.

'The plots of the treacherous Persian tyrant must be thwarted. Our magnanimity will not let the inhabitants of those distant places be corrupted. A mission will be sent. It will give gifts to those in power deserving of them. Furthermore, it will give them security against the barbarians of the north, against the Alani and other bloodthirsty Scythians. The walls and towers blocking the passes of the Caucasus are said to be in bad condition. The mission will repair the Caspian Gates.

'The most noble ex-consul Felix will head the mission. He will go personally to the rulers of Abasgia. Under his command, Marcus Clodius Ballista will go to the king of Suania; Marcus Aurelius Rutilus to the king of Iberia, and Gaius Aurelius Castricius to the king of Albania.'

Gallienus smiled regally. 'Unfortunately, soldiers cannot be spared to accompany them. Yet four more suitable men of *virtus* could not be found in the wide sweep of our *imperium*. We can be sure they will not fail. Their *mandata* will be issued today. They will meet at Byzantium as soon as the gods allow. A *trireme* will be waiting to convey them.'

The assembled men of power prostrated themselves. Gallienus held out the ring bearing the imperial seal. One by one the *comites* kissed it, and backed out of the audience chamber.

The *consilium* was over. Time for a bath and lunch. Gallienus was feeling better. He was extremely pleased with what he had decreed. The problems of the Caucasus had been addressed. More than that, four difficult men had been removed to a place where they could do no harm. No one was ever likely to raise a revolt and threaten the central power from such a remote spot. And Gallienus had kept his word to Demetrius. After lunch, the youth, doubtless, would find pleasing ways to express the depth of his gratitude.

Excursus

(The Caucasus, Spring, AD262)

Away with feminine fears,
Dress up your mind like your own cruel home.

–Seneca, *Medea* 42–3

The ox is wreathed; the end is near, the sacrificer to hand.

The young woman considered the oracle. It had been pro-claimed about something quite other, a long time ago, in a distant land. It had come into her mind unbidden. Yet it might not prove totally inapposite. Philip of Macedon had taken the Persians for the ox; himself for the sacrificer. Delphic obscurity had confounded him: the Persians had no part of it; Philip's role was the opposite.

The afternoon breeze from the Black Sea had brought its cus-tomary showers and vapours up to Suania. They had softened the outlines but somehow magnified the bulk of the Croucasis mountains above. It was warm enough, but all those waiting were damp through and through.

The procession came into sight around a turn in the track. The ox was pulling its sledge stolidly up the hill. It was led by the old priestess, her women attending her. More women walked behind. There was music. The only man in the procession rode the sledge. He wore a garland of spring flowers on his head; more were twined around his limbs. He looked serene – they often did, at this stage.

The young woman looked away from the approaching procession and at the trees bordering the track: mainly beech, but also birch, maple, alder and pine. Until her all too brief time away, she had never really noticed the thick woods of her childhood in Suania. Since she had been back, more than six years of disappointment and frustration, the endless trees oppressed her.

The procession passed, heading out to the centre of the broad upland meadow where the crowd waited. These rites of Selene were a recent innovation. The man was a temple slave of the goddess. He had vanished. A year ago to the day, he had been found in the high forests, wandering, frenzied, uttering prophesies. The old priestess and her helpers had taken him in their charge, binding him in the sacred fetters lest he hurt himself. Throughout the year they had tended him, bringing him the choicest delicacies, bathing him, putting out for his rest the softest mattress and coverings, taking care of all his animal needs.

The young woman's mother had imported the rites from her native Albania, changing them as she did so, appointing the aged priestess. Her mother had been strong. If only she were still alive. Then things would have been different these last six years and more – very different – and the young woman knew she would not have been forced to such desperate measures.

In the middle of the meadow, Polemo, king of Suania, sat on a high throne. He was resplendent in white: cloak and turban, both shot through with golden thread, studded with jewels. There was a large crowd below him, the majority of the three hundred councillors of the *synedrion*, many leading warriors. The young woman saw her three surviving brothers, standing tall and straight. The youngest turned and smiled. The scar on his cheek added to his presence. There was a man – one who did what his heart told him; no remorse, no compunction. If he had not been her brother . . . if they had belonged to another dynasty, the

Ptolemies, say, of ancient Egypt . . . he could have been the true partner of her greatness.

The young woman was mounted. Half a dozen of her own armed retainers on horseback around her, she sat apart. She was a priestess herself, but of a different, darker goddess. There was no place in this ritual for any women, except those who served the moon goddess Selene. Certainly no place for one dedicated to the bitch goddess, triple-faced Hecate.

The ox was taken from its traces. The crowd shifted to encircle the participants. Sat on her horse, the young woman had a good view of all, could easily see over the heads of the men. The old priestess raised her hands to the heavens, invoked Selene, daughter of the Titans, chariot driver, lover of Endymion. Two men stepped forward. Quick as a swallow, one stunned the ox with a blow from the back of an axe. The other slashed the razor-sharp edge of the sacred lance deep down one side of the beast's neck. The ox threw its head up. Blood pumped on to the grass. The men jumped back. In its agony, the ox paddled around in a tight, stamping circle. Its windpipe severed, it blew pink, frothy arterial blood from its nostrils and mouth. The beast collapsed. The attendants moved in again. They finished it off, rolled it on to its side, slit its belly and – plunging their arms in – drew out the ropes of intestines for divination. The aged priestess bent over the steaming coils. She considered them quietly. Then she announced all was propitious.

The next sacrifice still stood calmly. At this point, some of them began to fear, even to try and break free. Usually, however, the drugs kept them docile, as the goddess wished. The young woman knew all about drugs, every root and potion in Suania and beyond.

Gently, the young slave was led to the middle. His garland of flowers had slipped a little, but he was not struggling. He looked at the body of the ox, at the blood soaking into the lush green turf, with what appeared to be mild curiosity. The crowd was hushed, expectant. Unlike the young woman, they did not notice the two horsemen ride out of the trees.

The crone again raised her hands to the heavens, and began to call on the moon goddess in all her many names and sonorous titles.

The young woman watched one of the horsemen pass his reins to his companion and dismount. Despite the warmth of the spring afternoon, he was wearing a voluminous fur cloak. He walked, with a strange lack of urgency, to behind where her three brothers stood.

The old priestess finished. A man stood forward. The point of the sacred lance was still crimson. Now the victim seemed to become aware of his position. He raised his hands in a confused, placating gesture. It had no effect. The spear point took him in the stomach. He doubled up around it. His hands clawed at the shaft. He fell, screaming. The crowd leant forward, engrossed. In every dying twitch and gasp the will of the goddess was being revealed.

The late arrival stood for a moment behind the three brothers. Only the young woman paid him any attention. He pushed back his cloak. The naked steel was in his hand. He steadied himself. Three short, quick steps. He rammed the wicked sword into the unprotected back. Another voice screaming in agony.

The stabbed man fell to his knees. The tip of the blade protruded from his stomach. The murderer, hands empty, stepped back. Distracted by the writhing agony of another, those around were slow to understand. Only the youngest brother reacted. He spun around, drawing his sword. The killer took a step back, as if surprised. The youngest brother brought his blade up. The killer turned and started to run. He made just three or four steps before retribution found him. A wild, swinging blow. It caught him on the side of the head, half severing his jaw. Blood and teeth sprayed. He went down. The youngest brother was on him, blade chopping.

'There!' The young woman pointed. 'The accomplice, do not let him escape. Kill him!'

Her retinue of armed men booted their horses. The accomplice sawed his reins, dragged his horse's head around. All too late. The others were all about him. He toppled to the ground in a red mist, already hacked beyond salvation.

The young woman looked over at her youngest brother. He was standing over the assassin. Sword dripping, covered in gore; he was panting. No longer the least of four boys sat at a teacher's feet, she thought. Now her youngest brother was a man. He had come a long way in the last two years – they both had. Sealed and countersealed in blood, she said to herself. The oracle drifted back into her mind. *The ox is wreathed; the end is near, the sacrificer to hand.*

PART TWO
The Kindly Sea

(Ephesus to Phasis, Spring–Summer AD262)

To Phasis, where for ships is the furthermost run.

–Unknown tragedian, from Strabo 11.2.16

XIV

The problem of leave-taking, for a man with an imagination like Ballista's, was that each instance might turn out to be final. Standing on the quayside at Ephesus, he was waiting to say farewell. Offhand, he could not number the times he had endured such scenes. Rome, less than two years after he had married Julia, ordered north to summon Valerian, the journey that had ended at the battle of Spoletium and with a new dynasty on the throne. Rome again, Isangrim just three, when Ballista was sent east to defend Arete. One after another, the recollections jostled. The gaol in Emesa, when, leaving Julia terrified, Isangrim and Dernhelm crying, he had been hauled off to the malignant Quietus in the temple of Elagabalus. The memories went back to childhood; back beyond the awful day the *imperium* had reached out, in the form of the garlic-reeking centurion, and taken him from his native people, from the hall of his father and the embrace of his mother.

To dispel the clouds of unhappy memories, to take his mind from what was to come, Ballista thought about his trip to the commercial *agora* a couple of days earlier.

175

In almost every town through which he passed in the *imperium*, once he had enough money, Ballista visited the slave market. They were all much the same: the dejected human flotsam, the tools with voices watched over by cold-eyed men with cunning, brutal faces.

The slave market at Ephesus was situated in the north-east corner of the Tetragonos *agora*. Beyond the wooden livestock pens were the stone cells of the human goods. Ballista had been there before, four or five years earlier, when he had been in Ephesus as a deputy to the governor of Asia, tasked with the revolting duty of persecuting the misguided Christians. On that occasion, there had been no one that interested him. This time it had been different.

'Are there any Angles here?' Ballista always asked the question in his native language, always the same question. On half a dozen occasions over the years there had been a response. The first two of his people he had purchased Ballista had freed, given them money and sent north. They had never got there. Either they had taken his funds and decided to start a new life somewhere else, or something had happened. Since then, Ballista had kept the Angles he discovered as freedmen on his wife's estate in Sicily. There were fourteen of them now, men, women and children, living in and around Tauromenium.

'Are there any Angles here?' Ballista had repeated the question. Usually there was no answer; blank incomprehension on faces pinched with misery. Ballista started to turn to go. Then came a small voice. 'Here, over here.'

The youth spoke the language of northern Germania, but the accent was wrong. Ballista looked down at him. He had reddish hair, freckles, a black eye. 'You are not an Angle.'

'No, I am from the Frisii, but my friend here is one of your people.'

Sitting silently, his knees drawn up to his chin, was a youth of extraordinary beauty: blond hair, blue eyes, fine cheekbones, on one of which was an open cut. His gaze was fixed over Ballista's head. He betrayed no awareness of what was around him.

'What is your name, boy?' Ballista spoke gently. The boy shivered slightly, but did not respond.

'He is called Wulfstan,' said the Frisian. 'He has . . . had a bad time.'

The slave dealer sidled up. 'How much for the two,' Ballista snapped. The dealer named a price. Ballista snorted and offered him half. The man spread his hands and started to whine about feeding his family. Not trusting himself to bargain, Ballista indicated for Hippothous to pay him what he asked.

The coins in his hands, the dealer had been joviality itself. 'A fine choice, *Kyrios*, a fine choice. These two will . . .' Given a sharp look from Ballista, the dealer did not name the obvious way the youths might serve a new master. 'I am sure they will prove a good purchase,' he ended lamely.

As the Frisian helped the other youth to his feet, Ballista turned and looked where Wulfstan had been gazing. There, high above the *agora*, was the mountain, great slabs of limestone thrusting through the greenery. It was nothing like the far northern homelands of the Angles. But it was wild and free.

Dwelling on one's virtues, in this case *philanthropia*, had been an excellent diversion. Ballista was brought back to immediate circumstances by the arrival on the quayside of those who had come to see him off.

A dignified procession was emerging from the harbour gate; despite the earthquake, somehow its triple arches still stood. At the front, preceded by his *lictors* bearing the *fasces*, was Maximillianus, the governor of Asia. The *lictors*, their rods and axes symbolic of the proconsul's right to dispense punishment, both corporal and capital, were stepping carefully across the shattered marble paving. Close behind Maximillianus came the scribe to the *demos* Publius Vedius Antoninus, the *asiarch* Gaius Valerius Festus, and Flavius Damianus. The political and social hierarchy in the city were here to see Ballista go. While he had not saved Ephesus from the Goths, he was the hero of the defence of Miletus and Didyma. Whatever his personal history or merits, he was a man with *mandata* signed by the emperor. Respect had to be shown to such men.

Maximillianus made a formal speech, redolent of gravity and hard duty, with much invoking of the gods. The three leading notables did likewise.

After Ballista had replied in similar measured terms, his friend Corvus stepped forward and embraced him. The *eirenarch* said little, just wished him a safe journey. Unsurprisingly, as an Epicurean, Corvus made no mention of the divine.

Julia led the boys to him. She was tall, stately in the *stola* of a Roman matron. Things had not been completely good between them for many months. He did not know why. But it was a marriage of more than a decade, better than many. At times, when forced to be apart, he realized the degree to which he relied on her.

She kissed him, on the lips but very chaste. She wished him a good journey and a safe return. Succinctly, she outlined the latest arrangements for her taking the boys and the majority of the *familia* back to Tauromenium: a letter of recommendation for the ship's captain had arrived from one of her family friends; the vessel would coast up to Corfu and cross to southern Italy, rather than sail directly from Greece to Sicily. She told him she loved him. And that was that.

Julia's practicality, her very unfeminine lack of fuss, was one of the things that had drawn Ballista to his wife as he had got to know her after their wedding. But that had been when everything was good; now, he had half hoped for a more overt display of affection.

Ballista got down on one knee as Isangrim and Dernhelm came to him. He put an arm around each of his sons, kissed them. From the folds of his travelling cloak he produced a wooden toy, a horse, for Dernhelm. The boy squealed with pleasure. Time and distance were vague concepts to a three-year-old.

It was not the same for Isangrim. The boy was ten. He knew the Caucasus were at the far end of the world, knew he would not see his father for at least a year. The boy was trying to be brave.

Ballista hugged him, whispered in his ear. They both had to be strong, for each other, for Isangrim's mother and his brother.

'I wish I was old enough to come with you and Maximus and Calgacus,' said Isangrim.

'Next time you will be.'

Ballista turned to Maximus, who handed him a package. Ballista passed it to Isangrim. The boy unwrapped the coverings. It was a *gladius*: a man's sword, but short enough for Isangrim.

The boy thanked his father with an odd formality. Then he thought for a moment, before unbuckling the miniature sword on his hip. He held it out to his father. 'You can use it as a dagger.'

It had been the boy's treasured possession since Ballista had given it to him – was it four years before? – on his return to Antioch after his first trip to Ephesus.

Ballista thanked him, keeping a tight rein on his emotions. The boy would do well. If things had been different, if they had lived in Germania, he would have soon grown into a fine northern leader of men. Ballista could see his eldest son seated on the chief's throne in the hall, taking the golden rings from his arm, awarding them to the leading warriors of his *comitatus*.

It was time to go. A last kiss for each of his sons, and Ballista walked up the boarding ladder. Hippothous passed him a cup of wine. Ballista intoned a prayer to Artemis of the Ephesians; to Zeus, Protector of Strangers; to Poseidon, Lord of the Seas; to Apollo, God of Embarkation. He tipped the libation into the water. Nothing untoward happened: no one sneezed, no other things of ill omen. He gave the cup back to Hippothous, and gave the order to get under way.

The boarding ladder was pulled up, the mooring ropes slipped. At the rowing master's word, the oarsmen readied themselves. The blades dipped as one, bit the surface, and the *liburnian* eased away from the dock.

Slowly, the little, two-banked galley made its course out of the long harbour of Ephesus. Ballista stood in the stern and waved. Slowly, the mountain slid past to the right, the plain to the left. Slowly, the figures on the dock diminished: the tall, black-haired woman and the two blond boys.

When they were at sea, the dock itself was no more than a smudge below the white bowl of the theatre, no figures to be seen. Ballista turned his back. He looked north-west for Mount Korakion, the first landmark.

He was concerned for the safety of Julia and the boys. Any sea journey had its dangers. But he was not too worried. The Goths were long gone back to the Black Sea. They were reported to have passed through the Bosphorus some twenty days earlier. The squadron of Venerianus had arrived in the Aegean. It was resting close by on Chios, preparing to sweep north in the wake of the Goths. As for the danger of ordinary opportunistic piracy, Ballista had hired four veterans as bodyguards for his *familia*. These tough, grizzled men, added to the able-bodied of the crew, should give any fishermen or traders with an eye to kidnap and ransom serious pause for thought. There was nothing that could be done about storms, but it was eight days before the *kalends* of May, well within the outer limits of the sailing season, and the ship on which Julia and the boys would travel was sound, its captain vouched for.

Ballista was not excessively worried, but he would rest easier once he had news that they had made it back to Sicily. The island was far from either barbarian menace or likely Roman civil war. Surely there could be nowhere safer than the villa at Tauromenium, surrounded by their own slaves, freedmen and tenants. He wished he could have shipped Pale Horse with them. The gelding deserved a quiet retirement on the sunlit pastures of Sicily, but he would be well cared for on the estate of Corvus outside Ephesus. Ballista hoped to collect him on the way back.

Even after such a parting, even given the nature of the mission, Ballista felt the small spark of anticipation that came with the start of a journey. He had Maximus and Calgacus with him, as well as Hippothous. The two Greek slaves he had bought in Priene, Agathon and Polybius would act as body servants, along with the two northern boys, Bauto the Frisian and Wulfstan the Angle, when the latter was more recovered. Hippothous had bought his own slave in Ephesus.

The *liburnian* would run up to Chios, past Lesbos; plough against the current of the Hellespont, cross the Propontis and come to the Bosphorus and Byzantium. There, they would meet Rutilus, Castricius and the aged noble Felix. There, four eunuch slaves of the emperor would join them to act as interpreters. And there, a *trireme* would be waiting to carry all of them to the far end of the Black Sea. A line of iambic poetry came into Ballista's thoughts.

To Phasis, where for ships is the furthermost run.

It was not hard to see why these four men were commanded to the edge of the inhabited world. For once, Ballista had not needed Julia to explain the underlying politics. He had been briefly a pretender to the throne. Two of the others were his close associates in that short-lived usurpation. The fourth was the most prominent and vocal champion of senatorial independence and tradition, the self-styled embodiment of *mos maiorum*. All four had something of a military reputation. All four were an irritation, possibly even a potential source of unrest. Rather than execute them, they were being got out of the way. In legal terms, they were office holders. They might even do some good. But in real terms, they were heading for exile.

Many years before, as a hostage at the imperial court, Ballista had been instructed to study philosophy. Several of the treatises had been on the theme of exile. One had stuck in his mind. It was a speech by a man called Favorinus of Arelate. Like all philosophical tracts on the subject, it had argued that exile was not bad at all. The heart of the text was an extended image from the gymnasium. The exile was an athlete, alone on the dry sand, stripped naked to his very soul. His opponents were four: love of fatherland, of family and friends, of wealth and honour, and of liberty. They did not keep to the rules; all jumped forward and wrestled the exile at once.

Ballista could remember only a little of the arguments with which Favorinus considered he had vanquished these opponents. Love of possessions and repute seemed the least troubling to Ballista. Yes, it was good when people made way for you, stood up when you arrived, called you *Kyrios*. He had twice known imperial disfavour when living in Antioch. They had been unpleasant months. But Ballista had always claimed, and he hoped with some truth, that worldly success meant little to him. As long as he had enough to live comfortably, he believed he would be happy to be left alone to farm some land in quiet obscurity. He had not asked to be trained as a killer, had not sought the acclaim that came with being skilled at it.

The threat of losing your fatherland meant next to nothing to a man who had lost it many years before. More than half a lifetime, and Ballista, for all his imperial sponsored education, knew he had not become a Greek or Roman. Here, he remembered, he differed from Favorinus, who had boasted that culture had transformed him from a Gaul to a true Hellene. Ballista's time in the *imperium* had made him neither one thing nor the other. He suspected he would no longer feel totally at home if the emperor, for some reason of State, decreed he should return to Germania.

As for liberty, it all depended what was meant. If it was freedom to go where you wanted, do what you wished, Ballista could not see that he had had it either as the son of a war leader of the Angles or as a hostage and officer of Rome. Although, if liberty was free speech, he had had more of it as a youth in the north.

Loss of family and friends was the killer. Ballista recalled that Favorinus had concentrated on friends. An accident of nature had made that easy for him. In his speech, Favorinus had admitted that his mother and sister were dead. Born a eunuch, Favorinus was given no opportunity to make another family. Ballista had his two closest friends with him, but being away from his family, being away from his boys, that was the hardest thing.

Maximus touched his arm, and pointed ahead. A squall was blowing in from the north-west, from Chios, a line of dark clouds trailing tendrils of rain, flicking up white caps in front. The oarsmen would earn their money pulling through that to a safe haven. But it would be as nothing to the storms in the Black Sea, the

Kindly Sea, as, strangely, it was often called, before Ballista reached Phasis.

To Phasis, where for ships is the furthermost run.

Ballista could still not remember from which tragedy the line came.

XV

Byzantium was the last place in the world that Hippothous wanted to find himself. Even his home town of Perinthus would not have been as bad. It had been many years before, but some Byzantines would remember the murder of their fellow citizen Aristomachus the rhetorician, and they would not have forgotten his killer.

When the imperial *mandata* had reached Ephesus, Hippothous had seriously considered leaving the *familia* of Ballista. But somehow he felt he still had work to do as *accensus* to the northerner, and the role suited his predilections.

Even the journey to the Bosphorus had been painful. It had not been the two squalls. The first had hit them almost as soon as they left Ephesus. They had had to run north to a bay under Mount Korakion. The second had come on them in the Propontis, when they were rounding the peninsula of Arctonnesos. They had had to ride that one out in the open water, a thing for which no galley cared.

Hippothous had been no more scared of shipwreck than was to be expected in a man who had experienced that horror. What had troubled him much more was cruising past Lesbos on a calm spring morning. Virtually all the time the island had been in sight, he had remained in the prow. He had ceaselessly scanned the water, searching for the place where his original ship, all those years before, had foundered, for where Hyperanthes's life had slipped away in the churning black waters, for the spot where he himself eventually had crawled ashore, as close to death as life, and for the headland where he had buried his beloved boy under a simple stone with a makeshift epigram.

> A tomb unworthy of the death of a sacred citizen,
> The famous flower some evil daemon once plucked from the
>   land to the deep,
> On the sea it plucked him as a great storm wind blew.

Standing there, Hippothous recognized none of it. Admittedly, it had been dark then, and in the teeth of a gale, but it was as if it had happened to someone else. This had profoundly shaken Hippothous, in a way he could not explain.

Immediately Ballista had announced that they were bound for Byzantium, Hippothous had begun to alter his appearance. There had not been time to grow a full beard, but he had achieved a commendable short one of sandy stubble. He had had his head shaved. Old Calgacus had done it. By the time they reached Byzantium, the nicks had mostly healed.

Hippothous had wondered if he should affect a limp or a stoop. He had decided against it, as it was liable actually to draw attention to him. It was a long time since he had left. For twenty-four years he had lived among the *latrones*. That length of time, roaming from Cappadocia to Aethiopia with groups of bandits, must have altered his walk and manners.

At least there was no need to change his name. He had done

that – it seemed a lifetime ago – when he had first come to Cilicia and taken up banditry as a profession.

One thing beyond his control was that Ballista, Maximus and Calgacus knew his true story. He had told it to them the year before, for really nothing more than to pass the time as they had waited offshore on a *trireme*, for events to unfold at the town of Corycus. They had promised not to reveal his true identity while in Byzantium, but it was a worry.

The *liburnian*, like most shipping going north, had pursued a course against the sun as it negotiated the Propontis. This left a tricky pull from east to west across the mouth of the Bosphorus, across the current, to finally make port in Byzantium. As the rowers toiled, Hippothous had studied the city. The acropolis on its bluff, sticking like a dagger into swirling waters; the low sea walls and the high land ones; the roofs of the temples. It all might have brought back strong emotions, if Hippothous had let it.

Even though time and his own ingenuity had inscribed a new form on his body and movements, Hippothous had kept to the centre of Ballista's small *familia*, eyes down, as they walked from the northern military docks through the bustling commercial harbour – livestock, slaves, grain, saltfish from the north, olive oil and wine from the south – up into the city.

They were staying in one of the houses of a leading member of the *Boule* called Cleodamus. The house was a new acquisition. Until recently, it had been the home of one of the councillors executed by Gallienus. Cleodamus did not reside there himself. That was good: Hippothous knew Cleodamus had been a young junior magistrate when Aristomachus the rhetorician had been killed. Despite Cleodamus's absence, Hippothous had feigned illness and remained shut up in his room until today.

This morning's meeting could not be avoided. All the four men who constituted the mission to the Caucasus were arrived in

Byzantium. The imperial eunuchs sent by Gallienus to act as interpreters and advisors were to brief them. The room was quite bare. Presumably, the condemned councillor's household possessions had been sold separately from the building, and Cleodamus had yet to instruct his servants to complete the furnishing of his new property.

At one end was a portable altar, its fire lit. Arranged in a row along one side were four chairs. On the one nearest to the altar sat the elderly senator Felix. Next to him was Ballista. Then, in descending order of rank, came the other equestrians, Rutilus and Castricius. During Ballista's few days wearing the purple, Rutilus had served as his Praetorian Prefect, Castricius as his Prefect of Cavalry. Before that, together with Ballista, they had served the pretender Quietus. Hippothous knew the equestrians from that time. Behind each seated man stood his secretary. As his *accensus*, Hippothous was behind Ballista.

Opposite stood the four eunuchs. The two sides of the room presented a strong contrast. Each of the four seated men, including the ex-consul Felix, was dressed as a soldier: white tunic, dark trousers and cloak, practical boots, elaborate sword belts, with long *spatha* on left hip, short *pugio* on right. Their *accensi* had followed their sartorial lead. Felix, Hippothous and one of the other secretaries sported a beard. All except Ballista had cropped hair.

The court eunuchs were more exotic figures. Their snow-white tunics were unbelted. They had slippers on their feet, and from their shoulders red cloaks fringed with gold fell to the floor. Their unnaturally smooth faces were framed by the ringlets of their artfully curled long hair.

Felix got up and went to the altar. He pulled a fold of his cloak over his head. Throwing a pinch of incense into the flames, he delivered a prayer for the gods and the *genius* of the Augustus to guide their deliberations. Moving lightly for his age and stature, he walked back to the chair and sat down again.

Hippothous detected no obvious insincerity in the old nobleman's words. Indeed, a couple of times, Felix had tapped his boot on the floor to emphasize his seriousness. Hippothous decided to practise physiognomy. Felix had a full head of silver hair and a beard, both groomed but not too elaborate. His nose was large, and deep lines ran down from it to below his mouth. His gaze was dry, with the eyes quite close set. Although he moved easily, his breathing was heavy.

Hippothous observed Felix closely out of the corner of his eye. The consular rubbed one of his palms on the other. That was the sign which, to a skilled physiognomist, brought the others into focus, gave significance to the whole. Felix had the soul of a hypocrite.

For a time, the conclusion, arrived at so scientifically as to be inescapable, puzzled Hippothous. Nothing he knew of the life of the elderly nobleman particularly suggested hypocrisy. Felix had had a successful career. He had been consul many years before. An intimate of the emperor Valerian, he had set himself up as the embodiment of senatorial *dignitas* and tradition. Under Gallienus, he had commanded with distinction the infantry in the centre of the line at the battle of Mediolanum. Before this meeting, he had talked at some length of this and of his pleasure at being back in Byzantium, the city he had successfully saved from the Goths some five years before.

Hippothous turned it all over in his mind. The moment of revelation was exquisite. At Mediolanum, the infantry had really taken orders not from Felix but from the Praetorian Prefect Volusianus. Felix's actions in the defence of Byzantium might not have been everything he claimed. Felix was a liar. And what was a hypocrite, if not a liar? The highest knowledge physiognomy brought was not just revelations of what would happen in the future but what falsehoods were told of the past.

Eusebius, the chief eunuch, the one who would accompany Felix, took the floor. In a high but melodious voice he began to speak.

'The Caspian Gates is the name given to the passes which run north–south through the Caucasus mountains. To the north live the Alani and the other savage nomads they rule. There are many of them; all very warlike. The passes must be held to keep them at bay.'

Eusebius's eyes were wide, hard and bright like marble.

'There are two great passes. To the east is a plain between the Caucasus and the Caspian Sea. This pass sometimes is called the Caspian Gates, sometimes the Gates of the Alani. Herodotus tells us it was the route taken by the Scythians when they defeated the Medes and brought destruction and misery to the whole of Asia. It is in the country of Cosis, king of the Albanians.'

The head eunuch bowed in the direction of Castricius. 'It is to Albania that the *Vir Perfectissimus* Gaius Aurelius Castricius will travel with my colleague Amantius.'

Eusebius now turned his unsettling eyes on Ballista. 'The other famous pass, to the west, high in the heart of the mountains, also is often called the Caspian Gates, but is more properly the Caucasian Gates. Through it erupted the Alani, in the time of the Divine Hadrian, when they set upon the province of Cappadocia, and were only driven back by the valour of the historian Arrian. Now the pass is held by Polemo, king of Suania. It is here that the *Vir Ementissimus* Marcus Clodius Ballista, with my colleague Mastabates, will advise the king and rebuild the fortifications.'

Interesting, thought Hippothous, that this eunuch from the palace calls Ballista *Vir Ementissimus*, as if he were still one of the great equestrian prefects of the empire.

With a flaccid sweep of his hand, Eusebius continued.

'Although it is less well known, between the two great passes are several others. They are harder going, but usable. They debouch into the territory of Hamazasp, king of Iberia. The *Vir Perfectissimus* Marcus Aurelius Rutilus has *mandata* to go to him. He will be accompanied by my friend Gallicanus.'

Finally, Eusebius gave his attention to Felix. 'To the west of the main Caspian or Caucasian Gates are several more tracks across the mountains. They lead down to the Black Sea at the cities of Pityous, Sebastopolis and Cygnus. The most powerful rulers here are Rhesmagus and Spadagas, the kings of the western and eastern Abasgi. They have established a certain loose hegemony over such tribes as the Macropogones and the Phtheirophagi in the mountains, as well as the minor chiefs of the lowland Colchis behind the coastal city of Phasis.'

Eusebius bowed deeply. 'A situation of such complexity calls for the political acumen, and possibly the military skills, of such a man as Spurius Aemilius Felix, the hero of Byzantium and Mediolanum.'

Hippothous only smiled inwardly; for a physiognomist is not to be caught out himself. No matter how Eusebius dressed it up, the self-regarding consular Felix was unlikely to welcome a commission which would see him struggling up goat tracks at the end of the world to mountain tribes such as the Macropogones and Phtheirophagi. There was something pleasurable in contemplating the *Vir Clarissimus* Spurius Aemilius Felix in the huts of the chiefs of the 'longbeards' and the 'lice-eaters'.

The eunuch seemed to be moving to the close of his oration with the sort of courtly platitudes and gestures he thought suitable to the occasion. Hippothous found it hard to watch. The too smooth cheeks, the broad mouth, the long, thin neck, the fleshy arms and wrists, the womanly breasts and even hips: the complete repulsiveness of a man who is not like other men.

'Of course, men of understanding, such as yourselves, will long ago have unveiled the other reason for this mission; the one not to be spoken of with any outside this room.'

A neat rhetorical turn, thought Hippothous, whose mind had been elsewhere.

'Of course, it is important to keep the hordes of the Alani north of the Caucasus. But there is no especial reason to think they are intending to try to force the Caspian Gates now.'

The eunuch had all Hippothous's attention.

'Many reports, some casually received from merchants, others sent by *frumentarii*, indicate that, since the capture of the emperor Valerian, the minions of the Persian king have been assiduous in their courting of the rulers to whom you are being sent. There is hardly a petty chieftain south of the Caucasus that is not eating off a silver dinner service embossed with images of Shapur hunting lions or carrying out some other kingly pursuit. There is a Sassanid army, commanded by Shapur's son Prince Narseh, south-west of the Caspian Sea. It is there on the pretence of crushing a revolt among their subject tribes of the Mardi and the Cadusii, but it is poised to move up through Albania and Iberia. Unless we can restore our client kings in the region to their rightful loyalty to Rome, the *imperium* will find it has lost the whole Caucasian region as far as Colchis. Unless we succeed, next year, Sassanid horsemen will be riding west along the shores of the Black Sea.'

XVI

The *trireme* waiting for them at Byzantium that had orders to convey them the length of the Kindly Sea to the Caucasus was named the *Armata*. Its *trierarch* was called Bruteddius Niger. Ballista liked the look of both immediately. The big galley was taut, well run. Its captain was square set, the epitome of a grizzled seaman.

Yet not all was ideal. The *Armata* was not from the Classis Pontica which operated out of Trapezus in the Black Sea. Instead, she had been one of the squadron of Venerianus that had followed the Gothic pirates as far as Byzantium. When the rest of the flotilla sailed south, it had been seconded to remain. The *Armata* was an Italian ship based out of Ravenna. Neither it nor Bruteddius had ever been into the daunting Black Sea. Somehow that was typical of imperial bureaucracy.

Bruteddius had hired a local pilot to negotiate the Bosphorus. It had been a wise step. The current in the middle of the channel ran down from the Black Sea like a mill race. To proceed north with any ease, a galley, even one with nearly two hundred oarsmen, had to catch the counter-currents close to either shore, several times pulling across the rush of water from one side to the other.

Nevertheless, in a few hours, they passed the clashing rocks. These marked the entrance to the Black Sea. Once, they had floated, dashing together and crushing any vessel that attempted the passage. After Jason and the Argonauts had got through, the gods had fixed the dreadful obstacles in place. The pilot pointed them out with parochial pride. Ballista and the others were less than impressed. The dirty stubs of charcoal-green stone did not look the stuff of myth.

They had all heard terrible things about the Black Sea. Storms blew up out of nowhere. The southern coast was notorious for a wave pattern like no other: triple waves which could put even the most seaworthy craft on its beam ends. But the first day, the Kindly Sea was calm. The only thing that surprised the seamen used to the clear waters of the Mediterranean was its opaque quality. However, while they could not see into its depths, a helpful and strong current ran to the east.

The *Armata* raced along, leaving a long, straight wake like a path through a green meadow. Bruteddius wanted to push for a long day's row all the way to Heraclea. But Felix, true to the interests of his class, managed to turn the trip into a voyage of antiquarian sight-seeing. First, at lunch time, he insisted they delay at Calpe. Through the eyes of the cultured, the promontory was just as Xenophon had described it in the *Anabasis*: the harbour under the steep cliff, its beach facing west; close by, the spring of plentiful fresh water; the broad headland with the narrow, defensible neck connecting it to the mainland; the abundance of good, shipbuilding timber; to the south, before the mountains, the villages set on the rich soil. No wonder, Felix opined, Xenophon had wanted to settle the ten thousand there. Only the short-sightedness of the mercenaries had prevented the foundation of a magnificent Greek *polis*.

After Calpe, Felix desired to see the small island of Apollonia, where Apollo appeared to the Argonauts, and which was called Thynias by Apollonius of Rhodes in his epic of the voyage. Fortunately, there was a harbour of sorts at the bottom of the island. Bruteddius close berthed the *Armata* for the night, lashing her tight with double cables. As the rowers relaxed on the beach, Felix took Ballista and the other emissaries off with him. They wandered the shore, searching for the altar of the god and the sanctuary of Homonia which Jason had founded, and the place where the heroes had danced. Felix was not to be disappointed. A few indigenous inhabitants blended out of the trees and provided with utter certainty locales for every detail of the Argonauts' story; including several unmentioned by Apollonius. Furthermore, these sagacious guides encouraged the elderly senator to call for weapons and nets and set off after them, climbing the thickly wooded slopes to hunt the descendants of the very deer and wild goats pursued by the crew of the *Argo*.

At times like that evening, as, bow in hand, he strolled under the canopy of leaves, Ballista wondered if the education of the Roman elite really was the best training for governing their *imperium*. Some might consider expertise other than skilled rhetoric and an encyclopaedic knowledge of literature from or about the distant past might have more utility in holding together a far-flung empire threatened on all sides and from within in an age of iron and rust.

The second morning dawned bright and clear. At no particularly early hour, Felix led on to the *trireme* the envoys and their supernumeraries – friends, secretaries, servants and, in the case of the esteemed senator, who knew what else besides. The sailors and oarsmen had been waiting for some time. The members of the mission distributed themselves across the deck. Their numbers were such – no fewer than forty – that the galley's marines perforce had been left in Byzantium. As Bruteddius had been heard to say, the *Armata* now scarcely fitted her name. There would be Charon to pay, if they ran into trouble.

There was more of a swell than before, the sea oilier, but still no airs worth speaking about. The rowers bent to their task. With the current still flowing strong to the east, the *Armata* forged ahead. They cruised past the mouths of the rivers Sangarios, Hypios and Lykos, past the trading posts of Lilaion and Kales. Bruteddius had intended to try for another long day of rowing, all the way to the harbour of Amastris. But, shortly after they passed the *emporion* of Kales, the day dulled. A line of dark clouds appeared to the north-east. Sharp buffets of wind started to catch the ship crosswise, outriders of the coming storm. As the *trireme* skewed, Bruteddius consulted the pilot, then spoke to Felix. The consular needed no persuading. Bruteddius ordered the rowing master make all speed, and the helmsman shape a course for Cape Acherousias and the port of Heraclea that sheltered beneath its high rocks.

They had cut it fine. No sooner had they run into the Soonautes than the river lived up to its name: the 'Saviour of Sailors'. Walls of wind-driven rain screamed up the estuary and, in relentless succession, flailed across the ship. In the driving downpour, they made the *trireme* fast, wrestled the storm canvas into position, and huddled ashore.

The northern gale had no intention of relenting. Once, on the second day, Boreas teased them. The wind dropped, the sun even shone. They got as far as getting the rowers to their benches. The storm blew back in from the sea. Chastened, they all scrambled ashore again.

Heraclea was an ancient colony of the Megarians from mainland Hellas. It had all the amusements expected to be on offer in an ancient port city. Maximus and Hippothous, separately, and most of the crew of the *Armata* in groups, vanished into the backstreets near the wharves. After the abortive attempt to put to sea, Ballista had embarked on an epic drinking bout. He spent the subsequent day recovering. From then, Ballista decided to be more abstemious.

On the fourth day, bored, Ballista employed a local guide and ventured out of the town. On hired nags, the rain hard on their backs, they plodded inland up the road by the riverbank. The Soonautes river had once been called the Acheron. The entrance to Hades was a cave. As soon as he saw it, Ballista realized he had made a mistake. It was the narrowest of clefts in the rock. Inside, it was worse: a dark, twisting passage, slippery and descending precipitously. Sweating, heart racing, he forced himself to inch his way down. After an agony of time, they emerged into a great underground cavern. In the intervals when he managed to stop thinking about the pulverizing weight of rock above him and the narrowness of the passage back into the light, it was not too bad. There was a pool of water, statues, offerings of all sorts. The torchlight flickered atmospherically on the dripping walls. It was cold.

After the Mouth of Hades, they rode up to the tomb of Tiphys, the helmsman of the *Argo*. This was set high on Cape Acherousias, backed by a sacred grove of plane trees. The monument itself held little interest, but it commanded a magnificent view. Pummelled by the wind, leaning into it, Ballista revelled in the fury of the storm spread out before him, howling all around him. White-topped, great waves rolled down out of the murk. They crashed and roared on the rocks below. The spume, flung high, was snatched away. At the foot of the cliff, the sea had turned yellow. With some terrible, insentient anger, the wind scoured the headland and thrashed the plane trees, wrenching and torturing their branches, threatening to cast them down, god-loved or not.

'We should go, *Kyrios*.' The guide had to cup his hands and yell to be heard. Ballista laughed. The man was frightened. He was a coward. Ballista knew himself neither. He had descended to the Hades of the Greeks and Romans; had mastered his fear. Now, the reek of it was purged from him in the fierce embrace of this clean northern storm. At such rare times, his very own vitality made immortality, in Valhalla or elsewhere, seem certain.

'*Kyrios*, the trees, the horses . . . it is dangerous.'

Blinking the rain out of his eyes, Ballista smiled at the man, and turned to leave.

Like most towns, and many villages in the empire, Heraclea had an official rest house of the *cursus publicus*. In his room in the *mansio*, Ballista was drinking warm, spiced wine with Mastabates. The *conditum* tasted good. They had a brazier. It was snug, comfortably fuggy. Outside, it was still atrocious.

A tap on the door, and young Wulfstan's head popped round. 'That ferret-faced little fucker Castricius is here; big, ginger Rutilus with him.' The boy spoke in the language of the Angles. He was much recovered.

'They might understand,' said Ballista.

'These Romans and Greeks only learn each other's language.'

'Show them in.' The boy had a point.

'At once, *Atheling*.'

Ballista was finding it good to be addressed again by his title among his own people.

Mastabates bowed, blew a kiss to Castricius and Rutilus.

Ballista jumped up and embraced the newcomers. The northerner was glad to see them. Castricius was the older friend – all the way since the siege of Arete – and the more demonstrative. Yet Ballista owed much to both. At Zeugma, Castricius had saved Calgacus, Maximus and Demetrius. At Emesa, without the actions of the two, Ballista considered it unlikely that either himself or Julia and the boys would have survived. Such profundities aside, they were good company. Ballista was easy with them.

There were only two couches. Castricius got on one with Ballista. With just the faintest unease, Rutilus climbed on the other with Mastabates. Wulfstan brought more cups, more *conditum*.

'Mastabates here was about to tell me something of where we are going,' said Ballista.

'In the Caucasus they live off roots and berries, and all fuck outdoors like herd animals,' Castricius stated.

'You have read your Herodotus.' Mastabates' words were smooth, complimentary.

Castricius's small, lined face broke into a grin. 'No, just what I hear.'

'Even Maximus would be pushed in this weather,' said Ballista. 'Possibly Mastabates might give us a more informed view. Please start with the Albanians. It might help if Castricius loses some of his presuppositions before he tries to bend the king's daughter over in a field. It might hamper our diplomacy.'

Mastabates bowed, unsmiling. 'Albania is well watered. There is grass in the pastures all year round. The soil is fertile. But the Albanians lack foresight. They use wooden ploughshares, and only prune their vines every fifth year. Even so, they would be rich, if they did not bury all their wealth with their dead. Yet, oddly, once buried, the dead are never spoken of again.'

Typical of a Greek, thought Ballista, to start with the land; it is always the land that shapes the people.

'The Albanians favour a Cyclopeian lifestyle; living apart, each making his house where he will. They are a handsome race, large bodied. Most are shepherds but, despite that, they are not particularly ferocious.'

'How many men can they put in the field?' Castricius was nothing if not a long-service soldier. 'How do they fight?'

'It is said they resisted Pompey the Great with over eighty thousand warriors; more than a quarter of them mounted. They use javelins and bows, but some have armour and fight at close quarters. Often they are aided by the nomads from beyond the Caspian Gates.'

'And they are ruled by a king?' Ballista asked.

'Yes, the king is Cosis. Second in honour to him is his uncle, the high-priest Zober.'

Rutilus broke in. 'Tell me about the Iberians I will meet.'

Mastabates paused, as if choosing his words from a well-stocked store. 'They are different; to some extent, more civilized. They have tiled roofs and public buildings. There are four castes in Iberia: the royal family, the priests, the warriors and farmers, and the royal slaves. The next in line to the throne, the *pitiax*, commands the army and dispenses justice. King Hamazasp has no son, so his younger brother Oroezes is *pitiax*.'

Castricius laughed. 'Hamazasp has no son because our Ballista killed him at Arete.'

Ballista remembered the twang, slide, thump of the artillery piece, the long, steel-tipped bolt hurtling away, punching the young man from his horse; arms, legs, the long, empty sleeves of his coat, all flapping like a six-limbed insect. And he remembered Hamazasp. Himself a prisoner; Hamazasp coming into the cell under the palace at Edessa. He pushed down the thought of what had happened, what Hamazasp had nearly done to him; pushed it far down. But if he met the bastard again . . .

Mastabates was answering a question from Rutilus. '. . . armed like Persians, the ones from the mountains more like Scythians. There are fewer of them than the Albanians, but still tens of thousands.'

'Finally, what of my Suani?' Ballista asked.

'Very dirty people, no less filthy than the *Phtheirophagi*. They have to import grain from the lowlands. But they are not poor. They pan the mountain streams for gold. There are gems as well. They are ruled by King Polemo. He is advised by a council of three hundred they call the *synedrion*. There may be a problem at court. King Polemo's daughter was married to the prince of Iberia you killed. As a widow, she has returned to her father's domain – she is called Pythonissa.' The eunuch gestured in a way that had regard for Ballista's martial prowess in killing members of foreign dynasties while at the same time accepting the difficulties such behaviour brought.

'The king and his nobles are said to command two hundred thousand warriors. The Suani control the heights of the Caucasus. They are the foremost people of the mountains for courage – and for treachery. There is nothing they do not know of poison. One of them, they dip their arrows in and even the smell makes men suffer.'

'You are very well informed.'

Mastabates dipped his head. 'I have read the Greek geographer Strabo with attention.'

'I thought you were from those parts.'

'Nearby. I am from Abasgia.'

Ballista laughed. 'Let me guess, the imperial court has sent you with me to Suania, and one of the Suani with Felix to Abasgia.'

A shadow passed across Mastabates' handsome face. 'No, *Kyrios*, all four of us eunuchs are from Abasgia.'

No one else spoke. Mastabates continued. 'Some time ago, the rulers of the Abasgi found a new source of income. They began to search among their subjects for the most beautiful young boys. They have them castrated, and sell them to you Romans.'

'And how . . .' Ballista's question petered out.

'We were young, very young. It was a long time ago.'

Ballista noticed Rutilus cross his legs.

Mastabates rallied, keeping his voice very neutral. 'We know we are viewed as ill omened. If a man sees one of us first thing in the morning, he should return indoors, for that day will not go well for him. Composite, hybrid, monstrous, alien to human nature – many hold that eunuchs should be excluded from temples and public places.'

There was an embarrassed silence.

'The very contempt in which we are held by the many is our source of strength. We look to each other. Rulers give us their confidence. They look to us for unalloyed loyalty. Unable to have wives and children, who should a eunuch lavish his affection on, if not the ruler, the one who protects him from common brutality?'

'Yet is it not a life of regrets, without certain pleasures?' Ballista spoke gently.

Mastabates smiled. 'It is my pleasure to serve as Aphrodite served Ares.'

Rutilus moved slightly away.

'But it would be wrong to think of us all as weaklings. A gelded horse is still fit for war; a castrated bull does not lose its might. Even if it is true that some of us may be a little less endowed with bodily strength, on the field of battle, steel makes the weak equal with the strong.'

XVII

At dawn on the fifth day, Boreas finally gave over. High above, ragged dark clouds still scudded south, vanishing inland over the mountains. Yet down in the port of Heraclea all was calm. Ballista watched a pale, washed-out sun glitter in the puddles on the dockside.

The crew of the *Armata* were sullenly preparing her for sea. Great sluices of water fell unexpectedly from the storm canvas as it was removed. Fat drops fell from the rigging on to the oarsmen as they settled themselves on their benches. If only, some muttered, she were a fully decked *trireme*. 'Bugger that,' others replied. 'Easier to get trapped when she goes down.' 'Silence, fore and aft,' roared her officers.

Felix made the libation to Apollo, protector of travellers. Bruteddius ran his eye over all. The bow officer, rowing master and helmsman were at their stations: prow, midships and stern. They indicated they were ready. Bruteddius gave the order. The cables slipped, the *Armata* was heaved off from the wharf. *Oars outboard. Ready? Light pressure. Row!* Slowly, the vessel gathered her way, turned, and pointed her bronze ram out to the Kindly Sea.

The storm had left the surface of the sea muddy, with a quantity of flotsam. There was a swell. It demanded a shorter than usual stroke from the rowers. They were slow to make the adjustment, poor at keeping time. A run of four days ashore had done them no good. Bruteddius had considered attempting the passage to Sinope in one sailing. He had talked to local skippers. It would be a long day, very long and very hard; from well before dawn to after dark, if not to the next dawn. Yet he was told it was not impossible. He had settled on Amastris instead, just sixty or so miles. There was but one good harbour in the long stretch between Amastris and Sinope, and his men were not in good condition. What could you expect? Volunteers they might be, soldiers notionally, but in origin they were nothing but a bunch of soft freedmen and easterners; Greeks and Egyptians. A few days' drinking and whoring in a backwater town, and they were all out of sorts and as weak as women.

The voyage to Amastris passed without incident. No wind got up, so the men had to row all the way. No bad thing to knock them together again. They laboured hard past the tomb of Sthenelos. They took no more notice of the mouth of the river Kallichoros, where the god Dionysus danced, or that of the Parthenios, where the goddess Artemis bathed. They were unaware when they hauled the ship from the territory of the Bithynian Thracians to that of the Paphlagonians. And all the while the enormity of the sluggish sea stretched on their left.

Not long after the time for the midday meal, the *Armata* pulled into the neat, sheltered oval of the galley harbour at Amastris; pulled in most gladly. No one appeared happier to disembark than Felix. Ballista followed him down the boarding ladder. The elderly senator's joy was palpable. True, Felix had not been doing physical work. Far from it: a comfortable chair had been provided for him to view the tomb of the hero as they went by. After that, he had retired to the tiny cabin in the stern, declining all invitations to see rivers associated with divinities – unless there were an epiphany, that day, they were just rivers to him. Nevertheless, he was evidently glad to be back on *terra firma*. Ballista imagined that the consular was looking forward to some food and a drink, then a relaxing afternoon. These, followed by a massage at the baths and a good dinner, should suffice to restore his spirits. Ballista had some sympathy with the general idea.

Felix stopped so abruptly that Ballista almost barrelled into his back. A man had run out from between two warehouses. He was thin, in thin clothes; both hard worn. He ran straight at the senator. Two men, better set up, ran out after him. Belatedly, it occurred to Ballista that social precedence had left Felix's four bodyguards at the top of the boarding ladder. Ballista moved to intercept the thin man. He was too late. The man slid to his knees, and grabbed Felix around the thighs. The senator tried to step back; the man's arms pinioned him. If Rutilus had not caught Felix from behind, he would have fallen.

'Asylum, *Kyrios*, grant me asylum,' the man pleaded.

'Do not listen to him.' His pursuers, overawed by the *maiestas* of Rome, embodied in the elderly ex-consul, had pulled up short.

'In the name of Caesar, grant me a hearing, *Kyrios*.' The man clung to Felix like a shipwrecked sailor to driftwood.

'He is a slave, a runaway,' one of the others said.

'No, I am a free man, a Roman citizen, wrongly enslaved. Grant me a hearing, *Basileus*.'

Felix, his vanity flattered by being called a king, placed a hand, almost in benediction, on the cowering man. 'I shall hear the case at the start of the second hour tomorrow. The plaintiff will remain in custody until then.'

One of the bodyguards, a legionary detailed from Legio II

Parthica, had fought his way off the ship and now took the man away.

The second hour of the next day, the seventh day before the *ides* of May, found Ballista seated next to Felix, as one of his five *assessors*, in a pleasant portico overlooking the *agora*.

The thin man was asked the prescribed questions: Name? Race? Free or slave?

'Melissus, son of Charillus, *Kyrios*; from Erythrinoi, a village in the territory of Amastris. I am a free man, unjustly taken into slavery.'

He was given a chance to tell his story.

'I am a fisherman. I was out in my boat, the *Thalia*, when the Borani came. They captured me. The barbarians burnt my *Thalia*, just for their pleasure. They took me with them. When they went ashore for fresh water at the mouth of the Parthenios, I escaped.'

The men who claimed to own him started to voice their disagreement. Felix silenced them with a look.

'I had nothing but a tunic on my back. As I walked towards Amastris, I fell in with these men. At first, they spoke gently to me. When they had lulled me, they had four of their followers grab me. They bound me, beat me. With cruel humour, they renamed me Felix. They were laughing, joking it was a lucky name for a lucky slave.'

His captors ill-omened naming decided the case there and then. But Felix went through the formalities. The man's supposed owners were allowed a chance to state their case. Fully aware of how the wind was set, they made a very poor job of it. Witnesses appeared on both sides. Those for Melissus made far the better impression.

Felix made a show of consulting his assessors. Ballista, Rutilus, Castricius and two young, well-born friends of Felix gave their unanimous opinion. Then the consular delivered his judgement.

'Melissus, son of Charillus, of the village of Erythrinoi, is to be restored to freedom. The men who have so inhumanely preyed on a fellow citizen in misfortune are to be stripped and beaten. Their property is confiscated: half to the *fiscus* of our *dominus* Gallienus Augustus, half to Melissus, son of Charillus. Let the sentence be carried out now.'

Straightaway, eight burly soldiers from the *stationarii* based in Amastris seized the men, dragged them out into the *agora*.

Even before the first whip fell, the condemned were screaming.

'Cowardly *Graeculi*,' said Felix.

The words, even the screams, were cut across by a new voice, loud in its desperation: '*Kyrios*, hear my petition. I too have been wronged.'

Wearily, Felix said, 'Who spoke? Bring him forth.'

And so it started: an endless series of complaints, all different, but all having one thing in common. When the barbarians came, I hid in the hills, returning I found my neighbour had taken my goat, field, wife . . . When the barbarians came, in the chaos, my fellow citizen attacked my boat, home, daughter . . . When the barbarians came, my fellow townsman joined them, pointing out roads and houses, sharing in their depredations. When the barbarians departed, they left behind my silver bowl, my statue of Athena . . . My friend recovered it, but now will not return it to me.

All through the long day, Ballista listened to the stories of woe. He thought of the famous description by Thucydides of the breakdown of society during the civil war in Corcyra. He thought the coming of the barbarians might be worse; to domestic bad faith and betrayal was added the horror of the unknown.

A very small part of him felt an atavistic pride – this is what we northerners can do to you feeble men of the south. He suppressed the thought as unworthy. He concentrated on his dominant emotion, a genuine pity for peaceful men and women whose innocence had been no shield. Yet he did not suspend his critical faculties, trying hard to discern the victims from the liars and opportunists. A false accusation, if successful, brought the same rewards as a genuine one.

To give him his due, Felix worked hard. But, by the evening, the old senator was very tired. He had had more than enough. There were eight complaints still unheard. Felix announced that he must sail the following day; his duty to the *Res Publica* demanded it. The remaining cases must be taken to the governor of the province of Bithynia et Pontus, Vellius Macrinus, currently thought to be holding assizes in the city of Prusa. That many of those involved were poor men, poorer still after their disaster, and Prusa probably was over two hundred miles away, did not seem to occur to him.

The following morning, bright and early, the *Armata* pulled out of Amastris. At first there was a north-westerly breeze, but it was fitful; several times it disappeared and the oars had to be run out; as many times again, it returned and the oars were drawn inboard. Leaning on the starboard rail, Ballista commented to Bruteddius on the forbidding-looking coast. Big, wooded mountains; the trees ran down to the rocks, and the rocks jutted out into the sea. Stark precipices reared up from the water. There were coves, but most were rock bound, open to the weather; each more of a trap than a haven.

'Not good,' Bruteddius agreed. 'I wanted to get to Sinope today. The noble senator, however, seems to have rediscovered his pleasure in religion. He demands we spend the night at Ionopolis. I am told by the locals the mooring there is not secure. If another storm gets up . . .'

'I will talk to him,' Ballista said.

Felix, seated in comfort, was listening to one of his staff, a winsome youth, reading the *Argonautica* of Apollonius. Ballista waited for him to finish the passage. Then, choosing his words with care, he spoke in Greek. '*Kyrios*, this early in the sailing season the weather is unsettled. Ionopolis is just a grandiose name given to the obscure Paphlagonian town of Abonoutei-chos. We would have to ride at anchor. There is nothing to see except the temple built by the charlatan Alexander of Abonoutei-chos. Long ago, Lucian exposed the god Glycon as a fraud: a tame snake with a moulded human head, deceitful voices whispered through the windpipes of cranes, sham oracles created by greedy men. The consul Rutilianus became a laughing stock when he was taken in by it.'

Felix turned a cold, baleful face on Ballista. 'Publius Mummius Sisenna Rutilianus was my kinsman. In matters of religion, allow me to believe a Roman of high rank and unblemished character over a malicious scribbler like Lucian of Samosata.' He pronounced the latter with extreme distaste. 'Lucian, part *Graeculus*, part Syrian, all malevolent.'

Ballista nodded. 'Of course, *Kyrios*.' There was nothing else to say.

Despite the desolate coast, Ionopolis was reached without mishap. The elderly consular and his entourage went ashore. Ballista and the others stayed with the ship. Bruteddius allowed the crew no shore leave; two thirds camped on the beach, the rest remained aboard. Thankfully, the night was placid.

At first light, Felix climbed the boarding ladder, smiling, gracious, obviously buoyed up by an auspicious response from the oracle. Bruteddius assured the consular that everything was ready. Felix made the libations, asked for the favour of the gods. Ballista was irritated, but unsurprised to hear Glycon among the deities. *What has the snake god promised you, old man?* he thought. *A century ago your kinsman believed, so now you do; to you that passes for piety.*

There was no wind. The sea was dead calm, leaden. Even the eastward current seemed to have deserted them. The sun was a pale disc behind the haze. Intermittent patches of vapour curled on the surface of the water. The oarsmen would have a hard day of it.

Ballista sensed the unease of Bruteddius; something deeper than just scratching at his beard. The veteran *trierarch* had ordered that one of the three levels of rowers should rest at all times. He had taken the *Armata* well out into the deserted sea. A glance at the coastline showed why. Iron-bound promontory after iron-bound promontory; between each, open, rock-strewn coves.

Bruteddius had taken on another local pilot. There was but one safe anchorage in the sixty or seventy miles between Abonouteichos and Lepte Point. As it was pointed out, Bruteddius relaxed a little. As the *Armata* left it astern, he went back to worrying at his beard.

Across a grey sea, under an increasingly grey sky, the *trireme* laboured on, the men singing doleful songs to keep time. At the foot of the cliffs, jagged black-green rocks, frosted white on top with bird droppings. Above the precipices, rugged foothills, jagging up to wild mountains just visible through the mist. Only the occasional column of smoke, rising straight in the still air, showed the country was not deserted.

In the heavy fullness of time, the shoreline turned north. The *Armata* turned to follow. The high cliffs dropped away. Through the gathering mist, gentle meadows could be seen rolling down to the sea, on them tiny white dots, most likely sheep grazing, seemingly unattended. Ballista thought it might put some men in mind of pastoral poetry or Greek novels. He had never really cared for either. Demetrius would have enjoyed the view; probably Hippothous did.

'Lepte Point.' Bruteddius pointed. The headland ended in a low jumble of grey rocks. The water pushed and sucked sluggishly at them. Bruteddius kept the *Armata* well out. When he thought it completely safe, he brought her head around.

'Ship in sight,' the bow officer called out. Ballista, Maximus in tow, walked forward with Bruteddius. The three peered through the shifting obscurity. The bow officer pointed. 'A warship, a *liburnian* by the size of her. Must be from Trapezus, one of the Classis Pontica.'

It was hard to judge distance in the mist. Maybe a mile away to the south-east was a dark shape. The outline of a high prow and forward-sweeping sternpost indicated a Mediterranean-style war galley. Smaller than the *Armata*, she appeared motionless, seemingly sitting on her oars in the shipping lane just around Lepte Point.

'She is not alone.' Maximus had always had keen eyes. 'Beyond her.'

Ballista strained to penetrate the murk. Another dark shape, a second, then a third. 'How many do you see?'

'Six – there could be a seventh.'

Ballista could make out four now. The two he could see best had a prow at either end. 'Bruteddius, turn us around, and get us away from here.'

'Gothic longboats?' The *trierarch* was tugging his beard.

'Gothic longboats.'

Bruteddius shrugged. 'That explains the empty sea and the beacons.'

'We will fight them.' No one had noticed Felix arrive on the fo'c's'le. 'We will go to the aid of the *liburnian*. It is unfitting we should run.'

'They have seen us,' said the bow officer. 'They are getting under way.'

Ballista addressed Felix. 'It is too late for the *liburnian*. She is with them.'

'Unstep the masts; main and bowsprit.' Bruteddius's voice carried throughout the ship. The crew moved promptly at their *trierarch's* command.

'This is a *trireme*,' said Felix. 'We can fight them all.'

'No,' said Ballista bluntly. 'Our marines and artillery were left in Byzantium. None of our rowers are armed; all of their men will be.'

'We will manoeuvre, use the ram.' There was no doubting the old senator's martial spirit.

'They would grapple us.' Ballista shook his head. 'Seven or eight ships – they would be on us like a pack of hounds.'

Both masts were down. The gaggle of passengers was impeding them from being securely lashed to the deck, getting tangled in the coils of the back and forestays. 'All civilians sit down,' bellowed Bruteddius. 'Well spread out and not in the way.'

The *trierarch* led the men of rank back to the stern. Maximus had vanished.

'All rowers to benches. Prepare for fast turn to left. On the command, starboard oars full pressure; larboard side, back her down hard; steering-oars, hard over.'

A chair was produced for Felix. He waved it away.

'Now!' The rowing master and the bow officer repeated the call.

The great galley surged forward and heeled. Her starboard lowest-level oarports almost under water, her ear dipping towards the sea, she circumscribed a tight circle. In a matter of moments, Bruteddius had her levelled off and racing back to the west.

Ballista looked over the stern. The Goths had gained appreciably. Now he could see five longboats behind the *liburnian*. As he watched, the blast of a horn echoed across. It was answered by seven or eight more.

Bruteddius spat over the side. 'We have a start, and we have the legs on them. It has already been a longish row, but the boys have rested in turn. Anyway, fear gives a man stamina.'

No sooner were the words out than another horn rang out. It came from somewhere ahead and to the left. Another blast followed.

'We were being followed,' said Ballista.

'Helmsman, take us out to the north-west, out into the deep sea.' Clearly, Bruteddius was not given to panic. 'Clear for action. Spare oars to all levels. Spread sand on the deck. Complete silence. Only officers to speak.'

Ballista knew what orders had not been given. This called for some tact. He turned to Felix. '*Dominus*, I have commanded a *trireme* in action before. If the *trierarch* agrees, should I organize what fighting men we have?'

The elderly senator nodded gravely. 'That would be best. I have never been called to fight at sea. My four bodyguards and myself are at your disposal.'

The chase soon took on its pattern. The *Armata*, throwing a big bow wave, forged through the dull sea. Directly astern, a little more than half a mile away, mainly visible through the gloom, were the *liburnian* and eight longboats. Somewhat further back, off south-east, were two more northern warships; these drifted in and out of sight.

Normally, Bruteddius would have been right: the *trireme* most likely would have outrun her pursuers. But, despite his reassuring words, the oarsmen of the *Armata* had been rowing, more on than off, for hours, since shortly after dawn. The Goths seemed fresher. At least, they were keeping station, if not actually gaining a trifle.

Bruteddius spoke. 'The pilot says that, on this course, there is nothing between us and the Island of Achilles off the mouths of the Danube three hundred miles or more. We could edge to the north. The Crimean Bosphorus is no more than a hundred and sixty-odd miles.' No one stated the obvious: the Goths would run them down long before they reached either.

Maximus reappeared with his weapons and equipment and that of Ballista. With him were Calgacus and Hippothous, already kitted out. As he armed, Ballista ascertained the number of warriors aboard. Four in his *familia*. Felix's four bodyguards. The old man insisted on arming too. Rutilus and Castricius added just themselves. Bruteddius, of course, was a long-service centurion. Twelve men, one rather long in the tooth.

Ballista asked for volunteers from the entourages. Twenty answered the call. Ballista rejected six, among them the youths Wulfstan and Bauto. However, he gave each of the boys one of the many knives in his kit. They would not wish to be enslaved again. The eunuch Mastabates was one of those accepted. There were pikes and boarding axes aboard. These and the warriors' spare weapons were doled out. Twenty-six men in all, less than half trained. Hopeless.

The sun broke through the haze. Everything was suddenly illuminated. Through the tendrils of mist, nine Gothic vessels astern, two more further behind on the larboard quarter. Say a minimum of thirty warriors in each. Over three hundred armed men against fewer than thirty. No sort of odds. Utterly hopeless.

The sun went in again. Grey wisps of vapour rose again. The grim chase went on.

'I cannot understand why they would chase a warship,' said

214

Felix. 'There must be easier, richer pickings. They do not know we have no marines or engines.'

'They know everything about us.' Bruteddius spoke quietly.

'How?'

'Someone from Abonouteichos told them.'

'Never.' Flat disbelief in Felix's voice.

'They are Goths, but to some they are just pirates. All *latrones*, on land or sea, get information from locals.' Bruteddius sounded resigned.

'No citizen would do such a thing!'

Ballista gently intervened. 'The cases you heard at Amastris, *Dominus*? You condemned two men to the arena for joining in the barbarians' depredations.'

The chase ground on. The water still sang down the sides of the *Armata*, but slower now. The oarsmen were tiring fast. Their open-mouthed faces were masks from a tragedy. Their breathing came in sobs. Their sweat dripped on the men below, puddled in the hold. Individuals were starting to miss their stroke. The banks of oars were becoming ragged, like the damaged wings of a bird. The Goths were coming up hand over fist. No more than three hundred yards of clear water separated the sternpost of the *Armata* from the ram of the *liburnian*.

Ballista ran through his pre-battle ritual: the dagger, sword, the healing stone. Wordless, he embraced Calgacus and Maximus. He shook hands with Hippothous, Rutilus and Castricius. The latter hugged him close. The sombre, gathering darkness of the day was fitting. Ballista's main regret was not seeing his sons grow. Maybe in Valhalla, if there was such a thing or something like it.

Bruteddius had stopped tugging at his beard. The old seaman actually laughed.

Dull witted, everyone at the stern stopped gazing at the Goths and looked at Bruteddius. The *trierarch* called out loud to his rowers. 'One last effort, boys. Less than half an hour, *pueri*, and we are safe.'

Bruteddius turned and pointed ahead. There, curving across the Kindly Sea, was a solid bank of fog.

XVIII

The *Armata* slipped into the clammy embrace of the fog. Instantly, the temperature dropped. The sweat ran cold between the men's shoulderblades. Their breath plumed. Wraiths of mist slipped inboard past the bow post, snaked down among the benches. A pall of steam rose from the rowers, adding to the gloom. It was getting hard to see from one end of the boat to the other.

A murmur of tired voices from the oarsmen; the stroke became ragged, desultory. 'Silence!' Bruteddius's voice was pitched to carry, but not far. 'Not safe yet, *pueri*, just a little more. Easy pressure.'

The *Armata* ghosted through an opaque world. The creak and splash of the oars, the soft gurgle of water. The fog pearled on everything: deck, oars, rails. It dripped from the crew's beards.

Ballista watched Bruteddius staring over the stern into the fog. All the officers, everyone watched Bruteddius. Nothing visible, no sound of pursuit. Neither meant anything.

Bruteddius softly called for the purser. '*Pentekontarchos*, break out the food and water.' The officer padded away, the mist swirling behind him. 'Where is the *naupegos*?'

'Here, *Dominus*,' said the shipwright.

'Bring up the thin papyrus rope and all the tallow.' Bruteddius did not glance at the man, never looked inboard.

'*Dominus*.'

Under the eye of the *pentekontarchos*, the rear watch of the deck crew was piling wrapped bundles and amphorae on the quarterdeck.

Bruteddius turned to survey his ship. '*Thalamians*, cease rowing, oars inboard.' Gratefully, the rowers on the lowest level obeyed. '*Pentekontarchos*, feed the *thalamians* first.' Bruteddius turned back to the wall of fog beyond the sternpost.

Bread, both soggy and slightly stale, a lump of cheese, a raw onion, and a long drink of heavily watered wine; not having eaten since dawn, the *thalamians* wolfed it down. It was gone in seconds.

'*Zygians*, cease rowing, oars inboard.' The procedure was repeated with the middle level, leaving the top level, the elite *thranites*, rowing the boat on their own.

The *naupegos* announced the things were to hand.

'Good, shipwright,' Bruteddius said. '*Zygians* and *thalmians*, strip.'

Ballista and the other passengers watched, bemused, as the two lower levels of rowers stripped off their things with no question or complaint. The hundred or so men sat naked or in undergarments, most shivering with cold and exhaustion. Bruteddius glanced over his shoulder and smiled. 'Good, *pueri*. Now muffle your oars with your tunics; tie them tight with bits of rope. Grease the oarports.'

The cloying smell of rancid mutton fat wafted as the men began to rub the tallow into the leather sleeves which kept the water out of the oarports. It mingled with the stench from the bilges: stale water and sweat, human waste. No oarsman had left his bench for hours. They had had to relieve themselves where they sat. It had not been good for the men on the lower levels. They reeked of piss and shit. Ballista felt sick in the choking miasma.

'*Thalamians*, oars out. Gentle pressure. Row. *Thranites*, oars inboard; eat, then do the other things.'

'What do we do?' Ballista addressed the question to Bruteddius's back.

The *trierarch* tipped his head to one side, took his time answering. When he did, he did not look round. 'We could continue on our present course: three hundred miles of sea room to the Island of Achilles or the mouths of the Danube. It has the advantage that the Goths will not think we will do that. It has the disadvantage that, unless an easterly wind gets up, we would never get there. We have no more food, only enough water to last until the morning.'

Bruteddius paused, tipped his head to the other side. 'We could head north: a long day's row to the Crimea. But what sort of reception would we get?'

'Come.' Felix broke in. 'It is not the heroic age. They do not sacrifice strangers there any more. The king of the Crimean Bosphorus is a loyal client of Rome.'

'The Goths got the *liburnian* somewhere,' said Bruteddius thoughtfully.

Before Felix could reply, Ballista spoke. 'When the Borani first raided into the Black Sea, the time Successianus defended Pityus, they forced the cities of the north-west and the king . . . some of the subjects of the king of the Crimean Bosphorus to provide them with ships.'

'Or we could run south,' Bruteddius continued. 'We might run into the two Goths who were off to larboard. If we got there, would we be safe? The nearest detachment of auxiliaries is in

Heraclea, and precious few of them. It depends how badly the Goths want us.'

Again, Bruteddius paused. Ballista leant on the stern rail next to him. The *trierarch's* face was very still, but his eyes did not stop moving, probing the impenetrable fog. 'We could stay here, sit quiet,' Bruteddius continued. 'Hope that either the Goths pass us in the fog or give up when they see it. The men are exhausted. They could rest. But, if the Goths came on us, with no way on the boat, we would be a sitting target.'

This time Bruteddius was silent for longer.

'And our final option?' Ballista asked.

'Our final option is to turn back, try to run silently through them in the fog and the night, get to a safe harbour in Sinope, or even all the way to Trapezus. Best to try and take on water and food somewhere along the coast and then press on to Trapezus. There are troops there.'

'And that is what we will do?' said Ballista.

'That is what we will do,' said Bruteddius.

Half an hour, and the *Armata* was facing east again. During this time, the *thranites* had rested, but now they had to return to their work. The top level consisted of the chosen men, the best oarsmen in the boat. Hard men, nut brown; it was said they could row from dawn to dawn with just a sip or two of water. Now that claim would be put to the test. Their hard, callused hands played out the long, smooth shafts of fir. One rank of blades would make less noise. The *thranites* would row with more control, more quietly than the *zygians* or *thalamians*. It had to be them. They took pride in it. A soft word from the rowing master and they began. Slowly, the *Armata* got under way.

It was near sunset. Somewhere behind, the sun was going down. Only a faint lightness in the billowing clouds of fog, a strange hint of refracted colour, indicated the west.

The great galley slid forward. No pipes, no songs; the *thranites* kept time instinctively, watching the backs of the men in front. Catch, pull, twist and lift. A slight swell had got up from aft, gently lifting the stern, running under the keel. Nothing to trouble the *thranites*. The wings of oars rose and fell with the quietest of splashes. The ram nosed through the water with a restrained, sibilant hiss.

Ballista stood in the stern with Bruteddius. The *trierarch*, legs splayed, rocked as one with the movement of his boat. His eyes were never still. They flicked from the *thranites* to the prow, where the bow officer was leaning far forward, watching, listening.

The fog was thick, tangible. Yet every so often, a space cleared, like a glade in a forest. The boat pushed through, back into the gloom.

Bauto brought Ballista a small cup of unmixed wine. The Frisian was meant to be Calgacus's servant, but he and Wulfstan tended to Ballista and the old Caledonian indiscriminately. They were good boys.

As he sipped the alcohol, Ballista looked down the length of the long, narrow craft. Below the *thranites*, the other rowers were asleep on their benches, a hundred or so men huddled in strange attitudes. Beyond exhaustion, they lay, limbs overlapping, like animals in a malodorous den.

A seagull swooped from nowhere, its cry harsh and shocking. Bauto jumped. Ballista put a hand on his shoulder, smiled a reassurance he did not feel. The bird was gone.

The *Armata* slipped wraithlike through the coils of clinging vapour. Ballista's eyes itched with tiredness. Time had lost all meaning. It was darker. The rhythm of the *thranites* was hypnotic. They could have been rowing for hours.

The brazen note of a horn rang out. Horrible in its immediacy, it came from somewhere not far off the larboard bow. Everyone froze. Even the *thranites* faltered. A sharp, urgent whisper from the rowing master amidships, and the rhythm was resumed.

Another horn answered, then another, both off to starboard. Behind Ballista, a man sniffed loudly. He swung round to cuff him to silence. It was Felix. Ballista did nothing.

More horns, seemingly all around. Allfather, they were in the middle of the enemy. Ballista looked at the others on the quarter-deck. Everyone was unnaturally still. Maximus's eyes were shut; he was listening. Bruteddius glanced back; a tight smile. The boat glided on.

A disembodied voice floated through the fog. Ballista held his breath. The creak and splash of the oars was hideously strident. The voice came again; muffled, a little off to the left.

'Cease rowing.' Only the nearest oarsmen could hear Bruteddius. Those further away followed their lead. The boat's momentum carried her on.

Another voice, much nearer, to the right. It was German; a question, the words indistinct.

Ballista's breathing was shallow, panting. He was gripping the sternpost tight, sweating. Around him, the faces of the others were sheened with moisture. Their heads turned this way and that, peering at things they could not see.

The voice came again from the right, nearer still: a hail, a man's name.

Even the helmsman was trembling. No one was sleeping on the lower benches now. All the men kept glancing at Bruteddius. The *trierarch* was rock still. If the hail was aimed at them, it was over. The boat was losing way.

Off the starboard bow, something darker than the mist, more solid. A hundred feet, no more: the upswept stern of a galley – the *liburnian*. The *Armata* was nearly dead in the water.

222

A Gothic voice returned the call; clean over the *Armata*, from further away to the left.

The horns started up again, the notes eddying through the fog.

Bruteddius padded to the nearest oarsmen. He spoke so low that Ballista and the others by the helmsman did not hear. Drops of water fell from the oars as the *thranites* glanced over their shoulders at the men behind, readied themselves. Bruteddius, nodding calmly, gestured to the two rowers on either side closest to him. They looked at each other, began the stroke. The others copied.

The splash as the blades bit the surface, the creak of wood, the slosh of water. Surely the Goths must hear. One stroke, a second. No outcry yet. The many thousand wooden joints sighed as the ship gathered way. Still no alarm. Someone was muttering a prayer. Another hushed him.

Yet more horns, their piercing volume a blessing from the gods. The dark, solid shape to the right faded aft. In moments, the fog blanketed the sounds of the horns. Ballista drew an almost sobbing breath. The *Armata* sailed on into the opaque, dark night.

XIX

'Ships astern, three of them.'

Ballista surfaced from a dead sleep, trying to understand.

Maximus was shaking his shoulder. 'Goths, less than half a mile away.'

Ballista could barely move. He had slept in his mail coat on the hard wooden deck. Maximus offered him a hand. He saw Wulfstan and Bauto helping Calgacus to his feet. Hippothous, shaven head glinting, was already up.

A breeze had got up in the west. It was tearing away the last shreds of the fog. The sun had just risen. In its raking light, the enemy was in clear sight. Long, low vessels, a prow at either end – unmistakably, northern longboats.

How had they got there? Last night, after the too close encounter with the *liburnian*, the *Armata* had rowed on for another three hours; the first just the *thranites* pulling, then they had rested while the other two levels took over. They should have been well clear. It might be a trick of the current. Certainly, inshore, yesterday, it had run strongly to the east. There again, the Goths might have separated, scouring the sea for their prey. Ballista scanned the horizon through 360 degrees: no other ships anywhere.

A *hoom* sound rolled across from the Gothic ships: their warriors giving voice. Silhouetted by the newborn sun, there was no chance the *Armata* could have escaped detection. The Goths were putting out their oars, gathering way. Two of them hauled round to set towards the *Armata*. The other veered away towards the west, going to get the rest of the wolfpack.

Bruteddius and his officers were hazing the crew back to their stations. The oarsmen were moving stiffly, like old, tired men. No one ever wants to spend a night at sea in the cramped and damp discomfort of a war galley. 'Out oars, prepare to row, medium pressure. Row.' The rowing master's pipe squealed. The blades broke the surface: not too ragged, given the circumstances.

Horns blared from the northern boats. No longer deadened by the fog, the notes skimmed far out across the sea, summoning their kinsmen to the chase. Yesterday evening, the horns had masked the sound of the *Armata's* escape; today they were likely to bring its doom. This had the makings of another long, bad day.

The *Armata* was built for speed. Under oars, she could leave almost anything afloat far behind in her wake. But not when her rowers were tired, hungry and thirsty; not when they had not stepped off the boat for more than twenty-four hours; not when they had not eaten since the previous evening.

The oarsmen sat on sodden cushions. They wore soaking tunics – they had unmuffled their blades in the night. The salt had chafed their skin, their calluses were raw, bleeding. Below them, their own waste slopped and stank. Despite it all, the banks of oars, if they did not rise and fall quite as one, did nothing too dissimilar.

Under Bruteddius's order, the rowing master kept them only at medium or even light pressure. It was designed to preserve what little energy they still possessed. However, it did not make the Goths fall away astern. A little over three hundred yards of undulating green water separated the *Armata* from the longboats.

Bruteddius, as ever, stood near the helm. The swell had increased. Bruteddius moved as one with the motion of his ship. His eyes shifted endlessly; measuring, calculating. Behind his beard, he was haggard. Ballista wondered if he had slept at all.

The purser was summoned. Bruteddius ordered the last reserves of water to be rationed out; each man aboard to get the same meagre measure.

Next, Bruteddius called the shipwright to his side. 'When the men have drunk, clear the passengers out of the way as far as you can, and step the masts.' Like all the crew, the *naupegos* was under military discipline, yet he appeared just a little uncertain. Bruteddius looked hard at him. 'A storm is getting up in the west.' He smiled. 'Either it will save us, or kill us.'

A salute. *We will do what is ordered, and at every command we will be ready.*

The full deck crew, aided by a few of the able-bodied passengers pressed into service, unlashed the mainmast from its horizontal position on the deck and heaved the long, heavy trunk of pine into place to lift. They squared off the endless ropes and tackle, then hauled and hauled: slowly, slowly – with more than one heart-stopping shift and sway – the mast was coaxed upright and its heel slid home into its tabernacle.

'Rig double stays,' shouted Bruteddius. He turned to Ballista. 'The mast can take punishment. I selected her myself: a fine, straight tree, from a good, sunny aspect.' Then louder, to a wider audience: 'Sway up the yard.'

Against the squeal of pulleys and the hammering of mallets, Felix spoke. 'I have stores for myself and my *familia* in the cabin. They should be distributed to the men.'

The old senator's offer was accepted most gladly. And so it was that, there in the wastes of the Kindly Sea, the crew, the sweepings of the backstreets of Alexandria, Antioch and Smyrna, many of them brought up on slave bread, were fed by hand all the delicacies the *imperium* and beyond had to offer. Biscuits, soft and melting, a world apart from ship's biscuit or the *buccellatum* of the army, smoked eel from Spain, artichoke hearts in honey vinegar from Sicily, stems of silphium from who knew where, apricot halves in grape syrup ... one and all vanished into hungry mouths, delighted rough, untutored pallets.

Shared among two hundred, there was only a mouthful or two each, but it helped. Certainly, it raised spirits. There were smiles, even song – a croaking version of an old favourite about an unusually accomplished girl from Corinth: oh, the things she could do with your prick.

'I do not understand it at all,' said Felix almost plaintively. 'Barbarians, especially northern barbarians, are not noted for their persistence. But these Scythians seemingly would follow us across the Styx.'

'They know what we carry.' Bruteddius said, then roared, 'Tighten that fucking brace.'

Ballista and Maximus exchanged a look, one of total understanding, complete with a small, knowing smile. As Ballista looked away, he caught the eye of Hippothous. There was a strange light there. Of course, thought Ballista, you too know all about the bloodfeuds; if the Goths are Borani or Tervingi, the gold and silver, all the diplomatic gifts on board, are just bread, not the relish. What could you do? Wherever you go, old enemies will find you.

'Sponges, have we got any sponges, *Pentekontarchos*?'

The purser hastened to assure his captain they had plenty.

'Get the deckhands to wash down the men on the benches as

they row. Start at the top level. The *pueri* will feel better when they are not quite so covered in shit. And get the pump working; try to get some of that filthy water out of the bilges.'

The sun was getting higher, sparkling in the spray. Through it the unsmiling chase ran on. Like some punishment in Hades, ever labouring, never succeeding, the crew of the *Armata* drove her through the water, but never could escape their pursuers.

Bruteddius went into close conversation with the shipwright and the local pilot. There was much gesticulating, pointing, shaking and nodding of heads. At the end of it, the *naupegos* went off and returned with men carrying a second set of steering oars. These, with some considerable difficulty and much voluble swearing, were run out through the rear of the outriggers on both sides of the ship at the level of the topmost rowers. The tillers from these came in at right angles to where a second helmsman now took station in front of the first. This done, the *naupegos* and his men crawled around fitting hanging weather screens to the outside of the ship that were intended to give some measure of shelter to the *thranites*, who, although they had a deck over their heads, were otherwise exposed on the sides.

After inspecting the new arrangements, Bruteddius climbed some way up the sternpost and gazed aft. Eventually, he climbed stiffly down, and addressed the senior passengers on the quarterdeck.

'*Domini*, you see the cloud behind us over our starboard quarter. Most likely, it has formed over the high land behind Sinope. If that is right, we drifted further east in the night than we thought. With the Goths where they are, now there is no chance of us making Sinope.'

Those assembled received this in silence.

'The wind has moved to the north-west. The *Argestes*, the 'Cleanser', as it is known, is strengthening. Maybe it will 'cleanse' us of these Goths.' Bruteddius smiled with no great humour. 'The *Argestes* will blow a storm. The second, outer steering oars are there to help in a high sea. When it hits, we will run before it under sail. But we will try to keep it a touch on our larboard quarter. We do not want to be driven on to the coast to the east of Sinope. It is inhospitable, a fifty-mile bight of shifting shoals and banks. The local pilot and the *periplous* I studied both say the first safe harbour is Naustathmos. But it is in the marshes of the estuary of the Halys. Better we try for Amisus. It is only some fifteen miles further, and has an easy approach. Failing that, a little beyond, there is Ankon on the headland of the Daiantos Plain.'

'And failing that?' Ballista asked.

'Trapezus.'

'How far?'

'Better none of us think of that.' Bruteddius went back to studying his ship and the sea.

The storm did not come in one rush. It built gradually, wave on wave, the wind keening higher in the rigging. The fore and aft lift were increasing. The waves were showing white. The rowers were having trouble catching their strokes. Bruteddius, ignoring the pleading looks of his officers and men, bided his time.

Ballista, one arm holding the sternpost, the other firm around Wulfstan and Bauto, watched the Goths astern. The longboats were only about two hundred yards behind. They were rising and falling on the waves like seagulls. At times, they were completely lost from view in the troughs between the rollers. These were big – all the way from the mouth of the Borysthenes; three, four hundred miles of sea room to gather themselves, to build up into something terrifying.

'Are we going to die?' Wulfstan had to shout to be heard.

'We are not sailing on a mat. Old Bruteddius knows what he is doing.' Ballista squeezed the boys harder. 'The goddess Ran will not get us with her drowning net today.' He did what he could to convey reassurance.

Maximus, timing the roll, slid to his side. 'The Goths are gaining.'

Ballista flicked his head to get his long hair out of his eyes. 'There will be no fighting in this. Help me out of this mail shirt.' He released Wulfstan and Bauto. 'You boys hold on tight to the rail.'

Soon the waves were breaking and tumbling. The oarsmen were fighting for purchase on the broken sea. The deck was streaming. One of the *thalamians* was carried up from the depths of the ship. He was twitching, his face a bloody mess. He had missed his stroke; somehow the metal counterweight on his oar had smashed into his face.

'Deck crew,' Bruteddius bellowed above the elements, 'on my command, unfurl the mainsail – only a little canvas, steady on the brails. Rowing master, when she draws, on my second command, oars inboard; *zygians* and *thalamians*, all the way, seal the oarports; *thranites*, leave just the blades outside the weather screen.'

Bruteddius, moving easily across the wildly pitching deck, went to the rear helm. He placed his hands on the tillers, next to those of the helmsman. Braced, feeling the run of his ship, he gazed back over his shoulder towards the prow.

'Deck crew, now!'

The sail dropped, snapped and bellied out, tight as a drum in an instant. The mast groaned.

'Enough!'

The deck crew, leaning back, feet slipping, struggling for balance, wrestled the brails secure. There was just a few feet of sail showing. The ship shied like a racehorse.

'Rowing master, oars inboard!'

The poles rattled home, and the *Armata* twisted, straightened and forged ahead with a new urgency.

'Helmsmen, bring the wind a touch to larboard.'

The waves rushed under the high, curving stern of the *trireme*, tipped her nose down, lifted her. The long, delicate ship rode at a slant up the great face of water. At the top, she hung for a moment among the flying spume, ram high, then wriggled and slid down the far side. Again and again the threat was surmounted, the inhuman power negated.

'Oarsmen, lie on your benches. *Thranites*, listen for orders. More hands to the pump. Bow officer, get some men bailing.' A bigger wave brought Bruteddius to his knees. He was up in a moment. He bawled the traditional cry of seafarers: 'Alexander lives and reigns!'

Ballista had been in a galley caught in heavy weather before – the *Clementia*, out in the Adriatic, north of Corycra. He understood the risks. So many things could turn the boat side on to the waves – too much water in the bilges, rushing uncontrolled, making the boat unstable, unresponsive to the helm; an exposed rank of oars, caught by a wave, acting like a lever; the ram driven too deep, becoming a forward rudder; a broken steering oar – and caught side on, she would roll, and that would be an end to it. Bruteddius was doing everything he could. The pump and bailing. The double steering oars. Just enough sail to give the vessel steerage. The oars inboard, but the upper rank poised for a desperate attempt to claw her head around.

You could not fault Bruteddius's efforts. But they might well not be enough. A terrible wave could break over the ship, swamp her. If that happened, no despairing efforts would prevent her, sooner or later, turning broadside to the sea. The *Armata* might fail to ride a huge wave. Not reaching the crest, she would pitch poll; upended, stern over bow. If such a terrible wave came, it could simply drive the ship, ram first, down into the depths. That would be best – it would be the quickest.

The storm buffeted at their ears, yet not so loud they could not hear the groans and unnatural thumps as thousands of wooden joints flexed and ground together, not so deafening they were not aware of the high thrum of the rigging, and the roar and crash of the waves.

'*Dominus*, the water down below is rising. I think the *hypozomata* is working loose.'

'No,' Bruteddius reassured the shipwright, 'it is just the seams moving. Nail a patch over anywhere it is coming in too fast – and get more men bailing; keep changing the shifts on the pump.'

The *naupegos* reeled away below deck, clutching at the woodwork as he negotiated the steps.

'What is a *hypo– hypozoma–*?' Maximus asked.

'Nothing of importance,' replied Bruteddius.

The air was full of water, the sea raging, but still the ship swam; sliding, twisting, bucking beneath their feet, but she still swam.

'Hercules' hairy arse!'

The *Armata* ran into something. She was smashed sideways. Across the deck men were knocked off their feet, sent sliding down towards the starboard rail.

'All hands, larboard,' bellowed Bruteddius. 'Now!'

Ballista did not think. He skidded around the corner of the cabin, and set off between it and the back of the rear helmsman. The deck lurched up in front of him. He was thrown flat. He was slipping backwards in a deluge of water. His foot hit something, broke the momentum. His fingers found purchase in a join in the deck. Wulfstan was slithering past. Ballista put out a hand, grabbed the boy by the scruff of his tunic.

'Larboard now!' Bruteddius's voice was cracked. 'The next one will turn us over.'

A few steps and Ballista's chest collided with the rail. Locking his forearms under it, he gripped for dear life. A body banged in on either side, another from behind.

Looking up, Ballista saw that a mountain of water was heading straight for him. The third of the rogue triple waves towered over the boat.

Ballista forgot to breathe before the impact. Saltwater forced its way into his mouth, up his nose. It tried to rip him from the rail. The *Armata* was tipping. Ballista tried to breathe out. He failed. The boat reared still higher.

Ballista's body forced him to try and breathe. Nothing but water, choking, down into his lungs, drowning him. The boat literally hung in the balance.

Allfather, this is it, thought Ballista. I am going to die.

Then wonderful, sweet air. Gulping, coughing, Ballista felt the rail start to fall. Slowly at first, then faster, the *Armata* began to right herself.

'Rowers, back to your benches.' Bruteddius was indestructible, a thing of nature. 'Balance the boat.'

From below, the sounds of the starboard oarsmen stumbling, bumping to their places – a herd of weird migrating animals.

All around Ballista, cheering, faces with insane grins. Someone was thumping him on the back. Saved! Saved! Gods be praised!

The stern of the boat lifted on a normal wave.

'Man overboard!' The shout came from the stern. Ballista staggered towards it.

Hippothous was pointing. The *Armata* was sliding up the wave – nothing to be seen but water.

The boat crested the wave, and there was a small head in the water. Arms wide, thrashing in a wild crawl.

'Bauto!' Wulfstan screamed.

The Frisian boy was going up the front of the following wave. He went over the top.

Ballista hugged Wulfstan to him, as tight as his own child.

The *Armata* slid up the wave, hung on its peak. And Bauto was gone. Nothing but empty, pitiless water.

'The Goths! They are gone.'

It meant nothing to Ballista. There was no room in his thoughts for anything but a small boy lost in a wild sea.

The storm went as it came – gradually. All the long day, and most of the following night, the *Armata* ran, as far as could be told, a little east of south-east.

Dawn found the ship crawling past the mole into the miraculous safe harbour of Amisus. She was leaking like a sieve. Several planks sprung, the two great ropes of the *hypozomata* that girdled the hull and held her together were loose. The water had risen past the bilges. The pump and bailing barely held it at bay from the lower benches. Only the natural buoyancy of a wooden boat was stopping her sinking.

The human cost could have been worse. Five broken limbs, three arms, two legs. Several bad cuts and rope burns. Two men knocked senseless. Just one dead – a young boy drowned in the immensity of the Kindly Sea.

PART THREE
The Mountains of Prometheus

(The Caucasus, Summer–Autumn, AD262)

Slim indeed are our hopes, if we must entrust our safe return to women.

–Apollonius of Rhodes, *Argonautica*, 3, c. 488–9

XX

When the sea fret lifted, there, fine over the starboard bow, were the Caucasus mountains. Forty, fifty or more miles away, the immense green-grey slopes thrust up and, far behind them, cloud-topped, the jagged white peaks of the mountain wall. They were, thought Ballista, a fitting place for a high god to chain an immortal traitor.

Ballista had crossed the Alps several times, and as a young man he had served in the Atlas, but those mountains were as nothing to this eastern range. He could see why some men held that the Caucasus might stretch as far as India. Somewhere high in that wilderness of rock and snow, he had to seduce a king from his Persian inclination and cajole him back into friendship with Rome. Somewhere up there was a grim pass he had to defend from the savage northern nomads. It was the far edge of the world; a sort of armed exile.

'Arrian was right,' Hippothous said. 'The Phasis river does have a strange colour.'

Ballista looked. Mud carried down by the great river of Colchis stained the sea in a wide yellowish fan. The waters of the Phasis

237

were indeed light with a tawny shade, just as the bookish governor of Cappadocia had written more than a century before. For these Greeks and Romans, everything was seen through a filter of literary texts.

The *Armata* turned and nudged in towards Phasis. The last leg of the furthermost run had been slow. They had taken eight days at Amisus repairing the *trireme* after the storm. It had been a miserable time: hard, dirty work tightening the *hypozomata* around the vessel, making sound the sprung planks, caulking the seams, splicing and replacing damaged rigging, cleaning the fouled bilges. The spirits of the passengers as well as the labouring crew had been oddly oppressed by the fate of one young barbarian slave boy. The death on shore of one of the unconscious crewmen had passed almost unnoticed.

Two days out from Amisus, they had docked in the neat manmade harbour below the towers of Trapezus and a smoke-blackened temple to Hadrian and Rome, where a battered statue of the deified emperor pointed out to sea. They had gone ashore. The fold of his toga over his head, Felix had sacrificed an ox, inspected its entrails – nothing untoward – and poured a libation. Trapezus was the headquarters of the Black Sea fleet, and the most important garrison town for the army at the eastern end of the sea. The next morning, the consular, for all the world as if he were the governor of Cappadocia, had inspected the ships, the troops, their weapons, the walls, the trench, the sick, the muster rolls, and the food supplies. All were sadly depleted. Only a few years earlier, the Classis Pontica had boasted no fewer than forty warships here; there had been some ten thousand local troops as well as many regulars. But then the northmen had come, the garrison had failed in its duty and courage and the Borani had sacked the city. Now there were but ten *liburnians* – four of them laid up – and just three units of soldiers. The two units of local infantry,

Numeri I and II Trapezountioon, numbered no more than a hundred and fifty men each, and the cavalry regulars, Ala II Gallorum, about two hundred, even including those absent without leave and the ill.

The subsequent two days, a similar story had played out. Just down the coast at the fort of Hyssou Limen, the old, proud Cohors Apuleia Civium Romanorum Ysiporto had only two hundred and fifty men with the standards all told. Eighty miles to the east, things were yet worse at the city of Asparus. In the glory days of Arrian, Asparus had been home to five cohorts. Now Cohors II Claudiana and Cohors III Ulpia Patraeorum Milliaria Equitata Sagittariorum, despite a notional compliment of around fifteen hundred soldiers, could put just three hundred men on the parade ground. There was no reason to suppose things would be better at Phasis.

They entered the estuary slowly. The Phasis ceaselessly created new, shifting mud flats. A man in the bow swung the lead, calling back the soundings. When they were over the main bar, Felix poured out unmixed wine into the river, a libation to Earth, the divine genius of the emperor Gallienus, the gods who inhabited this land and the spirits of the dead heroes.

The *trireme* backed water to the military jetty. Longshoremen caught the ropes, made her fast. The boarding ladder was run out. Headed by the venerable senator Felix, the mission to the Caucasus clattered off the ship. Bruteddius called farewell. Five days before the *kalends* of June, twenty-six since they had weighed anchor at Byzantium, and the outward voyage of the latter-day Argonauts was over.

The prefect in command of the imperial troops greeted them. A Spaniard of a certain age, he had a careworn, placatory demeanour: the *Vir Clarissimus* and his esteemed *comites* had been expected much earlier – it had been necessary to return the soldiers of the welcoming party to other duties – they were terribly overstretched – he very much hoped the *Vir Clarissimus* would understand, that no one would take offence.

Felix, urbanely but firmly, cut through the apologia: all would be splendid, quite splendid, if their baggage could be conveyed to their quarters, and if lunch was in hand; nothing like a return to *terra firma* to give one an appetite.

'Just so, *Dominus*, just so.'

The prefect conducted them through the *vicus*. Ballista noted with approval the well-built brick wall and deep ditch which protected the landward approach to the settlement of veterans and traders. Better still, the fort itself had a double ditch before its walls and artillery visible on its towers. The state of the garrison remained to be discovered, but it was worth remembering that Phasis was one of the few localities that had not fallen in either of the great raids by the Borani.

The headquarters building was modest, and the lunch in keeping with its surroundings. When they were still on the hard-boiled eggs and pickled fish, one of Felix's bodyguards came and whispered in his ear. The consular's face flushed and assumed an appearance of *dignitas* outraged.

'Prefect,' Felix snapped, 'your men may have committed some dereliction, but the soldiers with me have done nothing to deserve punishment.'

Ballista's sympathy went out to the prefect, who appeared both baffled and anxious.

'Millet!' Felix said. 'My men are being served millet.'

Understanding dawned on the prefect's face, but not ease. 'Oh no, not a punishment, nothing of the sort.'

Felix continued to look like thunder.

'No slight intended,' the prefect floundered on. 'A forced measure, supplies of wheat have not been shipped to the garrison since . . . since the . . .' He seemed to be struggling to find the right words to describe the recent years of continuous usurpation, civil war and repeated barbarian triumph. 'Since the troubles,' he concluded lamely.

Now it was the elderly senator's turn for confusion. 'Why not purchase wheat locally?'

'We do, we do, but little is grown in Colchis. It is prohibitively expensive. Although, of course, we would never serve anything else to a *Vir Clarissimus* and his *comites*.'

'Then requisition the stuff.'

The prefect looked as if he were going to raise some objection, but did not. 'Of course, *Dominus*.'

Over the apples and nuts, Felix announced a desire to view the monuments and places associated with the heroic age, with Jason and the Argonauts, with princess Medea and her bloody-minded father Aeetes. So strong was his desire, he would set out straight after lunch.

'Of course, *Dominus*.'

And when he returned he would both inspect the garrison and conduct a *lustrum* of the expedition.

The Spanish prefect looked far from happy at this.

Felix smiled. 'Have no fears, Prefect, I am fully aware of the difficulties faced by commanders of far-flung forces in these difficult times.'

The prefect did not appear mollified. '*Dominus*, it is the *lustrum*.'

'No, no,' Felix said. 'I will, of course, reimburse you the price of the sacrificial beasts – only those our traditions require: a boar, a ram and a bull. You will be put to no expense.'

'*Dominus*.' Clearly the prefect was still unhappy. Ballista had no idea where the problem lay, but he suspected it was not about money.

'Make sure the attendants with them have propitious names –

and that there are plenty of musicians, all soldiers, or suitably martial instruments.'

As soon as the *Vir Clarissimus* had sipped the last of his *conditum*, they made a start. A local guide led them first to the temple of the Phasian goddess on the headland. Here, they were shown two anchors – one iron, one stone – both said to be from the *Argo*. Next, they were led across the heavily wooded Plain of Circe. Walking the sun-dappled path overhung by a profusion of elms and willows, they all felt a pleasurable frisson of horror. Just as they had been led to expect, from the uppermost branches hung any number of untreated ox-hides, each containing its corpse.

The guide laughed like a conjurer who had completed his trick. 'It is an abomination to us to cremate or bury a man. But do not think us barbarians, do not think we do not honour our mother the Earth – we give her the bodies of women.'

'Everywhere custom is king.' Felix sonorously quoted the famous line of Herodotus. This was the sort of exoticism hoped for at the edge of the world.

Ballista reflected that the Sassanid Persians, as Zoroastrians, exposed their dead too; men and women.

A brisk walk, the path damp underfoot, and they came to the palace of Aeetes. They stepped through the broad gates in the columned walls. There in the shady courtyard, the guide pointed out the bronze bulls crafted by the god Hephaistos and the four miraculous springs. The former no longer moved – indeed, they were now all bronze – and fire no longer belched from their mouths, and the channels of the latter no longer ran with milk, wine, unguent and water, but Felix seemed most impressed. Apart from a prurient interest in the bedroom of Medea – Ballista caught Maximus sniffing the sheets – the rest was less arresting; less opulent than many a senator's villa on the Bay of Naples.

A walkway of wooden boards led them down to the river. They passed the temple of Hecate. 'Think,' the guide urged them. 'The priestess Medea trod on that very threshold.' Felix nodded, struck by the worn stone. Ballista was less convinced they would have decorated temples or palaces with Corinthian columns in the age of heroes before the Trojan war.

A suitably Stygian ferry conveyed them across the river. They crossed the Plain of Ares, the water again squelching under their boots, until they came to the sacred grove of oaks and the vine-tangled temple of Phrixus. 'Nothing to fear now, ha, ha,' the guide prattled. 'The terrible *draco*, the serpent's teeth which bring forth the armed men from the soil, all vanquished by your predecessor Jason from the west. Of course, his life would have ended here if not for the love of the princess Medea.'

They studied for a time a particularly venerable oak, on which, the guide assured them, the golden fleece had hung. Felix declared it time to return. He resolutely declined invitations to view the *polis*, its *emporion* or anything else modern. The primitive ferry rowed them back to the *vicus* and the fort.

There were two units stationed at Phasis, the Vexillatio Fasiana and the Equites Singulares. Both were notionally composed of select soldiers drawn from other units from across the province of Cappadocia. In reality, they were little more than a local militia. Even on the small *campus martius* their inadequate numbers were evident: perhaps three hundred in all. The prefect hurried to inform the *Vir Clarissimus* and his *comites* that another hundred men, fifty from each, were upriver in the fort of Sarapanis.

Felix was at his most gracious – he was certain that the detachment was as well turned out as the soldiers in front of him; a most creditable sight in a difficult age; sharp in their movements, resolute in their demeanour; it spoke most highly of their officers. As the prefect and his under officers relaxed, Felix mentioned the *lustrum*.

'All is ready, *Dominus*.' The prefect looked as if he were about to be thrown into the arena.

'What is it? Are the animals not ready?'

'No, *Dominus*, they are all here.'

'Then what? Trouble finding musicians or men with the right sort of name?'

'It is the ram, *Dominus*.'

'Providing its entrails show the favour of Mars, it will not matter if it is not too good-looking a beast outwardly.'

The Spanish officer took a deep breath. '*Dominus*, I do not want you to think that we have in any way deserted the traditions of Rome, or her religious rites, which have given her *imperium* without end. Although stationed in a far-off place, we are soldiers of Rome. We renew our *sacramentum* every year. We will do what is ordered, and at every command we will be ready.'

'What is it?' Felix said, not unkindly.

'The majority of our men are drawn from the local population; have been as far back as our muster rolls go. It is against the customs of Colchis to sacrifice rams. It is the same in Iberia and Albania, throughout the region of the Caucasus. Tacitus mentioned it.'

Felix considered this seriously. 'Our expedition has been dogged by misfortune – Gothic pirates, storms – we have lost time and men. The gods have not been well disposed towards us. A new beginning is necessary. A *lustrum* is the time-honoured way for Romans to supplicate the gods in such a case. To alter the ritual might offend the natural gods of Rome. While I have no wish to offend our subjects, we have our *mandata* – Rome must come first. Let the *lustrum* be performed.'

To brazen tunes, the bull, the boar and the contentious ram

were brought out and led around the members of the expedition. Three circuits from their violent end.

Ballista thought about the elderly senator Felix. He was no more hidebound than most of his order. He had been faced with a difficult choice. He had made his decision. It was not the one Ballista would have made. But Ballista, unlike Felix, was far from convinced the natural gods of Rome existed, or any gods at all.

XXI

On the fifth day, the *kalends* of June, the expedition had divided. Felix sailed for the north-eastern shores of the Black Sea to pursue his diplomacy with the two kings of Abasgia and their clients the longbeards and the lice-eaters. As the *Armata* had already returned straightaway to Byzantium bound then for the west, the consular had been obliged to charter a merchant vessel. The best the put-upon prefect at Phasis could provide was a small *liburnian* as escort.

Hippothous noticed that, as soon as the self-appointed embodiment of old Roman values and virtue had left, the spirits of the others lifted. As a Hellene, Hippothous could understand. A little conspicuous western antique *mos maiorum* and *virtus* could go a long way, but there was something inherently wearing in constantly, if silently, being made aware that you fell somewhat short of the ideal.

The remainder of the expedition was to travel together up the river Phasis as far as a fort called Sarapanis, said to be set in a range of hills on the border between Colchis and Iberia at the very limit of navigation. This involved embarking themselves and their baggage on several native boats. Hippothous was most unimpressed with these so-called *camarae*. Long and narrow, they were dirty and uncomfortable. There was no cover; far from having a cabin, they were actually undecked. Each had benches for thirty rowers. The *camarae* were so cramped that, although the expedition now totalled just eighteen persons, they had to distribute themselves and their possessions across five of these squalid craft. And there was something more distinctly unsettling about these *camarae*. Clinker-built, they had a prow and steering oars at either end. To Hippothous's eye, they looked like nothing so much as small versions of the longboats of the Goths and Borani – hardly an auspicious thing.

At first, the river Phasis was very broad, wonderfully calm – like smoked glass – after the Kindly Sea. On either bank, beyond a thick screen of reeds, was low, marshy primeval forest. Everything was very green, very flat. The air was humid, misty. At clearer moments, the Caucasus loomed on the left.

The river meandered in great sweeps, little archipelagos of sodden, uninhabitable islands in the bends. Nothing but the splash of the oars, the water singing down the sides of the boats, and the endless croaking of innumerable frogs. However, not all was peace. A constant impediment, if not actual danger, was the great lashed-together rafts of logs the natives floated down to sell in the city for shipbuilding. Again and again, the *camarae* hurriedly had to pull to the banks to avoid collisions with the unwieldy masses of timber. It was, Hippothous thought sourly, the only time their oarsmen displayed the merest hint of energy or alacrity.

By the end of the second day, another problem materialized. The silt carried down by the river created an ever-changing pattern of shallows and mud banks. A man in the prow of the lead boat probed the riverbed with a long pole. The helmsman was faced with continual choices as the channels of the river divided again and again. Not all his choices were good. Although the *camarae* drew little water, they ran aground with increasing frequency. Here, the double-ended form of the boats came into its own. Quite often, the rowers merely reversed their position, the helmsman scurried to the other end of the boat, and the oars pulled her off. If that did not suffice, things became considerably more fraught. The crew had to go overboard and, standing waist or even neck deep in the turbid water, manhandle the boat free. This they were most reluctant to do. Like most of the great watercourses, the Phasis bred man-murdering monsters. The travellers were told these looked like catfish but were larger, blacker and stronger; as man-eating as any in existence, as deadly as the horrors that were hauled from the Danube with teams of horses or oxen.

Each time the men came back over the side, muddy but unmolested, the Colchians would laugh, clap, break into song. One solemnly assured Hippothous that their continued good fortune was owed to all on board heeding local wisdom. Before setting out, Hippothous and the others had been enjoined to empty all their water skins and the like. To carry alien water on the Phasis was to bring the very worst luck.

Whether it should have been credited to the absence of foreign water, or to the kindly hand of a deity, none of the dark monsters made an appearance. But with the searching for a channel, the logs and the groundings, the perceived idleness of the natives, progress was very slow.

Dawn on the fourth day, and the river narrowed and the forest thinned. Signs of habitation increased: fields, orchards, isolated log huts. Small, near-naked children tended flocks. They waved as they brought their charges to water at the riverbank. To the north, the Caucasus seemed only a little closer.

But to the south, the hills advanced near, rising in steep, timber-covered slopes.

The things that did not change were the dampness, the lushness and the interminable noise of the frogs: *brekeke-kex, ko-ax, ko-ax*. They preyed on everyone's nerves. *Brekeke-kex*. None more so than Maximus – what he would not do for some fucking peace. Sat in the stern of one of the stinking *camarae*, Hippothous told Maximus every fable of Aesop featuring frogs that he could recall. It was like soothing a child. The barbarian enjoyed the ones where the frogs suffered and died an unpleasant death. His favourite was the one where the frogs, tired of their democratic existence, asked Zeus for a king. The god sent them a log. Unimpressed with its inactivity, they petitioned for a new monarch. So Zeus sent them a water snake, which ate them.

'And the moral is?' Hippothous asked.

'Be very afraid of snakes.'

'No.' Sometimes Hippothous wondered if the barbarian was mocking him. 'It is better to be ruled by an indolent emperor than an active one who is malevolent.'

'Or,' Calgacus suddenly spoke, 'the obvious truth that all change is likely to make things infinitely fucking worse.' Hippothous was not sure he had ever met anyone more gloomy than Ballista's old Caledonian freedman.

They slept that night in a town with the happy name of Rhodopolis. There were indeed roses. The *polis* was set in a fertile plain. Once, maybe in the days of Hellenic freedom before Rome crossed the Adriatic and her greed impelled her to the ends of the earth, Rhodopolis had been a fine place: temples, *agora*, *Bouleuterion*; everything a Hellenic *polis* should have. But it was much decayed, and bore the signs of both violence and neglect. Possibly, Hippothous thought, in this case Rome was not to blame.

Rhodopolis had been sited with a view only to wealth and not defence.

On the fifth day, the hills crowded close on both sides. The stream was narrow and fast, the going slow. At the time when two thirds of the day had gone, the time when exhausted labourers pray for the dark to hurry, the *camarae* fought their way around the last corner, and gratefully moored at Sarapanis.

Sarapanis was a neat, small village of tiled houses, a touch run down. It clustered at the foot of a steep, conical hill. At the top was the fort. Its garrison proved to consist of only sixty men. But the walls were sound and they had two pieces of artillery. The whole – fort and village – was almost entirely encircled by the confluence of the Phasis and another river. To make good the fort's lack of a natural spring, an underground tunnel had been dug down to one of the rivers. It was an eminently defensible site, dominating the crossing from Colchis to Iberia. It was easy to see why the garrison of locals had been replaced with Roman regulars. It was a pity there were not more of them. Freed from the noble shadow of Felix, Ballista slipped easily into the role of senior Roman army commander: touring, inspecting, questioning, speaking words of encouragement. At such times, Hippothous thought, the northerner had an air of competent authority.

At Sarapanis, the expedition was to divide again. Rutilus and Castricius were to travel together as far as Harmozica, the capital of Iberia, to the court of King Hamazasp, the king whose son Ballista had killed. Whenever Hamazasp was mentioned, Hippothous noted, Ballista's face became hard, closed in: most likely guilt, possibly with an edge of fear. From Hamazasp's palace at Harmozica, Castricius would journey on to Albania to deal with King Cosis. The latest report placed Cosis at Tzour on the Caspian coast. Undoubtedly, the Albanian king was there keeping an eye on and ingratiating himself with the Sassanid prince Narseh, who was finishing off rebels among the Mardi and the Cadusii just to the south.

As their *contubernium* was to end, Ballista – subtly, if not indeed unconsciously asserting his primacy – decided that a feast was in order. Hippothous was instructed to produce money from their travelling funds, and soldiers were dispatched to procure the good things necessary. Ballista demanded these include his favourite suckling pig and black pudding, and amphorae of local wine – dozens of amphorae of local wine.

Hippothous came back to life reluctantly. His one servant, Narcissus, was talking to him. Hippothous wished he would stop. The slave continued talking. Hippothous opened his eyes. His head hurt. Narcissus passed him a cup of water. Hippothous sat up and drank it, held it out for more.

The local wine had not come in amphorae but goatskins. It had tasted of goatskins. Hippothous's mouth still tasted of goat-skins. However, he did not feel quite as bad as he had expected. Probably he was still drunk. It meant the full horror of the hang-over would overwhelm him later.

'*Kyrios*, the eunuch Mastabates is to talk to you all in an hour.'

In the small headquarters, Ballista, Rutilus and most of the others were waiting. They all looked crapulous. Castricius had not appeared yet.

'You do not look well, *Accensus*,' said Maximus.

Hippothous did not reply.

'I feel fine.' Maximus pulled down the neck of his tunic. 'You should get one of these amethysts. Sure, they are the finest pre-ventative of the effects of over-indulgence. Drink all you want, stay sober, feel good.'

Hippothous noticed that, as well as the gemstone on a thong, the freedman wore a fine golden necklace, Sassanid work. *And where did you steal that?* he wondered.

'Cabbage.' said Rutilus. 'Fried is best, but boiled will do. Or eat almonds before you start drinking.'

'Nonsense,' said Ballista. 'Old wives' tales. None of them works, amulets and gemstones least of all. Drink milk first, lines the stomach.'

'Olive oil, if you are not a barbarian,' said Rutilus.

Castricius entered to laughter from the rest. The little man looked half-dead.

'Now we are all here,' said Mastabates. 'Before we go our separate ways, I was ordered to remind you all of what information our noble Augustus Gallienus, long may he reign, has received of the three Caucasian kings whose fortifications you will repair and whose allegiance you must secure.' The young eunuch paused, seemed to swell slightly with pride. 'I do not think it indiscreet to mention that this order was given to me personally by the Praetorian Prefect Lucius Calpurnius Piso Censorinus. He assured me the information was as accurate as could be found, having been gathered from previous diplomacy, from merchants, and from specially instructed *frumentarii*.'

'First, Polemo the king of Suania. He is a man who cares little for either Rome or Persia. He is dominated by two passions – survival, a tricky proposition for a monarch of his race, and the acquisition of as much wealth as Croesus. Polemo's spirit is dominated by avarice. He taxes heavily those crossing the passes in his territories, and his mountains are said to produce much gold and many gems. Yet none of it is enough to satisfy him. So, he takes gifts from both the *imperium* and Persia, while keeping faith with neither. Frequently, his men raid the lowlands, as far as the client cities of Rome on the Black Sea coast. Pityous, Sebastopolis, Cygnus – all have suffered. Of course, he always denies responsibility; his warriors act without his permission – which, given his subjects, often may be true.'

Hippothous reached for some water on the table. He was annoyed that his hand was unsteady. He saw Maximus smile. You had better watch yourself, barbarian bastard, Hippothous thought savagely, I might yet mark you down for death.

'Polemo,' continued Mastabates, 'is important to Rome in two ways. First, as a check on the kings of Iberia and Albania, in case they should be misguided enough to throw in their lot with Shapur. Second, Polemo holds the Caspian or Caucasian Gates, the best pass through the central Caucasus. It keeps the nomadic hordes of the Alani away from civilization. There is a fort in the pass, but it is said to be in grave disrepair – hence our opportunity for the *Vir Ementissimus* Marcus Clodius Ballista to bring his experience as a siege engineer to win the favour of the king.'

'Now, as to the forces available to Polemo . . .'

The eunuch began to explore Polemo's military capabilities (large) in conjunction with the byways of his soul (devious, if not warped). Hippothous's attention wandered. He was running a cold sweat, felt sick. Fragments of the night before floated through the wine fumes clouding his thoughts. Castricius teasing Ballista about a girl from Arete, called Bathshiba or some such Syrian name: how had he not fucked her? Maximus joining in: tits and arse that would have made even Hippothous here change his position. It was shocking the informality Ballista allowed. But, then, they were all really barbarians; Rutilus was nothing but a Thracian, and Castricius a Celt from Nemausus; generations of Roman rule had hardly civilized them at all.

Deep into the *comissatio*, long after the food, drink flowing, the conversation had turned maudlin. *That poor bastard Mamurra*. He had been a Roman officer. For some reason, which the drink temporarily had removed from Hippothous's memory, Ballista had left him to die in a siege tunnel in Arete. The others who had been there – Castricius, Maximus, Calgacus – had vehemently and repetitively denied that Ballista should blame himself – *there was nothing else he could have done.* That was it – if Ballista had not collapsed the mine, the Persians would have poured into the town, killed everyone. *That poor, square-headed bastard Mamurra – sure, what a very square head he had – the squarest head you ever saw, like a block of fucking marble it was.* They had moved from misery to childish hilarity in a moment, wine sloshing from their cups. *Mamurra was destined to die, not like Castricius. Nothing could kill him. Sent to the mines, the little bastard survived; volunteered for a night raid, only three survivors, sure enough one of them was Castricius; the Sassanids massacre every living thing in Arete, but not the little man.* Castricius had risen to his feet, struck a mock-heroic pose: *it was all true, even the spirits of death dare not touch me.*

Hippothous felt his gorge rising. He looked around the headquarters – a sea of faces, the eunuch still talking. By the Graces, do not let me throw up. It would be too humiliating. Practise physiognomy: take your mind off your physical condition. Which one? Not Ballista: Hippothous was reserving judgement on him. Not Calgacus or Maximus: one too ugly, the other too disfigured – leave them for a later date. Hippothous thought physiognomy was easier with children, before a face became weathered by time and accident. Experience writes its story on the face, but chance – a broken nose, a scar – confuses things. Certainly not one of the eunuchs: he was feeling sick enough without dwelling on those monstrous, disgusting creatures. Castricius: he would do – little Castricius the survivor.

Slim lips in a small mouth, indicative of cowardice, weakness and complicity. The lower lip protruded, a sign of tenderness and a love of well being. But a sharp, pointed, small chin, meaning badness entering into evil, also boldness and killing. A thin nose, showing the presence of great anger. And, now Hippothous studied him, he saw that Castricius had beautiful eyes. There was nothing redeeming about that. A man with beautiful eyes was treacherous, concealing what was in his heart; also, he was bold, had potency of spirit and strength in action. Castricius was a complex case, but a bad, dangerous man. That was what physiognomy was for, to guard against the vices of the bad before having to experience them.

A real master of the science could go much further than generalities of *that man is bad, that one good*. A real master could read the specific actions that both had been and would be committed by any man. If Hippothous studied hard, devoted his mind to the science, he felt he might achieve that god-like mastery.

A question from Ballista brought Hippothous back from his physiognomic studies. 'Mastabates, at Heraclea you spoke of a problem at the Suanian court – the widow of the Iberian prince I killed.'

'Yes, Pythonissa. Despite her name, she is a priestess not of Apollo but Hecate. With her husband dead, there was no place for her in Iberia. She had produced no children and was not needed for the succession. Hamazasp has a brother, Oroezes. He in turn has grown sons, and they are married with sons. Pythonissa was sent back to her father. He proposed marrying her off to the ruler of the lice-eaters. She is a wilful young woman, said to be skilled with poisons. She would not accept the marriage, thought it beneath her. Pythonissa wished to marry her own father-in-law, old Hamazasp, become queen of Iberia, and breed an heir to the throne. Even Suanian sensibilities, such as they are, were revolted by the idea. So she remains, a discontented woman at the court of Polemo.'

Ballista grunted. 'What of the rest of the royal house of Suania?'

'We know of no other evident difficulties. Polemo has two surviving sons, Azo and Saurmag. They had a good Hellenic education. There is nothing to suggest a problem.' Mastabates smiled. 'Polemo had two other sons. They both died violent deaths, one recently. Nothing surprising there. It is hard to find a subject of Polemo that does not have at least one or two murders to his name.'

XXII

From the fort at Sarpanis to the Caspian Gates, as a bird would fly, Ballista guessed, was not more than one hundred miles. It had taken them fifteen days, and the village outside which they were now halted was still one short stage – maybe five, six miles – from the fortified pass.

Of course, no one in their right mind ever tried to travel in a straight line in hill country, let alone in mountains. Paths sometimes switched from low, clinging to the valleys and watercourses, to high, the shoulders or even the ridgeways. They often made wide detours around ravines or particularly severe slopes, as they tried to thread their way from one pass to another. Yet it was not so much the terrain that had detained them as the natives.

The travelling party was small, ten in all: Ballista himself, Hippothous, Maximus, Calgacus, and Mastabates, with just five servants – the boy Wulfstan; Agathon and Polybius, the slaves Ballista had bought at Priene; Hippothous's Narcissus; and the eunuch's man, who was called Pallas. Such a number needed only a small baggage train; the diplomatic gifts they carried were expensive but readily portable. Little was called for in the way of food, fodder or lodgings. Yet the difficulties in procuring these things had been legion. The Roman *cursus publicus* did not run out here. In this debatable zone of influence, rather than direct rule, it was uncertain if they were still in the *imperium* or not. Certainly, flourishing purple-sealed *diplomata* in Latin did not produce animals, men or materials. To achieve anything, coins had to appear, a surprising number of coins. The locals wanted old coins. Given the radical debasement of precious metal in recent imperial coins, that was to be expected, but they seemed to take caution to excessive lengths, preferring coins minted more than two and a half centuries before, in the reign of the first Augustus. Significantly, they were quite happy to take eastern coins, recent Sassanid ones as well as those from the previous dynasty, the Parthians.

Finding the right coins and enough of them had been merely the beginning. Local horizons were narrow. The owners would only let their animals go so far – two, maybe three valleys – then new ones had to be hired. The beasts never turned up on time, sometimes never arrived at all. When they did, either the animals themselves or the price had changed. It was the same with porters for the sections where the locals insisted that the going was too bad for animals, and little different with supplies. The majority of the negotiating fell on Hippothous, with Mastabates translating. The Greek often looked as if he wanted to kill someone, but then, to some extent, the irritation infected everyone. For sure, the delay was shared by all.

Yet when they were moving, out in the country, the early days of the march had been glorious, even uplifting. It was a land of rolling wooded hills and valleys; birch, beech and laurel, with white rhododendrons underneath. There were mists and showers, usually in the afternoons. Sometimes the latter were heavy, but both alternated with soft, warm sunshine. Broad, defined tracks, dappled in sunlight, ran alongside clear, babbling streams.

The villages had been another matter. Walled compounds clustered together, seemingly as much in suspicion of each other as for defence. Each was surmounted by one or more stone towers, tapering and forbidding. There was mud everywhere. Hairy pigs, geese and mangy dogs wallowed in it, or wandered, snapping and posturing in mutual hostility. There were children everywhere. They were half or totally naked, indescribably dirty, faces often bestial. Sometimes, they would ignore the arrivals, carry on playing noisy games involving stealing what little the others might possess. At other times, they joined the adults in silence, their dark stag eyes watchful, all unwelcoming.

The lodgings obtained – an upper room of a tower, the floor of a barn – matched the young in filth. The thick, dark smoke from the fires of moss and pine chips did nothing to discourage the biting insects. At least the food, although monotonous, was wholesome enough: roast mutton or pork, boiled fowl, the meat on flat bread, washed down with goatskin-tasting wine.

Further into the mountains, there were fewer trees: here a sheltered slope of firs, there an upland pool ringed by maple and beech, the occasional, isolated birch. But up there the flowers had come into their own: thick tangles of cream rhododendrons shot through with purple, and banks of yellow azaleas perfuming the air. Underfoot, the turf was enamelled with lupins, bluebells and cowslips.

There were still habitations in the higher reaches. But the party had mainly passed by those lonely, closed-in towers, stark up on their ridges. The locals had likewise ignored them. Ten heavily armed travellers – now the slaves were armed too – might have been a bit too tough a target. The party had camped where seemed good in the open: flattish spaces, as far as possible, with a view all around. It had been cold in the tents, and every night some lost sleep, as a watch had to be set.

It was healthy. So Ballista had claimed. Clean, fresh air, aromatic fires of rhododendron stalks and roots, trout caught by hand in the backwaters, flatbread toasted on the blades of their daggers. Ballista's slave Agathon was developing into a fine camp cook. Hippothous had not been convinced. The most elementary knowledge of medicine indicated that water from snow and ice was very bad for one; the light, sweet, sparkling part vanished when frozen and did not return. Drinking from these icy upland streams could only lead to gravel in the kidneys, stones, pain in the loins, and eventually rupture. Only Calgacus seemed to give his gloomy prognosis much credence.

One morning, the thick, thick mist had lifted suddenly, and there was the big mountain, still far away, seen beyond a jumble of boulders and between the green shoulders of its lesser brethren, but incredibly massive, snow covered and solitary. 'Strobilos,' the guide had said. 'Where Zeus chained Prometheus.' The mountain shone in the sun. In a moment, the mists had returned, and it was gone.

In the clinging, grey vapour, they had been walking up from a deep, green basin. A vague, tall shape shambled down out of the fog. Ballista and the others stopped. Bears were said to be common. They had drawn their weapons. Maximus had actually grunted with anticipation. The fog swirled. In it, the bear had started singing. Realizing it was a man, their guide had said something incomprehensible, and made the sign of the evil eye. The man came forward. Even by the standards of the mountain men, he was ragged and soiled. His body was emaciated. He was bleeding freely from several cuts and abrasions. His clothing appeared to consist of a stained, torn sack. The man had looked closely into Ballista's face. There was no comprehension in his eyes. He stank. The guide had given the creature food, spoken gentle things to him. 'One taken by the moon goddess Selene,' the guide had explained. 'When the servants of the goddess find him, he will live like a lord for a year.'

'One year?' Ballista had asked.

'One year.'

'And then?'

The guide had not answered.

They had left him where he was, and continued to climb. Their breath plumed. There was much snow still lying at the top of the pass. They descended via a steep slope of shale. Near the bottom, the mist had lifted again. There were yellow flowers in the grass. Ballista looked back. The locals had been avaricious. A Caucasian pony, even a nimble-footed horse could have made the crossing. No need for two guides and a dozen porters.

In front of them was the upper course of the Alontas river. It braided itself in many tiny channels across a broad, flat valley bottom. The rivulets twisted and turned. Banks of mud and stones were left exposed, each neatly curved, as if by the hand of a skilled potter. They were grey amid the prevailing lush green. The valley walls were precipitous and high. They were green, but bald, not a tree in sight. Here and there, they were riven by deep gullies. On the side of one, not far ahead, clung a grey village. There were horses and cattle grazing the flat pastures below it. It offered a chance to get in the saddle again, and the pleasure of dismissing all the grasping guides and porters.

A mile or so beyond the village, and the valley had turned. Another long valley, and then another turning. In the distance, more valley walls, higher and higher, fading from green to blue to misty grey. The ten small figures on horseback were dwarfed by the immensity. It did not matter; from that point, they had known all they had to do was follow the river and it would lead them to the Caspian Gates.

The Suani warriors were waiting for them here outside the last village before the Gates. There were thirty of them, mounted, spread out. They completely blocked the width of the valley floor. Some of the horses were in the various streams, hock deep. These drank or stamped and shook their manes as the mood took them. The men were well armed. Mail showed under the empty-sleeved Caucasian fur coats they wore loose over their shoulders. Some had metal helmets. Each had a lance or javelin in his right hand and a targe strapped to his left arm. From each saddlebow hung a combined bow case and quiver. They sat their horses well. They looked tough, if wild and ill disciplined.

Ballista wondered just how much danger he and the others were in.

The Suani rider with the most elaborate embroidery on his coat and on the *gorytus* suspended from his saddlebow paced his mount forward. 'Which of you is Marcus Clodius Ballista, the envoy of the *basileus* Gallienus?' The young man spoke in Greek. His words were moderately polite, but his tone arrogant, bordering on hostile.

Ballista nudged his horse out of the group.

'Dismount.' The order from the Suani was peremptory.

'Who are you?' Ballista kept his voice very level.

'I am Azo, son of King Polemo of the Suani. My father is in the village. He is with the *synedrion*. They are expecting you. It will be best for you if you have brought the tribute.'

Ballista did not reply. He swung down from the saddle, indicated for the others to do likewise. He told them to break out the first two parcels of gifts. Calgacus was to stay behind with the horses and the remainder of the baggage, Agathon and Polybius with him. The rest were to accompany Ballista.

Azo and some of the Suani dismounted. Those now on foot set off up into the village. The others stayed where they were.

Dikaiosyne the village was called, 'justice' in Greek. When Ballista had asked why, Mastabates admitted he had no idea. The place had another, native name. The eunuch had not known what that meant either. Ballista did not think it the moment to question the Suanian prince Azo on etymology. They walked up in silence.

The first buildings began a good way up from the floodplain. They were built on a thirty-degree slope. Dikaiosyne was backed by a sheer rockface, which reared up several thousand feet. Above the settlement there was snow in every declivity. They trudged up the usual muddy alleys formed by the blank outer walls of compounds. Hairy pigs grunted out of their way. Dogs barked.

They emerged into the village square. It was full of people, some two or three hundred, stood in an inverted U, the open side towards the newcomers. Ballista tried very hard not to appear surprised; tried to take in his surroundings. The square was wider than most; small alleyways opening off from the otherwise featureless walls all around. It had at its centre not an old oak tree, but an oversized circular well. Next to the well was an eastern type of altar with a lit fire.

It was easy to pick out King Polemo from his advisors and subjects. He was seated in the middle on a high throne. A dark-bearded, sharp-faced man in middle age, he wore a cloak and turban, both white with gold thread, both a little grubby. His sword belt, scabbard and red boots were set with what looked like pearls. By one of his hands stood a younger, lighter-coloured, less impressive version of himself – that must be Saurmag, the other prince. On the other was a tall, blond, statuesque young woman – the troublesome daughter Pythonissa, the priestess of Hecate.

263

The members of the *synedrion* of Suania stood in the front rank. The councillors tended to be tall, well-formed men with aquiline, attractive, if hard, faces. In their dress they followed their king: a mixture of western styles – tunics, trousers and boots not unlike an unarmoured Roman officer; with barbarian – eastern turbans or nomad caps with lappets. From what could be seen, the warriors in the rear ranks appeared to favour cheaper, rougher versions of the same. None of them seemed to have an obsession with the baths.

A group off to one side caught Ballista's eye. There were six of them. They were different – darker hair and beards, taller hats and baggier trousers, cleaner. They were not Suani. They were Persians – Zoroastrian priests. Of course, that explained the fire altar by the well. Ballista had been told by Mastabates that the chief of the Sassanid king's fire-worshipping priests, none other than Shapur's close confidant Kirder the *Herbed*, had led a mission of conversion to the Caucasus. Numerous fire altars had been founded throughout Albania, Iberia – across the whole region. Ballista looked hard. None of these men was Kirder. He had seen him once in Edessa. None of them was Hormizd, the Persian boy chance had briefly made Ballista's slave. Ballista would not recognize any other Zoroastrian priests. The *mobads* in this village square looked annoyed. It made Ballista again wonder how strong diplomatic immunity would prove among the mountaineers of the Caucasus.

'Marcus Clodius Ballista, *Vir Ementissimus*, welcome.' The king spoke Latin well. 'Your arrival is auspicious. The ceremonies are about to begin.'

A grey stallion was led out. Polemo got down from his throne. He fussed over the animal, breathing into its nose, playing with its ears. Once he had got its trust, he drove the knife deep into the base of its neck. He withdrew the blade. A thick, solid jet of blood, the diameter of a man's bicep, gushed out. The blood splashed the sleeve of Polemo's white tunic. The horse plunged, tried to rear. Polemo had to step back quickly. The stallion's legs gave way. Thrashing, it did not want to die. But it had no choice. It died slowly in its own blood.

Polemo, brushing at his stained sleeve, reascended his throne. Behind their big beards, the Zoroastrian *mobads* looked even less happy. Ballista thought he knew why. He had seen this Persian ceremony carried out in Edessa, by none other than the King of Kings himself. It had taken place at dawn. Now it was mid-afternoon. The king of Suania had been waiting for the envoy from Rome. And there was the manner of it. In Edessa, the stallion had been pure white, and it had gone consenting to the god.

'Bring out the impious,' called Polemo, this time in Greek.

A man and a woman were manhandled into the middle by a dozen or more guards. Their hands were tied. They were young, good-looking, naked. They looked terrified. The girl tried to cover her breasts and delta. With her arms bound it was impossible to cover all of herself. The crowd regarded both with prurient interest.

'Behold the impious adulterers,' said Polemo. 'If the white reeds are cut at dawn, at the time sacrifices are offered to Hecate, at the time the divine paean is chanted, at the beginning of the spring, the dark goddess will let there be no mistake.'

Ballista heard Mastabates mutter, 'Fascinating, I always thought it an old wives' tale.'

The naked girl crumpled to her knees, holding her bound wrists out to Polemo in supplication. She was crying. It did no good. She was hauled back to her feet. The king ignored her, carried on speaking.

'Such is the nature of the reeds that if they are placed somewhere in the woman's chamber and the adulterer enters, he will be robbed of his rational thoughts, and he will, drunk or sober, confess what he has wickedly done or intends to do. Such is the case here. They are condemned out of the man's own mouth. By the sacred judgement of our ancestors we commit them to the Mouth of the Impious.'

The girl screamed. The man shouted, things that were obviously defiant insults in the local language. He was knocked to the ground. Two large sacks were produced. At the sight of them, both gave way. The girl collapsed again, sobbing hysterically. The man's bladder failed. The crowd laughed as the urine ran down his legs.

The sacks appeared to be empty. Ballista was at a loss. In Rome, a parricide was sewn into a sack with a snake, dog, cock and monkey, then thrown in the Tiber. There were no animals to be seen here, and the Alontas river was both some way from the village square and, at the moment, too shallow to dispose of corpses with any guarantee of success.

The couple struggled madly, but the sacks were forced over their heads. They were held down while the sacks were sewn shut. The two bundles of coarse sacking were left to writhe on the ground for a time. Muffled yells came from inside. Both were kicked indiscriminately.

It took four strong men to lift and restrain each sack. They carried them towards the mouth of the well. It must be what Polemo had called the Mouth of the Impious. With no ceremony or delay, both were thrown in. The screams were cut off quickly, replaced by the sounds of heavy objects hitting water, then by silence.

'The punishment of the impious, those who have defiled the sacred nature of the hearth, have betrayed the hospitality of god and man, is not over.' Polemo's tone suggested he was rather pleased with the idea. 'From the Mouth of the Impious, the river

266

will bear them underground to Lake Maeotis. In thirty days they will emerge there, crawling with maggots and, as ever, the vultures will come from nowhere, tear the corpses to pieces, and devour them.'

All the *synedrion* and the rest shook back their cloaks and coats, gave evidence that they thought this a fine thing.

'Marcus Clodius Ballista, approach the throne.'

Ballista did as he was bidden, stepping across the blood-slick turf around the carcass of the stallion and between the fire altar and the Mouth of the Impious. In front of the king of the Suani he bowed and blew a kiss from his fingertips. If Polemo had been expecting full *proskynesis*, he would be disappointed. Ballista had no intention of grovelling in the dirt at the feet of this grubby, upcountry potentate.

'*Kyrios*, I bring you greetings from *autokrator* Publius Licinius Egnatius Gallienus *Sebastos*.' It was no effort for Ballista to translate the emperor's titles into Greek, for centuries the language of diplomacy employed by all powers in the east. 'And a letter from his own hand, for your eyes only.'

Ballista handed the gold-encased roll of purple papyrus to the prince Saurmag, who gave it to his father. A half-memory flashed through Ballista's mind – was it from Herodotus? – a man sent with a message that read 'Kill the bearer of this letter,' something like that. Had he been sent into a sort of unofficial exile, or to a remote place to be killed? The king did not read the letter but tucked the roll into his belt. Suddenly Ballista was very aware of the eyes of the daughter on him. It was only to be expected – he had killed Pythonissa's husband, unpicked the promising threads of her young life.

'*Kyrios*, the *sebastos* sends you gifts.' Ballista told Hippothous to unwrap the *ornamenta consularia*. Mastabates gave him a sharp glance. Ballista was reversing the order in which he had been told to present the first lot of gifts. Hippothous held forth the gleaming white toga with the broad purple stripe, the special, many-laced boots only a Roman senator might wear, then the twelve *fasces*, the rods symbolizing the power to beat, the axes they wrapped the power to kill.

'The ornaments of a Roman consul; tokens of the emperor's affection.'

Polemo grunted a less than fulsome appreciation. Ballista indicated the other gifts be presented. This time, as the covers came off, the king of the Suani leant forward. He had caught the gleam of precious metal. The extensive dinner service – wine jugs, coolers, plates, serving bowls, all in gold and silver – was spread out on cloths on the ground. Polemo's hawk-like face broke into the uncomplicated smile of an acquisitive child. He had some of the choicer pieces passed up to him. He turned them in his hands, admiring their cunningly worked designs.

Sometimes, Ballista thought, the Romans are blinkered like a chariot horse that only sees its own lane. Just because consular rank, the right to be addressed as *Vir Clarissimus*, was close to the greatest felicity imaginable among them, it never crossed their minds it might mean something less to anyone else; that it might have fallen as something of an anticlimax after the gold and silver. Ballista had been right: precious metals were the way to the affections, if such was the right term, of this avaricious kinglet dressed in his grubby tunic high in the Caucasian mountains.

Polemo continued to peer closely at the metalwork, running the tips of his fingers over the embossed figures. Allfather only knew what message, if any, he was reading in those images of eastern barbarians looking a bit like the Persian *mobads* on their knees in front of suitably naked, heroic westerners.

'We are pleased with the tribute sent by the *basileus* of the Romans,' said Polemo.

Ballista bowed, not taking issue with the expression tribute.

'You will stay the night here in the royal residence. At the feast, you will tell us of your plans to rebuild our fortifications at the Caspian Gates.'

As Ballista thanked the king in Attic Greek, he was sure the girl Pythonissa was smiling.

XXIII

Riding the last few miles to the Caspian Gates, Ballista felt the world close in around them. The valley twisted and turned. Its grey walls reared up impossibly high; jagged, naked rock – no birds, no animals, not even an ibex or mountain goat. Above, the sky seemed no more than a pale ribbon. Wraiths of mist often pursued one another up there. When they caught each other, they coalesced into a fog which cut off the heavens, oozed down the fissures and threatened to engulf the travellers. At the bottom, the track was little wider than an ox cart; the river filled the rest of the space. The Alontas tumbled and roared over the boulders in its shallow bed. Its surface was just a handspan below the level of the road. When the rains were heavy, when the snow melted fast on the peaks, obviously the Alontas would rise, fill the pass and sweep away almost everything in its way. Given this, the ever–present likelihood of rockfalls, and the character of the neighbouring peoples, the pass struck Ballista as a particularly dangerous place.

'Cumania,' the Suani prince Azo said. The gorge turned to the right here. The path was on the inside of the curve, hard up against the eastern wall. The river thundered along, trying to undermine the opposite rocks. Up above the waters, away to Ballista's left, there were stone walls, slate roofs: a small fort perched on an outcrop forty or fifty feet over the Alontas.

'The Gates,' Azo said.

Ballista looked north around the bend: the river, the track, fallen boulders, the walls of the ravine. He looked harder, and there, in the torrent, the stumps of three stone piers – all that remained of the famous Caspian Gates.

'Much work for you to do.'

The words of the Suani were borne out as the day wore on. While the prince sat on a sheepskin rug, drinking and talking with his warriors, Ballista and his *familia* scrambled and splashed about. The water was shockingly cold, the rocks slippery. Inspecting the fort, Ballista discovered that some of its roof timbers were rotten; parts of its walls needed replacing. Apart from raw stone and water, there were no building materials to hand.

'My sister,' Azo said. A mounted group was approaching. 'She likes to hunt. Our brother has a hunting lodge beyond the Gates in the hills to the north.' A slight look of distaste passed across the speaker's face. 'Saurmag often goes among the Alani barbarians.' Ballista got the impression that neither barbarians nor brother pleased Azo.

Pythonissa headed the cavalcade that clattered up from the direction of Dikaiosyne. She was dressed for the chase, armed like a man. She rode astride. Perhaps for a woman's respectability, there were two eunuchs in her train. The other twenty or so riders were warriors.

Azo and Ballista bowed where they stood in the road, blew a kiss. Pythonissa pulled up her mount a few paces short. She tossed the reins to one of the eunuchs, and jumped down. She bowed and blew a kiss back. She spoke to her brother in Greek about coverts and game, wild boar and deer, about nothing of any importance.

Ballista watched her. She reminded him of Bathshiba in Arete. Pythonissa was taller, her skin paler, her hair blond. She looked nothing like Bathshiba. But the wild Amazonian quality was the same.

The girl turned to Ballista. She stood unexpectedly close. He was terribly aware of what he had done to her life, no matter how indirectly. He framed a polite, neutral question. 'What quarry are you after?'

She continued to regard him wordlessly. Her eyes were grey-blue.

'You and your men are well armed,' he continued. 'Equipped to deal with big game.'

The girl spoke. 'It is a mistake to decide in advance. Hunting is a lesson in the philosophic life. You sight the thing you have sought for a long time, then you lose it. The hunter learns to deal with extreme emotions: elation, despair, boredom.' She delivered this in a mock-earnest tone. Then she became very serious. 'I wanted to speak to the man who killed my husband.'

'I am sorry it had to happen.'

'Tell me how you killed him.'

'I had set a trap for the King of Kings. Your husband rode at Shapur's side. The wrong man died.'

'An artillery bolt?'

'Yes.'

'Did he die well?'

'He rode out that morning as a man. Thousands mourned him, tried to revenge him.'

'His father, old Hamazasp, would have you dead.'

Ballista smiled. 'I know it.'

She nodded, stepped back. When she spoke again it was to her

272

brother as well. 'I will be gone some time. I will see you on the way back.'

'Not me,' said Azo. 'As soon as the Roman tells me what things he needs, I am leaving this desolate place.'

'So be it.' She got into the saddle unassisted, easily. She led her men off down the track, around the turning in the gorge. She did not look back. They watched her go off to the north, beyond the Gates.

Ballista decided that his first impression of Azo may not have done the young prince full justice. Certainly the Suani had a fine self-regard and a wariness close to hostility. Yet these, Ballista thought, might be the products of being brought up in a royal court, even one – possibly especially one – as obscure as that of Suania. At least Azo was capable, did what he said he would. After Pythonissa had left, Ballista had presented Azo with a lengthy list of the materials and men he needed: timber, cut stone, bricks, slates, sand, lime, rope, chains, nails, a forge; stone-masons, carpenters and a blacksmith, all with their tools, and as many labourers as could be gathered. Azo had summoned his secretary, told him to note it all down, and ridden south. Ballista had been impressed when the first deliveries began the very next day.

The fort of Cumania was the initial priority. A garrison in the pass had to have somewhere to live, and the gorge was narrow enough for arrows from the fort to dominate the track on the other side of the river. On its own it could not totally prevent people from using the track, but it could make it unpleasant and dangerous.

Cumania was a small, dark hold; roughly circular, no more than fifteen paces in diameter, four storeys high. There was a walkway around the roof. Luckily, the repairs needed were not too extensive. Only part of the roof needed replacing, and a few patches of the walls. Ballista had regular Roman crenellations added. In these he set three refinements – projections from the battlements, each with a protected hole opening on to the void below. The central of these was directly over the only entrance to the fort. The southern was fitted with pulleys, chains and buckets to raise fresh water coming from upstream. The northern had the opposite intention, being designed as a latrine from which the waste would be washed away downstream.

The fort was set on a crag in the western wall of the ravine. It was inaccessible from the heights far above. The sole door, a solid affair of iron-bound oak – Ballista tested it, replaced both frame and hinges – faced the river. It opened on to the second floor and could only be reached by a flight of stone steps which exposed the right, unshielded side of anyone ascending and rose straight from the water. The defenders now could drop missiles on the steps, while remaining in perfect safety directly overhead. The arrow slits were on the second floor and above, had stout wooded shutters and were not nearly wide enough to admit a man. With mines, ramps, siege towers and rams all equally out of the question, and with no artillery among the peoples of the mountains or the northern steppes, Ballista thought a handful of men could hold Cumania for ever. The only ways the fort could fall were starvation or treachery. He set about provisioning the place.

The actual 'gates' which would seal the pass demanded more thought. First, the easiest, part was to design a gate to block the road. This was to be of dressed stone, and bound into the natural rock. It would have a fighting platform above. It would look like almost any Roman gate anywhere. But detached buttresses would be built to the south in front of the main load-bearing sides of the gate. When the Alontas was in flood, hopefully these would catch some of the boulders and tree trunks carried downstream. If that worked, and the waters poured through the open gates, the structure might not be battered down and swept away.

Extending the gates across the river was the crucial problem. Ballista decided to employ the three existing stubs of piers as breakwaters. Like the buttresses on either side of the track, they might take the force of debris when the river was in full spate. He ordered three concrete pillars erected behind them. On these he planned to put a simple wooden walkway, with a palisade facing just north. Either end of the defences would be supported by the natural rock and his new stone gate. There was to be a wide clearance between the surface of the water and the walkway, to allow the river to rise several feet. To block this when the river was lower, to stop nomads creeping under the walkway, he designed a series of metal portcullises which could be raised and lowered.

Work on the 'gates' got under way slowly. Partly it was due to materials. There was no suitable sand or lime for the concrete in the whole of Suania. After a few days, a little was found in a royal store, just about enough for the new pillars in the river. Everything else would have to rely on local mortar. Again, the cut stone arrived slowly, in small quantities. But the sluggishness of the early stages of building was much more down to the workers. Azo had sent plenty of them, skilled and unskilled. The problem was not one of numbers but attitude. They were proud mountaineers, warriors. There was not one among these Suani, even if he had no shoes and wore a rag on his back, who did not regard such building work as far beneath him. They were worse than the Greeks and Romans; at least they reserved their contempt for labouring for money at the whim of another, rather than at the whole concept of hard, physical work.

Ballista suspected that his attempts to encourage by example – attempts he was sure would have worked with Roman soldiers – had failed completely. When Ballista, Maximus and the others stripped off their tunics and heaved buckets up the perilous timber scaffolding or stood waist deep in the fast, chill water to manhandle beams into position, the Suani just despised them all the more.

Ballista and old Calgacus wandered down the track, past the hammering and sawing, off to the north. It was hard getting any sustained work out of the Suani. The carpenters, stonemasons and blacksmith were not too bad – they had a craft – but the labourers . . . Ballista would have to ask Azo about it during the prince's next fleeting visit. Still, it was not raining; for once, there was not even any mist. The sun was actually out. The sky was a translucent blue, with a few very high white clouds.

'Another few weeks, even at this rate, and we are done,' said Ballista.

Calgacus shook his head. 'We might as well let the lazy bastards take their time. We cannot leave without imperial orders. Until we get new *mandata*, we are stuck here at the arse end of the world.'

Out of the noise and dust, Ballista was not going to let the Caledonian spoil his mood. Where the sun fell on the tops of the gorge, the rocks glowed pink. There was an incredible clarity to the air. 'Do you see that eagle up there?' They both craned their necks.

A terrible, loud crack, like a siege engine breaking. Ballista and Calgacus whirled around – hands on hilts. The noise echoed off the canyon walls, confusing its origin. A deep groaning of wood, followed by a volley of further cracks. Shouts and screams from back down the track. Men running towards them. Others running away, hurling themselves into the river. The scaffold high above the track over the beginnings of the gate shifted outward. It held for a second or two, slightly swaying. There were men clinging to the top of it. Another series of cracks, vicious splinters flying, a definitive lurch and the edifice collapsed out and down into the river. The limbs of those falling pumped futilely. With hideous abruptness, they vanished into the spray that masked the stony bed of the river.

A great pall of dust mushroomed up from where the timber structure had been. The noise of the river, the screams of the injured; all sounds seemed to come from a long way away. The water whirled a beam past where they stood. Then a man. He was floundering, but alive. He grabbed a half-submerged rock. Ballista shrugged out of his sword belt.

'No, you fucking fool,' Calgacus shouted.

The water was not deep, not up to Ballista's waist. It was icy cold, the bed treacherous, stones shifting underfoot. He waded out. His boots were full of water. The man was only three or four more paces away. He was clinging desperately. There was blood – a lot of it – on his arms, his head.

'Look out.'

Another chunk of timber was swirling down towards them. Ballista scrambled back – the curious, slow high-steps of a man in water. Not enough time. He hurled himself backwards. He went under, the water rushing in his ears, eyes blurred. As he came up, the shattered end of the beam caught him on the left shoulder. The pain was intense. There was blood in the water. He held the wound tight with his right hand.

'Come on.' Calgacus was with him.

'I am fine. Help me get him.'

They waited, timing it, while other debris scoured the space between them and the injured Suanian.

'Now!' They spoke at once. Five, six stumbling steps. They had him, a hand under each armpit, dragging. They made no attempt to keep his head above water – drowning was the least of his problems in those few moments to the riverbank. They were there – crawling out, spitting, spluttering.

XXIV

Sabotage. There could be no doubt. It had been sabotage. They squatted on their heels in the dust and inspected the evidence – the neat cuts where several of the support beams had been sawn part way through, and the contrasting tortured ends where the wood had twisted or snapped.

'Not too skilled,' Ballista said. 'They could have sawn through fewer beams and had a greater certainty of collapse.'

'Sure, that is good,' Maximus said. 'No need to confine our suspicions to the trained carpenters.'

'Two dead, two more likely to die, another dozen hurt; it will be bad for the spirits of the workers,' Mastabates said.

Calgacus snorted; a horrible sound mingling contempt and derision.

'Was it an attempt to kill you?' Mastabates asked Ballista.

It was Hippothous who answered. 'It is not likely. Ballista has been up on the scaffolding – we all have – but not continuously. The odds were exceedingly against him – any of us – being any-where near it when it fell.'

'Then who benefits by sabotaging our mission?' Mastabates

went on to begin to scout answers to his own question. 'The Caspian Gates are designed to keep out the Alani.'

'I have not seen any nomads around,' said Maximus.

'Would we recognize them?' Ballista shrugged, then the pain made him wish he had not. 'A lot of the Suani dress like men from the steppes – the caps with lappets, the furs, those animal-style buckles and clasps. I am still enough of a northerner to find it hard to tell one of these easterners from another. A Hellene such as Hippothous would be no better – worse probably. Apart from Mastabates, do any of us know enough of the language of the Suani to notice an unusual accent?'

'It is against Sassanid interests for us to do well.' Mastabates tried another tack. 'Those bushy-bearded *mobads* hanging around Polemo would be in a good position to organize something like this.'

Everyone nodded at the truth of the words.

'But it could be something more local, more personal,' the eunuch continued. 'Iberia is only a few valleys away. We all heard Pythonissa remind you that old King Hamazasp still hates you.'

This time Ballista remembered not to shrug. 'A reciprocal thing,' he murmured.

'Of course, it could be something yet closer to home.' Mastabates' thoughts pressed on. 'The eldest two sons of Polemo of Suania have met violent deaths. Members of that family do not die in their beds, nor does any dynasty in the Caucasus. Everyone in the mountains is enmeshed in feuds. If you have eyes to see, it is evident that the princes Azo and Saurmag hate each other. And who could tell what the girl Pythonissa wants – a priestess of Hecate, said to be skilled with poisons, angry, frustrated, a latter-day Medea.'

It was an informal *consilium* that advised Ballista on the banks of the Alontas: Maximus, Calgacus, Hippothous and Mastabates.

The four slaves, Agathon and Polybius along with Mastabates' Pallas and Hippothous's Narcissus, had been left across the river in Cumania to keep an eye on their possessions. It left just young Wulfstan in attendance. He had been joined by the Suanian who had been fished out of the water. His name was Tarchon. Despite all the blood, he had not been badly hurt. Now he would not let them out of his sight. Through the translation of Mastabates, Tarchon had repeatedly thanked them for saving his life. As far as could be understood, the incident had apparently made them his blood brothers in some obscure but fierce Suanian way. Now his honour seemed to demand that he die for them. Tarchon looked forward to it with pleasure.

The *consilium* was over. Nothing for it but to carry on: rebuild the scaffolding, keep more on their guard. They dispersed. Watching the labourers get back to work, Ballista let Calgacus and Wulfstan change the bandages on his shoulder. The ragged wood had torn the flesh nastily. Having the splinters out had been excruciating. It still hurt a great deal. He had a black eye and a range of other bruises from his tumble in the river.

'Pythonissa,' Tarchon said, then some things which probably meant a lot in his own language but merely sounded vaguely positive to the others.

The riders were rounding the next bend in the gorge, coming up from the north, moving at a gentle canter. The girl was in front. She was riding a chestnut with a nice action. Her blond hair was uncovered. Otherwise, it would not have been easy to distinguish her at a distance. She wore a baggy tunic, rode like a man.

One of the baggage animals had a deadweight lashed across its back; two others had something heavy slung between them. Ballista quickly counted heads: twenty-three, what he thought they had started out with.

Pythonissa reined in. '*Kyria*.' Ballista greeted her in Greek. He bowed, blew a kiss from his fingertips. The things on the pack-horses were game. He felt relieved.

'*Kyrios.*' She performed *proskynesis* from the saddle. In another it might have been offhand, in her it had an elegance. She looked around at the debris. 'Accident or design?' She appeared to have the laconic style of her brother Azo.

'Sabotage.'

She nodded, as if it were to be expected. 'Artemis smiled on us, we have a boar, a deer and several brace of partridge and snipe. If you have bread and wine, we can have a feast.'

The cooking was a drawn-out and rather fraught business. The language barrier separating Ballista's Agathon and the various self-styled experts in field cooking in the train of Pythonissa simmered all afternoon, often threatening culinary disaster, if not physical violence. The linguistic and diplomatic skills of Mastabates were pushed to their owner's exasperation. Yet when the sun went down, all was ready.

The majority were to eat where the food had been cooked, in front of their tents and shelters along the track, not far from the animal lines. Only the select were to dine in the little fort of Cumania: Ballista and the four citizens in his *familia*, Pythonissa and four of her leading warriors.

It was dim and fuggy in the circular second-floor room. The shutters were pulled back from the arrow slits, but little of the smoke from the torches escaped. Ballista remembered someone once remarking to him that civilization ended where candles and torches replaced lamps. Couches and low tables had been found or improvised. Ballista shared a couch with Pythonissa. Wulfstan and one of her eunuchs stood at the foot to serve them.

The first course was a soup made from dried peas heavily fla-voured with cumin. It was a local favourite; the embassy had eaten it several times since reaching Colchis. Usually, Ballista enjoyed it.

This evening he was distracted, trying to think of things to talk about with this strange girl. What came into his mind was crashingly inappropriate. *Are you involved in many bloodfeuds? Have you poisoned many people?* He pulled the bread into little pieces. Pythonissa herself was quiet, seemingly preoccupied. Left to the two of them, conversation soon would have ground to a halt.

Fortunately, the others made a better show. The four Suani spoke Greek. Maximus was his customary ebullient self. His hands waved and chopped as he elaborated ever more implausible stories. He had to gulp his drink whenever his flow of words allowed him a chance. Mastabates also did well. Paradoxically, he was so urbane he did not seem out of place in this rough fort in a wilderness of mountains. Little in these circumstances was to be expected from Calgacus, but he was polite enough when called upon to make an answer. Hippothous, however, was a disappointment. He spoke seldom; instead, he sat intently staring at one of the Suani. *Allfather*, Ballista thought, *it better be physiognomy – if the Greek tries to fuck him there will be bloodshed.*

The main course arrived. There was plate after plate of roast meat: venison and boar, partridge and snipe. Not boiling the game birds had been the essence of Suanian objections to Agathon's cooking. There were few vegetables – just some cabbage and garlic – but more flat bread, and more, much more, goatskin-flavoured wine.

Ballista rallied a little. Pythonissa had asked him about the battle at Soli where he had defeated the Sassanid king. Ballista explained the overall strategy and the specific tactics in some detail. She gave every sign of being interested. Although warmed by the wine, he knew he was being humoured and led. But, far from minding, he felt grateful.

A burst of laughter from the Suani followed Maximus telling the inevitable joke about the young tribune at a remote fort and the camel. Things were going well. They were enjoying themselves. Even Ballista was beginning to relax. Then she asked him, with what might have been an arch look, about his capture of the Sassanid royal harem – *was it very opulent, very decadent?* She put a certain emphasis on the last. His words dried up.

Ballista preferred not to think about the things he had done in the purple shadows of that silken pavilion. Tipping wine on the altar to extinguish the sacred flame. The two servants – eunuchs – killed on a whim. His treatment of Shapur's favourite concubine Roxanne. Afterwards, slumped half naked on the throne of the house of Sasan, drinking, the girl crying. Even Maximus, when he came in, looking aghast. Of course, Ballista had thought his wife and boys dead; he had not been in his right mind. But the memory was painful – his complete loss of self-control, his descent to what any Greek or Roman would see as his true bestial barbarian nature.

Seeing something was wrong, Pythonissa took up the conversational running. She talked to him confidingly about the ghastliness of her ex-father-in-law Hamazasp; his ignorance, alarming table manners, and extraordinary taste in women and not just boys but men. The latter was a subject Ballista did not want to dwell on, but he appreciated her flow of talk.

After some pears poached in wine – with an unusual aftertaste of goat – the serious food was over. Just some walnuts, cheese, honey, dried apples, roasted broad beans and yet more bread were put out to soak up the serious drinking.

The talk flowed around and over Ballista. He knew what was troubling him. It was her proximity. The way she spoke and smiled and moved; everything made him intensely aware of her physical proximity.

Eventually, Ballista was relieved to call an end to things. He stood, slightly unsteadily, wished them goodnight. The guests left. Ballista went to the top floor, which he had taken as his quarters. Wulfstan helped him out of his best tunic, put out a bowl of water, and left. Ballista was washing when Calgacus stuck his head around the door.

'The woman has sent you a gift.'

The two eunuchs entered. Between them they carried a strangely heavy-looking roll of silk carpet. Carefully, they placed it on the floor. One stood forward, bowed. 'Our *kyria* said we were to open the gift only when you were on your own, *Kyrios*.'

Ballista gave Calgacus a look which said that, even naked with an injured shoulder, he had nothing to fear from a couple of court eunuchs. The Caledonian made a strange face – possibly a smile – and withdrew.

The eunuchs gently unrolled the soft, embroidered material. A tangle of white limbs, a mass of blond hair. They helped her to her feet. She was naked. She was biting her thumb to stop herself laughing out loud. The eunuchs bowed to her, to him, and backed from the room.

She took her arms away so he could see her. She was smiling. A necklace, a bangle or two, nothing else. 'Just like Cleopatra to Caesar,' she said.

He walked across. She put her arms around his neck, careful to avoid his injured shoulder. He put his around her waist. She tipped up her face. He leant down. They kissed, her tongue in his mouth. He slid his hands down to the small of her back, pulled her to him. Her breasts pressed against his chest. She was tall. He smelt her perfume, her body. She leant back, looking up at him. Her blue-grey eyes were shining. He felt the familiar surge of powerful lust. It was going to be all right, more than all right.

Ballista woke in the early hours of the morning. A feeling of dread was on him. He was sweating, heart racing. The girl was asleep beside him. Moonlight slanted in from the narrow arrow slits. Ballista forced himself to sit up, look across the room at what he knew he would see. There by the door, as he knew it would be, was the tall, hooded figure. The huge, pale face, the grey eyes full of hatred.

'Speak,' Ballista said.

'I will see you again at Aquileia.' Maximinus Thrax spoke, although he had been dead these more than twenty years.

Holding his courage tight, as he had every time before, Ballista replied. 'I will see you then.'

Pythonissa stirred, put her arm across him. Ballista looked down at her. She opened her eyes. He looked back towards the door. The daemon was gone, just the odour of the waxed canvas of its cloak lingering.

'What is wrong?' She suddenly was very awake. She quickly scanned the room for threats. Seeing nothing, she relaxed. 'You look as if you had seen Hecate herself.'

Ballista tried to smile, to speak – he could do neither. He lay back.

'Tell me,' she said.

He told her – the centurion who had taken him from the hall of his father to be an imperial hostage, the siege of Aquileia, the conspiracy, the wild fight, stabbing the iron stylus deep into the throat of the emperor, the decapitation of Maximinus, the desecration of his body, the daemon that walked by night, the threat of Aquileia – told her all of it.

Pythonissa listened until he was finished. She kissed his chest.

'You think it is more than a dream?' he asked.

'It could be a dream, but of course the dead walk.' She kissed his chest again. 'Avoid the Italian city of Aquileia and nothing more will happen.'

Now he could half smile. 'Unless it is another place of that name, or Aquileia is something else – a state of mind.'

Her blue-grey eyes regarded him. 'Does the daemon ever return the same night?'

'No.'

She kissed his lips, then his chest. He felt her hair slide down his body, her tongue licking. She started doing what will take almost any man's mind off his troubles. At least while it lasts.

Her eunuchs returned an hour before dawn. She told them to wait, turned to him.

'I am not a young man any more.'

She took no notice.

After she had gone, he had to endure the sly smiles of Wulfstan, Calgacus and the others as he washed, dressed, had breakfast. Maximus kept tiresomely remarking how tired he looked. Ballista wondered what it would be like to live in a culture where you had privacy. In Germania, in the *imperium* – everywhere he had been it was the same. The poor lived many to a room. The houses of the rich were packed with servants. As some satirist had written, 'When Andromache mounted Hector their slaves stood with their ears glued to the door, masturbating.' It would be good to live somewhere where you could have sex with reasonable certainty that no one was listening. Despite such thoughts, Ballista found himself smiling a smile he would have found smug and annoying on someone else. It was interesting that Hector had liked his wife to get on top.

Someone came to say the *kyria* was leaving. They crossed the river by the stepping stones, arriving only moderately damp at the other side. Pythonissa walked her horse forward from her entourage. Ballista bowed, blew a kiss; wished her a safe journey. Very formal, she returned the *proskynesis*; asked the gods to hold their hands over him. He had a sudden vision of her naked, on her hands and knees, of him taking her from behind. He had to have her again. She smiled, full of mischief, as if she could tell what he was thinking. She leant down from the saddle, passed him something.

It was an ice-white gem hung on a golden chain. 'From the peak where Prometheus was chained,' she said. 'A cure for nightmares.' He thanked her, slipped it around his neck. She turned her horse and rode away to the south.

They got back to work. There was a change in the Suani. While they would never labour like *helots* promised their freedom, they were better than they had been. It might have been connected to the visit of Pythonissa, or possibly to Ballista saving Tarchon. Whatever the reason, they were a little more assiduous.

Within a few days, progress was apparent. Once the scaffolding was rebuilt, the gate on the track began to take shape. The new piers in the Alontas were put in place, and the first tentative spans of timber began to connect them. The final finishes were made to the tower of Cumania.

There was a new purpose and a better routine to the day. At first light, sacrifices were made to Prometheus and Heracles. Respect for local sentiment meant that nothing was ever offered to Zeus or Athena. The workers were fed hot bread with cheese. This was prepared by native cooks at fires on the side of the road. To spare the inhabitants of the fort from being choked by smoke, Agathon cooked their breakfast with the others, then carried it across the stepping stones. Their favoured deities and their stomachs placated, the workers went to their assigned places. Lunch was a simple affair – more flat bread, this time with soup or millet porridge – taken where they toiled. An afternoon's work, another set of sacrifices, and the Suani were free to pass the evening with more eating, drinking and singing their sad songs by their fires.

The sixth morning found Ballista on the battlements as the sun hit the peaks above the gorge. He had a panoramic view over the dark river, the road, the sawing camp fires and the as yet quiet half-built fortifications. Pythonissa was much on his mind. For years, he had amazed his friends and, if he were honest, himself, with his fidelity to his wife. Maximus had never been able to understand it at all. Not even on the many occasions, inevitably when they were drinking, when Ballista had tried to explain the true reasons. Apart from Roxanne – and he felt nothing but guilt about that – he had not had another woman in part because he loved his wife but also because he had developed a strange super-stition. He had somehow convinced himself that if he had another woman, the next time he was in combat he would be killed. Almost every fighting man he had ever known had a talis-man he hoped would keep him safe – the belts of Roman soldiers were covered in the things. Ballista had clutched his uxorious faithfulness to himself like a sealskin amulet, a rabbit's foot, or some such trinket. But at Soli he had taken Roxanne, and he had not died at Sebaste, or in any of the other places where the spirits of death had hovered close, not in Galilee, Emesa, Ephesus or Didyma. Things had not been right between him and Julia, not since he had returned from Galilee. He had no idea why. Yes, he supposed he felt guilt, but man was not built for monogamy. Celi-bacy was bad for the health of man or woman. Julia was far away. And Pythonissa was ... wilder than any girl he had known, wilder than any of the whores of his youth. He drifted into a rev-erie about her body, the things she did.

Across the river, something was wrong. Shouting, a crowd gathering by one of the camp fires. A man was staggering, flail-ing about. It was Agathon. Ballista went to the trapdoor, climbed down the ladder. He grabbed his sword belt from his quarters, carried on down.

Calgacus met him on the floor below. 'Agathon . . .'

'I know – stay here, post a guard, shut the door after us.'

The others were on the second floor. 'Maximus, come with me. The rest of you stay here.'

As Ballista and Maximus went down the outer steps, Tarchon joined them. There was no shaking the Suanian. The heavy oak door slammed behind them. Ballista wondered if they should have taken the time to put on their mail coats.

When they reached the other side, they had to shoulder through a dense throng of onlookers. Agathon was on the ground. He was clawing at his eyes, his body jerking. He had fouled himself. The Suani watched him with expressionless black eyes. Ballista and Maximus knelt either side, gripped him hard, restrained him. A final convulsion and Agathon died.

In the complete silence, Tarchon got to his knees and cradled the head of the dead slave. He put his face very close to but not touching that of the corpse. Tarchon sniffed. He said something in his native tongue, then one word in Greek: poison.

XXV

The killing of Agathon changed things. Ballista and the *familia* now habitually went fully armed. By day, pickets were posted. At night, Cumania was shuttered and bolted. A watch was kept. All food and drink for the *familia* was kept in the fort, where it was prepared by Polybius and Wulfstan. It had been brought home to them that they were far from help, hemmed in by wild mountains and any number of potential enemies. At least Cumania was virtually impregnable. A siege mentality was fast developing.

Yet the construction proceeded well. The Suani outside the fort seemed unaffected by the poisoning. Seen so much of it, Maximus suggested. The dressed stones of the gate went up tier by tier. The wooden walkway over the river was completed. There were practical difficulties tying it into the natural rockface to the west, but nothing Ballista could not resolve.

It was seven days before the *kalends* of August, fifteen since Agathon had been murdered. Nothing else bad had happened. The fortifications were nearly ready. Ballista thought they might be finished by the *kalends*. It was all in hand.

The messenger arrived mid-afternoon. He came from the

south, had a letter for Ballista. It was in Greek, in a woman's hand. She hoped it found him well, asked if the gemstone had helped, thanked him for entertaining her so well. He had no doubt it came from Pythonissa. She wanted him to ride down to the house she had in Dikaiosyne that night. For discretion, it was better he came alone.

With the exception of Maximus, the *familia* was unanimous that he should not go. It was madness. The letter might not be from her. Even if it were, it could be a trap. From her or not, the situation was too dangerous. Someone in these ghastly mountains wanted them dead. These Suani were not to be trusted.

Ballista was determined. He would go. If so, they said, he could not ride alone. Even Maximus joined in the chorus. These mountaineers would cut a lone stranger's throat soon as look at him. Ballista relented: he would take one man. The Suani Tarchon, in the little Greek he had picked up, demanded that he accompany the *kyrios*: blood oath, he had sworn blood oath, very happy to die. Words failing him, he mimed covering his head, sneaking along. Maximus was having none of it: all these years, and he was not going to be elbowed aside by some filthy fucking goat boy who probably did not know one end of a fucking sword from another.

Ballista exercised tact. He reminded Tarchon that Calgacus had also saved him. The blood oath was to the old man as well. Tarchon must stay and keep him safe; if that failed, he could die happy for him. With much doubt in his eyes, Tarchon agreed. Maximus would accompany Ballista. They would return the following night. On the day they were away, Calgacus would command. Everyone must take their orders unquestioningly from him. No Suani, with the exception of Tarchon, were to enter the fort. Did they all understand?

Not long after dusk, when the sky in the west was still purple, three men in native costume crossed the stepping stones over the

292

Alontas and went to the horse lines. They tacked up, mounted and rode south.

At first they rode in silence. The night darkened, the heavens were painted with stars. It was good to be out of the fort, away from the pass. It was good to be riding at night. The Alontas rattled away past them, the horses stepping quietly. Sometimes they pricked up their ears, looked out into the darkness at things the men could not see.

When the rock walls rolled back and the country opened they felt like talking. Maximus untied the folds of the native turban that had been covering the lower part of his face. 'Do you think I will catch something from this?'

'Almost certainly: lice.'

They spoke in the language of Maximus's home.

'Are you thinking it is altogether wise us risking our lives just so you can fuck her?'

'Muirtagh of the Long Road would never do anything like that.'

'Never in six lifetimes. Do you think she might have a maid or two?'

'No, just the eunuchs. But I am sure they will be grateful for your attentions.'

They crossed a stream joining the Alontas. Water splashed up in the starlight, stones clinked under the horses' hooves.

'You remember that night we dressed up to walk the walls at Arete?'

'When that soldier said Ballista's bodyguard was one of the ugliest fuckers he had ever seen?'

'That is the one. Then there was us as fishermen at Corycus.'

'Sebaste.'

'What?'

'It was Sebaste.'

'Wherever, gods below it took me days to get rid of the smell. And that time at Ephesus you had me blacked up as the king of the Saturnalia to start a riot.'

'Happy days. You remember what you were wearing in Massilia?'

'Sure, you always have to bring that up, just when I am happy.'

About the middle watch, they came to a place where two small rivers came down on either side to join the Alontas. Beyond was Dikaiosyne. The villages of Suania had no walls. There was no need for them with every home a miniature fortress. The messenger led them through the alleys to a closed gate in a blank wall. He whistled and the gate opened.

Ballista left Maximus with the porter and the horses. He followed the messenger up several flights of stairs. The house was large, a more Mediterranean style than most. On the top floor, one of the eunuchs sat, dozing on a tasselled cushion outside an ornate door. As he got to his feet, the messenger wordlessly went back down the stairs.

'Wait please, *Kyrios*.' The eunuch tapped on the door, slipped inside.

Ballista waited – a long time.

The eunuch re-emerged. With a courtly bow, he waved Ballista to enter.

There were several little lamps burning, but the wide, tall room was still dim. It was perfumed and opulent with rugs and hangings. A large bed against the far wall was plump with mattresses and cushions. Pythonissa walked out of the shadows. This time she was not naked, not quite. She wore a silk gown, diaphanous and clinging like a statue of a goddess. It emphasized her body, more than nudity ever could.

'*Kyrios*,' she said. As she bowed the gown slid open. He could see her breasts. There was a sheen to her skin.

Pythonissa pulled her gown together. Her nipples stood out through the thin material. She firmly pushed away his hands. She took his native headdress and coat, helped him out of his sword belt and mail coat. She placed them away in a corner. Coming back with a bowl of water and towels, she told him to sit. She washed and dried his hands, helped him off with his boots, washed and dried his feet; all the time fending off his hands.

She went to fetch him a drink. This time he grabbed her. The wine spilt as he dragged her on to his lap. He kissed her, his hands moving greedily over her. She broke her mouth away, laughing. 'I wondered how long I could make you wait.' They kissed, pulling at each other's clothes. They ended up on the floor.

Afterwards, not bothering to dress, she padded to the door. She opened it and told the eunuch to bring food and drink. Ballista stood up, stretched. She came and stood in front of him. She was tall, little shorter than him. She looked at the healing scars on his shoulder, traced them with her fingertips. She dipped her head, her red lips parted, and her tongue traced along the wounds.

The eunuch glided into the room. He set the things out on a table. Pythonissa took no notice at all of him. Her hand reached down, fondling. Ballista went to push her away, stopped himself. She was shameless, impudent. The eunuch bowed. As the servant backed out of the room, she sank to her knees.

Ballista woke late the next day. He was in her big bed. His head ached slightly from the wine, but he felt good. He could smell her on him.

Pythonissa was already up. Wearing another sheer gown, she was telling her servants where to place the breakfast trays. There was an aroma of warm bread, bacon, other good things. She smiled knowingly at Ballista. 'They have brought a lot of food. It would be indiscreet for you to leave until tonight. You might need to keep your strength up.'

The day passed languorously. The eunuchs carried in a bath, hot water. Ballista and Pythonissa bathed, oiled each other. They ate, drank, talked. At midday, Maximus arrived, asked if he needed anything. He did not. Maximus went away again. Twice more in the afternoon Pythonissa mounted Ballista as Andromache mounted Hector. He had almost forgotten the vigour that came with a new lover.

When it began to get dark he said he should go. She said, 'Not yet,' arranged herself on the bed. He took her from behind, hard, almost brutal. It was just as he had remembered it from the first time. When it was over, they lay together, flushed, out of breath.

The door crashed open. Harsh light flooded the room. Men crowded in. Ballista rolled from the bed. Two men were between him and his weapons. Drawn blades covered him.

'My whore of a sister.' It was Saurmag. There were six armed men with him – not Suani, nomads from the north. There were more outside.

'What are you doing?' Pythonissa was on her feet. Her face white with anger, she made little attempt to cover her breasts, her delta. Inconsequentially, Ballista thought of the Aphrodite of Cnidus.

Saurmag did not answer her. From his coat he produced some white reeds, scattered them negligently on the floor. 'Cut at dawn at the beginning of the spring. Cut by you, when you sacrificed to Hecate, sang the paean to your bitch goddess. Now they will condemn you.'

Ballista stood very still, measuring, calculating. Only a small table to hand, nothing to use as a weapon. The two men nearest did not take their eyes off him.

'You fool, Saurmag,' she hissed. 'A word from me to our father – what you did to our brothers.'

Saurmag smiled. 'You forget, I was not alone in killing Mithridates and Tzathius.'

'Our father will not believe you, nor will Azo.'

Saurmag actually laughed. 'That really does not matter. They are being hunted down now.' His face hardened. 'Because you betrayed me, I have been forced to act sooner than I wished.'

The Suanian prince stepped forward. His men's eyes did not waver. Ballista wondered where Maximus was.

Saurmag slapped his sister hard. She took a step back, recovered herself. Saurmag pointed at Ballista. 'I sent you to kill this barbarian. Instead, like the whore you are, you took him to your bed. Because you let him live, the Caspian Gates are nearly complete.'

He slapped her again. 'Nearly complete, but not finished. The Alani rode through today.'

'You are a fool.' Her voice was low, full of menace. 'The Alani will not let you rule. They will take Suania for themselves.'

'You underestimate me; like our father, our brothers, the *synedrion* – all of you.' Saurmag shrugged. 'Anyway, you will never know. Your shameless lust has delivered you and your barbarian into my hands. By tomorrow you will both be gone into the Mouth of the Impious. In thirty days' time the vultures of Maeotis will be tearing at your flesh.'

XXVI

The dark was not absolute. Tiny squints of light peeped through the trapdoor above his head. Ballista wished they did not. They showed just how small was the space.

The cell was underground, apparently cut from the living rock. Ballista had to be careful how he shifted his weight. The surfaces behind his back, under his arse, his heels, were rough, jagged. There was not enough room for him to stand or, sitting, straighten his legs. He could feel the mass of the rock all around, pressing in, restricting him, crushing him. The fear of confined spaces was hard on him. He sat, arms around his knees, in the dark, in the filth. He had no idea how long he had been there.

Up in Pythonissa's room, Saurmag had been in no hurry to end his pleasure. The Suanian prince had slapped his sister again. She had raised her arms to protect her face. He had laughed, caught her wrists, slapped her two, three more times. Some of the Alani grinned, enjoying her nakedness, her pain. But the eyes of the two watching Ballista did not shift. The northerner slumped, trying to look defeated, hoping for an opportunity.

Saurmag had said something to the nomads in their language. One, probably the leader, had replied. He was grinning, eying the girl. 'I asked if his men would enjoy you,' Saurmag had said. He yanked her wrists high, fully exposing her body. She spat. The spittle ran down his cheek. He hit her hard with his fist. There was blood on her lips. Her brother looked her up and down, slowly, nothing fraternal about it. 'No, if I . . .' He hit her again. 'You can die no more defiled than this barbarian and all the others have left you.'

'Neither with steel nor poison.' Her voice had been just in control.

Saurmag had smiled. 'No poison, no steel. I keep my word: just the Mouth of the Impious. Take them away.'

Down in the cell, the dark pushed in on Ballista. He tried to control his breathing, drive down his fear. Where was Maximus? What had happened to him? 'Do you need anything?' 'No, I do not.' Inadequate words, if they were to prove their last. Saurmag had not mentioned the Hibernian. There had been no sight of him. Pythonissa had been dragged off. Ballista did not know where. After she had gone, four Alani had hustled him down to the bottom of her house. He had stumbled along, the picture of dejection – waiting for a chance. They had not bound his hands. The chance had not come. At the end of a rock-cut corridor, the trapdoor had been hauled up. He had been shoved down into this solitary cell. The trapdoor had slammed down. Allfather, he prayed Maximus had got away.

The Alani had come up through the Caspian Gates. What of Calgacus and the others? The small fortress of Cumania was as near impregnable as any Ballista had seen. But surprise, treachery, could take any place. If they had had time to secure the fort, they had provisions to last for months. But had they had enough warning? Had they let any others take shelter with them? Others

299

who might turn traitor? If they were attacked night and day, how long before exhaustion wore them down?

Alone in the dark, he thought of his sons, his wife. Perhaps he had been right all those years – take another woman and he would die. *The mills of the gods are slow in grinding, but grind fine.* From the proverb his thoughts drifted to lines of Euripides:

> Not to your face, no fear, not to any miscreant's
> Will justice strike the fatal blow; but soft
> And slow of tread, she will, in her own season,
> Stalking the wicked, seize them unawares.

He refused to give way to self-pity. If nothing else, he might as well die fighting before he let them sew him in the sack.

There were indistinct noises from above. They resolved themselves into footsteps. A heavy tread coming nearer. More than one man. No, thought Ballista, not like Edessa. The horror of that cell came back to him. A Persian called Vardan and Hamizasp of Iberia: beating him, rolling him over, tugging at his clothes. Only a near miracle – the arrival of the Persian boy, the Zoroastrian *mobad* called Hormizd – had saved him.

The footfalls were directly above. Might as well die today without suffering that, better than dying tomorrow afterwards. Ballista tried to get up into a crouch. His legs were dead, arms shaking.

The light blinded him as the trapdoor was opened. 'Get him out,' someone said. He tried to rise. Hands gripped him, hauled him up. He was set on his feet. They were still holding him.

'Hecate, you stink.' A woman's voice. Ballista forced his eyes open. It was Pythonissa – and better, much better than that – behind her was Maximus.

'How?' Ballista was swaying, grinning like an idiot, trying to kiss them both. They were alive – free – they had freed him. All-father, but this was good.

'Get dressed now,' She was not grinning. There was a third person, a Suanian warrior. He passed over a bundle of clothes. Ballista started to put on the trousers, tunic, boots, other things; all native costume. He was clumsy with cramp. Maximus helped him.

'I was out looking for a place where a man might have some fun.' Maximus shook his head sorrowfully. 'Nothing at all, dullest place I have ever set foot. No bars, no brothels, no baths, not a drink or a girl to be had in the whole fucking place. You have got your arm down the wrong sleeve. Anyway, I was on my way back, all my hopes dashed to the ground, when who should I see but your man Saurmag coming up the road, and not on his own either. So, I ran back, whistled up our faithful messenger, old Kobrias here' – he nodded to the Suanian – 'and one of his friends. We went over the back wall as Saurmag and his boys came bursting in the front. Kobrias's brother lives an alley or two over. He hid us. Gods, will you concentrate – hold your fucking foot still; it is like dressing a child. We got a boy to watch. The lad comes back, tells us Saurmag has just ridden out as if he were late for his own funeral, taken all but ten of his men with him. So we thought we would come back. There you go. Very fetching you look too, a proper barbarous mountaineer.'

'He has a gift for killing,' Pythonissa said.

'Thank you, *Kyria*.' Maximus bowed to her then smiled at Ballista. 'Your armour and weapons are in the courtyard with the horses.'

'How many?' Ballista asked.

'He killed five of the ten,' Pythonissa said. 'Now we must go. Put the hats on, cover your faces. No talking until we are clear of the village. There are others of my brother's men here.'

301

There were two bodies, much blood, at the end of the corridor. Several more outside.

In the bone-white moonlight, a warrior and a eunuch held the horses. Ballista, more himself now, wriggled into his mail coat, buckled on the belts that held his weapons. His war gear clinked and glittered reassuringly. Maximus tossed him two more knives. He hid one in each boot.

'Put the hats on,' Pythonissa hissed.

Ballista and Maximus did as they were told. 'Your helmet is in the bed roll on the saddle,' Maximus whispered. 'There is food and drink.'

'Enough talk,' she said.

Ballista noted with approval the bow case hanging from his saddle.

They mounted. A woman appeared from nowhere, unbarred the gate of the house. As the six riders went past, she performed *proskynesis* full length in the dirt. The gate shut quietly as they rode away.

There was always something strange about riding through a town or village in the dead of night – the flat quality of the light, a stray cat or two where there should be people, a dog barking loud in the stillness – and never more so than when riding through an enemy-held place, when any human encounter most likely would mean discovery and disaster. The priestess of Hecate led the muffled figures down one alley after another, past crossroads haunted by the servants of her infernal deity. The clop of hooves, the creak of leather, the jingle of tack echoing back from the blank walls, the shuttered windows – all inviting anyone awake to wonder who was abroad at such an hour, inviting scrutiny.

At long, long last, they left the last sleeping houses behind. Relief washed through them all. Even the horses seemed to move more freely. Pythonissa quickened the pace to a round canter.

They rode on without speaking: the priestess, her lover, his body-guard, two warriors and a eunuch – a strange company bound by circumstance. The sounds of their passing floated off up the bare slopes.

After half an hour or so, Pythonissa reined in. They slid from the saddle, walked next to the horses to let them get their wind back. The night was quiet all around.

'Why are we heading south?' Ballista asked.

'Saurmag and the Alani have gone to besiege Cumania. Our brother Azo is there.' She gave a snort of laughter. 'It seems a rumour had reached my eldest brother that the northern barbarian Ballista had behaved with impropriety towards a member of his family. He is very keen on both family honour and propriety – I think I have been a great trial to him. Yesterday, Azo was on his way to see you. Somehow he slipped past the Alani, and ended up having to take refuge with your men.'

'How many were with him?'

'Only half a dozen.'

Ballista calculated: Calgacus, Hippothous, Mastabates, the three slaves and young Wulfstan, the Suani Tarchon, joined by seven other Suani – fourteen of fighting age and a boy. The additional numbers meant less danger of the tiny garrison succumbing to fatigue. If the siege were very long, it might put a strain on supplies. More worrying, Ballista's men were outnumbered. If one of the Suani turned traitor, things would not be good.

In the gloom, Pythonissa turned a serious face to Ballista. 'Saurmag has to kill Azo. If he does not then, irrespective of his Alani allies, he will not be king of Suania. With Azo still alive, neither the *synedrion* nor the rest of the Suani will accept him as king.'

'What about your father?'

'He is dead.'

They walked on in silence until it was time to mount up again.

'If not north to the Caspian Gates, where are we going?' Ballista asked.

Pythonissa smiled, spoke with a playful edge. 'To the low country, so the renowned general Marcus Clodius Ballista can gather troops from the Roman garrison in Colchis. With the hero of Soli at their head, they will win a great victory, drive the nomads back beyond the Gates, kill the patricidal usurper Saurmag, place the rightful heir Azo on the throne of Suania, and in so doing both make the new monarch grateful to his sister and ensure he is a friend of Rome. A happy outcome for everyone, except all those you kill and all those connected to Saurmag.'

Ballista settled himself in the saddle. He snorted sadly. 'A good plan for a Greek novel. There are not enough Roman troops in the whole of the Kindly Sea, let alone Colchis.'

'Then we will go to Iberia,' Pythonissa rallied. 'Hamazasp will give us troops. He will drive a hard bargain, but I was married to his beloved son.'

'Hamazasp will kill me, unfortunately, not quite as soon as look at me.' Ballista took her lack of response for agreement. He clicked his tongue and the horse walked on.

'Albania then.' Pythonissa was full of resource. 'You said your friend Castricius is at the court there. My mother was Albanian. King Cosis will welcome the chance to acquire influence in Suania.'

'Which is why Hamazasp of Iberia will never let Albanian troops cross his territories to get to Suania.'

This time Pythonissa had no more ideas. The horses walked on down the track.

Ballista made up his mind. 'If we need warriors to defeat Saurmag and his Alani, there is only one place we can raise them – to the south-west of the Caspian Sea in the lands of the Mardi and the Cadusii.'

Pythonissa looked at him with incomprehension. 'Their revolt has been crushed by the Sassanid prince Narseh. There is still a Persian army there.'

'Yes.'

She saw what he meant. 'They will kill you.'

'They might not.'

XXVII

As the dawn chased away the night, they came to another pass – perhaps fifteen miles south of Dikaiosyne, certainly less than twenty. Its native name was unpronounceable by Ballista and Maximus. Rendered into Greek, it was Dareine. They could smell the camp fires a way off, before the smoke was visible in the mist. They halted: six huddled centaurs in the dimness.

'Fuck,' said Maximus.

'Is there a way round?' Ballista asked.

Pythonissa made a negative gesture with a hand. 'Not unless we go a long way back towards the village.'

'Fuck,' said Maximus.

'And they will be Saurmag's men?' Ballista asked.

'Yes.'

'Fuck,' said Maximus again.

Ballista looked all around. The bare slopes were grey in the half light. Above, the snow of the peaks was pink with the morning sun, the rocks showing through a deeper red. Resting on them, the sky was blue, but with ugly scrawls of dark cloud which promised foul weather. Down below on the pale track were the six muffled riders, much alike in their cloaks and bulky coats.

Ballista spoke to Pythonissa. 'Your two warriors go in front. They must try and talk us through. Maximus and I go next. We may have to cut our way out. If someone goes down, no one can stop.' He looked over at Maximus and knew the falsity of his words.

Pythonissa spoke in their own language to the two Suani warriors. Their identical, dark-eyed faces regarded her dispassionately. When she had finished, they moved their horses to the front. She backed her horse next to the eunuch. They all set off at a walk.

The tide of sunshine was flowing down the western slope. The bottom of the pass was still in shade. Clouds of fresh smoke billowed out from the small camp fire on the side of the track. There were four guards feeding the flames. The smell was aromatic, homely. The other, larger fire was some way off on a shelf to the left. Above it there was just a waver of smoke. It had not been made up for hours. The unreckoned number of men there were not yet stirring. The tethered horses looked down solemnly.

A challenge was called from ahead. One of Pythonissa's men answered. The men by the fire were not Alani but Suani. It might help. The travellers walked their horses up to the picket and stopped. The sentinels had spread out; two in the track, one to either side; bows in hand, arrows notched. They kept their distance. There was an exchange of words. By the larger fire, men were getting to their feet.

Unslinging a goatskin of wine from one of the horns of his saddle, Ballista unstoppered it and took a swig. He used his knees to pace his mount towards the guard off the track on the right. Getting close, he leant down and offered the drink. As the warrior reached for it, Ballista stabbed him in the side of the neck. The dagger went in hard to the hilt. The man dropped the flask and his bow. He did not scream. His hands grabbed Ballista's forearm. Ballista used his boot to shove him away. The man fell back with a frothy, choking sound.

Shouts – a prolonged scream. Ballista wheeled his horse. Automatically wiping the blade of his dagger on his thigh, he sheathed it and drew his sword. His hand was sticky with blood. Another of the guards was down, not moving. A third guard was dodging this way and that. Pythonissa's two Suani were circling him, cutting down with their long swords at his head. The man had his arms up. Blood was running down them. He was screaming. The final guard was running up the slope towards his companions at the larger camp fire. They were snatching up their weapons, throwing saddles on to their horses, untethering them.

'Move!' Maximus was already a little way down the track. His horse was stamping, throwing its head about at the scent of blood.

Pythonissa's mount surged past. Ballista brought his around behind that of her eunuch, slapped the flat of his blade across its rump. The eunuch's horse leapt forward like a scalded cat. Ballista booted his after it.

The two Suani were still chopping at the remaining guard. 'Leave him,' Ballista shouted as he passed. The two men sawed at their reins. As they came around, an arrow took one in the face. He was knocked sideways in the saddle. His horse shied. The Suanian crashed to the ground. More arrows were slicing down. 'Leave him,' Ballista shouted over his shoulder.

The fallen Suanian was alive. The arrow protruding from his jaw, he was struggling to his feet. His face a mask of blood, he reached for his horse. It skittered back, and bolted after the others. His companion sat in indecision. Arrows fell around him. One thumped into the baggage strapped across the rear of his mount. He kicked his heels, and raced after Ballista.

The five remaining riders were strung out along the track, the loose horse running with them, threatening mayhem. Maximus slowed, pulled to the side, let Pythonissa and the eunuch overtake him. The Hibernian fell in beside Ballista. Their surviving Suanian was only a dozen lengths behind.

'How many?' Ballista said above the thunder of hooves.

'Twenty, maybe more.'

'Suani or nomads?'

'Plenty of both.'

'Fuck,' Ballista said.

The first few miles were a straight chase. They were in the pass; there was nowhere else to go but down it. They rode as fast as they could. Stones rattled and flicked up from the horses' feet. Thankfully, the loose horse dropped back. Again and again they forded the stream in a chill spray of their own making. The day was not getting lighter. The clouds were coming down. The pass twisted. On the longer straights they could see the dark mass of their pursuers, a mile or so behind, an amorphous animal set on revenge.

Pythonissa reined in at the entrance to the pass. They pulled up around her, horses and riders steaming. A steep slope down to a green valley, a river winding through it. 'The Aragos,' she said. 'We follow it.'

Leaning far back in the saddle, carefully, they negotiated the incline. At the foot, she led them to the left, downstream. They had covered no great distance when those hunting them appeared at the top. Despite the hunters whooping at the sight of their prey, Ballista called for Pythonissa to slacken the pace. They would draw ahead again as the hunters came down the slope. This was going to be a long chase.

Some of the hills along the Aragos were timbered, but not enough to offer concealment. The fissures in its flanks were equally unpromising. Of course, they could not be like the two north of Dikaiosyne, Ballista thought bitterly. You could hide any number in them, or in the one they had ridden by between the village and the pass.

Although, generally, the valley of the Aragos was wide, at times it hemmed in on them. At these places the cliffs were vertical; devoid of vegetation, grooved as if by the chisel of some inexpert giant stonemason. Ballista contemplated making a stand, only to dismiss it as a futile last resort.

The ceiling of cloud was getting lower, the day darker. The horses were very tired. They rode on at a pushed canter but sitting straight, well back in the saddle.

When they had not seen or heard those chasing them for some time, Ballista called a halt. No sight of the sun, but he thought it about mid-morning. The mountain horses were tough, but needed spelling. They dismounted, let them drink just a little, led them onward.

The sound of a horn – echoing through the granite hills, impossible to tell how far – drove them to horseback again. They rode on downriver. The threatened rain still did not fall. Out of the murk, high on a terrace, a work of man suddenly would emerge, each one startling in its incongruity. Here a ruined stone tower, there a shepherd's hut; never anything that offered them safety.

When the horses were staggering, they got down again, walked by their heads.

'Have we crossed into the territory of Iberia?' Ballista asked. 'Will they not turn back?'

'In the Croucasis, territory is a fluid concept,' Pythonissa said. 'Its only meaning is where a ruler can get away with what he wishes.'

'It has always been a rule that the weak should be subject to the strong,' Ballista said.

She gave him a strange look. 'The Athenians in Thucydides. It is easy to forget you have become a Greek.'

'I have been in the *imperium* a long time.'

'If my brother's men recognized us, they will not dare turn back.'

They struggled on through the afternoon. Riding, walking, riding, walking – the times in the saddle getting ever shorter. It was amazing what a horse or a person could do when forced. Eating, drinking, relieving themselves on the track; even Pythonissa taking but a few steps for privacy. Humanity and beasts rendered near one in extremity.

Eventually, Ballista saw a large, tumbledown stone building off up one of the slopes. They could not go on. They would camp there. He sent Maximus back to the last turn of the valley. He would replace him in a couple of hours. The rest plodded into the ruin. It looked as if it had been a barn. Now, roofless in this bleak place, it seemed a monument to misguided optimism.

They lit no fire. After perfunctorily rubbing down and seeing to the horses, they slumped to the floor. Too tired to eat more than a mouthful or two, they tried to settle themselves to get what sleep they could. The Suanian warrior sat a little apart, sobbing quietly but unceasingly.

'What is the matter with him?' Ballista asked not so he could hear.

'Kobrias is mourning. His brother Oroezes was the one we left behind,' Pythonissa said.

Ballista could think of nothing to say. He went to sleep.

About two hours later, he woke, cold and stiff in every joint. His first thought was of his sons. He forced himself to saddle his horse, and lead it out to go and take over the watch. Maximus walked his animal to the barn. The rain still had not come. But the clouds were there, blotting out the moon and stars. Even when Ballista had been out some time, visibility was negligible.

It was cold. Ballista wriggled his toes in his boots, kept the

311

hand that was not holding the reins under his coat. He did not want to move too much: it would make him easier to spot. Sometimes, however, the cold forced him to get up, stamp his feet, walk the horse about. He did not really think the hunters would come up in the night. There may be Alani among them, as Maximus had said, but if so the nomads had no spare mounts with them. Their horses would be as done in as those of their quarry.

Time passed incredibly slowly. The river lapped past in the dark. From far away came the sound of jackals; once, the howl of a wolf. He calmed the horse. Ballista sat in the dark on the abysmal hillside. He thought of his sons, his wife. They would be asleep in warm, comfortable beds in the villa in Tauromenium. He wished he were in Sicily with them. Sicily, in these troubled times, the age of iron and rust: he could not think of a safer place. No Roman army had campaigned there since the civil wars as the old Republic died, nearly three centuries previously. No barbarian incursion had troubled the island for much longer. Nothing since the great slave uprisings, and they were what? – three and a half, four centuries ago. He wanted to be at home with his family. As he framed the thought, Pythonissa's words slid into his mind. *It is easy to forget you have become a Greek*. But he knew it was not true, not completely true. He would never be wholly a Greek. Yet now he would never again be wholly an Angle of Germania. Separated from the culture of his birth, he knew he would never fully be accepted as either Greek or Roman. Wherever he went he would be in exile. Whatever, all he wanted now was not to be on this dismal fucking hillside in the middle of nowhere.

The eunuch came along to take his place. Ballista took his horse back to the barn. Maximus was fast asleep. The Hibernian twitched and muttered, caught in a dream of who could tell what lubricious nature. Pythonissa and the other Suanian were awake, heads close together, talking. Ballista felt a pang of jealousy. He dismissed it – she was not his woman. At least the barbarian had stopped crying. Ballista hunkered down, fell asleep thinking again about his sons.

They were up an hour before dawn. Kobrias was on watch. They ate, fed the horses. They were tacking up when the Suanian galloped back. The hunters were coming. Still more than a mile before the turn in the valley, but riding fast. Ballista and the others climbed into the saddle, the threat banishing their fatigue.

Pythonissa led the Suanian warrior aside. She spoke urgently to him in their own tongue. Ballista said they should set off. She gestured for him to wait. She spoke some more to the Suanian. The warrior obviously agreed. She passed him a phial. He drank. She embraced him. 'Now we go,' she said.

As the others turned their horses down towards the track, the Suanian sat motionless.

'What is he doing?' Ballista asked.

'He will lead them to the barn. With luck, they will think they have trapped us all inside.'

'Why?'

'Yesterday he left his brother to die. Today Kobrias will make amends.'

'He will die.'

'And save us. He will have made amends. The thing I gave him will keep his courage up.'

They splashed across the stream, and around the next corner, out of sight.

XXVIII

By nightfall, the four riders came to the confluence of the Aragos and another river flowing from the north. Here, Pythonissa said they should leave the valley and strike due east into hills covered in stands of trees. They did not go far before camping. Again, they made no fire but, away from the valleys, in the immensity of the wilderness, their pursuers were unlikely to discover them.

They rode on the next day across gentle slopes of birch, ash and hazel. In the glades were lupins and hollyhocks. The big rain-clouds had gone and the day was warmer, alternating between short showers and soft sunshine. They made camp early, mid-afternoon, by a stream fringed with raspberry bushes. Pythonissa showed them how the locals caught trout by digging under the stones to uncover creatures muck like small black scorpions, fitting them to hooks. They bathed in an upland pool. First Ballista and Maximus, then, as they built a fire, Pythonissa and her eunuch.

'You know,' said Maximus, 'some eunuchs can get it up. It all depends on what age they were castrated and how.'

'You know,' said Ballista, 'I could not give a fuck.'

They cooked the trout, ate them with toasted flat bread.

When they had finished, Pythonissa came to Ballista, led him away, back to the pool. They had sex almost fully clothed, without talking. There was a chill to the evening. Afterwards, they lay together.

'Tell me about your brothers,' Ballista said.

'Saurmag and Azo . . .'

'No, the two who were killed.'

She was silent.

'What happened to them?' he prompted.

'In Suania, the more sons a warrior has, the more he is thought a man. Often, if a girl is born, they put a pinch of hot ash in the baby's mouth.'

Ballista considered this. 'In the story, Medea was not treated well by her father, but no one thinks she was right to dismember her brother.'

'So you think I am a new Medea.' She smiled. 'After you killed my husband, I was returned like an unwanted purchase to my father's court. My father wanted to marry me off to the king of the lice-eaters. Saurmag promised me more. If he took the throne, he would find me a better match. He talked much of the king of the Bosphorus.'

'So you helped him kill your brothers.'

Pythonissa did not reply.

'Why did you turn against him?'

'Like all men, Saurmag is only interested in fucking women or using them in other ways. He realized he could only rid himself of our father and Azo if he had help from outside Suania. He decided to summon the barbarian Alani. As an inducement, I was to be given to the Alani chief. I would have shared a tent with the nomad as his fourth wife.'

'And you discovered this when hunting north of the mountains.'

'No, I went there to make certain my suspicions were right.'

'And on your return, you came to my bed.'

She smiled. 'Do you regret it?'

'And now you think I can rid you and Suania of Saurmag and the Alani, making your brother Azo grateful to you.'

'As you say.' She turned to look at him with her blue-grey eyes. 'If you think I am a new Medea, remember what she did when Jason deserted her.'

The next day, they picked up the headwaters of the Alazonios river and followed them down out of the high country. They emerged on to a broad, grassy plain dotted with isolated Albanian farmsteads. It was the threshing season. Small boys stopped their work and regarded them from out of clouds of chaff. The river meandered beneath bald hills to the right. The greener foothills of the Caucasus were some miles away to the left. They rode by the trees that bordered the Alazonios. At night, they went down to the banks and camped. And Ballista worried about Calgacus and young Wulfstan and the others.

After four days by their side, the Alazonios turned south through the hills. Down there, the river was the border between Albania and Iberia. Wanting to keep well clear of Hamazasp, they kept on to the south-east, tracking a tributary upstream. For another three days they crossed more high country, fording fast streams where the waters surged dangerously around the animals' bellies. The evening before the *nones* of August they reached an Albanian settlement called Chabala.

The headman of Chabala was welcoming. He told them what they wanted to know. Cosis, king of Albania, was on the Caspian coast, south of the big peninsula, in the territory of the Cadusii. His uncle, Zober the high-priest, was with him. They had gone to confer with Prince Narseh, the son of Shapur. Yes, Narseh had his troops with him – many myriads – for there were still those unpunished among the Cadusii. Yes, the headman thought the Roman Castricius was with Cosis.

They rested for a day in the headman's house. When they left, he gave them gifts and food, provided two warriors who would act as guides. A day in the saddle brought them down to an immense lowland plain. It was hot down there. Yet not so hot they would put off their armour.

They rode hard for three days, but the news of their coming preceded them. No fewer than one hundred mounted Albanian warriors were waiting for them. They were large, handsome men, dressed much like Persians or Armenians. They were armed to the teeth: bows, javelins, swords, many daggers; wearing breastplates and curious helmets made from the skins of wild animals. The leader at least spoke Greek. He welcomed the *kyria* Pythonissa with all politeness – his *basileus* Cosis greatly looked forward to entertaining her. With Ballista he was more reserved – it was his duty to take him with all speed to Narseh, the glorious son of the house of Sasan. On the type of welcome Ballista might receive he would not be drawn.

To reach the sea, they crossed the strangest landscape Ballista had ever seen. The path ran through nothing but miles of crazed, cracked mud. In places it pushed up to resemble small hillocks or large anthills. From these eminences, hot, liquid mud flowed; darker than its solidified antecedents. There was no animal or plant life. The smell was repulsive, like naphtha. It was like riding back into primordial chaos, back before Prometheus had moulded man from the foul stuff around them.

Finally, there were clumps of coarse grass, patches of sand. The mud gave way to the shore. The sea breeze blew away most of the stench. And there on the silted coastline was the camp. The horselines stretched into the distance. To Ballista's experienced eye, there were some ten thousand horsemen and a horde of others – infantry and camp followers, Persians and Albanians all indiscriminate.

The camp was dominated by two pavilions, both purple, one larger than the other. The men were led in front of them, told to dismount. Pythonissa and her eunuch were ushered straight inside the smaller of the tents. Ballista and Maximus were told to wait. The Albanian guards were replaced by Persians. Beyond the camp, the line of the sea was decorated with men impaled on poles. It could have been the wind coming off the sea, but one or two of them seemed still to be moving.

'Did you know, the Caspian is a lake?' Maximus asked.

'No, it is not.'

'Sure it is – sweet water and snakes. I know about snakes.'

'Did you know that among the many poisonous snakes in Albania there is one whose bite causes men to die laughing?'

'Fuck off.'

'And another with venom that brings you to death weeping and mourning for your ancestors.'

'What if you did not know who your father was?'

'You would probably cry about that.' Ballista inclined his head. 'We are drawing a crowd.'

'Well, you cannot blame them, it is not every day Nasu the daemon of death comes calling cap in hand.' Maximus looked somewhere else. 'Do you think we will be joining the boys on the shore?'

'No, I would not have come if I thought that.'

'You do not sound so sure now.'

'No, I am not so sure now.'

A Sassanid noble walked out of the pavilion. He was tall, broad-shouldered with slim hips. The silk surcoat over his steel was heavily embroidered, predominantly light blue. His beard was dyed bright red, and his eyes were lined with kohl. Some years before, Ballista would have laughed. That was before he had seen such men fight.

The Persian greeted them suavely in Greek. He asked them to accompany him into the presence of Prince Narseh. Ballista knew that such civility was only to be expected in a man of such rank from the Orient. It signified nothing about their fate.

They passed through the outer chamber of the marquee, where petitioners waited in silence. They were not told to remove their weapons – that might be a good sign.

The inner sanctum was a slightly smaller version of that of the King of Kings Shapur himself: purple and gold opulence in everything. Ballista pushed away the memories. He had to keep his concentration. Everything might depend on it.

The son of Shapur sat on a throne at the far end. Ballista and Maximus advanced – not too close – and made full *proskynesis*. Face down on a Persian rug, Ballista accepted that this was not the time for an assertion of either Roman *dignitas* or Germanic freedom. Having blown the ritual kiss, they got to their knees, then their feet.

Prince Narseh was a good-looking young man, with an aquiline nose above a curly blue-black beard. He wore a tiara and an enormous pearl hanging from each ear. He was flanked on his right by officers, on his left by *mobads*. Ballista did not recognize any of them. A Zoroastrian fire altar burnt in front of the priests. Soldiers in armour lined the walls.

'I know you well, Dernhelm son of Isangrim.' Narseh spoke excellent old-fashioned Attic Greek. 'The barbarian from the frozen north where lies the mouth of hell. Marcus Clodius Ballista, the man who would have been king of the Romans – if only for five days, in just one town in Syria.'

The courtiers laughed.

'The man who tried to kill my father at Arete, who raped the

319

favourite concubine of the King of Kings at Soli. The oath-breaker who reneged on what he promised at Edessa.'

No one in the pavilion was laughing now.

'The unrighteous one who defiled the purity of fire with the corpses of the slain at Circesium, the sacrilegious one who extinguished the fire altar in the tent of Shapur. The servant of Ahriman who has the temerity to style himself Nasu the daemon of death. And he brings with him his heartless killer, the ex-gladiator Maximus.'

It was very still in the pavilion. The sacred fire crackled.

'Mazda is the supreme requiter – none of the wicked is so high or low as to escape him either by force or by stealth. We of the house of the Mazda-loving king Sasan follow the customs laid down by our ancestors. The torture of the boats is an ancient Persian punishment. The malefactor is laid on his back in a boat. Another boat, carefully adjusted, is nailed over the first. Only the criminal's head, hands and feet protrude. He is given good food to eat, milk and honey to drink. If he refuses, his eyes are pricked until he takes it. The sweet drink is tipped over his face. He is left, facing the sun. A swarm of flies descends to cover his face. Inside the boat, sooner or later, he does what must needs be done when men eat and drink. In time, worms and maggots seethe up from the corruption and rottenness of his excrement. Slowly they devour his body, eat their way into his vitals. It is not a quick death. Men have lived as long as seventeen days in the torture of the boats.'

Ballista held himself on such a tight rein he could not speak. Even his thoughts were stifled. He had been a fool to come here. Now he would be killed, and he had brought Maximus to this horrible death.

'The Greeks and Romans traduce us when they talk of Persian cruelty.' Narseh continued in the same flat tone of voice. 'With us, even a slave has his services weighed against the number and gravity of his crimes before he is sentenced. It is true that you, Ballista, were gracious when mischance and the evil of the tent-dwelling Arabs brought one of the *mobads* into your house as a slave. Again, no one can deny that in Cilicia at the place of blood you saved the life of my brother Valash, the joy of our father Shapur.'

The faint flicker of hope in Ballista was stamped out by the next words of Narseh.

'There are many crimes born in the darkness in the hearts of men. Mazda inspired our ancestors to create as many fitting punishments. Bring in the crosses.'

Six men in the soiled costume of labourers dragged in two crosses. They rolled back the carpets, set the crosses upright. In the previously quiet space the noise was fearsome as they hammered the wicked-looking things into the sandy soil.

The workmen left. They were replaced by four executioners; two held knotted whips, and two long swords.

This was all happening too fast. Ballista knew he had to do something. 'Prince Narseh, son of . . .'

'Silence,' Narseh ordered. 'Your words will change nothing. Strip them.'

It was no sooner said than done. Strong arms seized Ballista and Maximus. They were disarmed. Their hats, cloaks and armour were pulled off. They were left standing in their travel-stained tunics.

'Five hundred lashes. Cut off their ears and then their heads. Carry out the punishment.'

Allfather, Ballista began to pray. He doubted they would survive the scourging to feel the severing of their ears. *Allfather* . . .

The executioners draped the cloaks of Ballista and Maximus over the crosses, tied them in place, fixed their native hats firmly on top. The ones with the whips steadied themselves, and then swung. With the utmost seriousness they went about their work.

After a few strokes, the knots in the whips had torn great rents in the cloaks.

The condemned men began to laugh. A court official told them it was customary for men in their position to beg for mercy. Sheepishly, they both bleated, 'Mercy,' once or twice, quietly.

The men with the whips were running with sweat, panting hard, by the time they had finished. It had taken a long time. They had not stinted themselves. The cloaks were in shreds. The two with the swords approached the crosses. With a deftness approaching artistry, they sliced the lappets from the native caps – first one ear, then the other. A flourish of the blades, and the headgear was cut in two.

'Humanity and piety are the kindly sisters of the virtues,' Narseh said. 'Valash and I have always been close. I could not stand my brother's anger if I had killed his saviour. Besides, I believe we have much to discuss.'

XXIX

This paradise turned out to be roughly circular. As such places went, it was rather smaller than Ballista had imagined, not much more than a couple of miles in diameter from wall to wall. But there, it was an Albanian paradise, not a Persian one. They rode apart from one another. The horses, thin legs skittering, were dark shapes moving at a fast trot through the verticals of the trees. The riders were taking care not to catch their long spears in the branches.

Ballista was worried at the time it was all taking. Four days had passed in the camp on the Caspian shore after the symbolic punishment of him and Maximus. It had taken two days to ride up here into the foothills. Another three days had elapsed while the paradise was prepared. It was now, he reckoned, just short of a month since Saurmag had welcomed the Alani through the Caspian Gates. If they still held out, Calgacus and the others had been besieged in Cumania for twenty-five days. If they still held out. The little fort was strong, very strong. They should have more than enough provisions, ready access to water. But anything could have happened: treachery was an ever-present danger. Ballista was far from complacent.

The bright coats of the beaters flared through the shadows of the trees. The hounds, leashed now, surged about their legs, snarling. The riders trotted up, swung down, passed the reins to attendants and hefted the stout spears with the broad blades and wide cross-pieces.

'He is in there.' The chief huntsman pointed to a thick, broad tangle of undergrowth on the banks of a stream. There was clear ground in front, the only obstructions the wide-spaced trunks of a stand of mature beech trees. Prince Narseh told the head of the beaters to take his men across the stream, wait for the command and then slip in the hounds all at once from that side. Narseh spoke in Persian. Ballista considered whether the Sassanid prince knew that he and Maximus understood. They had been careful not to speak the language since they arrived at the camp. It was important to keep close anything that might be of advantage.

'We will take our stand here. Spread out among the trees, in the shape of the half-moon, we will cut off all ways of escape.' Now Narseh spoke in Greek to those around him. He turned to Pythonissa. '*Kyria*, it would be best if you were with the guards.'

'I have done this before,' she said.

'I do not doubt it, *Kyria*. Did not Xenophon write that all men who have loved hunting have been good, and also those women who have been given this blessing? But think of the consequences for Suania should something happen to you.'

Pythonissa acknowledged this gracefully. With an attendant leading her horse, she walked a little way back to where twenty or so Sassanid *clibanarii* stood in a body, weapons ready. They moved to hem around her like a wall.

The faces of the hunting party were strained. Ballista did not doubt that his was the same. It was no small thing they were undertaking. Ballista thought of the famous hunt in Calydon, not of the hero Meleager or the huntress Atalanta but of Ancaios in the dirt, castrated and disembowelled.

'Among my people, the Macedonians, it used to be that a youth could not recline at table among the men until he had taken a boar,' Castricius said. All murmured their approval of this hard old custom. Ballista wondered if the Macedonians had used nets and caltrops. Certainly the Greek Xenophon did not seem to have imagined doing without them. To face the fury of the beast in the open, with just a spear, as they would now, was the sternest of tests, bordering on the foolhardy. Oddly, Ballista had always thought Castricius came from Nemausus in Gaul. He was sure he had heard him say it many times. Perhaps there was some reason behind the little man's shifting *patria* – Ballista would have to ask him about it one day when they were on their own.

Narseh arranged the hunters. The prince himself took the middle. To his right went the two Albanians, King Cosis and his uncle the high-priest Zober, and two Romans, Castricius and Maximus. To the left were stationed Ballista and the three other Persians, the young commander Gondofarr, the *mobad* Manzik and the old general Tir-mihr.

The clear, sweet note of Narseh's hunting horn echoed through the paradise. Beyond the thicket and the stream, out of sight, the hounds sang. Ballista gripped the cornel shaft of the spear – left hand in front of right, side on, crouching, left foot following left hand, feet no further apart than in wrestling. He waited, his neck soon aching from looking over his left shoulder. Sun dappled down through the beeches. The leaf mould was soft under his boots.

From the covert came furious barking, crashing – animals moving fast – a high yelp of pain. The shouts of the beaters: *now, hounds, now*. Ballista felt his sweat slick on the spear. Branches breaking, getting closer. The howling of the hounds ever louder.

A half-seen movement, and then – straight in front of Ballista – the nearest bush exploded.

The boar stood in the sunlight. It was a mighty beast. Its head swung to either side, evil white tusks glinting. *Oho, hounds, oho!* Like Bacchic revellers, the handlers drove on the madness. *Oho, hounds, oho!* The hounds tumbled out. Teeth bared, eyes popping, they darted in, snapping at the legs and flanks of their quarry.

The boar lunged. It gored a hound, tossing it high, paws over back. The hound landed in a heap. Its side was laid open, the blood bright on the fallen leaves. The others, hackles up, fell back a moment.

The beast's piggy, malevolent little eyes locked on Ballista. Its humpback bristled. Faster than seemed possible, the boar accelerated. Ballista got lower in his stance, braced for the inevitable impact. Hooves drumming, the curved tusks, all bloodied, raced at him.

At the last second, the boar jinked to Ballista's left. He tried to realign his spear. It took the boar in the shoulder. Not a clean blow. The blade was not embedded. The shaft was torn from Ballista's grip. The spear spun away. Its momentum took the boar past. Ballista heard it scrabbling to turn, get at him. He threw himself full length. He dug in his fingers, the toes of his boots, pressed his face, all of him down, down into the soft forest floor. There was damp soil in his nostrils. His eyes were shut, waiting for the pain. There was shouting, as if from a great distance. The earth under him shifted. He smelt the evil, hot breath of the thing on his neck, smelt its hot blood. It drew back, seeking another angle to get its tusks under him, to prise him from the ground, to gore his soft flesh.

A shout – sharp, insistent – close at hand. Ballista felt the boar swing away. He risked a glance. He had grit in his eyes. The boar charged full on to the spear of young Gondofarr. The steel penetrated its mouth. The shock drove the young Persian back one pace, another. He dug in his heels, stayed big and strong. In its madness, the beast snapped its way up the shaft, driving the broad blade deeper down its own throat, deeper into its own vitals. Still, somehow, the young Persian denied its elemental force, held the frothing, murderous thing at bay. The boar reached the cross-piece and died.

Solicitous hands picked Ballista from the dirt, brushed him down. *Are you all right? Did it get you?* Ballista felt unsteady. He said he was fine. He did not say so, but he needed to piss. Gondofarr stood in front of him. Ballista bowed, blew a kiss from the tips of his fingers, thanked him, called him hero, in Persian. Gondofarr embraced Ballista – the scent of hot boar strong – spoke back to him in that language, called him *framadar*.

All nine hunters huddled together, slapping each other on the back. They were laughing, eyes bright with relief, good fellowship overflowing – closer than men after much drinking. The great beast – skewered by Gondofarr's spear – lay at their feet: the irrefutable proof of their shared courage, their very manhood.

Manzik the *mobad* cut some hairs from the creature's back, laid a few on its tusks, watched them shrivel in the heat. He tossed the rest into the air, said a prayer to Mazda.

Prince Narseh told his chief huntsman to butcher the beast, light a fire. Others should fetch bread, wine, other good things. They would feast here in the paradise. As men scurried to do his bidding, Narseh called for their mounts, asked Pythonissa to accompany them. They would ride, water the horses, divert themselves with conversation.

Downstream, they soon came to a pool. They sat around it in a circle, dropped their reins, let the horses drink. Gondofarr and Maximus produced flasks. They passed them from hand to hand with no ceremony. Ballista drank greedily, the need to piss forgotten.

'There are many good things to hunting,' said Narseh. 'It

conditions the body, toughens the soul – only a fool or an effeminate would think differently. An almost sly look came over his face: 'And it can bring a certain privacy.'

Indeed, there were just the ten of them in sight or earshot.

'When do we march?' Ballista asked.

Narseh smiled, as if at the impetuousness of a younger relative, even though Ballista probably was some years the elder. 'If one believes, as I myself do, Persia and Rome to be the twin lamps in the darkness of humanity, then it is a duty to act. It is as much against the interests of my father, the Mazda-worshipping divine Shapur, King of Kings, of Aryans and non-Aryans, of the race of the gods, son of the Mazda-worshipping Ardashir, as it is against those of Gallienus Augustus to tolerate the nomads south of the Caspian Gates. If they get a base in Suania or anywhere south of the Caucasus, the Alani will spread destruction far and wide. Those in Colchis whom the Romans claim owe them allegiance, and the loyal dependants of the King of Kings in Iberia and here in Albania will be just the first to suffer. In their lust for plunder, the bloodthirsty nomads will look to ride their ponies down through the Roman province of Cappadocia into Syria and west to the Aegean. In their savage ignorance, they might even have the temerity to try to encroach through the lands of the Cadusii and Mardi into the Aryan heartland ruled by my father.'

The Sassanid prince paused for a drink but clearly had not finished his speech. The others politely waited.

'The *framadar* Ballista stresses the need for haste.' The Persian word sat oddly amidst the Greek. 'It precludes asking the advice of my father. On my own authority, I will lead the Persians to the Caspian Gates.' Narseh turned to Cosis and Zober. 'I take it that, faithful to your oaths, your Albanian warriors will march with us?'

328

Both the king and the high-priest assured him that they would support him to the extremity of their powers, if not beyond. 'But' – King Cosis cleared his throat – 'what of Hamazasp? The Iberian king has always been untrustworthy. Will he ride with us? Will he even let us cross his territories?'

Ballista almost smiled. Of course the king of Iberia was untrustworthy, and few men alive had more reason than Ballista to hate him. Yet Cosis was the hereditary enemy of Hamazasp, and the attempt to do him down had been too transparent.

'Hamazasp will do his duty,' said Narseh. 'No king of Iberia, no vassal king of any people, will bring down on himself the anger of the King of Kings. Velenus of the Cadusii will see to that.' The rebel Velenus had been despatched to Shapur. Things did not look good for him. A punishment of exemplary cruelty was expected – no scourging of a cloak, lopping the ears off a hat, for him.

'Let us turn to practicalities,' Narseh said. 'Speak your minds freely. Leave nothing unexpressed that we might later regret.'

'We still have no real report of how many Alani have crossed the mountains, nor the numbers of Suani that have gone over to Saurmag,' Tir-mihr said.

'The majority of Suani will remain loyal to the memory of King Polemo and to his chosen heir Azo,' said Pythonissa. 'The members of the *synedrion* have never trusted Saurmag.'

Narseh dipped his head to Pythonissa but spoke to Tir-mihr. 'In this case, numbers may matter less than in many operations. No one can fight a battle on a mountain. All engagements will be in the river valleys and passes. In an enclosed space, a multitude of the enemy will count for less than our equipment, training and courage, Mazda willing.'

'Then how many we march upcountry should be determined by two things,' said Tir-mihr. 'How many we can spare from the occupying army among the Cadusii and Mardi, and how much forage we think available in Suania.'

Ballista liked the old Persian general. Tir-mihr had the good sense born of long experience. He said what was needed straight-forwardly, without elaboration.

'We will ride with two thousand *clibanarii* and three thou-sand light horse,' said Narseh. 'It will leave our cousin Sasan Farrak enough to keep the tribes to the south-west of the Caspian from any further rebellion. It is the haymaking season; the *kyria* Pythonissa assures me that the high valleys of Suania can feed many more horses than that.' He addressed himself to the Albanians. 'A contribution of another one thousand allied horse – half with heavy armour – would be welcome.'

Cosis and Zober made haste to pledge their men.

'It would be an honour if the king himself led his men,' suggested Narseh.

Cosis said the honour would be all his. Ballista realized that the Albanians would be as much hostages as a military asset – a posi-tion he knew all too well.

'Good,' said Narseh. 'We will gather another thousand riders from Hamazasp on the march.'

The Sassanid's horse raised its head from the water, tossed it. Narseh waved the flies from its eyes, quieted it. 'One thing still concerns me. While I accept the need for speed, urged by both the *framadar* Ballista and the *kyria* Pythonissa, is it wise to go into the Caucasus with cavalry alone?'

Ballista knew it was time for him to justify the gamble he was asking them to make. '*Kyrios*, infantry usually are essential for hill fighting – to hold ground, to guard the heights flanking the col-umn. But, as the *kyria* says, the tribesmen will not be united against us. The Alani, like the Persians, prefer to fight on horse-back. They and Saurmag are pinned to the fort of Cumania. The

330

pretender has to take Azo, and the Alani have to ensure the pass back to the steppes. They will have to meet us in open battle before the Caspian Gates.' Ballista tried to sound like Tir-mihr, sagacious and certain. He hoped he was not leading them all to disaster.

Narseh laughed, his teeth very white behind the blue-black beard. 'I hope you are right, *Framadar*. I hope your desire to rescue your friends has not clouded your judgement.' He was no fool, this handsome young prince. 'We Persians remember what happened when the Achaemenid Cyrus went against the nomad Massagetae. Their barbarian queen used the King of King's skull as a drinking cup.'

XXX

It was a tradition among the Persians not to begin a march until after sunrise. It was not, as the Greeks held, a result of sloth, but down to the demands of religion. After the necessary dawn sacrifice, with the day already well advanced, the signal was given by trumpet from the tent of Prince Narseh.

It was four days after the hunt in the paradise that they finally set out. Despite his eagerness to get to his *familia* in Suania, Ballista was not unhappy at the delay. Certainly, the first day had been a godsend. The problem had been another Persian tradition. Something they had decided on drunk had to be discussed again sober to see if it still seemed a good idea – and vice versa. They had ridden back from the pool and eaten roast boar. Then, with the servants dismissed and a ring of particularly trusted *clibanarii* posted, they had started to drink and talked it through again. They had drunk a great deal. Pythonissa had left early – which, given nine very drunk men, had been a good thing. They had drunk through until the stars paled above the treetops. The next day, Ballista had been unable to get out of bed. He was good for nothing, except perhaps one thing. Pythonissa had visited him. While it lasted, sex gave a hungover man an unfounded sense of well being. Afterwards, of course, he felt far worse. Even on the subsequent two days, Ballista had felt washed out. He was sure he could drink less than when he was younger.

Narseh had been busy while Ballista moped about. The Sassanid prince had made great efforts to circumvent yet another Persian custom. Eastern armies – and those of the house of Sasan were no exception – liked to take their comforts with them. Huge meteor trails of wagons and carts, slaves and concubines; all manner of camp followers streamed in their wake. The length of the column was much increased, its rate of march and cohesion drastically reduced. The civilians got in the way of the warriors, and were very given to panic. To venture into the mountains thus encumbered was to invite disaster.

Issued by the authorized general and a son of the Mazda-worshipping divine King of Kings, the word of Narseh was not to be ignored. But his *ukase* was unpopular. Each *clibanarius* was to be accompanied by just one servant. Every ten light horsemen could have one servant. The hierarchical nature of Sassanid society was further reflected. Each commander of a hundred might have five servants; each commander of a thousand, ten. The prince himself – appearances had to be kept up in the sight of foreigners – would travel with one hundred. All servants were to ride. It did not have to be a horse – a donkey, mule or camel would do – but there were to be no wheeled vehicles at all. Cosis was instructed that the same regulations were to apply to his Albanians.

Ballista rode off with Maximus and Castricius to a spur of the foothills to watch the army come down into the plains. It was a warm morning; going to be a hot day. The horses stamped, swished their tails as the flies got at them. Ballista wondered whether to question Castricius about his newly claimed Macedonian ethnicity. A sophist he had once heard had claimed that we reinvent ourselves with every action, if not every thought. But publicly changing from a Gaul to a Macedonian seemed somewhat excessive.

A swarm of light horse came out from the tree line. The bowmen swooped across the grassland, wheeling this way and that out of sheer high spirits. With their bright tunics and turbans, the colourful saddlecloths of their mounts, they resembled a migration of exotic, fierce birds. Ballista estimated their number – about five hundred. It was odd watching them in amity. He remembered seeing their like on the march down to Circesium, and the fear they had induced.

Two more distinct bodies of light cavalry emerged, the numbers of each about the same as the previous division. The newcomers cantered off to right and left to flank the march. They may be deep in allied territory, but Ballista approved that Narseh was taking all precautions. He suspected the hand of the dependable Tir-mihr.

Narseh led out the main body. Above him floated a great lilac banner with an abstract design picked out in silver. The *mobad* Manzik carried the prince's sacred flame, boxed for travel. Ballista was unsure about these Zoroastrian symbols. He thought each Bahram fire was lit from another; forming, as it were, an extended family.

Behind Narseh, the *clibanarii* rode five abreast: big men on big horses, splendid in silk and steel, bristling with lances, hung about with bow cases, maces, long swords. The column was four hundred deep – a sight both beautiful and terrible.

The baggage train was next. Ballista could see Tir-mihr and young Gondofarr spurring up and down its length, trying to chivvy it into some order. Given Narseh's instructions, it should consist of less than three and a half thousand mounted men. It was impossible to be sure, but there seemed more. Yet many would drop out before the mountains, and at least there were no wheeled carriages.

After the camp followers came the remaining five hundred Sassanid light cavalry, with Cosis and his Albanians bringing up the rear. For the first morning of a march, it was none too bad. Ballista had seen a lot worse. He remembered old Valerian's army straggling along by the Euphrates up towards Samosata.

'These Zoroastrians, you have to say, have a far better afterlife than your Greeks and Romans,' Maximus said. 'Lots and lots of virgins.'

'I thought that was Manichaeans,' said Castricius.

'Maybe them too. Either way, it is a fucking sight better than all that fluttering and squeaking in the dark like a bat. It is no wonder your Greeks will hardly fight at all.'

'And the Romans?' Ballista asked.

'Nowadays, they prefer to let the likes of us do it – just proves my point,' Maximus said.

'I am sure it is Manichaeans,' said Castricius.

'But you do not know,' said Maximus. 'Hippothous now, he would know.'

'I doubt it,' said Castricius. 'Like most Greeks, he only knows about Greek things.'

'But he knows a fuck of a lot about physi–'

'Physiognomy,' said Ballista.

'Exactly,' said Maximus. 'He could take one look at Castricius here, read that pointy little face and see straight into his soul – and what a horrible sight it would be.'

'And then he could tell us why he has started pretending to be Macedonian,' said Ballista.

'It is a long story,' said Castricius.

'Are you going to tell us?' Ballista asked.

'Not now, no,' Castricius said.

'I am not sure I would want an eternity of virgins,' said Maximus. 'Me, I often like a woman with a bit of experience. And all the virgins are ever so willing. What about a bit of reluctance? Rip her clothes off, throw her on the bed.'

'Stop it,' said Ballista.

'I am just thinking, with no concubines among the baggage, those servants are going to get very sore arses. You know what these easterners are like – obsessed with sex.'

'Let us go down and join them.'

It was hot down on the plain, very hot and humid. It was still August, nine days before the *kalends* of September. They rode to the north-west, between the foothills on the right and a seemingly endless marsh on the left. They forded numerous watercourses running down from the high ground. Despite the thatched farmsteads dotted across the country, there was much unworked land. It was good cavalry country.

On the second day, they came to a place where the marsh and the hills came close together, leaving a gap of no more than four or five miles. The following day, the barriers drew back and the plain spread out in freedom. Ballista thought about Calgacus and Wulfstan and the others. If Cumania had not fallen, they had been imprisoned within its walls for thirty-one days. The fort would make a very circumscribed prison: four identical circular rooms, stacked on top of each other, each no more than fifteen paces across – dark, damp and depressing. The strain of continual vigilance, of continual fear, both robbing the goodness from the defenders' sleep. And worse in a way for Calgacus: the views of freedom from the roof walk – the Booted Eagles and Black Vultures soaring above the crags, the Alontas river tumbling down the gorge, past the walls of the fort, and then off to the north, unrestrained by the encircling horde of barbarians through which it ran.

Maximus would smile to hear such poetic views ascribed to Calgacus. But the Hibernian might be wrong. He did not know Calgacus as Ballista did. All Ballista's life the old Caledonian had been there – from the time childhood memories stopped being isolated incidents and pictures and became something which could, at least with creative hindsight, be ordered into a rough narrative. Beneath the wheezing, cursing and foul-mouthed muttering, Calgacus was a kind man of surprising sensitivity. Ballista was determined to get the old bastard out.

Despite the sunshine, Ballista's thoughts took a dark turn. If he raised the siege, Calgacus would not be free, merely returned to the strange armed exile to which Gallienus had sentenced them. There was no time limit to the sentence. They had no idea where it would be served next. It was unlikely they would be allowed to return home any day soon. It was as if a capricious deity had his eye on them. Who alive was closest to a god, if not the Roman emperor? The eye of Cronus was upon them.

Yet, in a way, Ballista could not help a feeling of almost gratitude towards Gallienus. The emperor had not killed them. He had not condemned them to a small island, to pointlessly wandering the beaches of Gyaros or Pandateria. It showed practicality – the *imperium* was getting use out of them at the ends of the world – and a certain magnanimity of soul.

Something from the treatise *On Exile* by Favorinus came to mind. Something about the philosopher wandering vast swathes of territory, Greek and barbarian, seeing and hearing what happened there and, by memorizing it, making it part of an education in virtue. From what Ballista could remember, there was nothing at all in the work that even hinted at the acquisition of alien wisdom. It was all Greek.

A Roman might have been a little different. They always boasted of their willingness to adopt the best of foreign things. But, apart

337

from Greek culture, that really boiled down to weapons and military practices – a Spanish sword, a German war cry, the Punic word for 'tent'. Ballista would follow them in that. He actually relished the chance to ride with the Sassanid *clibanarii* and see what war was like with them. And he had the dangerous opportunity to fight the nomadic Alani and see how they waged war.

But Ballista wanted to go further. He wanted to find out how the other peoples he was thrust among did things, how they regarded the world and the things in it. He was not going to fall into the trap of considering the customs of every people as good as each other. The Suani were too murderous; the Persians too god-haunted. But by looking at their attitudes, his own values might come more clearly into focus. The fable told that each man had a wallet on his back containing his failings. Those of others were easy to see; your own very difficult. Maybe exile could provide the chance to sit down, unstrap the wallet, bring it around to the front and examine its contents with care.

Duty, friends, family – in ascending order, Ballista had decided that these were what he was about. Trying not to let any of those three down, trying not to do things of which he would be too much ashamed. Pythonissa slipped into his thoughts. How did she fit into the image he was constructing of a man made better by being refined and tempered by exile? Allfather, what if Julia found out?

The warriors of Hamazasp were waiting for them on the far bank of the Alazonios river. It was a serious levy, twenty thousand or more, arrayed for war. The Iberian king was in the centre, mounted on a black Nisean charger, beneath a great black banner embroidered with a red bull. The men with Hamazasp outnumbered those with Narseh several times.

The Sassanid forces neatly manoeuvred into position: the *cliba-*

narii in the centre with Narseh, the light horse on either side, the Albanians out on the right flank.

The two armies watched each other across the water. The Iberians looked much like the Persians. But they were less well armed, and showed less discipline. The Persians sat quiet in their units, awaiting the words of command. The Iberians surged about, horse and foot intermingled. Their nobles caracoled their horses, sang out things in their native tongue.

Ballista spotted the tall, red-headed figure of Rutilus stationed with the nobility near Hamazasp.

Hamazasp and another rider, backed by half a dozen others, walked their horses out to midstream. The Alazonios was the border between Albania and Iberia. It was neutral ground, watched over by the deity of the river.

Narseh told just the *mobad* Manzik, young Gondofarr, Ballista and Pythonissa to accompany him. Obviously, the veteran Tirmihr was to take command, should anything happen to the prince. The five riders splashed out into the river. Narseh halted the length of a horse from Hamazasp.

It was for Hamazasp to speak first. The water ran around the horses' legs. The king of Iberia looked over those with the Sassanid prince. When he reached Ballista, he sneered.

At length, Hamazasp bowed in the saddle, blew a kiss. 'Welcome the glorious Prince Narseh, son of the Mazda-worshipping divine Shapur, King of Kings of the race of the gods, grandson of the Mazda-worshipping divine Ardashir, King of Kings of the race of the gods, great-grandson of King Papak of the house of Sasan. I, Hamazasp, by the grace of Mazda king of Iberia, and my brother the *pitiax*, Oroezes, welcome you. How may we and the warriors of Iberia serve you?'

With a slight movement of the head, Narseh acknowledged this. 'We thank you for the gracious words. In the name of my father Shapur, we wish to cross your land unhindered to drive the nomad Alani back through the Caspian Gates to the sea of grass.'

'It shall be as you say.'

'Furthermore, we wish you to provide food for our men, fodder for their horses.'

'It shall be as you say.'

'Furthermore, we wish you or your brother, the *pitiax* Oroezes, to join our expedition with one thousand horsemen, and to take a binding oath to these things.'

'I will be honoured to lead my men to war with you.' Hamazasp could not prevent the sly look on his face. 'All will be as you wish, noble prince of the house of Sasan. But I have a petition. The late King Polemo of Suania unjustly seized territory from Iberia. If his daughter who rides with you will take an oath to return all the land up to the Dareine Pass, my warriors will fight all the more courageously in a just cause with friendship restored between the Iberians and the Suani.'

Narseh turned to Pythonissa. She curtly bowed her head.

Hamazasp took his oath first. It was in the Persian fashion. The *mobad* Manzik produced the salt, and the king of Iberia swore with his hand on that.

Pythonissa nudged her horse nose to tail with that of Hamazasp. The *pitiax* reached across her and tied her thumb to that of Hamazasp. The king of Iberia produced a knife. He cut his own thumb, then hers. 'Neither with steel nor poison,' he said. Raising their bound hands, he licked the blood from his own thumb then from that of the woman who had once been his daughter-in-law. 'Sealed and countersealed in blood.'

As Pythonissa repeated the oath, Ballista knew full well that neither of them would keep it.

XXXI

The prince Narseh of the house of Sasan with his warriors and his father's Caucasian vassals marched out of the north gate of the Iberian town of Harmozike five days before the *ides* of September. Ballista's odyssey to rescue Calgacus was going to be decided soon, one way or the other. Yet he feared it may all have taken too long. After they had met Hamazasp down at the Alazonios, etiquette had demanded they remain camped on the riverbanks for two days. First, the king of Iberia had feasted the son of the Sassanid king, then Narseh had returned the compliment. These had been uncomfortable occasions for Ballista. Beyond a formal greeting, he had managed to keep from having to talk to Hamazasp – there were many present – but he could not avoid the Iberian's glances. The monarch did not attempt to disguise his hatred. Ballista knew the man would like to eat his liver raw.

Another six days had passed as the combined forces wended their way up to Harmozike. There, two more precious days had been consumed by yet larger, yet more extravagant dinners. Wedging himself among Rutilus, Castricius and Maximus, and using Pythonissa as a screen, Ballista again had avoided any conversation with Hamazasp. But in his own residence the king had become bolder, especially when fortified with wine. Several times, Ballista had looked up the hall to realize that Hamazasp was talking about him, laughing with his nobles. Ballista was certain of it. He could not hear the words, but they had glanced over. Had Hamazasp been telling them what he had nearly done to Ballista in the cell in Edessa? Was he claiming more than the truth – claiming that he had gained some revenge for the death of his son by raping his killer? Ballista was furious. If the Iberian said something in Ballista's hearing, the northerner would have to try to kill him – even though the chances of success were minimal and the likelihood of himself being killed almost certain. But unless that happened, there was nothing he could do.

Pythonissa had said that there was much more than sexual innuendo to be concerned about. Ballista had argued that, as he was doubly protected as an envoy of Rome and a companion of Narseh, the king of Iberia would not dare harm him. Pythonissa's withering reply had surprised Ballista in the crudity of its language. Did he not understand that they were lodged in the palace? Hamazasp hated him – the northerner had killed his son, and now was fucking his daughter-in-law under his own roof. Pythonissa's father had not countenanced her remarriage to the old king, but Hamazasp himself had given every indication of wanting to fuck her. Hecate knew, he had tried often enough, in this very building, when she was married to his son. Of course, Hamazasp would not make an overt move against Ballista, just as he would say nothing that Ballista could hear – the Iberian may be a filthy, perverted goat who had tried to fuck his son's wife – but he was not a fool. Yet had Ballista failed to notice that, in the Caucasus, poison was a way of life? Anyway, she was as concerned for herself as for Ballista. Her relationship with the northerner had made her an enemy in Hamazasp, that and not going to the king's bed. She had insisted neither Ballista nor she ate or drank anything that had not been tasted by her poor eunuch. She advised Ballista not even to touch anything that others had not already handled. Such procedures were hard to carry out unobtrusively. She did not seem to even try. It had not helped the general atmosphere at court. Nor had Pythonissa's open nocturnal visits to Ballista's chamber. At least the eunuch had not died yet.

It was a fine morning as they rode out of Harmozike. The early autumn had taken the intense heat out of the weather. Ballista felt better. He was fully armed and mounted on a good horse – a Nisean stallion lent by young Gondofarr. Ballista's three Roman friends were around him. They rode at the head of the army, just behind Narseh, well away from the Iberians.

The order of march remained as before, with two thousand of Hamazasp's Iberians added to the rear. At a last-moment command of Tir-mihr, the rearmost group of Sassanid light horse were divided into two, and one half was placed between the Albanians and the Iberians. Old ethnic animosities might flare at any time. Ballista was confirmed in his admiration for the elderly Persian general.

They rode past the confluence of the Cyrus and Aragos rivers and followed the valley of the latter to the north. The Aragos was broad. It ran in several shallow streams, separated by low shingle banks. The green hills descended some distance away. Every so often they were cut by tributaries that came down in reed-fringed, wooded gorges of their own making.

At the end of the second day, they made camp just beyond where Ballista and Pythonissa had left the Aragos and taken to the hills in their flight to the east. From there, it took the army two days to reach the Dareine Pass. Now the hills were closer.

Small figures could be seen on the higher slopes, watching them. It was impossible to say if they were Alani, or followers of Saurmag, or Suani loyal to Azo. Although in dribs and drabs, small numbers of the latter began to appear in the camp to perform *proskynesis* to Pythonissa. Some stayed to fall in behind her with their weapons.

As they progressed upriver, they were riding back over the ground where Ballista and Pythonissa had been pursued. They went by the ruined barn where the Suanian Kobrias had died so that they could escape. Ballista would have said a prayer to the Allfather for him, but that deity of the distant north had no interest in men from Suania. Ballista was unsure how much interest Woden had even in his own descendants.

At the Dareine Pass, Hamazasp invoked the oath sworn by Pythonissa. In that desolate place he installed a garrison of one thousand of his Iberians, under the command of his younger brother, the *pitiax* Oroezes. High on one of the bare shoulders of rock, they got busy pitching tents, setting out horse lines, building fires. The smell of the dung they used as fuel wafted down to where the army camped along the path in marching order.

Ballista sought out Tir-mihr. He spoke quietly in Persian. Since his involuntary use of that language in the paradise after the charge of the boar, there was no further point in reticence. 'This is the main pass down from the Caspian Gates out of the Caucasus. Now the *pitiax* holds it, have we not put ourselves in Hamazasp's hands?'

Tir-mihr inclined his head, a gesture acknowledging the force of the argument, but not accepting it. 'If we lose, very few of us will escape these mountains. The Alani will hunt us down and the Caucasian tribes will turn on us: Iberians, Albanians, Suani – all of them. It will be a disaster like that suffered by the Achaemenid Cyrus at the hands of the Massagetae If we win,

Hamazasp will not dare oppose us, nor would he have the power. But I imagine the king of Iberia thinks, as you did, that he has got the better of us. Mazda willing, he will be proved wrong.'

The army turned right out of the Dareine Pass and followed the Alontas river to the north-east. Ballista had ridden this route twice before – arriving in Suania and in his flight. It looked familiar, if far from welcoming. High above the slopes, eagles soared, riding the updrafts on wide, feathery wings. Many among the Caucasians made the sign of the evil eye or openly cursed them.

The army was moving with no great haste. It was settling in for the night when a Suanian galloped in from the north. The Alani were breaking their camp before Cumania, ready to move south. Already their scouts had been seen before Dikaiosyne. Narseh ordered Tir-mihr to take one thousand Sassanid horse ahead in a night march to the village. The main body would set out before dawn the next day to join them.

Breaking their camp before Cumania . . . the words reverberated in Ballista's thoughts. *Their camp before Cumania* . . . the fort had not fallen. Do not tempt the gods but, most likely, Calgacus was alive; most likely Wulfstan and the others were too. *Allfather, Grey-hood, Deep-thinker, let it be so, let the miserable old Caledonian bastard be alive.*

It was raining as they rode into Dikaiosyne. The place looked no more prepossessing than before – tall, gloomy stone towers, narrow lanes and mud. There were hairy pigs and yapping dogs everywhere – under the horses' hooves, unsettling them. As they crossed the village square, Ballista eyed the Mouth of the Impious. From Germania or Rome, this really was the far end of the world. They did things differently here: cursing eagles and protecting rams, sacrificing madmen and throwing adulterers into underground rivers, eating millet – no end to their strangeness.

Narseh quartered the troops then held a brief council of war.

They stood on the flat roof of a tower, looking north. The Alontas was braided in several shallow streams. Its broad valley was rain-swept, its flanks bare, except for the two tangled ravines about half a mile away, where mountain streams came down, one on either side. A straightforward battle plan was outlined. *Clibanarii* and allied heavy horse in front. Narseh himself, Tir-mihr and the kings Cosis and Hamazasp would command. The light horse were to form up behind under the orders of Gondofarr. In both lines, the Persians would hold the centre, with the Albanians on the right, the Iberians the left. The topography dictated a frontal clash. The baggage was to stay in Dikaiosyne. With no danger of outflanking, just one hundred Sassanids would be sufficient to guard it from local banditry. It would be best if the *mobad* Manzik, the Romans, the *kyria* Pythonissa and her Suani remained in the village to over-see it. Tomorrow would bring the battle – let everyone get what rest they could.

Pythonissa led Ballista and the other three Romans to her house. After they had eaten, she took Ballista to her room. Beds were made for the others elsewhere. When they were alone, Pythonissa was eager, wanton. She tugged at Ballista's clothes, pushed him on the bed, mounted him. Leaning forward, her breasts just above his face, she rode him, all the time saying the things that excite men.

Ballista woke in the middle of the night, sometime around the sixth hour of darkness. There was an odd smell, oily with a note of burnt almonds. Without moving, he opened his eyes. Pytho-nissa was not beside him. He sensed a presence in the far corner. Silently, he raised his head.

A single lamp was burning. Pythonissa was naked. She held his drawn sword. She was rubbing a liquid from a phial into the steel. Ballista watched her for a time. 'What is that? Poison?'

'No.'

'Is it poison?'

'No, it gives strength. It is what Medea gave Jason.'

Ballista grunted his disbelief.

'You still wear the ice-white gem I gave you. Have your nights been disturbed?'

'Coincidence.'

She laughed, walked towards him. 'The unguent works on flesh too.'

'You should have been a *hetaira*.'

'You are not the first man to call me a whore.'

In the morning there was a thick mist. It haloed the many torches in the village square. Prince Narseh approached one of the huge panniers by the Mouth of the Impious. He drew an arrow from the *gorytus* on his hip. He dropped it in. One by one, the nobles and officers did the same. The *clibanarii* and light horsemen would throw in their arrows with less ceremony. Ballista knew from Herodotus that, long ago, the Persians had marked out an area of ground, marched in their men in their thousands. After the battle, they had repeated the procedure. From the empty space, they had estimated casualties. The new Sassanid system gave far greater accuracy. At the end of the day, every man took back an arrow. Those shafts remaining in the panniers indicated the number fallen.

An Iberian nobleman approached Narseh and performed lesser *proskynesis*; understandable, given the mud. 'I bring bad news, Prince. The noble king Hamazasp sends his apologies. He has been struck down by illness. He is unable to ride with you to battle and share your glory. My name is Ztathius, son of Gobazes, I have been given the honour of leading the warriors of Iberia. Hamazasp will keep back only a hundred of his men as guards.'

The words of Ztathius were received in silence. Young

Gondofarr looked openly sceptical. Tir-mihr scowled behind his beard. But there was little that could be done. 'So be it,' said Narseh at last. 'Mazda watches you, and your king.'

With Pythonissa and the other Romans, Ballista climbed to the top of the tower where the council of war had been held. It must have been dawn, for there was light behind the mist. But the vapour was still thick, limiting vision to no further than a boy could throw a stick.

A trumpet sounded, muffled in the fog. A detachment of Sassanid horse bowmen trotted out below the tower. They disappeared north into the gloom, fanning out to screen the deployment of the main force. A drum began to beat. Below the tower, Narseh led out the *clibanarii*. At a stately pace, they manoeuvred into line. The Iberian heavy horse followed, taking their station to the left, then the armoured Albanians moved out to hold the right. The three thousand cavalry, eight deep, filled the valley like a phalanx of iron statues. Where they stood in the streams of the Alontas, the water swirled around the hocks of the horses.

At a trumpet call, the screen of bowmen trotted back through the narrow gaps between the divisions. The rest of the light horse rode out of Dikaiosyne to join them. Until the army moved forward, there was not room for all the four thousand unarmoured to take their places. Many were left still jostling in the lanes of the village.

The fog was thinning. Ballista could see a hundred yards or more. Below the great lilac standard of Narseh, he could make out the *mobad* Manzik. The priest was on foot, praying, arms raised. A white ram was being led up. With no warning, arrows arced out of the vapour. Most fell short. Some clattered off the armour of the *clibanarii*. A few landed near the sacrifice. The *mobad* took no notice. He pulled up the ram's head, slit its throat.

The beast collapsed. The priest again raised his arms and invoked his god. The arrows were falling thicker. Nomad horns howled in the mist. Manzik prostrated himself before Narseh, unhurriedly got up and, as if strolling in a peaceful garden, made his way through the ranks back to the village.

A Sassanid war drum thundered. The *clibanarii* drew their composite bows. A flight of three thousand arrows shot blind into the gloom. Like rain blown in from the sea, a dark squall of shafts came back. Here and there among the *clibanarii* a horse plunged as an arrow tip found its way through mail, plate and hardened leather. The Persian light horse joined the exchange, aiming a high trajectory over the heads of the armoured men. The arrow storm intensified. Above the thrum of numberless arrows came the screams of men and horses. Men were dying in the Persian ranks. Out of sight, men would be falling among the Alani. There was something uncanny about this fight with an unseen enemy.

'This cannot last,' Rutilus said. 'Their quivers will soon be empty.'

'It is impossible to tell, but the Persians should be getting the better of it,' Castricius said. 'Their armour will be heavier than the nomads. The Alani will have to do something.'

As if in response to their words, the incoming arrows slackened. Dark shapes emerged at the front of the wall of fog. A frenzy of horns, drums and yells sounded from the enemy.

'Here they come,' Maximus said.

Three closepacked wedges of horsemen burst from the curtain of moisture. Strange standards flew above: animal skulls, pelts, horse tails, the outstretched wings of birds of prey. Tatters of mist swirled about them.

The standard of Narseh inclined forward, trumpets blared, the war drums beat faster. The mighty Nisean chargers stepped out.

Like a great wave building, ponderous but terrible, the Persian force surged towards the foe.

The nomads covered the ground fast. The Sassanids were still at a slow walk when the forces collided. The noise of the clash rolled back down the valley to the Romans watching on the roof. The Alani were outnumbered, but momentum drove the tips of their wedges into the Persian formation. The hideous cacophony of combat stunned the senses.

The lilac standard of Narseh dipped – seemed like to fall – then straightened. The fighting was fiercest around the Sassanid prince. The Alani advance here slowed as Persian numbers told. The other two wedges were already stationary. A great roar went up. Narseh and his retainers had stifled the central thrust of the nomads.

Across the valley, the combatants were pressed close. Often with no room to wield spears or swords, men wrestled on horseback. Clawing with their fingers at each other's throats, gouging their eyes, seeking to fling them down among the stamping hooves.

'More like an infantry battle,' Castricius said.

'Unless they cut Narseh down, the nomads will lose,' Rutilus said.

The nomads fought with ferocity, but it could not last. The collapse started at the rear, among those still uncommitted. In ones and twos, then in small clumps, finally in whole groups, nomads pulled their horses' heads around and bolted back up the valley into the obscurity of the fog.

Peroz! Peroz! Screaming victory, the Sassanids and their allies – heavy cavalry and light horse – poured after them.

As if swept by the hand of a deity, the battlefield was empty. There was the inevitable detritus of war – broken and discarded weapons, dead and injured men and beasts, unscrupulous and avaricious men from the victors, men of no honour, already dismounted and scavenging the field – but the combatants were gone.

The watchers on the tower were silent. There seemed nothing to say. The fog had receded further. It still hung on the hilltops, made a ceiling to the valley. Yet now Ballista could see almost a mile or so up the valley. It was not far enough to see the rout. Everything was eerily quiet. They could hear the river. It ran on as before. From there, or somewhere, came the sound of frogs: *brekeke-kex*.

The first vultures were dropping down on to the stricken field. Some Suani were slinking out from Dikaiosyne to join those robbing the dead and sending the wounded to join them, so they could take what they had also. Persians were said to carry all their wealth on them. Their allies the Suani would go to them first.

'Is it all over?' Pythonissa asked.

'Yes,' said Castricius. 'It is hard to believe thousands of men are being slaughtered just up there.'

A movement caught Ballista's eye.

'Fuck,' Maximus said.

Half a mile away, in the gully to the right, where a tributary came down to the Alontas, the trees and bushes were moving. There was no wind.

'Fuck,' Maximus said.

The dark, hunched shapes of the steppe ponies and their riders moved out on to the floor of the valley. They milled for a time. Five hundred, a thousand – the exact number was hard to tell. With a whoop, the majority rode away to the north and vanished into the mist. They were behind the advancing Persians. Their arrival would be a complete surprise, most likely change the entire course of events. It was a perfect ambush. The Alani charge and withdrawal had been planned from the start. All the time the ambushers in the gulley had been waiting their moment.

About two hundred Alani remained in sight. In no particular order, they trotted south towards Dikaiosyne. They halted in a rough line about a hundred yards from the village.

Ballista turned to Pythonissa. 'How many armed Suani do you have here?'

'Around three hundred.' She was admirably calm.

'How many of them have horses?'

'One in ten.'

'Have the mounted gather in the village square. Those on foot must block the entrances to the alleyways that face north.'

She told an attendant to see to it. 'What are you going to do?' she asked Ballista.

'Talk to Hamazasp, then the *mobad* Manzik.'

'Hamazasp will kill you.'

'I will have the others with me.' He pointed to Maximus, Castricius and Rutilus.

'It is not enough. Ten of my mounted Suani are below; take them with you.'

The king of Iberia was quartered in another tower facing north. It was surrounded by his warriors. They did not seem unduly concerned by what had happened. They eyed the men who rode up with some hostility.

Ballista addressed a man in elaborate armour, obviously a leader. 'I need to speak to Hamazasp.'

'He is ill.' The man spoke Greek with a heavy accent; his tone was dismissive.

'I need to speak to him.'

'No.'

'If you do not tell him, Narseh will have you impaled.'

'Narseh might not return. You are in no position to issue

threats, Roman.' He touched the hilt of his sword. His men shifted.

A figure appeared on the roof of the tower, looking down. It was the Iberian king. He did not speak.

'Hamazasp,' Ballista called up, 'you must lead the warriors with you. We can brush aside the nomads before the village. If we are quick, we can save the day.'

Hamazasp stared down at Ballista with loathing. Still he did not speak. Then he turned away and was gone.

'Not long for you now, *Kinaidos*.' The Iberian laughed.

Ballista swallowed a retort to the insult – that bastard Hamazasp would suffer for saying he took it up the arse. Ballista backed his horse. The others did the same. When they were out of weapon reach, they wheeled and rode away.

Appropriately enough, Manzik the *mobad* was praying when they arrived at the house he had taken. He finished as Ballista burst into the courtyard and said what he wanted.

'I am afraid I cannot lead the Sassanids,' Manzik said. 'We *mobads*, with our own hands, can kill everything – ants, snakes, anything that walks, crawls or flies – we take pride in it. But we are forbidden to kill dogs or men.'

'Tell your men to take orders from me.' Ballista knew time was fast running out.

'What about the baggage? Prince Narseh ordered us to guard it.'

'If the army is defeated, the baggage will be the least of our concerns.'

'Of course, you are right. Take the men. I will remain and attempt to protect the property of the prince and the warriors.'

Ballista had just over a hundred and thirty mounted men: Persians, some Suani, just four Romans. All well mounted, with good armour: enough for the first task. The second was another matter. He divided the cavalry into two columns, each waiting out of sight in an alley. Ballista was at the head of one, Rutilus the other. Castricius was to bring up the Suani foot. Pythonissa had been told to barricade herself in her house. Allfather knew if she would.

The Alani out in the valley before the village were not expecting trouble. Their line had disintegrated. Apart from forty or so gathered around a ragged standard in the centre, most had dismounted and were looting the dead. Even those still on horse had dropped their reins, were sitting all unconcerned; drinking, eating, chatting.

'Now!' Ballista said, and kicked his heels into the flanks of his horse. Behind him, a Sassanid trumpet relayed the order. The Suani infantry, who had been blocking the mouth of the lane, leapt aside at the last moment. Ballista's mount accelerated out into the open. There was a reassuring thunder of hooves behind. To his left, he saw the tall figure of Rutilus leading the other charge.

The nomads dropped their pickings, ran for their ponies, swung up into the saddle. All too late. Ballista saw the closest of the looters go down under Rutilus's blade. The Alani around the standard were not caught so unprepared. A few managed to loose off arrows. They shrieked through the air, but none came close to Ballista. The nomads dragged swords clear of scabbards, made to stand up to the charge.

Ballista splashed through a strand of the Alontas and put the big Nisean charger straight at the pony of the Alan chief. The collision sent the shaggy small beast, still snapping, back on its haunches. The chief fought to retain his seat. Surging past, Ballista swung his blade overhand. The chief instinctively flung up an arm to protect his head. Ballista's blade severed it below the elbow.

An Alan cut down at Ballista from the left. The northerner took the blow on his shield, without looking thrust his sword around the side of it, felt the steel tip catch, kicked on. A nomad in front was yanking his horse around to flee. Ballista smashed the edge of his blade backhanded down into the man's left shoulder. The pony took off. The nomad toppled into the stony bed of the river. The stones ran red.

Ballista reined in, checked all around for threats. There were none. Probably half the Alani were down – loose ponies bolting everywhere – the rest were scattered in all directions, hunched low over the necks of their mounts, pushing hard for their individual safety.

'Rally on me,' Ballista bawled, first in Persian, then in Greek. His voice had been trained over the years to carry across a battlefield. 'Form one wedge.'

The Sassanid *clibanarii* were good warriors. None spurred off in mindless pursuit. Within moments, they were jingling into formation. The thirty or so Suani were slower, some had to canter back from the beginnings of a chase. But soon they began to fall in behind.

Ballista looked back towards the village. A ragged column of Suani warriors on foot was jogging out. Castricius had them in hand.

'At the trot, advance.'

Almost at once they rode into the wall of fog. The world was reduced to a few yards of shifting greyness. Sounds – the snort of a horse, the clink of metal touching metal – were muted. The air smelt of mist, water, wet stone and damp horse. It was like riding into the demesne of some bleak underworld.

Ballista glanced over each shoulder. Rutilus on one side, Maximus the other; serried ranks of Sassanids behind. The fog pearled on beards and cloaks. The damned croaking of frogs started up

– *brekeke-kek, ko-ax, ko-ax.* From further away came an indistinct roaring, like surf on a rocky shore.

Ballista flinched. With a whir of wings, a flock of white doves dived out of the mist. They wheeled just over the column, and were gone. Shouts, curses from the rear. Ballista turned to the Persian officer tucked in behind him. 'Pass the word for silence.'

'Those birds are unclean. Like lepers, they must be driven out,' the Persian said.

'Surprise is our only hope. We must not let them know we are coming.'

The order to be quiet hissed back through the ranks.

The roaring was getting louder, sharp sounds within it becoming distinct.

'Not far now,' Ballista muttered.

Rutilus leant forward, whispered near Ballista's ear, 'Hamazasp can take us in the rear.'

Ballista actually laughed. 'Allfather, I hope not.' He stopped laughing. 'It depends how active is his treachery; how brave he feels. I think he will wait and see who wins.'

A black, moving mass appeared ahead through the vapour; not above fifty yards. The clash of weapons, yells, and screams of men and horses. Ballista flung up his hand. They halted, automatically dressed their ranks. Ballista turned in the saddle. 'We are there,' he said softly. 'They are still fighting. We are in time. Now – on my word, ride hard, but keep closed up, stop for nothing. Our infantry will be here to add their weight soon.'

'Now!'

They moved off at a walk and went straight up to a close-in-hand canter. The noise of fighting swelled.

Even the Alani at the very rear did not see or hear them coming. The nomads were too noisily intent on the trapped Sassanid warriors in a tight-wedged knot beneath the lilac standard. The

356

Alani were circling, pouring arrows in from all sides, from every trajectory.

The first of the Alani Ballista killed literally never knew what hit him. He had just released an arrow, was reaching for another, when Ballista's sword caved in the back of his skull. Ballista neatly retrieved his weapon. The next man looked around, an arrow notched in his bowstring. Ballista's heavy blade smashed bow, arrow, hands to ruin. The Nisean stallion barrelled a pony aside. Ballista forged on. Behind him welled up a chant of 'Peroz, Peroz.' In front rose cries of fright.

A warrior with a shaggy sheepskin cap sliced at Ballista. Long training let the northerner watch the blade, take it on his own, roll his wrist to force it wide, and repost; all one fluid movement. The nomad jerked back. Not far enough – the steel sliced across his face. The blood sprayed into Ballista's eyes; hot, stinging. Half blinded, Ballista finished the man with two chopping blows.

Ballista kicked on. He wiped his eyes, and his Nisean went down. He used a horn of the saddle to push himself off, throwing himself away from his falling horse. The ground rushed up. He landed awkwardly. His helmet rang on a stone. The great weight of the stallion crashed beside him.

Ballista tried to get up. Stay on the ground, and he would die. Sharp hooves were stamping all around. A wave of nausea engulfed him. His legs gave way. Curling up tight, his arms covering his head, the blackness overtook him.

Ballista did not know how long he had been unconscious – he was still in the same position – probably but moments. Legs straddled him. He groped for his sword. It was gone: the wrist loop must have snapped. He looked up. His eyes were gummed with blood; he did not know if it was his own. Maximus and Rutilus, back to back, stood over him. Suani warriors on foot ran past. They were cheering, laughing with the courage that comes from spearing fleeing enemies in the back.

'This time it is over,' Rutilus said. 'They are broken.'

Ballista was helped to his feet by Maximus. As if from a great distance, he heard '*Peroz, Peroz.*' He drew a deep breath, made to give orders to keep some men together in case Hamazasp tried anything. The nausea rushed up to his throat, his mouth – a cloying, oily taste of burnt almonds. He got back on his hands and knees, and painfully started to throw up.

Peroz! Peroz!

XXXII

Prince Narseh and Azo, the man who would be king of Suania, were regarding the Caspian Gates. It was a desolate sight. Ballista's reconstruction had not been completed before the Alani arrived. During their siege of Cumania, the nomads had removed and burnt all the woodwork from the Gates. They had even begun to demolish the stone gate across the track at the eastern end.

Yet, despite their ruinous state, the Caspian Gates had been a choke point in the rout of the nomads. The path down which Ballista rode towards the royal entourage had been mainly cleared of the dead, but they were everywhere else. Sassanid work parties were busy. They were gathering their own dead, treating them with respect, getting them ready for exposure to the birds of the air, as was the Zoroastrian way. Things were different with the corpses of the Alani and those Suani who had fallen supporting Saurmag. Stripped naked, sometimes mutilated, they were unceremoniously being thrown into piles out in the valley. It was the natural order, Ballista thought, for some things to be stacked: sheaves of wheat, amphorae, barrels. Corpses were not in that category. The pallid, blue-white tangles of limbs were grotesque. They said something deeply troubling about the inhumanity of mankind.

Ballista climbed down from the saddle, passed Maximus the reins. Narseh and Azo turned to him. Ballista bowed to each, blew them a kiss. If he had performed full *proskynesis*, he was not sure he could have got up again unaided. He was still dizzy; the taste of bile and burnt almonds remained strong in his gorge.

'Ballista, *Framadar*.' Narseh stepped forward. He was smiling, but his dark eyes were melancholy. 'Nasu, the very daemon of death.' He embraced the northerner; kissed him on each cheek, the eyes, the lips. His blue-black beard rasped across Ballista's face. 'I am in your debt. Your intervention turned the battle. It broke the Alani. Maybe, in the mist, they thought the numbers with you larger. We will never know.' The prince stepped back, studied Ballista. 'I was told you took a bad fall. Are you hurt?'

'I will live.' Ballista smiled. 'But, I am afraid, I cannot return the charger Gondofarr lent to me.'

'Gondofarr is dead.'

'I am sorry.'

'Tir-mihr is badly wounded. Our losses are heavy.'

'How badly wounded?'

'He has been carried to the village. It will be as Mazda decrees. The *mobad* will send word.'

'Hamazasp betrayed us.'

Narseh rubbed his eyes; the gesture of a tired man. 'His Iberians fought well. His man Ztathius was killed.'

'He sacrificed them. He was not ill. He was waiting to see who won.'

'There is no proof.'

'When the Alani sprung the ambush, the Iberians in the village were not surprised. Hamazasp must have been forewarned.'

'He has sent his congratulations. We must leave things as they are.' Narseh lapsed into silence.

Azo took Ballista into his arms, kissed him. The Suani prince was laughing. Unlike Narseh, the death of his men did not seem heavy on him. 'I am doubly in your debt. Both for today and for when my snake of a brother and his barbaric allies rode up the pass. Saurmag would have taken me, if your men had not welcomed me into Cumania. Although "welcome" might not be quite the right word. Fifty-one days is a long time confined with your man Calgacus. Does he ever stop moaning? And the Greek called Hippothous – he has a most disconcerting habit of staring at one.'

'They are the companions the gods have given me.'

'If I were you, I would worship at new shrines.'

'What happened to Saurmag?'

A cloud of anger passed over Azo's face. 'He escaped north to the steppe. I saw him pass. From the battlements, my arrow killed one of the traitors who rode at his side.' The Suanian brightened. 'A temporary reprieve. I will close the passes next spring. With his subjects unable to cross south for the summer pasture and unable to trade for iron and salt, a suitable gift should induce the chief of the Alani to hand Saurmag over.'

'And then things will not go well for him.'

'As you say, things will go badly for Saurmag at my hands.' Azo's eyes were dancing. 'There was another I had intended to suffer. But a man who helped put the diadem on the king's head should perhaps be allowed certain intimacies with the royal family.'

Ballista said nothing. Your whole family is rotten to the core, Ballista thought.

'Your own household is waiting for you in the fort,' Narseh said.

'You took your fucking time,' Calgacus said.

'How was it?' Ballista asked. They were alone on the steps of Cumania.

'I have had better times. At first Azo hardly spoke. But since a Suanian sneaked into the fort a few days ago with the news that you and Narseh were coming, the little shite has never drawn breath. He has an inventive mind when it comes to torture. Good job he has got used to the idea of you fucking his sister.'

'How are the others?'

'Waiting inside. Young Wulfstan is strong. Hippothous is off his head – does nothing but stare at people and mutter about physiognomy telling him the future. Fuck me, another few days and I would have had to kill him.'

The eunuch Mastabates came down the steps. He had a gold-trimmed ivory codicil in his hands. '*Ave*, Marcus Clodius Ballista, *Vir Ementissimus*.' He spoke formally in Latin.

'What is that?'

Mastabates handed it to Ballista. 'Your new *mandata*.'

'What?'

'Your new *mandata*. Signed by the hand of the pious, invincible Augustus Publius Licinius Egnatius Gallienus himself.'

'How did you get this?'

The eunuch said nothing.

'You have had it all the time?'

Mastabates acknowledged this with a dip of the head. 'My instructions were to give you this when your mission in Suania was complete.'

'And it is?'

'Without doubt. The first task was to ensure that the nomads

362

were contained beyond the Caspian Gates. That you accomplished today. But the other half was to win back the peoples of the Caucasus to Rome. There is a Persian army at the Gates. The kings of Albania, Iberia and Suania have never been more under the influence of the Sassanids. You, Rutilus and Castricius can hardly be said to have succeeded. Still, you have not failed as spectacularly as the noble senator sent to Abasgia.'

'What happened to Felix?'

'He has been expelled from Abasgia for being an accomplice to attempted murder. He is lucky to be alive. My colleague Eusebius was apprehended trying to kill King Spadagas.'

'Why?'

Mastabates gave a thin smile. 'What would you do to the man who castrated you for money?'

'He did not succeed?'

'No, but he died well.'

'Did Felix help him?'

'I very much doubt it.'

Ballista opened and read the codicil. 'The Heruli?'

'Yes.'

'I have to go to the north-east of the Black Sea, beyond Maeotis?'

'Up the Tanais river.'

'Out on to the sea of grass?'

'A not altogether pleasing destination,' Mastabates agreed. 'But you will have Castricius and Rutilus as companions. And, I fear, I am ordered to accompany you.'

'Why?'

'His imperial majesty did not divulge his thinking to me, but I assume that you, like an Abasgian eunuch such as myself, are supremely expendable.'

*

Pythonissa came to the chamber at the top of the fort of Cumania where Ballista was going to spend the night. This time there were no carpets, no flirtatious subterfuge. She dismissed her men outside, walked in and told Wulfstan to leave. The boy had been bandaging Ballista's various grazes from his fall. She did not offer to take over.

'When did you intend to tell me?'

'Tomorrow,' Ballista said.

'When are you leaving?'

'Tomorrow.'

'Take me with you.'

Ballista had been dreading this since he had been given the *mandata*. If he were honest with himself, he had been dreading this since the start.

'No. I have a wife.'

'Take another wife.'

'It is not permitted among my people.' It came out easily. It was close to the truth. He had rehearsed it.

'I have read Tacitus. Leading men among the German tribes can have more than one wife.'

'I am not a German any longer. I am Marcus Clodius Ballista, a Roman equestrian. I live in Sicily with my wife. Romans have one wife.'

'Gallienus has taken a second wife.'

Ballista smiled – rueful, placating; he was not sure which. 'Emperors do not encourage their subjects to follow all their practices. Anyway, Pippa is not a wife but a concubine.'

'Take me with you as a concubine.'

'It would not answer. You would not be content. Anyway, I am ordered to travel to the nomads.'

Pythonissa came close. 'Take me with you.'

'You will be better here. Without your help, your brother

would not have reached the throne. He will be grateful, find you the sort of match you seek.'

Pythonissa waved the idea away angrily. 'Gratitude does not run in my family. Take me with you.'

'No.' There – it was said.

'I saved your life.' Her blue-grey eyes looked into his. 'I love you.'

'There is nothing to be done.'

She stepped away – tall, straight-backed, angry. 'They told me you were sick on the battlefield. Did you think I had poisoned you?'

'It crossed my mind. I thought my usefulness might have ended.'

'I wish I had.' She turned and left the room.

Under a lowering sky, Ballista led the small column south up the pass towards Dikaiosyne. It was an oddly assorted company: six fighting men in Roman armour, three eunuchs, eight slaves and a Suanian called Tarchon who would not be left behind – eighteen horsemen with five baggage animals.

It was raining. Groups of Sassanids paused from the grisly work of sorting cadavers and watched them pass. Nothing was said.

The path ran through the village. The horses stepped carefully in the mud of the alleys. The blank, forbidding walls of the towers were black in the rain. They came out into the village square. She was there. Dressed in black, standing in the rain, hair unbound. Standing by the Mouth of the Impious.

Ballista reined in.

Pythonissa did not look at Ballista. She stretched her hands down to the earth. 'Hecate triple-formed, who walks the night, hear my curse. Vengeful furies, punishers of sinners, black torches in your bloody hands, hear my curse.'

Now she turned her blue-grey eyes on him. 'Kill his wife. Kill his sons. Kill all his family, all those he loves. But do not kill him. Let him live – in poverty, in impotence, loneliness and fear. Let him wander the face of the earth, through strange towns, among strange peoples, always in exile, homeless and hated.'

Appendix

Historical Afterword

At the end of his wonderful *Human Traces* (2005), Sebastian Faulks writes that he does 'not think that novels should contain bibliographies . . . as though all art aspired to the condition of a student essay'. However, in that case, he made an exception, and the discussion of his sources runs for seven pages. Undoubtedly, he has a point. But the classical pedant in me has an affinity for lists – in my books and in others' – and I always like to make an exception.

History and Fiction

As with all the *Warrior of Rome* novels, I have worked hard to try to make the underlying history as accurate as possible – the geopolitics, the *Realien* (clothes, weapons, food, and the like) and the *Mentalités*. (And what could be a surer sign of scholarship than delineating two concepts with words from two foreign languages in one sentence?) But, as always in these novels, the story in the foreground is fiction. After the Sassanids' victory over Valerian in the battle 'beyond Edessa' (most probably in AD260), the influence of the Sassanids in the kingdoms of the Caucasus seems to have increased. Both Shapur and the *mobad*

Kirder later boasted in inscriptions of their successes there. Archaeological finds of Sassanid silverware from the period in the region have
plausibly been interpreted as diplomatic gifts (*see* Braund, below, under
'The Caucasus', pp. 242–3). We have no evidence of Roman efforts to
counter this – unsurprising, given the general paucity of evidence –
although we know that missions were sent at other times. Similarly,
there is no evidence of an attempt by the Alani to force the Caspian
Gates at this point in history, although they did try on other occasions
(e.g. *see* Arrian's small work *Expedition against the Alani*).

People

Gallienus

The emperor Gallienus was a controversial figure in antiquity. On the
one hand, the Latin sources vilify him either as degenerating into the
worst sort of effeminate, ineffectual tyrant (Eutropius), or having been
of that nature from the very start (Aurelius Victor; the *Historia Augusta*).
On the other hand, the Greek sources (Zonaras; Zozimus) portray him
in a far more positive light, as struggling manfully to hold the empire
together in the face of overwhelming odds. There is an obvious line of
explanation. Gallienus got on badly with the Senate – he promoted
men of obscure origins and may have excluded Senators from army
commands – and Senatorial opinion dominated Latin historiography.

The only modern, book-length scholarly study known to me is L. de
Blois, *The Policy of the Emperor Gallienus* (Leiden, 1976).

There is no certainty about when Gallienus was born. Estimates usually range between AD215 and AD218. I arrived at a slightly later date via the
following steps. Gallienus's father, Valerian, was 'old' when he came to the
throne in AD253 – let us say sixty. So, Valerian was born around AD193. Elite
Roman men tended to marry in their late twenties. Thus, Valerian probably would have wedded just before AD223. Gallienus seems to have been

his eldest child – so may have been born in AD222. I had worked this through before I realized that it, most usefully, made Gallienus and my fictional Ballista exact coevals. Of course, every assumption and every stage of the reasoning may well be completely wrong.

Hippothous

In *Lion of the Sun* and *The Caspian Gates*, the life story Hippothous tells himself and others follows that of his namesake in *An Ephesian Tale* by Xenophon of Ephesus, up until the death of the old woman he married in Tauromenium. In the ancient novel, the character then travelled to Italy, Rhodes and Ephesus. In mine, he headed back to Cilicia, where he set himself up, via successful banditry, as a leading man of the town of Dometiopolis, until the Sassanid invasion caused him to throw in his lot with Ballista and become his *accensus*. An oddly unreliable narrator, Hippothous is lucky that Ballista's former *accensus* Demetrius is away in the west and that none of the rest of the *familia* read Greek novels. (Ballista tried *The Aithiopika* of I Ieliodorus in *Lion of the Sun*, but did not get on with it.)

There is an excellent translation of Xenophon of Ephesus by Graham Anderson in B.P. Rearden (ed.), *Collected Greek Novels* (Berkeley, Los Angeles & London, 1989, pp.125–69).

Peoples

The Goths

There has been something of a boom in the last twenty-five years or so in scholarly studies of the Goths. Outstanding among them are H. Wolfram, *History of the Goths* (English translation, Berkeley, Los Angeles & London, 1988); and P. Heather, *The Goths* (Malden MA, Oxford & Carlton, 1996). Many of the most important sources are collected and translated in P. Heather, and J. Matthews, *The Goths in the Fourth*

Century (Liverpool, 2004). Recently, M. Kulikowski's *Rome's Gothic Wars* (Cambridge, 2007) makes a revisionist argument that the Goths as a group only came into existence in the region of the Danube in the third century due to the influence of Rome. For this to be true, the first century Gotones mentioned in Tacitus, *Germania* 44 have not to be Goths, and Jordanes, *Getica* 3–4 on the origins of the Goths has to be completely wrong. It should be remembered that Jordanes was a Goth, and his evidence shows, at the very least, that Goths in the sixth century believed that their ancestors had migrated from the Baltic in the third.

The chronology of Gothic raids in the Black Sea and the Aegean during the AD250s–260s is hopelessly confused. As the Goths were a very loose confederation at this time, I have assumed a Viking model of raiding: endemic, low-level piracy, with occasional large-scale assaults.

The Sassanids

To the reading on the Sassanids (also known as Sasanids, Sassanians, and Sasanians) given in *Fire in the East* and *Lion of the Sun* can be added the provocative and wide-ranging overview 'The Sasanid Monarchy' by Z. Rubin in *The Cambridge Ancient History* XIV, edited by A. Cameron, B. Ward-Perkins and M. Whitby (Cambridge, 2000, pp. 638–61.

Places

Ephesus

Sources for this city were given in *King of Kings*.

Priene

Situated on the lower slopes of the Mycale mountain range, with views out over the Maeander plain and the sea, Priene is a magical and little visited site. Far and away the best book, although very difficult to find (at least in English; it was also published in German and Turkish) is F. Rumscheid, *Priene: A Guide to the 'Pompeii of Asia Minor'* (Istanbul, 1998). Useful short introductions can be found in G.E. Bean, *Aegean Turkey: An Archaeological Guide* (London, 1966, pp. 197–216); and E. Akurgal, *Ancient Civilizations and Ruins of Turkey* (London, New York & Bahrain, 2002, pp. 185–206).

Miletus

Published to tie in with an exhibition in Berlin in 2009–10, the essential work on Roman Miletus, with wonderful maps, plans and pictures, is *Zeiträume: Milet in Kaiserzeit und Spätantike*, edited by O. Dally et al (Berlin, 2009). As with Priene, above, brief introductions are in Bean, *op. cit.*, 219–80; and Akurgal, *op. cit.*, 206–22. Although focused on earlier periods, there are various informative studies by Alan Greaves, especially 'Miletos and the Sea: A Stormy Relationship', in *The Sea in Antiquity*, edited by G.J. Oliver et al (Oxford, 2000, pp. 39–61); and *Miletos: A History* (London & New York, 2002, pp. 1–38; 137–42).

Didyma

The standard book is J. Fontenrose, *Didyma: Apollo's Oracle, Cult, and Companions* (Berkeley, Los Angeles & London, 1988), although, splendidly, the author only spent 'a good part' of one day on the site (p. x). Again, introductions in Bean, *op. cit.*, 231–48; and Akurgal, *op. cit.*, 222–31.

The Black Sea

My interest in the Black Sea was sparked by two texts, one ancient and one modern. Dio Chrysostom, *Oration 36, The Borysthenetic Discourse*, includes an incredible account of a trip the philosopher claims to have made to the city of Olbia (or Borysthenes, as it was also called) on the north-west coast. Neil Ascherson's *The Black Sea* (London, 1995) is a fine mixture of popular history and travelogue. The latter has recently been joined by Charles King, *The Black Sea: A History* (Oxford, 2004): a splendid work of historical synthesis.

For anyone wanting to journey in their imagination in the Black Sea of antiquity, there are three essential classical texts. Voyaging west to east, Arrian, *Periplus Ponti Euxini* (in the edition of A. Liddle, London, 2003, with introduction, translation and commentary), and Apollonius of Rhodes, *The Argonautica* (several translations in print); heading in the other direction, Xenophon, *The Anabasis* (available in many translations).

For seafaring, as in *Fire in the East*, I have drawn heavily on the practical experiences of Tim Severin, *The Jason Voyage: The Quest for the Golden Fleece* (London, 1985), and the scholarship of J.S. Morrison, J.E. Coates and N.B. Rankov, *The Athenian Trireme: The History and Reconstruction of an Ancient Greek Warship* (2nd edn, Cambridge, 2000). The litmus test of an under-researched historical novel set in the classical world is the inclusion of slave oarsmen, usually complemented with anachronistic whips, chains and drums. The briefest glance at the magisterial *Ships and Seamanship in the Ancient World* by Lionel Casson (2nd edn, Baltimore, 1995, pp. 322–7), dispels any such notion.

The Caucasus

The outstanding work of modern scholarship is D. Braund, *Georgia in Antiquity: A History of Colchis and Transcaucasian Iberia 550BC–AD562* (Oxford, 1994). The single most important ancient text is Strabo 11.2.1–5.8.

I have drawn much from travellers' accounts. Among Victorian ones, particularly useful are two by D.W. Freshfield, *Travels in the Central Caucasus and Bashan* (London, 1869; facsimile, 2005) and *The Exploration of the Caucasus* (2 vols., London, 1902; facsimile, 2005); and one by A.T. Cunynghame, *Travels in the Eastern Caucasus, on the Cas-*

pian and Black Seas, especially in Daghestan and on the Frontiers of Persia and Turkey during the Summer of 1871 (London, 1872; facsimile, 2005). Two enjoyable modern ones are T. Anderson, *Bread and Ashes: A Walk through the Mountains of Georgia* (London, 2003); and O. Bullough, *Let Our Fame be Great: Journeys among the Defiant People of the Caucasus* (London, 2010).

Fluidity of boundaries, both political and cultural, marked the peoples of the ancient Caucasus. Given this, I have moved some things around for this novel. The Mouth of the Impious (Ps-Plutarch, *On Rivers* 5) – which probably never existed at all – has migrated from Colchis to Suania. Albanian scapegoats (Strabo 11.4.7) have been imported to Suania, complete with a fictitious explanation. Control over the Dariel (or Daryal) Pass (the Caspian Gates in this novel) has been handed to the king of Suania. Usually, the king of Iberia is thought to have controlled it. Procopius (1.10.9–12), however, wrote that it 'was held by many men in turn as time went on', and, at the time he was writing about (a rare occasion when we have any evidence at all), it was not held by the Iberian king. Unable to find a classical name for the Cross pass, I named it the Dareine Pass from an unidentified pass through the Caucasus in the work of Menander Guardsman (10.5).

It is a pity the three Caucasian rivers in the novel had such similar names. The Alontas is the modern-day Terek, the Alazonios the Alazani, and the Aragos the Aragvi.

Things

Earthquake

For the physical effects of the earthquake that struck Ephesus, probably in AD262, I borrowed heavily from Edward Paice's enthralling *Wrath of God: The Great Lisbon Earthquake of 1755* (London, 2008). The classical ideas about earthquakes come mainly from Aristotle, *Meteorologica* II.7–8; and Ammianus Marcellinus XVII.7.9–14.

Exile

For the elite of the classical world, exile was an ever-present fear. The Roman emperors' frequent imposition of the punishment on intellectuals encouraged a great deal of literature on the subject. The main texts used in this novel are Musonius Rufus, *That Exile is Not an Evil* (text and translation, C.E. Lutz in *Yale Classical Studies* 10, 1947, pp.68–77); Dio Chrysostom, *Oration* 13, *In Athens, On Exile* (text and translation in Loeb series, J.W. Cohoon, 1939); and Favorinus, *On Exile* (translated by Tim Whitmarsh as an appendix in his *Greek Literature and the Roman Empire: The Politics of Imitation*, Oxford, 2001, pp. 302–24).

Physiognomy

The ancient 'science' of reading physical externals to reveal character and thus uncover both deeds that have been committed as well as those still to come has been brought to the attention of students of mainstream aspects of the classical world by S. Swain (ed.), *Seeing the Face, Seeing the Soul: Polemon's Physiognomy from Classical Antiquity to Medieval Islam* (Oxford, 2007) – a model of collaborative, wide-ranging scholarship.

Philosophers

In chapter six, the views of Gallienus on philosophers in the Roman empire are very close to those of H. Sidebottom, 'Philostratus and the Symbolic Roles of the Sophist and Philosopher', in E. Bowie and J. Elsner (eds.), *Philostratus* (Cambridge, 2009, pp.69–99) – which some might consider unsurprising.

Eunuchs

There has been less scholarship on this subject than one might imagine. Modern interest begins with K. Hopkins, 'The Political Power of Eunuchs', in his *Conquerors and Slaves: Sociological Studies in Roman History, vol. I* (Cambridge, 1978, pp.172–96). Things are taken much further in the essays collected in S. Tougher (ed.), *Eunuchs in Antiquity and Beyond* (London & Swansea, 2002) and S. Tougher, *The Eunuch in Byzantine History and Society* (London, 2008).

For the views of Mastabates in chapter sixteen on the prejudices of others against his kind, I played with two works of Lucian: *The Eunuch* and *The False Critic*.

Persian Punishments

In chapter 28, the ghastly Persian punishment is from Plutarch, *Artaxerxes* 16; variants of the symbolic one are found in Plutarch, *Moralia* 565A; Favorinus, *Corinthian Oration* (preserved in the works of Dio Chrysostom, *Oration* 37.47); and Ammianus Marcellinus 30.8.4. The historicity of them is uncertain. All come from non-Persian sources, and all refer to the Achaemenid dynasty. However, it is probable that the Sassanid dynasty regarded themselves as heirs to the ancient Achaemenids (although some scholars deny this), and it seems that the Sassanid royal court was to some extent Hellenized. Given those two things, it is conceivable that these punishments might have been 'invented traditions': the Sassanids reading them in sources from the Roman empire and then 'importing' them as 'genuine Ancient Persian customs'. Whatever, they were too good not to include in this novel.

Other Historical Novels

As in all the novels in this series, I have included deliberate homages to a couple of historical novelists whose work has both proved an inspiration and given me a lot of pleasure.

The evocative *hooming* sound the Goths make is taken from Robert Low's wonderful *Oathsworn* series – *The Whale Road* (2007), *The Wolf Sea* (2008), *The White Raven* (2009) and *The Prow Beast* (2010) – the very best of Viking novels.

Ballista's habit of calling on his distant ancestor Woden as Allfather derives from *Votan* (1966) and *Not for All the Gold in Ireland* (1968) by John James. I had forgotten this, until I reread them last year. Both are enthralling works and do not deserve to be out of print.

Quotes

The lines from Seneca's *Medea* at the heading of sections of the novel are from the splendid translation by Emily Gowers, *Seneca, Six Tragedies* (Oxford, 2010), which also underlies Pythonissa's curse at the end of the book.

Thanks

In every novel, I thank mainly the same people, but neither my gratitude nor pleasure diminish.

First, the professionals: Alex Clarke, Jen Doyle, Tom Chicken, Francesca Russell, Katya Shipster at Penguin; Sarah Day for copy-editing; and James Gill at United Agents.

Next, Oxford: Maria Stamatopoulou, Louise Durning, and Janie Anderson at Lincoln College; and John Eidinow at St Benet's Hall. A couple of colleagues – Al Moreno at Magdalen College, and Lisa Kallet at University College; and a couple of postgraduates – Richard Marshall at Wadham, and Chris Noon at Christ Church – have helped more than they know by teaching some of my students. Two of the latter, Matt Elstrop and Will Gibbs, escaped neither my tutorials nor endless talk of Ballista.

Then friends: Jeremy Tinton for Maximus-related stuff; Adi Nell for the killing of animals, especially horses; Jeremy Haberley for inhabiting Rutilus; Kate Haberley for what remains the best obscenity in the novel; Steve Miller for the Turkish driving ('anticipation'); and Peter Cosgrove for the foreign travel, the photos, the office, and lots of other stuff.

Finally, my family for their love and support. In Suffolk, my mother Frances and aunt Terry. In Woodstock, my wife Lisa and sons Tom and Jack.

Glossary

The definitions given here are geared to *The Caspian Gates*. If a word or phrase has several meanings, only that or those relevant to this novel tend to be given.

Ab Admissionibus: Official who controlled admission into the presence of the Roman emperor.

Abasgia: Kingdom on the north-east shore of the Black Sea, divided into an eastern and a western half, each with its own king.

Ab Epistulis: Official in charge of imperial correspondence, who usually wrote the emperor's letters.

Abonouteichos: Town in Pontus where the holy man / charlatan Alexander founded the cult of a serpent-bodied god named Glycon. The town was renamed Ionopolis.

Abritus: Town south of the Danube; in marshes nearby, the Goths defeated and killed the Roman emperor Decius in AD251.

Accensus: Secretary of a Roman governor or official.

Achaea: Roman province of Greece.

Achaemenid: Persian dynasty, empire founded by Cyrus the Great *c.* 550BC, and ended by Alexander the Great 330BC.

Adyton: Greek, inner sanctuary.

Agora: Greek, marketplace and civic centre.

Ala: Unit of Roman auxiliary cavalry; usually around five hundred-, sometimes a thousand-strong; literally, a wing.

Ala II Gallorum: Roman cavalry unit, originally raised in Gaul, stationed at Trapezus on the Black Sea (modern-day Trabzon in Turkey).

Alamanni: Confederation of German tribes.

Alani: Nomadic people north of the Caucasus.

Alazonios: Alazani river in modern Georgia.

Albania: Kingdom to the south of the Caucasus, bordering the Caspian Sea (not to be confused with modern Albania).

Alontas: River in the Caucasus, the modern Terek.

Amastris: Greek town on Black Sea, modern-day town of Amasra in Turkey.

A Memoria: Official responsible for reminding high-status Romans, and especially the emperor, of the names of the people they meet.

Amicitia: Latin, friendship, might be as much political as emotional; opposite of *inamicitia*.

Amicus: Latin, friend.

Andreia: Greek, courage; literally, man-ness.

Andron: Room(s) reserved for the men in a traditional Greek house; in practice, the functions of rooms may have changed during the course of the day, i.e. the *andron* may have been occupied by women during much of the day when the men would be out.

Angles: North German tribe, living in the area of modern Denmark.

Aphrodite of Cnidus: Famous nude sculpture of the goddess of love by Praxiteles.

Aquileia: Town in north-eastern Italy, where the emperor Maximinus Thrax was killed in AD238.

Aragos: River in the Caucasus, the modern Aragvi in Georgia.

Argonautica: Greek epic poem of the voyage of Jason and the Argonauts written by Apollonius of Rhodes in the third century BC.

A Rationibus: In the principate, the official in charge of the emperor's finances; later overshadowed by the *Comes Sacrarum Largitionum*.

Ares: Greek god of war.

Armata: Latin, 'the armed one'; in *The Caspian Gates*, the name of a war ship.

Aromeus: Good but heavy wine from the region of Ephesus, said to induce headaches.

Asiarch: Head priest of the imperial cult in a *polis* in the province of Asia which had imperial permission to build a temple to the emperors.

Asneis: Gothic, a lowly day labourer.

Assessors: Advisors to a Roman judge.

A Studiis: Official who aided the literary and intellectual studies of the Roman emperor.

Atheling: Anglo-Saxon, prince or lord.

Atrium: Open court in a Roman house.

Autarkeia: Greek, self-sufficiency; concept amenable to vastly different interpretation but vital in all schools of Greek philosophy.

Auxiliary: Roman regular soldier serving in a unit other than a legion.

Autokrator: Greek, sole ruler; used of the Roman emperor.

Bahram fires: Sacred fires of the Zoroastrian religion.

Ballista, plural *ballistae*: Torsion-powered artillery piece; some shot bolts, others stones.

Ballistarius, plural *ballistarii*: Roman artilleryman.

Barritus: German war cry; adopted by the Roman army.

Basileus: Greek, king; used of the Roman emperor; could also carry a philosophical connotation as the good opposite of the tyrant.

Bithynia et Pontus: Roman province along the south shore of the Black Sea.

Borani (also *Boranoi*): German tribe, one of the tribes that made up the confederation of the Goths, notorious for their piratical raids into the Aegean.

Bosphorus: Latin, from the Greek *bosporos*, literally, ox-ford; the name of several straits, above all those on which Byzantium stood and that in the Crimea. The latter gives its name to the Roman client kingdom of the Bosphorus.

Boule: Council of a Greek city; in the Roman period made up of local men of wealth and influence.

Bouleuterion: Greek, council house, where the *Boule* met; equivalent to the *curia* in Latin.

Buccelatum: Army biscuit, hard-tack.

Cadusii: Tribe to the south-west of the Caspian Sea.

Caledonia: Modern Scotland.

Camara, plural *camarae*: Double-prowed boat local to the Black Sea region.

Campus Martius: Latin, literally, field of Mars; name of famous space in Rome; in general, name for a parade ground.

Campus Serenus: Area of rich farmland north-west of Byzantium.

Capax Imperii: Latin, capable of (governing the) empire; a memorable Tacitean phrase.

Cappadocia: Roman province north of the Euphrates.

Caspian Gates: Name given to the passes through the Caucasus mountains.

Caucasian Gates: Alternative name for the Caspian Gates; sometimes specifically applied to the Dariel (or Daryal) Pass.

Chaldean: Cover-all label given to 'eastern' magicians under the Roman empire.

Cilicia: Roman province in the south of Asia Minor, divided into an eastern 'smooth' half and a western 'rough'.

Cinaedus, plural *cinaedi*: Derogatory Latin term (taken from Greek, *kinaidos*; Romans liked to pretend that all such habits came from the Greeks) for the passive one in male–male sex.

Classis Pontica: Roman Black Sea fleet.

Clementia: Latin, the virtue of mercy.

Clibanarius, plural *clibanarii*: heavily armed cavalryman; possibly derived from 'baking oven'.

Cohors: Unit of Roman soldiers, usually about five-hundred strong.

Cohors Apuleia Civium Romanorum Ysiporto: Unit of auxiliary infantry, originally raised from Roman citizens in Apulia in Italy, now stationed at the fort of Hyssou Limen on the southern shore of the Black Sea.

Cohors II Claudiana: Auxiliary infantry unit stationed at Asparus on the Black Sea.

Cohors III Ulpia Patraeorum Milliaria Equitata Sagittariorum: Double-strength (*milliaria*) auxiliary unit of bowmen with both cavalry and infantry components, originally raised in Petra, now stationed at Asparus on the Black Sea.

Colchis: Rather vague geographic term for eastern end of Black Sea; often used for land bounded by Iberia to the east and the Black Sea to the west; for Greeks and Romans, the name was heavy with mythic connotations.

Collegium, plural *collegia*: Latin, literally, colleges; associations, sometimes religious or burial clubs, often formed by the lower classes, always regarded with suspicion by the elite.

Colonia Agrippinensis: Important Roman city on the Rhine; modern Cologne.

Comes Augusti, plural *comites Augusti*: Companion of Augustus; name given to members of the imperial *consilium* when the emperor was on campaign or on a journey.

Comes Sacrarum Largitionum: Count of the Sacred Largess; very important official in the late empire, who controlled mints, mines, monetary taxation and the pay and clothing of soldiers and officials.

Comissatio: Drinking that followed the eating at a Roman feast.

Comitatus: Latin, a following; name given to barbarian war bands, and then to the mobile, mainly cavalry forces set up by Gallienus to accompany the emperor.

Conditum: Spiced wine, often taken as an aperitif, sometimes served warm.

Consilium: Council, cabinet of advisors, of a Roman emperor, official or elite private person.

Contubernium: Group of ten (or maybe eight) soldiers who share a tent; by extension, comradeship.

Corrector Totius Orientis: Overseer of all the Orient; a title applied to Odenathus of Palmyra.

Crimean Bosphorus: Client kingdom of Rome based on the Crimea, sometimes simply referred to as the kingdom of the Bosphorus.

Cronus: In myth, the reluctant father of the gods; as each was born, he swallowed them. Thus the expression 'having the eye of Cronos on you' meaning that something bad is about to happen.

Croucasis: Scythian name for the Caucasus; said to mean gleaming white with snow.

Cumania: Fort in the Dariel (or Daryal) Pass.

Curia: Latin, senate or council house; in Greek, *Bouleuterion*.

Cursus Publicus: Imperial Roman posting service whereby those with official passes (*diplomata*) could send messengers and get remounts.

Custos: Latin, chaperone, literally, a guardian; one would accompany an upper-class woman, in addition to her maids, when she went out in public.

Cyrus river: The modern Kura or Mtkvari river running through Georgia and Azerbaijan.

Dacia: Roman province north of the Danube, in the region around modern Romania.

Daemon: Supernatural being; could be applied to many different types: good/bad, individual/collective, internal/external, and ghosts.

Dareine: Unidentified pass through the Caucasus mentioned by Menander Guardsman (10.5); in this novel applied to the Cross Pass in modern Georgia.

Decennalia: Festival to mark ten years of an emperor's rule; few were celebrated in the third century AD.

Demos: Greek, the people; also sometimes used to indicate the poor.

Derband Pass: Plain between the Causasus mountains and the Caspian Sea.

Didyma: Sanctuary, with oracle of Apollo, south of Miletus.

Didymeia: Festival held every fourth year at Didyma (every *fifth* in ancient inclusive counting).

Dignitas: Important Roman concept which covers our idea of dignity but goes much further; famously, Julius Caesar claimed that his *dignitas* meant more to him than life itself.

Dikaiosyne: Fictional village, 'justice', in Greek; roughly on the site of the modern settlement of Kasbeki.

Diogmitai: Constables in Greek cities; commanded by an *eirenarch*.

Diplomata: Official passes which allowed the bearer access to the *cursus publicus*.

Domina: Latin, lady or madam; the feminine of *dominus*.

Dominus: Latin, lord, master, sir; a title of respect.

Draco: Latin, literally, snake or dragon; name given to a windsock-style military standard shaped like a dragon.

Dulths: Gothic festival of the full moon.

Dux: Latin, a high military command, often of a frontier.

Eirenarch: Title of chief of police in many Greek cities, including Ephesus.

Elagabalus: Patron god of the town of Emesa in Syria, a sun god; also name often given (sometimes in the form Heliogabalus) to one of his priests who became the Roman emperor formally known as Marcus Aurelius Antoninus (AD218–22).

Embolos: The Sacred Way, the main street of Ephesus.

Emesa: Town in Syria (modern Homs), where the short-lived emperor Quietus was killed.

Emporion: Greek, trading place; lacking some of the amenities that made a *polis*.

Ephebes: Young men of a Greek city, the upperclass among them often enrolled in some form of paramilitary organization, to mark them out from the hoi polloi.

Epicureanism: Greek philosophical system whose followers either denied that the gods existed or held that they were far away and did not intervene in the affairs of mankind.

Equestrian: Second rank down in the Roman social pyramid: the elite order just below the senators.

Equites Singulares: Cavalry bodyguards; in Rome, one of the permanent units protecting the emperors; in the provinces, ad hoc units set up by military commanders; at Phasis in Colchis, the name of the permanent cavalry garrison.

Erastes: Greek, the older male lover of a boy (the *eromenos*).

Eromenos: Greek, a boy too young to grow a beard beloved by a mature *erastes*; just how far either with decency should go was debatable.

Etruscan: Native of Etruria in Italy, a place with a reputation for magic.

Eumenides: 'The kindly ones', a euphemism for the terrible furies from the underworld that pursued and tormented wrongdoers.

Eupatrid: From the Greek, meaning well-born, an aristocrat.

Fairguneis: One of the high gods of the Goths.

Familia: Latin, family, and by extension the entire household, including slaves, freedmen and the rest of an entourage.

Fasces: Bundles of wooden rods tied round a single-bladed axe, carried by *lictors*, the symbols of power of Roman magistrates.

Fiscus: Imperial treasury.

Framadar: Persian, a military officer or hero.

Franks: Confederation of German tribes.

Frisii: North German tribe.

Frumentarius, plural *frumentarii*: Military unit based on the Caelian Hill in Rome; the emperors' secret police; messengers, spies and assassins.

Gates of the Alani: Alternative name for the Caspian Gates; sometimes specifically applied to the Derbend Pass.

Genius: Divine part of man; some ambiguity as to whether it is external (like a guardian angel) or internal (a divine spark); that of the head of a household worshipped as part of household gods, that of the emperor publicly worshipped.

Germania: Lands where the German tribes lived; 'free' Germany.

Germania Inferior: More northerly of Rome's two provinces of Germany; mainly confined to the west bank of the Rhine.

Germania Superior: More southerly of Rome's two German provinces.

Getae: Tribe in the Balkans.

Gladius: Roman military short sword; generally superseded by the *spatha* by the mid-third century AD; also slang for penis.

Gorgons: Female monsters in Greek mythology, the most infamous being Medusa. Their terrible appearance, including snakes in their hair, turned men to stone.

Gorytus: Combined bow case and quiver.

Goths: Loose confederation of Germanic tribes.

Graeculus, plural *Graeculi*: Latin, little Greek; Greeks called themselves Hellenes, but Romans tended not to extend that courtesy but called them *Graeci*; with casual contempt, Romans often went further, to *Graeculi*.

Gudja: Gothic priest.

Gyaros: Small Aegean island just off Andros; Roman emperors sentenced men to exile there.

Hansa: Division of Gothic warriors.

Harmozica: Important town in ancient Iberia (modern Baginetti in Georgia).

Hecate: Sinister three-headed underworld goddess of magic, the night, crossroads and doorways.

Hegemon, plural *hegemones*: Greek, leading man.

Helots: Serf-type underclass in classical Sparta.

Heracles: Latin, Hercules; God who was once a man.

Herbed: Zoroastrian priest, possibly chief priest.

Heroon: Shrine to a hero; at Ephesus to the founder of the city, Androclos.

Heruli: Germanic nomads from north-east of the Black Sea.

Hetaira: Greek, literally, a female companion, girl who provided sex for 'gifts'; should be skilled at conversation as well, a cut above a common *porne* (prostitute); often translated as courtesan.

Hibernia: Modern Ireland.

Himation: Greek cloak.

Hippodamian: Name given to a planned street grid; after Hippodamus of Miletus, the famous fifth-century BC town planner.

Hispania Tarraconensis: One of the three provinces into which the Romans divided the Spanish peninsula, the north-east corner.

Homonoia: Greek, harmony; a philosophical concept and a divine personification; in the disputatious world of the principate, often invoked on civic coinage.

Humiliores: Latin, the humble, the lower class; a social expression which transforms in the late empire into a legal group, distinguished from the *honestiores* (the upper class).

Hydrophor: Priestess of Artemis at Didyma.

Hypochrestes: Aide to the *prophetes* at Didyma.

Hypozomata: Rope forming the under-girdle of a *trireme*; there were usually two of them.

Iberia: Kingdom to the south of the Caucasus (the name led some ancient writers to state that its inhabitants had migrated from Spain).

Ides: Thirteenth day of the month in short months, the fifteenth in long months.

Ientaculum: Latin, breakfast.

Imperium: Power to issue orders and exact obedience; official military command.

Imperium Romanum: Power of the Romans, i.e. the Roman empire, often referred to simply as the *imperium*.

Inamicitia: Latin, hostility, the opposite of *amicitia*.

Insula: Latin, literally an island; an urban block of dwellings surrounded by roads or paths.

Iustitia: Latin, justice; a virtue ascribed to Roman emperors.

Jormungand: In Norse mythology, the world serpent which lay in the depths of the ocean waiting for Ragnarok.

Kalends: First day of the month.

Kinaidos: *See* Cinaedus.

Kyria: Greek, lady, mistress; the feminine of *kyrios*; a title of respect.

Kyrios: Greek, lord, master, sir; a title of respect.

Latrones: Latin, robbers/ bandits.

Legio II Adiutrix Pia Fidelis: 'The Second Legion, the help-giver, loyal and faithful' based at Aquincum in Pannonia Inferior.

Legio II Parthica Pia Fidelis Felix Aeterna: 'The Second Legion, the Parthian, eternally loyal, faithful and fortunate' based in Rome.

Legio XXX Ulpia Victrix: 'The Thirtieth Legion, ulpian and victorious', stationed at Vetera (modern Xanten) in Germania Inferior.

Legion: Unit of heavy infantry, usually about five thousand strong; from mythical times, the backbone of the Roman army; the numbers in a legion and the legions' dominance in the army declined during the third century AD as more and more detachments (*vexillationes*), served away from the parent unit and became more or less independent units.

Libitinarii: Funerary Men, the carriers out of the dead; they had to reside beyond the town limits, and to ring a bell when they came into town to perform their duties.

Liburnian: Name given in the time of the Roman empire to a small war ship, possibly rowed on two levels.

Lictors: Ceremonial attendants of a Roman magistrate.

Limes: Latin, frontier.

Loki: In Norse mythology, the trickster, a mischievous, evil god.

Lustrum: Roman religious ceremony of purification, carried out when a new beginning was considered necessary.

Lydia: Kingdom in Asia Minor, conquered by the Persians in 546BC.

Macropogones: Literally, longbeards, a tribe to the north-east of the Black Sea.

Maeotis: Sea of Azov.

Magi: Name given by Greeks and Romans to Persian priests, often thought of as sorcerers.

Maiestas: Latin, majesty; offences against the majesty of the Roman people were treason; a charge of *maiestas* was a grave fear among the elite of the *imperium*.

Mandata: Instructions issued by the emperors to their governors and officials.

Manichaeans: The followers of the religious leader Mani (AD216–76).

Mansio: Rest house of the *cursus publicus*.

Marcomanni: German tribe.

Mardi: Tribe to the south-west of the Caspian Sea.

Massagetae: Nomad tribe to the north-east of Persia; famous, via Herodotus, for defeating Cyrus the Great of Persia.

Mazda (also *Ahuramazda*): The wise lord, the supreme god of Zoroastrianism.

Mediolanum: Major Roman city in northern Italy; modern Milan.

Miles, plural *milites*: Latin, soldier.

Milesian: From the town of Miletus in Asia Minor.

Milesian Tales: Greek genre of erotic stories, their most famous author being Aristides.

Mobads: Persian Zoroastrian priests; *see* magi.

Moesia Inferior: Roman province south of the Danube, running from Moesia Superior in the west to the Black Sea in the east.

Moesia Superior: Roman province to the south of the Danube, bounded by Panonnia Inferior to the north-west and Moesia Inferior to the north-east.

Mos Maiorum: Important Roman concept; traditional customs, the way of the ancestors.

Mouth of the Impious: According to Ps-Plutarch, *On Rivers* 5, an opening in the ground in Colchis which led to an underground river. Those condemned for impiety were thrown into it and re-emerged, very dead, thirty days later, in Lake Maeotis (the Sea of Azov).

Nasu: Persian, the daemon of death.

Naupegos: Shipwright of a Greek or Roman war ship.

Negotium: Latin, business time, time devoted to the service of the *Res Publica*; the opposite of *otium*.

Nemausus: Town in Gaul (modern Nîmes); possibly the birthplace of Castricius.

Nobilis, plural *nobiles*: Latin, nobleman,; a man from a patrician family or a plebeian family one of whose ancestors had been consul.

Nones: Ninth day of a month before the *ides*, i.e. the fifth day of a short month, the seventh of a long month.

Noricum: Roman province to the north-east of the Alps.

Novae: Town on south bank of Danube; successfully defended from Gothic attack by the future emperor Gallus in AD250.

Numerus, plural *numeri*: Latin name given to a Roman army unit, especially to ad hoc units outside the regular army structure; often units raised from semi or non-Romanized peoples which retained their indigenous fighting techniques.

Numerus I Trapezountioon: Unit of locally raised infantry at Trapezus.

Numerus II Trapezountioon: Unit of locally raised infantry at Trapezus.

Numidia: Roman province in North Africa.

Nymphaeum: Fountain house.

Obol: Small-denomination Greek coin.

Optio: Junior officer in the Roman army, ranked below a centurion.

Ornamenta Consularia: The ornaments of a consul; the symbols of consular office often used by Rome as a diplomatic gift to foreigner potentates.

Otium: Latin, leisure time, the opposite of *negotium*; it was thought important to get the balance right between the two for a civilized life.

Paideia: Culture; Greeks considered that it marked them off from the rest of the world, and the Greek elite considered that it marked them off from the rest of the Greeks; some knowledge of it was considered necessary to be thought a member of the Roman elite.

Palatium: Latin, palace, residence of an emperor.

Pandateria: Small island off the western coast of Italy; Roman emperors favoured it as a destination for those sentenced to exile.

Panonnia Inferior: Roman province south of the Danube, to the east of Panonnia Superior.

Panonnia Superior: Roman province south of the Danube, to the west of Panonnia Inferior.

Paphlagonia: Area of northern Asia Minor.

Paraphylax: Head of the temple guards at Didyma.

Parrhesia: Greek, free speech; vital concept in all Greek philosophical systems.

Pater Patriae: Latin, Father of the Fatherland; a title of the emperors.

Patrician: The highest social status in Rome; originally descendants of those men who sat in the very first meeting of the free senate after the expulsion of the last of the mythical kings of Rome in 509BC; under the principate, emperors awarded other families patrician status.

Patronus: Latin, patron; once a slave had been manumitted and become a freedman, his former owner became his *patronus*; there were duties and obligations on both sides.

Pax Deorum: Very important Roman concept of the peace between the Roman *Res Publica* and the gods.

Pentekontarchos: Purser or quartermaster of a ship.

Periplous: Greek, literally, a sailing around, a list of ports and anchorages and landmarks along a coast.

Peroz: Persian, victory.

Phasis: Main river in Colchis.

Philanthropia: Greek, love of mankind; underpinned by philosophy, the concept acted as a powerful influence on the perceptions and actions of the Greek and Roman elites.

Philotimia: Greek, love of honour; a virtue the Greek elite liked to believe they possessed.

Phtheirophagi: literally, 'lice-eaters', a tribe to the north-east of the Black Sea.

Physiognomy: The ancient 'science' of studying people's faces, bodies and deportment to discover their character, and thus both their past and future.

Pietas: Latin, piety; the human side of the *Pax Deorum*.

Pitiax: Title of the heir to the throne of Iberia.

Platonist: Follower of the philosophy of Plato.

Plebs: Technically, all Romans who were not patricians; more usually, the non-elite.

Plebs Urbana: Poor of the city of Rome, in literary compositions usually coupled with an adjective labelling them as dirty, superstitious, lazy, distinguished from the *plebs rustica*, whose rural lifestyle might make them less morally dubious.

Polis: Greek, a city state; living in one was a key marker in being considered Greek and/ or civilized.

Pontifex Maximus: Chief priest of Rome, a position held by the emperors.

Praefectus: Prefect, a flexible Latin title for many civilian officials and military officers; typically, the commander of an auxiliary unit.

Praetorian Prefect: Commander of the Praetorian Guard, an equestrian.

Prefect of Cavalry: Senior military post introduced in the mid-third century AD.

Prefect of the City: Senior senatorial post in the city of Rome.

Princeps: Latin, first man or leading man; thus a polite way to refer to the emperor (*see* Principatus), in the plural, *principes*, it often meant the senators or the great men of the *imperium*.

Princeps Peregrinorum: Literally, the leader of the foreigners, the commander of the *frumentarii*, usually a senior centurion.

Principatus: In English, the principate; rule of the *Princeps*, the rule of the Roman *imperium* by the emperors.

Prometheus: Divine figure, one of the Titans; variously believed to have created mankind out of clay, tricked the gods into accepting only the bones and fat of sacrifices, and stolen fire – hidden in a fennel stalk – from Olympus for mortals. Zeus chained him to a peak in the Caucasus, where an eagle daily ate his liver. Heracles shot the eagle and freed him.

Pronoia: Greek concept of foresight.

Prophetes: Title of priest who delivers oracular responses of Apollo at Didyma.

Propylon: Greek, portico.

Proskynesis: Greek, literally, kissing towards, adoration; given to the gods and in some periods to some rulers, including emperors in the third century AD. There were two types: full prostration on the ground, or bowing and blowing a kiss with the fingertips.

Protector, plural *protectores*: a group of military officers singled out by the emperor Gallienus.

Prusa: Town in Asia Minor; birthplace of the celebrated philosopher Dio Chrysostom.

Ptolemies: Macedonian dynasty who ruled Egypt from 323–30BC.

Puer, plural *pueri*: Latin, boy; interestingly, used by owners to describe male slaves and by soldiers of each other.

Pugio: Roman military dagger; one of the symbols that marked a soldier.

Raetia: Roman province; roughly equivalent to modern Switzerland.

Ragnarok: In Norse paganism, the death of gods and men, the end of time.

Ran: Norse goddess of the sea.

Reiks: Gothic, a chief.

Relegatio: Latin, lesser form of exile under the principate; the victim was banished from Italy and his home province, and was usually allowed to retain his property.

Res Publica: Latin, the Roman Republic; under the emperors continued to mean the Roman empire.

Rhodope Mountains: Mountain range in Thrace; in modern Bulgaria and Greece.

Rugii: German tribe in the far north of Europe.

Sacramentum: Roman military oath, taken extremely seriously.

Sacred Boys: Name for temple slaves at Didyma.

Sarapanis: Fort on the border between ancient Colchis and Iberia.

Sarmatians: Nomadic barbarian peoples living north of the Danube.

Sassanids (sometimes *Sasanids*, *Sasanians*, or *Sassanians*): Persian dynasty that overthrew the Parthians in the 220s AD and were Rome's great eastern rivals until the seventh century AD.

Scribe to the Demos: The most important annual magistrate in Ephesus.

Scythians: Greek and Latin name for various northern and often nomadic barbarian peoples, vaguely applied, thus the Goths and later the Huns were described as Scythians.

Sebastos: Greek, literally, the reverenced; used as translation of the Roman title Augustus.

Senate: Council of Rome, under the emperors composed of about six hundred men, the vast majority ex-magistrates, with some imperial favourites. The senatorial order was the richest and most prestigious group in the empire, but suspicious emperors were beginning to exclude them from military commands in the mid-third century AD.

Serdica: Roman town; modern Sofia.

Shieldburg: Northern shieldwall or phalanx.

Silentarius: Roman official who, as his title indicates, was to keep silence and decorum at the imperial court.

Silphium: Spice from Cyrene in North Africa much prized in the classical world; after it became extinct, a substitute was imported from Asia.

Sirmium: Roman town in Panonnia Inferior, modern Sremska Mitrovica in Serbia.

Skalks: Gothic, slave.

Spatha: Long Roman sword; the usual type of sword carried by all troops by the mid-third century AD.

Spoletium: Ancient town in northern Italy where in AD253 the short-lived emperor Aemilianus was killed, bringing Valerian and Gallienus to the throne, modern-day Spoleto.

Stationarii: Roman soldiers on detached duty from their main units.

Stephanephoros: Greek, literally, crown-wearer; title of magistrate in some Greek citics.

Stoic: Follower of the philosophy of Stoicism; should believe that everything which does not affect one's moral purpose is an irrelevance; so poverty, illness, bereavement and death cease to be things to fear.

Stola: Roman matron's gown.

Strategos: Greek, general.

Strobilos: Local name for peak in Caucasus where Prometheus was chained; possibly Mount Kazbek.

Suania: Kingdom in the high Caucasus; included the modern district of Georgia called Svaneti.

Synedrion: Greek, council; in Suania, a body of three hundred who advise the king.

Tamias: Treasurer of Didyma.

Tanais River: The Don.

Tauromenium: Town in Sicily (modern Taormina), where Ballista and Julia own a villa.

Teiws: God worshipped by the Goths.

Telones: Greek, customs official.

Tervingi: One of the tribes that made up the loose confederation known as the Goths.

Testudo: Latin, literally, tortoise, by analogy both a Roman infantry formation with overlapping shields, similar to a northern shieldburg, and a mobile shed protecting a siege engine.

Thalamians: Lowest of the three levels of rowers on a *trireme*.

Thalia: Greek, abundance or good fortune; in *The Caspian Gates*, the name of a fishing boat.

Thranites: Highest of three levels of rowers on a *trireme*; the elite oarsmen of the vessel.

Titans: Generation of gods defeated by the Olympians.

Toga: Voluminous garment, reserved for Roman male citizens, worn on formal occasions.

Toga Virilis: Garment given to mark a Roman's coming of age, usually at about fourteen.

Trapezus: Ancient town on the southern shore of the Black Sea, modern Trabzon in Turkey.

Trierarch: Commander of a *trireme*; in the Roman military, equivalent in rank to a centurion.

Trireme: Ancient war ship, a galley rowed by about two hundred men on three levels.

Tzour: Town in ancient Albania on the coast of the Caspian Sea, possibly modern Derbend in Dagestan, Russia.

Valhalla: In Norse paganism, the hall in which selected heroes who had fallen in battle would feast until Ragnarok.

Vexillatio: Sub-unit of Roman troops detached from its parent unit.

Vexillatio Fasiana: Unit of infantry stationed at Phasis.

Vexillium: Roman military standard.

Vicus: Latin, settlement outside a fort.

Vir Clarissimus: Title of a Roman senator.

Vir Egregius: Knight of Rome, a man of the equestrian order.

Vir Ementissimus: Highest rank an equestrian could attain; e.g. Praetorian Prefect.

Vir Perfectissimus: Equestrian rank above *Vir Egregius* but below *Vir Ementissimus*.

Virtus: Latin, courage, manliness, virtue; far stronger and more active than English 'virtue'.

Woden: High god of the Angles and other northern peoples.

Zygians: Middle of three levels of rowers on a *trireme*.

List of Roman Emperors of the time of
The Caspian Gates

AD193–211	Septimius Severus
AD198–217	Caracalla
AD210–11	Geta
AD217–18	Macrinus
AD218–22	Elagabalus
AD222–35	Alexander Severus
AD235–8	Maximinus Thrax
AD238	Gordian I
AD238	Gordian II
AD238	Pupienus
AD238	Balbinus
AD238–44	Gordian III
AD244–9	Philip the Arab
AD249–51	Decius
AD251–3	Trebonianus Gallus
AD253	Aemilianus
AD253–60	Valerian
AD253–	Gallienus

List of Characters

To avoid giving away any of the plot, characters usually are only described as first encountered in *The Caspian Gates*.

Achilleus: Iulius Achilleus, Gallienus's *a Memoria*.

Aeetes: Mythical king of Colchis, father of Medea.

Aelius Aelianus: Prefect of Legio II Adiutrix.

Aelius Restutus: Governor of province of Noricum.

Aemilianus (1): Marcus Aemilius Aemilianus, briefly Roman emperor AD253.

Aemilianus (2): Senatorial governor of Hispania Tarraconensis; organized defection of Spain to Postumus; made 'Gallic consul' for AD262.

Aemilianus (3): Mussius Aemilianus, prefect of Egypt, joined Macriani in AD260, then declared himself emperor in AD261.

Agathon: Slave purchased by Ballista in Priene.

Alexander the Great: 356–23BC, son of Philip, king of Macedon, conqueror of Achaemenid Persia.

Alexander Severus: Marcus Aurelius Severus Alexander, Roman emperor AD222–35.

Alexander of Abonouteichos: Second century AD holy man, or religious charlatan, ridiculed by the satirist Lucian.

Alexandra: *Hydrophor* (virgin priestess) of Artemis at Didyma; daughter of Selandros.

Amantius: Eunuch in the service of the Roman emperor, a native of Abasgia.

Androclos: Mythic founder of Ephesus.

Antigonus: One of Ballista's Equites Singulares, who died at Arete.

Anthia: Maid of Julia's.

Apollonius of Rhodes: Third century BC writer, author of the *Argonautica*.

Apollonius of Tyana: A philosopher/wonder-worker of the first century AD.

Ardashir I: Sassanid king, father of Shapur.

Ariarathes V: Second century BC king of Cappadocia.

Aristides: Author of non-extant erotic work called the *Milesian Tales*.

Aristodicus: Wise man of Cyme, whose story is in Herodotus.

Aristomachus: Byzantine teacher of rhetoric, whom Hippothous claims to have killed.

Arrian: Lucius Flavius Arrianus, Greek author and Roman consul, c. AD86–160. Several of his works survive, including the *Anabasis of Alexander*, the *Expedition against the Alani*, and the *Periplus Ponti Euxini*.

Arsinoe: Younger sister of Cleopatra of Egypt, murdered in 41BC in Ephesus, where her tomb was on the *Embolos*.

Athenaeus: Member of the *Boule* of Byzantium.

Attalus: King of the Marcomanni, father of Pippa.

Attalus II: Second century BC king of Pergamum.

Augustus: First Roman emperor, 31BC–AD14.

Aulus Valerius Festus: Christian, brother of the Ephesian *asiarch* Gaius Valerius Festus.

Aureolus: Manius Acilius Aureolus, once a Getan shepherd from near the Danube, now Gallienus's Prefect of Cavalry, one of the *protectores*.

Azo: Third son of King Polemo of Suania.

Bagoas: 'The Persian boy', at one time a slave owned by Ballista; now a Zoroastrian *mobad* called Hormizd.

Ballista: Marcus Clodius Ballista, originally named Dernhelm, son of Isangrim the *Dux* (war-leader) of the Angles. A diplomatic hostage in the Roman empire, he has been granted Roman citizenship and equestrian status, having served in the Roman army in Africa, in the far west, and on the Danube and Euphrates. Having defeated the Sassanid Persians at the battles of Circesium, Soli and Sebaste and killed the pretender Quietus, he was briefly acclaimed Roman emperor in the city of Emesa the year before this novel starts.

Bathshiba: Daughter of the late Iarhai, a *synodiarch* (caravan protector) of Arete, now married to Haddudad.

Bauto: Young Frisian slave purchased by Ballista in Ephesus.

Bonitus: Roman siege engineer; one of the *protectores*.

Bruteddius Niger: *Trierarch* of the *Armata*.

Calgacus: Marcus Clodius Calgacus, a Caledonian ex-slave, originally owned by Isangrim and sent by him to serve as a body servant to his son Ballista in the Roman empire; manumitted by the latter, now a freedman with Roman citizenship.

Caligula: Gaius Julius Caligula, Roman emperor AD37–41. As a child, nicknamed 'Little Boots'/ Caligula, because his father the general Germanicus had him dressed in miniature soldier's uniform.

Camsisoleus: Egyptian officer of Gallienus; brother of Theodotus; one of the *protectores*.

Castricius: Gaius Aurelius Castricius, Roman army officer risen from the ranks, Prefect of Cavalry under both Quietus and Ballista, thought to be originally from Nemausus in Gaul.

Celer: Roman siege engineer, one of the *protectores*.

Celsus: Pretender to the throne from Africa, killed in AD260.

Censorinus: Lucius Calpurnius Piso Censorinus. *Princeps Peregrinorum* under Valerian and the pretenders Macrianus and Quietus; now serving as deputy Praetorian Prefect under Gallienus.

Chrysogonus: Greek who has gone over to the Goths.

Claudius (1): Tiberius Claudius Nero Germanicus, Roman emperor AD37–54.

Claudius (2): Marcus Aurelius Claudius, a Danubian officer of Gallienus, one of the *protectores*.

Claudius Natalianus: Governor of the province of Moesia Inferior.

Cleisthenes: Well-bred youth of Tauromenium in Sicily, whom Hippothous claims to have loved.

Clementius Silvius: Titus Clementius Silvius, governor of both the provinces of Panonnia, Superior and Inferior.

Cleodamus: Member of the *Boule* of Byzantium.

Constans: Body-servant to Ballista.

Cornelius Octavianus: Marcus Cornelius Octavianus, governor of Mauretania and *Dux* of the Libyan frontier.

Corvus: Marcus Aurelius Corvus, the *eirenarch* (police chief) of Ephesus.

Cosis: King of Georgian Albania.

Croesus: The last king of Lydia, *c.* 560–46BC; proverbial for his wealth.

Cyrus: Cyrus the Great, king of Persia *c.* 557–30BC, founder of the Achaemenid dynasty.

Decianus: Governor of Numidia in Africa.

Demetrius: Marcus Clodius Demetrius, 'the Greek boy', a slave purchased by Julia to serve as her husband Ballista's secretary; manumitted by the latter, now a freedman with Roman citizenship living in the household of the emperor Gallienus.

Demosthenes: 384–22BC, Athenian orator.

Dernhelm (1): Original name of Ballista.

Dernhelm (2): Lucius Clodius Dernhelm, second son of Ballista and Julia.

Dio of Prusa: Dio Chrysostom, the 'Golden-mouthed'; a Greek philosopher of the first to second centuries AD.

Dio of Syracuse: *c.* 408–353BC, soldier, statesman and Platonist; returned from exile to free his own city from tyranny.

Diogenes: The cynic philosopher, *c.* 412/ 403–*c.*324/ 321BC.

Domitian: Titus Flavius Domitian, Roman emperor AD81–96.

Domitianus: Italian officer of Gallienus, one of the *protectores*; claims descent from the emperor Domitian.

Epicurus: Greek philosopher, 341–270BC, founder of Epicurean philosophy.

Euripides: Fifth century BC Athenian tragic playwright.

Eusebius: Eunuch in the service of the Roman emperor, a native of Abasgia.

Faraxen: A native rebel in Africa against Rome, rumoured still to be alive.

Favorinus: First to second century AD Greek philosopher, from Arelate in Gaul, born a eunuch.

Felix: Spurius Aemilius Felix, an elderly senator; defended Byzantium from the Goths in AD257.

Flavius Damianus: Member of the *Boule* of Ephesus, descendant of a famous sophist of the same name.

Freki the Alamann: German bodyguard of Gallienus.

Gaius Valerius Festus: Member of the *Boule* of Ephesus; *asiarch* (high-priest) of the imperial cult in that city.

Galen: AD129–?199/216, famous Greek doctor, court physician to Marcus Aurelius.

Galliena: Female cousin of Gallienus.

Gallienus: Publius Licinius Egnatius Gallienus, declared joint Roman emperor by his father the emperor Valerian in AD253, sole emperor after the capture of his father by the Persians in AD260.

Gallus: Gaius Vibius Trebonianus Gallus, a successful general on the Danube. He defended Novae from the Goths in AD250; emperor AD251–3.

Genialis: Simplicinius Genialis, acting governor of Raetia, defected to Postumus in AD260.

Gondofarr: Sassanid commander.

Haddudad: Mercenary captain who served Iarhai, Bathshiba's father; now an officer in the service of Odenathus of Palmyra.

Hadrian: Publius Aelius Hadrianus, Roman emperor AD117–38.

Hamazasp: King of Georgian Iberia.

Hermianus: Caecilus Hermianus, *ab Admissionibus* of Gallienus.

Herodotus: 'The father of history'; fifth century BC Greek historian of the Persian wars.

Hippothous: Claims to be from Perinthus originally; joined Ballista as *accensus* in Rough Cilicia.

Hormizd: Zoroastrian *mobad*; once when a slave of Ballista called Bagoas.

Hyperanthes: *Ephebe* of Perinthus, the great love of Hippothous; lost at sea off Lesbos.

Iarhai: A caravan protector who was killed in the fall of Arete; father of Bathshiba.

Ingenuous: One-time governor of Pannonia Superior and one of Gallienus's *protectores*; rebelled and was killed in AD260.

Isangrim (1): *Dux* (war-leader) of the Angles, father of Dernhelm/ Ballista.

Isangrim (2): Marcus Clodius Isangrim, first son of Ballista and Julia.

Jason: Leader of the Argonauts.

Juba: Titus Destricius Juba, senatorial governor of Britannia Superior; organized defection of Britain to Postumus; made 'Gallic consul' for AD262.

Julia: Daughter of the senator Gaius Julius Volcatius Gallicanus; wife of Ballista.

Kirder the mobad: Zoroastrian high-priest (*herbed*), of Shapur.

Kobrias: Suanian warrior.

Licinius: Gallienus's brother.

Longinus: Cassius Longinus, *c.* AD213–73, a philosopher; at the time of this novel teaching in Athens.

Lucius Verus: Roman emperor AD161–9.

Macarius: Marcus Aurelius Macarius, *stephanephor* (leading magistrate) and *asiarch* (imperial priest) of Miletus.

Macrianus (1): Marcus Fulvius Macrianus ('the Elder'); *Comes Sacrarum*

Largitionum et Praefectus Annonae of Valerian; behind the proclamation of his sons as emperors in AD260; killed with his eldest son in AD261.

Macrianus (2): Titus Fulvius Junius Macrianus ('the Younger'); son of Macrianus (1); acclaimed emperor with his brother Quietus in AD260, killed in AD261.

Mamurra: Ballista's *Praefectus Fabrum* and friend; entombed in a siege tunnel at Arete.

Manzik: Zoroastrian *mobad*.

Marcus Aurelius: Roman emperor AD161–80; author of philosophical reflections in Greek *To Himself* (often known as *The Meditations*).

Marinianus: Third son of Gallienus.

Marius: Gaius Marius, *c.* 157–87BC, Roman general who returned from exile to briefly take over the city.

Mastabates: Eunuch in the service of the Roman emperor, a native of Abasgia.

Maximillianus: Governor of the province of Asia.

Maximinus Thrax: Gaius Iulius Verus Maximinus, Roman emperor AD235–8, known as 'Thrax' (the Thracian') because of his lowly origins.

Maximus: Marcus Clodius Maximus, bodyguard to Ballista; originally a Hibernian warrior known as Muirtagh of the Long Road, sold to slave traders and trained as a boxer then gladiator before being purchased by Ballista, now a freedman.

Medea: Daughter of Aeetes, Colchian princess and sorceress, lover of Jason who helps him win the Golden Fleece.

Melissus: Fisherman from a village in the territory of Amastris.

Memor: African officer of Gallicnus; one of the *protectores*.

Mithridates: Eldest son of King Polemo of Suania.

Musonius: Gaius Musonius Rufus, first century AD Stoic philosopher, 'the Roman Socrates'. Like Socrates, Musonius left no writings; the works preserved in his name claim to be a record of his teaching written up by one of his pupils.

Narcissus: Slave purchased by Hippothous in Ephesus.

Narseh: Prince Narseh, a son of Shapur, King of Persia; commanding a Sassanid army on the south-west shores of the Caspian Sea.

Nero: Nero Claudius Caesar, Roman emperor AD54–68.

Nicomachus: Stoic philosopher.

Nikeso: Wife of Corvus.

Nummius Ceionius Albinus: Senator, prefect of the city of Rome.

Nummius Faustinianus: Senator, consul ordinarius with Gallienus AD262.

Odenathus: Septimius Odenathus, Lord of Palmyra / Tadmor, known as the Lion of the Sun; appointed by Gallienus as *corrector* over the eastern provinces of the Roman empire.

Oroezes (1): *Pitiax* (heir to the throne) of Georgian Iberia, younger brother of King Hamazasp.

Oroezes (2): Suanian warrior, brother of Kobrias.

Pactyes: Lydian rebel against the Achaemenid Persians.

Palfurius Sura: *Ab Epistulis* of Gallienus.

Pallas: Servant of Mastabates'.

Patavinus: Roman auxiliary soldier, standard bearer to Ballista at Miletus and Didyma.

Petronius: First century AD author of the Latin novel *The Satyricon* (better Latin would be *Satyrica*); usually identified with Petronius Arbiter, the sometime friend of Nero.

Philip of Macedon: 382–36BC, father of Alexander the Great.

Philip V: 238–179BC, king of Macedonia; of the Antigonid dynasty.

Pippa (or Pipa): Daughter of Attalus of the Marcomanni; wife / concubine of Gallienus, who called her Pippara.

Piso: Gaius Calpurnius Piso Frugi, senator and *nobilis*, one-time supporter of Macrianus; killed in a bid for the throne in AD260.

Plato: Athenian philosopher, *c.* 429–347BC.

Plotinus: Neoplatonist philosopher, AD205–69 / 70.

Polemo: King Polemo of Suania.

Polemon: Marcus Antonius Polemon, *c.* AD88–144, famous sophist and physiognomist.

Polybius: Slave purchased by Ballista in Priene.

Pompey the Great: Gnaeus Pompeius Magnus, 106–48BC; Roman general.

Postumus: Marcus Cassianus Latinius Postumus, once governor of Lower Germany; from AD262 Roman emperor of the breakaway 'Gallic empire'; killer of Gallienus's son Saloninus.

Pythagoras: Sixth century BC philosopher.

Pythonissa: Only daughter of King Polemo of Suania; a priestess of Hecate.

Quietus: Titus Fulvius Iunius Quietus, son of Macrianus the Elder, proclaimed Roman emperor with his brother Macrianus the Younger in AD260, and killed by Ballista in AD261, the year before this novel starts.

Quirinius: Aurelius Quirinius, Gallienus's *a Rationibus*.

Rebecca: Jewish slave woman bought by Ballista.

Regalianus: One-time governor of Pannonia Inferior, who claimed descent from the kings of Dacia before the Roman conquest; rebelled and was killed in AD260.

Respa: Son of Gunteric, brother of Tharuaro; Gothic warrior of the Tervingi.

Rhesmagus: King of the western Abasgi.

Romulus: Standard bearer to Ballista; died outside Arete.

Roxanne: Concubine of Shapur, captured by Ballista at Soli.

Rufinus: Gallienus's *Princeps Peregrinorum*, spymaster, commander of the *frumentarii*.

Rutilianus: Publius Mummius Sisenna Rutilianus, ex-consul ridiculed by the satirist Lucian for being taken in by Alexander of Abonouteichos.

Rutilus: Marcus Aurelius Rutilus, Roman army officer, Praetorian Prefect under both Quietus and Ballista.

Salonina: Empress Egnatia Salonina, wife of Gallienus.

Saloninus: Publius Cornelius Licinius Saloninus Valerianus, second son of Gallienus, made Caesar in AD258 on the death of his elder brother, Valerian II; executed by Postumus in AD260.

Sasan: Founder of the Sassanid royal house of Persia.

Saurmag: Fourth son of King Polemo of Suania.

Selandros: *Prophetes* of Apollo at Didyma; of the ancient Milesian Euangelidai clan.

Septimius Severus: Lucius Septimius Severus, Roman emperor AD193–211.

Shapur I (or Sapor) : Second Sassanid King of Kings, son of Ardashir I.

Simon: Young Jewish boy rescued from a cave in Arbela in Judea by Ballista.

Spadagas: King of the eastern Abasgi.

Strabo: Greek author of a universal history and a geography (the latter is extant), *c.* 64BC–*c.* AD23; the most important Greek writer whose work survives from the Augustan age.

Successianus: Roman officer who defended the town of Pityus from the Goths; later Praetorian Prefect to Valerian, with whom he was captured by the Sassanids in AD260.

Suren: Parthian nobleman, the head of the house of Suren, vassal of Shapur.

Tacitus (1): Cornelius Tacitus, *c.* AD56–*c.* 118, the greatest Latin historian.

Tacitus (2): Marcus Claudius Tacitus, Roman senator of the third century AD (most likely) of Danubian origins; one of the *protectores*; may have claimed kinship with or even descent from the famous historian, but it is unlikely to be true.

Tarchon: Suanian saved from drowning by Ballista and Calgacus.

Tatianus: Marcus Aurelius Tatianus, *Stephanephoros* (leading magistrate) of Priene.

Thales of Miletus: One of the 'Seven Sages' of antiquity.

Tharuaro: Son of Gunteric, brother of Respa, leader of the Tervingi longboats in the Gothic fleet in the Aegean.

Theodotus: Egyptian officer of Gallienus; brother of Camsisoleus; one of the *protectores*.

Thucydides: Athenian historian, *c.* 460–400BC.

Tir-mihr: A Sassanid general.

Trajan: Marcus Ulpius Traianus, Roman emperor AD98–117.

Tzathius: Second son of King Polemo of Suania.

Valash: Prince Valash, 'the joy of Shapur', a son of Shapur; rescued from violent death by Ballista in Cilicia.

Valens: Pretender to the throne, killed in AD260.

Valentinus: Governor of the province of Moesia Superior.

Valerian (1): Publius Licinius Valerianus, an elderly Italian senator elevated to Roman emperor in AD253; captured by Shapur I in AD260.

Valerian (2): Publius Cornelius Licinius Valerianus, eldest son of Gallienus, grandson of Valerian; made Caesar in AD256; died in AD258.

Vardan: Sassanid captain serving under the Lord Suren.

Vedius Antoninus: Publius Vedius Antoninus, a member of the *Boule* and the scribe to the *demos* at Ephesus.

Velenus: King of the Cadusii.

Vellius Macrinus: Senator; governor of the province of Bithynia et Pontus.

Venerianus: Celer Venerianus, Italian officer of Gallienus; one of the *protectores*.

Veteranus: Marcus Aurelius Veteranus, governor of Dacia.

Volusianus: Lucius Petronius Taurus Volusianus, Gallienus's Praetorian Prefect, risen from the ranks, consul in AD261; one of the *protectores*.

Wulfstan: Young Angle slave purchased by Ballista in Ephesus.

Xenophon: Athenian soldier and writer of the fifth to fourth centuries BC.

Zeno: Aulus Voconius Zeno, a Roman equestrian, once governor of Cilicia, now *a Studiis* to Gallienus.

Zober: High-priest of Georgian Albania, uncle of King Cosis.

Ztathius: Warrior and noble of Georgian Iberia.